The Soldier's Bride

Maggie Ford

W F HOWES LTD

This large print edition published in 2014 by
W F Howes Ltd
Unit 4, Rearsby Business Park, Gaddesby Lane,
Rearsby, Leicester LE7 4YH

1 3 5 7 9 10 8 6 4 2

First published as *Stolen Years* in the United Kingdom
in 1994 by Judy Piatkus (Publishers) Ltd

A CIP catalogue record for this book is available
from the British Library

ISBN 978 1 47125 414 7

Typeset by Palimpsest Book Production Limited,
Falkirk, Stirlingshire
Printed and bound by
www.printondemand-worldwide.com of Peterborough, England

This book is made entirely of chain-of-custody materials

Dedicated to Charles Titchen, my late husband and patient friend, and to my loving children, John, Janet and Clare

CHAPTER 1

Letty Bancroft shivered deliciously, a tingle of anticipation briefly replacing tension. Not long now and she'd be wearing her new corset.

Stiffened with whalebone, strengthened with buckram, moulding her already narrow waist as near the rich and fashionable 'S' bend as its cheaper version allowed, it had cost twelve shillings and elevenpence.

'How much?' Mum had looked disparaging. 'It'll kill yer wearing a thing like that, trying to be something you ain't.' But Letty had been eighteen two weeks ago. Now she wanted to be transformed, to look rich and fashionable, even if she was only a bridesmaid. At least, when she could get into the bedroom to put the thing on and *be* transformed!

Letty, or as her dad insisted, Letitia, drew back her head from out of the open parlour window above his second-hand shop, the sash pushed up as far as it would go for a bit of fresh air, and glanced again at the clock on the mantelshelf. Eleven-thirty! She'd never be ready in time.

It was Saturday 15 June 1908. Her eldest sister, Vinny, was getting married at one-thirty at Holy Trinity church in Old Nichol Street. Letty and her other sister, Lucy, were bridesmaids.

From the bedroom along the passage came girlish voices, high with excitement. All right for them! Lucy was ready, Vinny almost. And here she stood, still in her old everyday frock, hair tumbled around her shoulders in an auburn mass, waiting for Lucy to comb it, pin it up and puff it out fashionably over cloth rats.

Her mother looked round the parlour door. 'You orright, Letty, luv?' The tone sounded weary, almost like a sigh.

Letitia looked at the thin face, flushed by the disease that afflicted so many in the East End; squalor, narrow back alleys, lack of fresh air, it was said, made a perfect breeding ground. Mum had contracted it about ten months ago but had been determined it wouldn't spread to her three pretty daughters with all their lives ahead of them. She never kissed them now, which hurt a little; used a hanky for her smallest cough; had her own crockery, her own utensils, her own towel and face flannel, the family being just a bit better off than some who could hardly afford a towel between them at times. If Dad's shop did only moderately well, at least it managed to keep their heads above water.

'I'm orright, Mum,' Letty answered her enquiry. 'Just a bit fed up of waitin', that's all.'

'Never mind, luv,' Mabel Bancroft soothed. 'Not much longer. It do take a bit of time fer a bride to get ready.'

'Hmm!' Letty pulled a face, the grimace in no way marring its looks. She got her retroussé nose, her firm oval chin and high brow from Dad; her tallness she'd inherited from both parents, rare in a Cockney.

Her wide green eyes could make any boy blush to the roots of his hair when she treated him to that sideways glance of hers, a natural action, but she could make the most of it when she wanted to. Trouble was, she seldom wanted to, certainly not with the class of boy round here. Oh, for a well off young man like Vinny had found. She envied Vinny her luck. It would never be hers.

'Looks like I'll still be dressin' when everyone else is leaving,' she mumbled sulkily. 'I should of known I'd look a mess. Some bridesmaid I'll make – me hair all over the place.'

'It won't be all over the place, luv,' Mum said in a tired voice. 'Lucy'll do yer 'air lovely.'

The wan face withdrawn to save further argument, Letty turned back to the window and stuck her head out again. Her face framed by the heavy lace curtains, elbows folded on the soot-grimed sill for support, black-stockinged feet up on tiptoe, she peered down.

The street below was quiet. On Saturdays most people went to Brick Lane market a few streets away, the faint cries of the stallholders could be heard from here, above the rattle of trams on the main road. Tomorrow morning, however, would see the quiet street below erupt in a confusion of song birds, thousands of them, their concerted twittering like the sound of huge sheets of crisp tissue paper being vigorously rubbed together.

This was Club Row, London's caged bird market. Running off from the Shoreditch end of Bethnal Green Road, its stalls spilling across into Sclater Street and Hare Street, people came here on Sunday mornings to buy pigeons, chickens, but mostly to look for a caged bird as a pet – a linnet, a goldfinch or a canary.

In summer London's streets echoed to their sweet trills and warbles when new owners hung the tiny cages outside tenement windows. In winter the streets lay silent when the birds were taken indoors out of the cold, but even in winter Club Row had birdsong; cages stacked high in doorways, on stalls, each little captive singing as if to keep itself warm until someone bought it and took it home out of the cold.

Sunday morning the air would vibrate with the confused chatter of people buying, and stallholders yelling their heads off. The street would be a jostle of people milling between the fuliginous brick and dirty shop windows and the tatty awnings of stalls. Letty always loved looking down on the swirling river of hats; men's faces hidden beneath greasy cloth caps or dusty bowlers, ladies' beneath straw hats, plain sombre black or cream or yellow, banded with blue or red or brown ribbon; a few wide-brimmed hats decorated with wax fruit, half a yard of tulle, a feather or two, the poor of the East End aping the more opulent West End fashions.

This was still the same impoverished area Letty had known as a kid, but things were gradually changing. It was 1908. The well-to-do set the fashions, and every girl from scullery maid upward copied them. A girl could, with a paper pattern, a bit of cheap material and ribbon, make a dress for almost next to nothing and stroll in the park on Sunday looking quite the lady, even if she was in reality a mere factory worker.

Reminded sharply that shortly she too would look very much a lady in her bridesmaid's dress, Letty drew her head back inside finding the room dim after the brilliance outside.

'You two goin' ter be much longer, Lucy?' she yelled, petulance heightening the cockney accent Dad was always trying to curb in her.

'Ooh, keep yer 'air on!' Lucy's reply came back in the same vernacular, forgetting that she had been practising rounding her vowels and sounding her aitches, because she was going out with a boy who did. 'Nearly ready. Vinny looks a picture! Wait till you see 'er, Let.'

'And oo's *Let*, when she's at 'ome?' Dad's voice came sharply from the bedroom across the passage; Dad, who tried to practise what he preached, sometimes didn't do so well. 'She's got a name yet know. Letitia!'

'What, Dad?' Letty called back automatically, hearing her full name. Arthur Bancroft's voice became even more irascible. 'I wasn't talkin' to you!'

'I thought you was.'

His narrow face with its bristling sandy-grey moustache came round the edge of the door, followed by his tall thin frame. At fifty, he still bore traces of the handsome man he'd once been.

'Not so much of your lip, my girl! I was talking to Lucilla. And you, I ain't 'aving you bawling out like some factory 'and. I brought you up to behave a bit better than that. Lucilla watches her words – or do sometimes.' Lucy's reply was still grating in his head. 'And Lavinia is a proper lady since she met 'er Albert. So I ain't 'aving you talking like that in front of 'er 'usband to be and his people. I ain't havin' you show us up.'

He looked agitated, even less ready than before he'd started dressing for the ceremony. In his shirt and braces, his Sunday best trousers even so held up by a belt, his stiff celluloid collar popped off its stud, protruded at right angles from his neck like a seagull's broken wing. His hair, touched faintly with grey, parted in the centre and brushed flat as a natural wave allowed, shone with brilliantine to keep it so, except that one wave with its own ideas was sticking up like a cockscomb. The bane of his life, was his persistently wavy hair.

Letty smothered a giggle, kept her face straight. 'Sorry, Dad,' she said hastily, then tittered as he disappeared.

High ideals had Dad, bless him. With never quite the means to carry any of them out, he'd tried to disguise his own lack of education, his poor background, by concentrating on his daughters, insisting they behaved like ladies, tried to be a little better than he ever had been.

Even his choice of their names – Lavinia, Lucilla, Letitia – suited more to girls from Barnet than Bethnal Green, reflected that effort. Mum, more down to earth, had shortened them to Vinny, Lucy and Letty; neighbourhood mates went one better: Vin, Luce and Let. Dad gritted his teeth, and clung religiously to their original names.

From her sisters' bedroom came a wail: 'Be careful, Lucy. You'll break my neck, pulling my hair like that!'

Far better spoken than any of them Vinny had become, since meeting Albert Worth whose people came from Hackney.

At twenty-one, the same age as Vinny, Albert looked older. Round-faced and, to Letty's idea, a bit pompous, he was training as an accountant in his father's firm. Vinny had met him last year when the three girls had gone to see the Boat Race at Putney. He had accompanied her home when she'd torn the frilled hem of her summer dress and had taken to calling on her every Sunday afterwards, not put off by her background. Vinny could put on the posh talk when she wanted. She had won his family over and finally become engaged to him in January.

Letty glanced again at the ornate ormolu clock on its marble stand where figures of a gallant and his lady posed decoratively on either side of the oval face under a huge glass dome. Tight-faced, she hurried to the parlour door.

Leaning out of it, she blared into the dim passage: 'It's five to twelve!'

'Ooh, you are impatient!' Lucy's reply, yelled from the bedroom, was no panacea. 'I'm doin' me best!'

'That don't help me much though, do it?' Letty yelled back. 'I can't even use me own bedroom with all Vinny's stuff in it.'

A few stairs up were two tiny rooms, one hers, one full of Dad's junk. Letty's bedroom measured just six by eight. For weeks it had been full of Vinny's wedding stuff with nowhere else to put it. Living space above the shop was in short supply. Besides the two tiny rooms at the top, there were just two slightly larger bedrooms, a kitchen and parlour, all of which opened on to a long dim passage with a flight of stairs down to the shop. The parlour was of a decent size if it hadn't been crammed with Dad's bric-a-brac and what had once belonged to Mum's parents.

At one end, the top of the piano was home to several big Victorian vases with painted pastoral scenes, some sepia photographs of various relatives staring out with fixed expressions, and some smaller vases. The piano had belonged to Mum's mother. So had the six tall-backed chairs and the round dining table with extensions that opened with a winder, its polished mahogany usually protected by a chenille cover with bobbled fringes, an aspidistra in an ornate pot in the centre. Today its extensions were fully out, covered with a snowy Irish linen cloth and Grandma's best cutlery laid for the wedding breakfast. The two-tiered wedding cake stood in the middle, like a silent honoured guest, in place of the aspidistra.

At the other end of the parlour was a horsehair sofa with an armchair to match, the other one being wooden, with a padded back and padded wooden arms, such as Mum liked to use. 'Keeps the back nice and straight,' she maintained. 'Floppy sitting makes a woman ungainly.' She was still very Victorian in her ways, and it was too late to change her now. A lovely straight back she'd had once, a habit passed on to all three girls. It was sad to see how bent those shoulders had become over her slowly collapsing chest.

Letty wandered to the piano, lifting the lid with one hand and picking out two bars of 'I Dreamt I Dwelt in Marble Halls' with the other. Mum used to play on Sunday evenings. They'd sing their favourite songs, Dad's voice powerful, Mum's sweet, the girls' mostly indifferent. They'd not done it much since Mum had become so tired and worn. Letty closed the lid despondently.

What would Dad do if anything happened to Mum? She'd always had to push him, being a bit of a dreamer, always talking of what he'd do but never doing it. He wasn't hard enough, more of a leaner really. Mum's people had been metal merchants, brought up hard on business. Had she been a bit sterner with him, Arthur too might have been harder, made good money. But he was in love with beautiful things. He and Mum used to argue a lot once, over some fine piece he refused to resell after buying it off someone trying to raise a bit more cash than the pawn would give. He could be stubborn sometimes, Mum said, in a silly way. But they no longer argued, hadn't for months.

A lot of his treasured finds graced the mantelpiece that reared above the fireplace like a mahogany monarch almost to the ceiling in whirls and scrolls and shelves on fluted columns, backed by small mirrors. Each piece reflected Dad's passion for beautiful things.

Letty knew how he felt. She felt the same. She loved to wander around the shop touching the smoothness of polished wood, the silkiness of good china, looking at shapes, staring at pictures.

She heard Mum call out: 'Time's getting on, Lucy dear.'

And Lucy call back: 'The church is only in the next street, Mum. We ain't going all the way to Timbuctoo!'

'I know, luv. But it's time Vinny got herself sorted out, then 'as a cup of tea and a bit to eat. She 'as to sustain 'erself through the ceremony till we all get back 'ere for the wedding breakfast. Vinny, don't you forget to wear yer gran's garter . . .

10

something old. An' you'll have to borrer something too. You got a clean 'anky, luv? Can I help?'

'No!' Lucy's cry was just a little panicky. 'Don't come in 'till Vinny's ready. It'll spoil the surprise.'

Dad's voice rasped irritably: "Er name's Lavinia! Damn this bloody collar! See if yer can fix it, Mum.' He seldom called her Mabel.

A sudden outburst came from the bedroom. 'Lucy – it'll fall down, I know it will! Right in the middle of the service. My veil will pull it down. I shall feel such a lemon.'

'It won't fall down!' Lucy's voice was full of effrontery, her effort with Vinny's hair being criticised. 'It's well pinned.'

'If it falls down, I'll blame you! I won't get married. I'll run out of the church, I will!'

'Lucy! Vinny!' Mum was making for their bedroom. 'You'll spoil yer pretty face, Vinny, if yer start crying.'

'But just look at it, Mum!' she was wailing. 'It's all floppy.'

Letty leapt into action, running in behind her mother, Dad following. There the bride stood in all her glory, except for a face creased in pique. Letty made her eyes grow wide with admiration. Not all in pretence either for Vinny was delicately pretty.

'Luvaduck!' she gasped. 'I ain't never seen anyone look so . . . so beautiful!'

Vinny's grey-green eyes grew hopeful. 'Do you think so?'

'Think so? I think your Albert might faint away at the sight of you. I think the vicar might too. You look . . . you look as pretty as Carol McComas.'

She couldn't have quoted a more apt example of loveliness. Carol McComas was Vinny's favourite actress on whose swan neck, small perfectly balanced features, clear skin as delicately blushed as a peach, Vinny strived to model herself. In her high-necked, white satin wedding gown, its bodice a froth of lace, with more flaring at the elbows and the train, Vinny looked so like her, it took Letty's breath away.

'Your Albert don't know just 'ow lucky he is,' she sighed, wishing for a brief moment it was she who stood there.

Lavinia's face sobered with uncertainty. 'Oh, I do hope he'll like the way I look.'

Mum put her hands to her lips and stood back to survey her. Letty felt with a searing of sadness that Mum would much rather have cuddled her eldest daughter, soon to leave her family to share a new life with her husband, but dare not let this beautiful girl catch what she had. 'He won't be able to 'elp himself, luv,' she whispered, and her voice wavered.

The only man in a family of women, Arthur Bancroft risked a surreptitious wipe of one finger beneath his suddenly moist eyes. 'You best make yerself scarce now, Lavinia. Before people start arriving,' he said huskily. 'Can't 'ave 'em see yer before yer walk down that aisle.'

Master of himself again, he ushered his eldest

daughter out of the bedroom to be safely hidden in her parents' room until her entrance in church would take everyone's breath away.

At last Letty was free to place herself in Lucy's deft hands to be helped into her new undergarments and the dress that had been hanging behind the door under a sheet since being made up by Mum's friend Mrs Hall, a widow who lived above the Knave of Clubs on the corner of Bethnal Green Road. The material had been bought at Debenham & Freebody's departmental store just off Oxford Street – apple green crepe-de-chine – and went well with her auburn hair. Lucy's dress was pale blue, and a wonderful job Mrs Hall had made of them both.

Not too fancy, all right for Sunday dresses afterwards: the bodices pintucked and frilled, with tiny bunches of tulle rosebuds, satin ribbon at the waists, skirts that flared to a small train. Mrs Hall had made the hats as well and they were a sight for sore eyes; a good twenty inches across, a mound of tulle bows with masses of tiny artificial flowers, to be anchored to the hair by huge pearl-headed hatpins.

Uncomplaining, Letty submitted herself to Lucy's quick, sure hands. Lucy would have made a good lady assistant in one of those high-class departmental stores like Dickens & Jones, except Dad had never let any of them go out to work as girls of poorer families did. He didn't seem to think that helping in the shop for just a bit of pocket money was work, and always made sure they never went short.

Lucy stepped back as far as the bed behind her allowed to view her handiwork just as the shop doorbell tinkled. The shop was closed, of course, a handwritten sign on the door stating the reason.

'There!' she breathed, satisfied with her accomplishment, as well she might be – for Letty, seeing herself in the mirror on the ancient chest of drawers, couldn't have faulted her. They stood, the two of them, one eighteen, one twenty, both a dream in crepe-de-chine, beautiful hats, long gloves, waists elegantly slim, faces glowing with pride and excitement. 'Just in time. Hope it's none of Albert's posh lot. After where they live, it will look so cluttered to them here.'

Lucy had suddenly acquired a much posher voice. Throwing a reluctant look at the cramped and narrow bedroom, she went to the window and glanced down to where the new arrivals stood waiting to be let in.

In an instant she had withdrawn her head, eyes brilliant, her face animated.

'It's him! It's Jack! I thought he was going straight to the church but he's come here first. Oh, Letty – pr'aps he intends to pop the question. D'you think he does?'

'He's been calling on you for the last seven months,' Letty said, smiling at her excitement. 'Time he did. Not this very minute though.'

But Lucy wasn't even listening. 'I know he's been thinking about it, the way he talks. I'm sure he'll get around to asking Dad soon.'

She'd met Jack Morecross when Vinny's Albert had brought him one Sunday to meet her. Three years older than Lucy, he was a pleasant-looking, lanky young man with flat gingery hair and earnest blue eyes. He lived not far from Albert, his father having a small printing works inherited from his own father who had retired. A far better catch than the boys from around here, most of whom had no prospects and even less initiative, Lucy had lost no time in hooking handsome Jack.

Letty couldn't help feeling a little envious and faintly put out that she wasn't even walking out with a boy at the moment, not one she'd call halfway worth it anyway. The local boys hung around her hoping one day she'd ask one of them home to meet her dad, but she kept every one of them at arm's length, her mind set on the Prince Charming who would one day sweep her off her feet. Some hopes of that!

'You'll meet a nice boy one day, with your looks,' Mum would say, and immediately refer to Billy Beans whose parents had the grocer's shop further along Club Row. Rudely handsome and thick-set, about her own age, he was always setting his cap at her, hanging around. Trouble was, she liked Billy but not his name. Fancy – Letty Beans!

Lucy was back at the window, peering down as

Mum's footsteps echoed on the narrow lino-covered stairs down to the shop.

'He's brought his friend, he said he would. Yoo-hoo, Jack!' Leaning out, waving, Lucy's joyous giggle told of her wave being returned. She withdrew her head as the shop door was opened to admit him. 'His dad's a friend of Jack's dad. Jack and me thought he'd be company for you.'

Letty felt distinctly annoyed. 'You thought . . . Honestly, Lucy, you do take a lot on yourself! I can find me own company, thank you.'

Lucy looked a little ruffled. 'I thought you might like someone a bit more interesting than them around here. He's ever so educated.'

'I don't care if he's Tolstoy,' retorted Letty, having once had *War and Peace* inflicted on her at school. 'I don't want someone I don't know tagging around after me all day, telling me how educated he is. What do I say to 'im? I wish you hadn't of done it.'

Lucy was pouting, her good intentions in ruins. 'Well, better than the weeds around here. Jack says he's ever so handsome. He's got pots of money. His name's David Baron. He's twenty-eight and . . .'

'Twenty-eight! I don't want no twenty-eight . . .'

She broke off as the arrivals were shown into the parlour, but Lucy already had her by the hand, pulling her along, hurrying to welcome Jack. They reached the parlour as the doorbell tinkled once again, compelling Mum to go back downstairs.

Jack was standing self-consciously by the sofa,

16

staring down at his hat held in both hands. His friend was also politely bare-headed, but if he felt at all ill at ease in a strange home, he didn't show it. He was tall and dark-haired, and stood very still with his eyes steady. Dark eyes, Letty saw as Lucy dragged her into the room after her. He certainly did look well off, and so very mature in a well-cut charcoal grey suit that Letty felt her cheeks begin to burn, feeling even more angry with Lucy who left her standing to rush over and take Jack's hand.

Someone coughed and Letty turned to the window. Dad stood there semi-obscured by the sunlight pouring through the thick lace curtains. Neither expecting nor approving of this invasion by his second daughter's admirer and some complete stranger to boot, when both would have been better going straight to the church, he was busying himself filling his pipe to cover the resulting embarrassment.

Lucy's hand was confidently on the stranger's arm, drawing him towards her sister. 'Letty,' she began in her very nicest voice, 'this is Mr David Baron, Jack's friend. David, this is my sister, Letty . . .'

''Er name's Letitia,' came a deep rumble from behind the smokescreen of Dad's now kindled pipe. A reek of Navy Cut had filled the room. 'If yer goin' er introduce people properly, Lucilla, then get their names right.'

Her aplomb shaken, Lucy threw him a look, but

any hope of further introductions was stopped short by an invasion of relatives surging like the hordes of Gengis Khan through the door: Uncle Will, who was Mabel's brother, his wife Hetty, and three adolescent cousins, Bert, George and Ethel; then Arthur's sister Mildred, husband Charlie, and two more cousins, Violet and Emma, just coming up to adolescence. The room was suddenly a mass of people, with everyone kissing everyone else as if they'd all come together from the ends of the earth, when in fact all of them lived just a tram ride away, Uncle Charlie's lot from Whitechapel and Uncle Will's from Stepney.

'We all met up at the door,' Charlie of the constant ribald jokes explained jovially. 'Thought we'd pop in instead of going straight to the church. Funny you thinkin' the same thing, Will. So we all met up together at the door, didn't we? Funny that. Funny coincidence.'

Mabel, out of breath, hid a cough with her hand-kerchief. Letty, her mind taken off Mr David Baron for the moment, saw her sink into her chair set between the sofa and the fireplace. She looked like a little ailing mouse, wanting only to crawl away into a hole, out of sight. Letty's eyes tingled with sudden tears, the lining of her nose became acutely sensitive and her throat constricted. She fought the emotion, sniffed, bit on her lip. Couldn't start dissolving into tears in front of everyone, especially in front of the self-assured stranger.

'You all right, Mum?' she said, knowing

immediately she'd intruded on her privacy as all eyes turned to her.

Mabel smiled and got up out of her chair, her tone terse with the effort to sound unconcerned. 'Them blessed stairs. Wear you out, them stairs do.'

She even managed a laugh, but not enough to allay embarrassment in those who knew that their arrival had put her to an inconvenience they could have avoided.

'We've got ter start walking to the church in a few minutes,' she went on quickly. 'I'll go and see how Vinny's doin'. Her carriage'll be 'ere soon. Arthur.' She looked over to her husband, still puffing his pipe. 'You stay with the bride and bridesmaids to wait for it. You 'ave ter be with the bride to give 'er away.' She gave the company a broad smile. 'Lot ter think about when it's yer first.'

An outbreak of garbled conversation after a brief awkward silence following her departure. Making up their minds to get ready to leave, everyone began to draw together, face the door in a ragged group like a platoon of raw recruits, uncertain if they'd been given orders or not. Letty wanted to run after Mum with some odd idea of apologising, but Mum probably wouldn't have had any idea why, so she stayed where she was on the far side of Lucy, away from David Baron.

She became aware of him watching her, his eyes softening with understanding. She felt he knew what was wrong with her mother, though no one could have told him. You didn't talk about things like that, and if you did, only with family, and then only in a whisper, the word itself forbidding anything louder.

He seemed to know just how she was feeling too, but she hadn't invited his sympathy and her reaction was to take immediate umbrage that a total stranger was seeing right into her soul. And because annoyance was an unreasonable reaction, she felt all the more put out, her face growing hot.

'Who does he think he is?' she hissed at Lucy, and heard her giggle. She risked a glance at him as her relations at last decided to jostle out through the doorway and down the stairs, her cheeks on fire when she saw he had come closer to her. Oh Gawd, what was he going to say to her? What could she say in answer? He probably spoke like a toff, and she . . . she'd probably make a real fool of herself . . .

She acted instinctively. Grabbing the arm of her fifteen-year-old cousin Bert, she gushed loudly, 'Come on. Let's go and tell Mum you're all off now.'

CHAPTER 2

Those guests intending to, finally left in the small hours, their footsteps echoing along a silent and deserted Club Row. Letty closed the door behind them.

'I could kill you, Luce, honest I could,' she hissed, bolting the door top and bottom, throwing the bolts home with fierce energy, taking her spite out on them instead of her sister. 'Thank God he left early! I don't know what he'd have thought, us 'aving a knees up. I would have died. That sort's used ter sittin' in a circle drinkin' tea with his little finger stuck out, sipping champagne and nibblin' lady's fingers biscuits.'

She couldn't imagine him bothering to come calling on her after tonight. She wouldn't be seeing him again. Too much of a toff.

'And been married an' all!'

The sickly glimmer from the upstairs gas lamp guided them back through the cluttered shop that always smelled faintly musty. Lucy's affronted gaze sought out Letty's dim silhouette.

'He's not married now. It must 'ave been tragic, his wife dying, and him so young.'

Letty paused, her foot on the first stair. 'What d'you mean, young? He was ten years older than me.'

Lucy paused too. 'Well, he wouldn't have been when he lost his wife, would he? It was four years ago. You make him sound like Methuselah. Ten years ain't nothing. And he was ever so handsome.'

'I didn't think he was handsome,' Letty retorted. 'And what made you think I'd fancy someone second hand anyway? And his wife had a baby.'

'Born dead!' Lucy was rapidly becoming short-tempered. 'Ain't you got no feelings, Let? What he must've gone through, losing wife and baby all at the same time. And all you can think of is how *you* felt 'cos he'd been married and ten years older than you.'

To this Letty could find no reply. She'd been so busy trying to avoid David Baron when she'd discovered he'd been married once, the tragedy he must have endured had not really registered. Now, like a sudden thump in the chest, it did, and she felt so ashamed. But Lucy, overflowing with righteous anger, hadn't noticed.

'Ten years ain't so awful. He had nice manners and talked nice like Jack. You don't know what you want, that's your trouble. Jack just mentioned he had this handsome friend, and I thought . . .'

'All right!' Letty cut in waspishly, and began mounting the stairs. 'I should have been more sociable. But I wasn't, so there!' She slowed a little halfway up, Lucy coming up behind her. 'Anyway,

22

I don't think he was that good-looking. His nose was too long, and he'd got lines at the corners of his eyes too.'

'Laughter lines,' Lucy interpreted.

'Well, I never saw 'im laugh. All he did was look at me, all lah-di-dah like.'

At the top of the stairs, they paused to peer in at the men sitting around the parlour table at their game of pontoon.

Tense faces were lit by the ornamental oil lamp in the centre of the table, replacing the now demolished wedding cake; gone was the noise and laughter of an earlier game of Newmarket in which even the kids could take part, farthings given by parents to put on the four Kings, to be excitedly scooped up if they got as far as laying down a Queen of the corresponding suit. Now all that could be heard was the terse commands breaking an edgy silence. Buy one! Twist! Pay twenty-ones! Bust! And the chink of coins dropped on to a growing pile.

It had been a good wedding. Those who could play the piano taking their turn, everyone gathered around to join in the tunes. Uncle Will, maudlin drunk, had done several recitations, prompted at intervals by those who knew the words better than he did.

Uncle Charlie's store of near the knuckle jokes had got everyone rolling about, Albert's people looking a bit bewildered, Vinny going all red and flustered that they should hear such things, as if they were above it all. Aunt Elsie, Dad's sister, had brought up the tone a bit, playing one or two classical pieces with more gusto than skill. A friend of Dad's had sung, 'We've bin tergevver now fer forty yers, an' it don' seem a day too much', his eyes trained lovingly on his chubby wife as he continued, 'there ain't a lidy livin' in the land as I'd swap fer me dear ole Dutch.'

One of the younger cousins had done a tiptoe dance, exacting sentimental sighs from the women; one even younger had recited a little poem to even greater sighs of appreciation; an older cousin with a very pleasing voice had la-la'd the tune from *The Merry Widow* and had been so well applauded that she'd sung some more from other musical shows until she'd become thoroughly boring, pleasing voice or not.

The happy pair finally leaving for their new home, a nice rented house in Victoria Park Road, Albert's side departed not long after with Lucy's Jack and Mr David Baron. Afterwards the party consisting of close family and friends had developed into a good booze-up.

Everyone had raised the roof in song, shaken the ceiling of the shop underneath to the stamp of 'Knees Up, Mother Brown', men's boots pounding, women lifting their skirts, petticoats flying.

In the small hours, exhausted, they'd slumped down on chairs or the wooden planks set up on beer crates especially for this gathering. They'd gathered around the table to play Newmarket until

24

those who could still walk home finally left, the rest staying until the trams resumed running on Sunday morning, the men to play Pontoon while the women went off to find a bed to fall on for the few remaining hours.

Lucy yawned as they moved past the smoky parlour. 'All the fun's over. I'm going to bed.'

'If we can find one.' Letty quietly pushed open their parents' door, knowing exactly what she'd see there. Dresses draped over the chair, hung on the wardrobe doors and from the picture rail, aunts in chemise, petticoats and drawers lying dead to the world on the bed, only half under the counterpane on this warm night, limbs flung wide in the unladylike need for coolness, kids sprawled sound asleep across their legs.

'Cheek!' Lucy said as they closed the door on the second bedroom, just as crammed full of bodies. Mum, of course, had gone up to Letty's little room to find a little peace away from the rest. 'Our home and nowhere to sleep.'

She brightened. 'There's that mattress at the back of the shop. We could pinch a quilt. Gawd knows, I could sleep on a clothes line!'

Stretched out beside her sister, Letty's sleepy thoughts drifted. In her head she could hear David Baron's cultured voice. It had made her so conscious of her own that to protect herself she'd behaved like the brash Cockney she was. She'd laughed raucously, spoken too loudly, got her aitches mixed up, forgot to sound her ts, and all those East End colloquialisms she'd used without even thinking came echoing back to her, stark and hideous, hearing them as David Baron must have done.

He hadn't batted an eyelid though. The perfect gentleman, behaving as if she was Lady Muck herself. It had made her all the more self-conscious, saying things she hadn't meant to say. Like when he'd asked if she would like another glass of port, she'd shot back, 'I can 'elp meself, thank you!' Lordey – it had sounded awful.

'Myself,' she muttered into the darkness at the back of the shop, rectifying the error fruitlessly. 'Help myself . . . Help . . .'

Beside her Lucy stirred in her sleep, murmuring, 'What?'

Letty kept very still until she settled again, trying to obliterate her bruised pride in sleep, but David Baron kept getting in the way. Thanking Mum and Dad for their hospitality, turning to her: 'Delighted to have made your acquaintance, Miss Bancroft,' so formal she could have screamed. She had shrugged as if it hadn't mattered a jot to her. But it had mattered. It hurt that he hadn't asked to see her again. It was no compensation that his last glance had been for her; she interpreted it as one of reproach for the way she had shown herself up.

Furious with herself, she turned over. Facing away from Lucy, she stared into the darkness of the shop, its faint mustiness enveloping her. How could Lucy call him handsome? The boys around here were much better looking and far more robust. They spoke roughly but you knew how you stood with them. But David's maturity had given him a certain attractiveness . . . Oh, well, too late now. She closed her eyes before the morning light became too strong to let her sleep.

'I should have been nicer to 'im,' said Letty, desultorily flicking a feather duster over the vases on the piano. The last of their guests had gone home, leaving the flat with a forsaken air, having been so full of people the night before.

Lucy had her mind more on Jack and when he'd get around to talking to Dad about their engagement. 'Nothing you can do about it now,' she murmured, disinterested, her arm working like a piston rod to bring up the dining table's mahogany shine.

Letty gave the feather duster another listless flick. 'He might be coming with your Jack this afternoon?' she suggested hopefully.

Jack called every Sunday. He and Lucy usually took a tram to Victoria Park, the only bit of decent open space in the East End and a wonderful place for courting couples and family picnics. It had deer, a lake with a Chinese pagoda on an island in the centre, a huge ornate Victorian drinking fountain, lots of shrubberies and secluded walks, football fields, tennis courts. It extended all the way to Hackney Downs, almost like being in the country.

Lucy would return after kissing Jack goodbye, eyes sparkling, face glowing – and not all from the fresh air. Mum would give her a quick glance, then look away, and Dad's face would bear an anxious expression.

Letty wished someone was taking her to Victoria Park so she could be looked at like that. 'Don't suppose I'll see him again, anyway,' she muttered.

'Don't suppose you will.' Lucy's tone was offhand. 'You made it plain you didn't want nothing to do with him.'

'I didn't make it *that* plain. I just didn't want him thinkin' I was chucking meself at him.'

She gave the vases a last flick and transferred her attention to the gilt frames of two large pictures hanging side by side on the wall by the door. They'd come out of Dad's shop years ago, had been on the wall for as long as she could remember, hadn't been moved for years, the wallpaper behind them still light while the rest had darkened.

One of them depicted a young woman with the classical softly round face and figure and fair abundant tresses beloved by the Victorians. She was clad in flowing diaphanous amber material. Her back to a low, seawashed obelisk, she was bound loosely by golden chains, wrists crossed upon her breast, a dramatic love-lorn gaze cast heavenwards. A green and angry sea foamed about her thighs and dark storm clouds rolled above her, split by the occasional patch of palest blue.

The other showed the same maiden, unchained

and embracing the stone while the sea receded though her gaze was still cast heavenwards at the clouds and still wore the same forsaken expression. Letty had often wondered what story the pictures told, but no one could ever tell her.

Lucy had slid the chenille cover back in place and was starting on the piano.

'All I can say,' she went on, removing the vases one by one before polishing, 'is that after my Jack put 'imself out to bring him, you could have been more civil to him. Anyway, it's your lookout, not mine. Me and Jack's got more serious things to talk about today.'

What she meant was, she was going to have to push him again to talk to Dad, though it was hard to see why Jack was so scared. Her father was a quiet man, a bit stubborn but never the argumentative sort, and he already looked on Jack as a very worthy young man, very suitable.

Jack always came about two o'clock, after Sunday dinner. Washing up done, Mum having her usual Sunday afternoon lie down with a glass of Guinness – to do her blood good, as she always said – Dad down in his shop, Lucy sat by the window in her Sunday best. Her bridesmaid's dress still to be modified, she was in her dark blue suit and a high-necked cream blouse, her cream straw hat pinned to her hair. She looked a picture, her back stiff with anticipation as she waited for Jack.

Letty sat at the table, her weekly copy of *Peg's Paper* under her elbows, her chin in her hands.

She too was in her Sunday best, though she wasn't going anywhere. But just in case.

It was another lovely sunny day. The sash window pushed up as far as it would go for some fresh air, was also admitting a musty taint of bird droppings from the cages stacked against the shop front next door. The voices of the dealers loading them on to barrows to cart away, the market having closed, seemed to be almost in the room.

'I wish we didn't have to live here.' Lucy, her speech grown very cultured in preparation for Jack's arrival, wrinkled her nose delicately. 'It does stink sometimes. *And* I can smell the brewery.'

Her remark suddenly awoke Letty's senses to odours that normally passed unnoticed, acclimatised as she was, having lived with them all her life: a compound of rotten cabbage leaves, sewage, horse manure, and the sour reek of Trueman's Black Eagle Brewery in Brick Lane that hung in the air day and night, worse some days than others, especially when they cleaned out their vats. Today it wasn't so bad, being Sunday, but Letty found herself suddenly embarrassed by the combination of odours.

If David Baron did appear with Lucy's Jack, what on earth would he think, his nostrils assaulted by this stink of the East End, having to pass by the market traders, their language somewhat more than ripe at times? The market being closed yesterday, the street had been quiet. But today. . . For the first time in her life Letty too found herself wishing she lived in some more wholesome area.

'Vinny's lucky, moving out to Hackney,' Lucy muttered petulantly, playing with her gloves and gazing out of the window.

'Well, when you marry Jack, you'll be leaving too,' Letty said, but Lucy gave her a petulant look.

'When he gets down to talking to Dad! You'd think he was an ogre or something. Jack don't seem to have any courage sometimes.'

When he did arrive, he'd obviously found some degree of it. He didn't come upstairs immediately as he usually did. To Lucy that meant only one thing, and her hopes were rising.

'He's talking to Dad about us.'

Unable to sit any longer, she began roaming the room, peeping out of the door, straining her ears. Hearing her prowling outside her bedroom, Mum got up, and came into the parlour, her rest having imparted a high colour to her parchment cheeks, giving her a deceptively healthy look.

'Jack's talking to Dad,' Lucy told her, her own cheeks aglow with premature delight. 'It must be about us!'

'Now don't get excited, luv.' Mabel smiled tolerantly, but there was no holding Lucy who continued to pace the floor.

When Jack came upstairs he was with Dad. Arthur had opened a couple of bottles of brown ale, which was enough for Lucy. Her face radiant, she threw herself at Jack, all but upsetting his glass in the impact.

'Jack! You did it! You did it!' she shrieked. 'Oh, you did it!'

She and Jack went up West to buy her engagement ring, a band of three diamonds and two deep red rubies few boys around here could have afforded and which she flourished whenever anyone came near. She drove everyone half round the bend talking about her wedding.

'We have planned the wedding for next April,' she said, her speech almost on par with Vinny's these days. 'I shall be a spring bride.'

And: 'Jack's grandparents are buying us a house near where they live, in Chingford,' she made a big thing of telling her elder sister. 'It's got a long garden and a proper bathroom and you pump hot water into the bath through pipes from a boiler in the kitchen. They're ever so well off, Jack's grandparents.'

The look on Vinny's face was enough to pull shades down on, Letty thought; Vinny, who'd become so stuck up since marrying Albert, having her nose put out of joint!

Jack began coming for Sunday dinner, part of the family now, and Lucy's cheeks glowed even brighter than usual when she and Jack came back from Victoria Park, enough to make Dad remark, 'All I 'ope is they're be'aving themselves. If she gets in trouble before she's wed, I won't be giving 'er away, yer can bet your last farthin'.'

Letty had given up wondering if Jack would ever

bring his friend along with him. He wouldn't now. It was obvious David Baron had found her tiresome company, had merely been polite in saying he'd been delighted to meet her. Well, he hadn't been her type, anyway.

'Don't know as I'd fancy all that bother tryin' to be someone I ain't,' she confessed to Mum. 'I suppose I'll end up with someone like Billy Beans or Bert Wilkins.' She'd given up the effort to improve her speech, since as she said, she'd probably settle down with a local boy. 'But it don't seem fair, do it? Vinny movin' away to a different area now she's all toffee-nosed. And Lucy'll get just like her when she goes to live in 'er posh Chingford. Never mind, Mum, I won't leave you and Dad on your own. Billy Beans does like me. If I was ter marry him eventually, you'll always 'ave me near you.'

'You could do worse, luv,' her mother said philosophically, but her face was that of one who feared she might never see another marriage take place. 'Both of them lads is nice-looking and presentable. And that young Wilkins boy from Ebor Street ain't exactly hard up, him working at Watney's Brewery in Whitechapel Road where his dad's foreman, he'll soon get promotion. And Billy Beans' people are trade like us. You wouldn't ever 'ave ter scrimp and scrape. You ain't been brought up to that. And young Billy's always bin keen on you, luv.'

Billy with his bright shoe-button eyes, his broad smile on broad features, blond hair always neatly brilliantined down from a centre parting, was a better choice than sallow-faced Bert Wilkins, though Letty would never let on to Billy, mostly because it sort of spoiled the romance, imagining herself as Letty Beans. Letitia Baron would have sounded much nicer, but she shrugged off that speculation as an airy-fairy dream. Men from outside the East End didn't marry girls from inside it. It had happened with Vinny, of course, and again with Lucy, but three times in a row was just too much to ask.

'That's Jack, I expect.' Lucy's voice was off-hand as the doorbell jangled. She didn't even look up from the *Rational Dress Gazette* she bought every week from the newspaper shop next door to Beans Grocers. She was usually up and halfway down the stairs before the bell had stopped swinging on its single coiled spring.

Letty heard Dad open the door, then call up, his voice sounding a little perplexed: 'Your Jack's down 'ere, Lucilla.'

'Ain't you going down?' Letty prompted from the sofa. Lucy was all dressed and ready to go out. Letty herself hadn't bothered putting on her Sunday frock. She might later, if one of her friends called, when the girls would sit and scan through back copies of old magazines.

Lucy's mouth was set into a sulky pout. 'He's got legs – let him come up.'

'You ain't had a row with him, 'ave yer?'

Something inside Letty perked up to find that all didn't always go well with true love – compensating in some way for that nagging sense of defeat still lingering inside her even after all these weeks.

'No, I haven't had a row with him,' Lucy said sharply, then bit at a lower lip that had begun to work. 'Well, who does he think he is – telling me them suffragettes are getting too big for their boots and he'd soon put a stop to me if I behaved like that? Just because I said women *should* have more rights. He said a woman should know her place. Well then, let him do the running and come up here instead!'

Dad's voice came down again. 'He's coming up. And tell Letitia there's someone down 'ere for 'er too, if she cares ter come down.'

Letty looked enquiringly at her sister, but Lucy was already on her feet, doing a lot of hurried hair patting and frill pinking, in a fine old two-and-eight for one vowing a second ago to keep her fiancé dangling.

As Letty passed Jack at the top of the stairs, she smiled at his worried expression, stifling an impulse to say, 'Don't worry – she's not planning to be a suffragette!'

Mum's weary voice followed her down the stairs. 'Whoever it is, you can't go out until after dinner. I've only just got the 'taters on, and the meat's only 'alf done.'

'Orright, Mum,' she called back, prepared to relay the fact to her friend Ethel who was always calling before dinner. Her mum never got dinner until she came back from the Carpenters Arms in Hare Street, her chosen local rather than the Knave of Clubs on the corner. Her meal was often as late as four or five o'clock and Mum's heart had too often melted at her pinched longing expression at the aroma of cooking and put a bit on a plate for her. Ethel would gollop it down, saying, 'Yer won't tell me mum will yer? She'll get ever so annoyed. She don't like everyone feedin' me.' Mrs Bock liked her pint or two at the Carpenters Arms, could hardly afford to feed her brood, but had her pride. And someone else feeding her kids did it no good at all.

It wasn't Ethel Bock standing by the door as the shop came into view at the bottom of the stairs, but a tall figure, his hat in his hands – a pale grey homburg that matched an immaculate suit cut in the latest fashion Letty only ever saw in the West End when she and Ethel went to gape at the toffs.

She stopped abruptly on the last stair as her caller's resonant voice met her.

'Good morning, Letitia.'

Her first thought was her dress – the old blue dress, worn for much of the week. What sort of awful picture must she present to this well-dressed man? She shot a desperate glance towards her father, beaming his approval at her caller for having spoken her full name to his satisfaction.

Her voice, when she found it, sounded high and squeaky. 'Mr Baron . . . I . . . didn't expect to see you.'

She was put in an even greater fluster by Dad quietly passing by her, prudently going upstairs to leave the two of them alone, his face split in that silly grin of approval.

As David Baron came slowly towards her, Letty found her shoulders hunching forward, her hands fluttering about the front of the faded dress in some attempt to hide its appearance. She wanted to say something but her lips felt stiff. It was David Baron who spoke, completely in charge of himself when she was standing there like a chastised child, almost trembling embarrassment.

'I've wanted to call on you since your sister's wedding,' she heard him saying through her confusion. 'My work kept me away. You must have thought I'd forgotten you. I'm sorry.'

'Oh,' Letty said awkwardly. Outside she could hear the shouts of the street traders. People passing were glancing casually through the dusty window at the bits of bric-a-brac lying there. 'What do yer . . .What do you do then, your work?' she amended hurriedly, her vowels still flat to her ear for all she was watching the ts and aitches, though he didn't seem to notice.

'My father has a draper's shop in Highgate. Not far from where we live,' he said evenly.

Letty's tension relaxed instantly. His people were trade, same as hers. For all his posh talk he helped his father in a shop, just as she did. And here she had been, putting on airs and graces, or trying to, and all the time he was just a tradesman's son!

Even the ten years' difference in their ages seemed to diminish. Yes, he *was* good-looking she decided, his face lean and strong, though that longish narrow nose still spoiled the balance a little.

'You never said your dad had a shop,' she burst out. He had quite a gentle smile, not at all superior or patronising.

'You were so enjoying yourself at your sister's wedding reception, I thought you wouldn't be interested in such dull conversation.'

'Oh, I would have been,' she blurted. 'I am. Ever so.' She caught herself hastily, slowing what could have become a gabble. 'I didn't think you were very interested in me, so I . . . Well, I . . .'

Words faltered, died away awkwardly. She couldn't tell him how she had felt about him, could she?

It didn't seem to matter. He was looking at her as if she was something really special; she might have been wearing a ballgown and tiara the way his eyes took her in.

'Your dad, do . . . does he 'ave . . . a big shop?' She was stammering in her haste to sound right. 'It ain't . . . isn't a departmental stores, is it?'

'Just a shop,' he said, his eyes holding hers. 'It does quite well and it needs to be larger. That isn't possible, so we've had to find bigger premises nearby, and it's taken up a lot of time getting things into shape. That's why I couldn't come to call on you.'

Oh, help! her mind exploded. There were shop

38

people and shop people. Her father was one of the lesser ones against his. 'I didn't know that,' she said lamely. 'I just thought . . .'

It didn't matter what she thought, being polite and good-mannered, David Baron had merely called to apologise for any oversight on his part, no more than that. Disappointment dragged through her and she looked down at herself again.

'Well, thanks fer calling anyway. It was nice.'

'Letitia.' He had come closer. She glanced up to see him gazing at her. 'I've called to ask . . .'

He broke off, the shop bell jangling. Customers, a middle-aged couple, quite well dressed. Excusing herself hastily, Letty hurried over to stand by as they picked up a small flower-encrusted vase.

The woman turned to her, unsmiling, vase in hand. 'How much?'

Letty craned her neck politely, ignoring the rudeness. 'It says four and six on the ticket.'

'You can't possibly expect that much for something that is damaged! It has a chip on the rim.'

'Some stuff does come in a bit damaged,' Letty said, politely as she could. Used to this type of treatment from customers, her diction seemed to improve naturally when dealing with them. But in front of Mr David Baron, she felt suddenly demeaned, felt the heat come to her cheeks. 'We are second hand dealers, you see. But if you want to look around, there may be something you'd like that is in good condition.'

'No, I want this, Alfred.' The woman turned to

the man who was obviously her husband. 'It's very like the one Alice broke, and she's paying for it.' She turned to Letty, her eyes hard. 'But four and six really is far too much for something in this condition. We'll give you three shillings and sixpence for it.'

'I'd better ask the proprietor,' Letty began, but as the woman put down the ornament with a somewhat heavy thud, signifying an obvious intention to leave, Letty came to a decision. 'I could take four shillings for it,' she said cautiously.

She waited, watching the woman take up the article again, examine it, frown at it, turn it over in her gloved hands. She knew the signs and waited patiently to one side, not prompting or persuading. The woman would make up her own mind; the slightest wrong word would put her on her guard, drive her away. David Baron forgotten, Letty's main concern, her pleasure, was to see this customer, so certain of her rights, persuade herself into buying. Letty saw the signs, saw the woman take a deep breath, her neck lengthen, her head tilt. A decision had been made.

'Very well. Four shillings! It's still too much.'

Letty resisted the temptation to proffer: 'A bargain, madam.' She had heard so many traders say that. But the sale had been made; she'd not cheapen herself further.

'Thank you, madam,' she said sedately, taking the purchase and wrapping it as nicely as a piece of newspaper allowed. Only when the money was in the cash register and the customers departed with their find, did she remember David Baron again.

He was regarding her, not with sympathy but with a look of honest appreciation, though he, a stranger, had no call to patronise her, she thought, her pride faintly pricked.

'You handle customers very well,' he said frankly, but her chin had gone up.

'It's me . . . my dad's shop. I do know what I'm doing. I suppose you know what you're doing in your dad's shop.'

'That's true,' he conceded seriously, but there was light dancing in his eyes as hers regarded him defiantly.

No, she decided, he wasn't at all good-looking. His nose was definitely too long and his face too narrow. But his eyes were brown and his lashes thick. And his mouth . . . oh, luv, his mouth! Generous and wide, with lips that curved upward at the corners.

'Well then!' she challenged, trying to stop the strange thumping inside her chest. She was startled by his light laugh, realising instantly that it wasn't directed at her.

'I wonder who Alice is?' he chuckled. 'Madam's poor little skivvy, I don't doubt, paying out of her paltry wages for breaking madam's precious ornament! I don't suppose her bit of money would allow for anything more expensive, but by the look of *madam*, she'll exact more from that poor girl than you asked for it!'

She'd never heard him say so much in one go, and it revealed a nature sympathetic and understanding beneath the whimsy that made her laugh with him, suddenly at ease.

David was smiling at her. 'I called,' he said, 'to ask if you might care to take a stroll with me this afternoon? It *is* a lovely day.'

Letty did not hesitate. 'Oh, I would like that!' she burst out.

CHAPTER 3

It was a wonderful Sunday dinner. The small piece of beef stretched to accommodate David, a few less vegetables on each plate, Yorkshire pudding cut in smaller portions, gravy thinned down a fraction to go further, and Dad at his most affable, talking shop to David.

Lucy, magnanimous for once, agreed to the four of them going off to Victoria Park for the afternoon but made it plain that once there, she and Jack would leave the other two to their own company.

The journey there felt totally different from all the other visits when conversations with Letty's friends were yelled over the tram's clatter, its whine fluctuating when it slowed or accelerated. With David sitting beside her on the slatted seat, protecting her from the vehicle's more erratic jolts, there seemed no need for conversation.

Letty and her friends would spend all afternoon in the park, passing and repassing the boys with sly glances, pretending not to notice their reaction, tossing their heads at each cheeky remark and sending back as good as they got. Being *with* a boy was never the same.

She'd once let Billy Beans take her. It hadn't been half so much fun. But today with David at her side, a man, she felt strangely and wonderfully cherished and protected by the way he guided her, one hand gently beneath her elbow. She was shy about putting her arm through his as yet. Perhaps next time, if he asked to take her out again. She prayed fervently that he would.

She also prayed Lucy and Jack would stay with them, the idea of being left alone with David conversely putting her all in a fluster. What on earth would she find to talk about? Fortunately, Lucy didn't seem inclined to rush off as they approached the deer enclosure to see the fawn creatures with their slim cream muzzles.

'Aah . . . they're gorgeous!' Letty sighed, one or two coming close enough for a dry black nose to be touched. She felt David's hand under her elbow tighten a fraction, ready to pull her away from any danger. There was none from these gentle creatures, but it felt wonderful being watched over.

'I wish we had bought something to feed to them,' she said, taking care over her words.

A doe nibbled her finger, plucking at the thin cotton of her glove, but losing interest began to move away.

'Oh, it's going!'

Pulling off the glove, Letty pushed the tip through the wire mesh, wriggling it, tempting the animal back. It sniffed delicately at the fabric, touching the material with an exploratory tongue, gently took the tip of the glove between its protruding teeth, pulled a little.

'Oh, it do feel funny!' Letty giggled and heard David chuckle. She jiggled the glove, feeling the doe's grip tighten, grow stronger. But as she made to pull away, her giggle became a squeak of alarm.

'David! It's got me glove. It won't let go. Oh, 'elp!' Lucy too was emitting anxious little squeaks.

David's hand, warm and strong, covered Letty's, pulled, but what had appeared a gentle creature proved to have hidden strength. The cotton ripped, leaving Letty with the wrist end, staring in dismay as the remainder dangled from the deer's mouth, slowly disappearing behind the buck-teeth which masticated the morsel with relish. With a contented glaze in the animal's eyes, its prize slipped down the slender throat in one visible swallow.

Distressed, expecting to see the creature fall dead at any moment, Letty's studied speech went completely. 'Oh, crikey! What'll we do? I'll 'ave ter pay for it if it dies!'

Lucy had started to giggle. Letty rounded on her. 'Go on – have a good laugh! They was me best gloves. Dad bought 'em for me birthday. He won't half be annoyed!'

Lucy's giggles subsided abruptly, deeming Letty's attitude uncalled for. 'He's never annoyed with you, his little favourite.'

Letty stared at her, gloves forgotten. 'I'm not his favourite! He don't think any more of me than he does of you and Vinny.'

Lucy's face tightened. 'He's always thought more of you than me and Vinny. Ever since he lost the boys, you've been his favourite.'

Letty winced. Her younger brothers had died five years ago, Arthur from meningitis at the age of eight and Jimmie from appendicitis at the age of eleven, both within two months of each other. Dad had never really recovered from it.

'I know why, of course,' Lucy continued, not even realising what she'd said. 'You purring over that old junk of his. He laps it up.'

'I don't purr. Me and Dad just like the same things.'

'That old rubbish he calls art?' Lucy gave a derisive titter. 'None of it's worth a light.'

'You wouldn't understand,' Letty snapped. 'One day he'll find something really good and make a lot of money and get a better shop and deal in real works of art, what he's always wanted . . .'

Lucy's laugh was cynical. 'What *you've* always wanted!'

Blood rushed to Letty's cheeks. 'What's that supposed ter mean?'

Jack had clutched at Lucy, his smooth blunt features creased with concern as he strove to pour oil on troubled waters.

David, in his turn, took hold of Letty. 'I'll buy you new gloves,' he said in a tone firm enough to calm her instantly. And as she did, attempting to disguise threatening tears by brushing down the front of her beige skirt with trembling hands, his tone moderated. 'I shall take you out to buy them, Letitia.'

'There's no need,' she said ungraciously as Lucy marched off, head in the air, Jack trailing behind, reasoning with her.

'I would like to,' David said. He took her arm gently and threaded it through his. 'That is, if you don't mind?'

'I don't mind,' she managed to say as the angry beat of her heart began to slow a little. The feel of her hand lying on his arm spread a feeling of warmth through her, her anger against Lucy slowly diminishing.

'He has his own house and everything,' she told her sister that evening, already practising speaking like a lady; rather overdoing it, but pleased with her achievement so far. 'That's where we would live.'

'He's got to ask you to marry him first,' Lucy said, still a little chilly towards her. 'What if he don't?'

But Letty was full of confidence. He would never offer to buy her gloves if his intentions weren't serious, would he? Green eyes wide with visions of her future, she now, however, knew a fear she'd never before experienced. What if he met someone else and tired of her? Or what if anything dreadful, a terrible accident or something, happened to put an end to this wonderful thing that was happening to her?

★   ★   ★

47

Letty was seeing David every Sunday, he and Jack turning up together. But now it was she who spurned Lucy and Jack's company.

Weekends had become bliss to her. She felt a little sad about Billy Beans when he called, having to tell him she was otherwise engaged. But a girl had to make the best choice. David took her to museums and art galleries. She particularly enjoyed the art galleries – the splendid paintings, the fine sculptures, the delicate porcelain, all the things Dad would have liked to deal in.

There were afternoons in Hyde Park, afternoons rowing on the Serpentine. He looked so manly, rowing with sure strokes, jacket off, shirt sleeves rolled up. He was more sinewy than muscular. She thought of Billy Beans' solid frame, deciding she much preferred sinewy men.

Then there was the theatre. David would sometimes take her up West on a Saturday evening, with the full blessing of her dad, who once would never have sanctioned his daughter being up West after dark. But now she was escorted properly it was different. And where she used to be queuing outside to go into the gods while well off theatre goers in their carriages looked down their noses at the queues, she now went in on David's arm, seats booked. Proper theatres too, squashing into the Hackney Empire or the Cambridge a thing of the past.

No longer did she walk all the way up West with Ethel Bock to watch the carriage folk drive round

Piccadilly Circus. With David she rode in style. In her modified bridesmaid's dress and hat and the gloves he'd bought her, she'd watch with pride, as he gave directions to the cabby. Sometimes she almost had to pinch herself to prove she wasn't dreaming.

'Fancy,' she said to Mum. 'Me riding in a taxicab. I never dreamed I'd ever be doing that.'

'It's lovely for yer,' her mum said, while Dad smiled wistfully.

'Looks like you'll be next ter be married after Lucilla. Then all me daughters'll be gone.'

'He ain't asked me yet,' Letty laughed, aware of nothing beyond her own happiness.

'He will. And when 'e do, you'll be off, like the other two.'

Something in his tone struck a small chord of conscience, took the laughter from her lips. 'Well, if he does, Dad, I'll insist on staying around here. There are some nice places to live in Bethnal Green.'

She saw the lips under his moustache tighten. She felt his sense of desolation that with all of them flown to a better way of life than he had, his would never be the same again. She could almost feel the emptiness inside him. Overwhelmed by an explosion of love for him, she went and folded her hands over his as he sat by the sun-lit window, already wrapped in his own little winter.

'I promise, Dad,' she said emphatically. 'I won't ever go away.'

She meant it. But life was too wonderful for a young head to stay filled with dreary thoughts. David was wonderful. Whatever he did was wonderful: taking her to have tea in the nicest West End tea rooms, or after a show to restaurants where the rich went, feeling both opulent and conscious of shortcomings which she tried hard to rectify.

The weather being exceptional, David took her to Southend by train. She'd never been before. The tide was in, all clean and sparkly in the sunshine. The air smelled fresh, salty and strange. 'It's the seaweed,' David said. All she knew was that to her nose more used to the dead reek of smoke and soot, it smelled grand. And she felt grand, strolling sedately on the promenade, her hand on David's arm, him in straw boater and sporting jacket, she in a lightweight skirt and fawn blouse she'd bought herself, passing well-dressed folk, watching the bathers and long lines of bathing machines. They'd eaten Italian ice cream, had lunch, then a cream tea in a restaurant along the seafront.

Lucy had been jealous and badgered Jack into taking her. Vinny even more envious, but now pregnant and suffering morning sickness, made a great pretence of being disinterested and said, 'I can't see the point, sitting staring at a lot of water.'

Amazing how quickly autumn arrived, itself passing swiftly. Letty realised she and David had been going out together for five months, doing little more than that. Something she had at first thought too impertinent to ask was fast becoming very relevant.

'When will I meet your parents, David?' They were coming home from the National Art Gallery in Trafalgar Square. It was mid-November, and Letty huddled beside him in the cold taxicab they'd got from the station.

It probably wasn't the time to ask. He had been a little withdrawn all day and she remembered his telling her some time ago that November was the month his wife Ann and baby had died. He'd never mentioned them again, as if it was too painful to speak of. She was glad he didn't. It was bad enough feeling vaguely second best, merely filling the gap his loss had left. The more he spoke about it, the worse she'd have felt. Did he love her as much as he had clearly loved his wife? It wasn't something she could easily ask. She doubted she ever could.

'When will you be taking me to meet them, David?' she persisted as he gave a deep sigh, coming out of his reverie.

She'd touched on it last week but beyond saying, yes, he must sort something out, as if he was really saying he must prepare them for someone like her, nothing had yet come of it.

'You're not ashamed of me, are you, David?' Her bluntness, sharp and exasperated, surprised even herself. She'd never seen him look so hurt.

'How can you think that, Letitia?' He always said

her full name, much to Dad's approval. 'You *know* I love you?'

You know I love you. Never that breathless, desperate sigh: 'I love you – I love you – I need you!' A gentle kiss on leaving, that was his way, his hand lingering on hers. But, oh, for the ardent trembling of passion, crushed in desperate embrace.

She would of course have pushed him away, for decency's sake, but to have the opportunity . . . All these months, and they were no closer physically than when they'd first met. Oh, yes, he took her out to places most girls in her neighbourhood would have given their eye teeth to see, treated her handsomely, but that something that should have developed between them just hadn't. Why did he seem always to hold her away? But she knew why. It was where she lived, this rat hole. She saw it in that look of distaste when he came calling on Sundays, pushing through the coarse-mouthed bedlam of Club Row, past stallholders who spat on the cobbles and street traders who accosted everyone within arm's reach.

Until she'd met David she had never really taken a good look at the place, but now had become increasingly conscious of down-at-heel streets, of alleys reeking of urine; alleys where prostitutes lurked, and where men, faces scarred by razors, met to do deals and plot revenge; where a beating up or a stabbing nearly every night of the week only just evaded the police murder files.

Despite the authorities having swept away the

Nichol which had been a so-called rookery of thieves and prostitutes operating from squalid lodging houses, and despite their having put up blocks of flats where decent if poor families tried to keep up appearances, it had changed only outwardly. It was still there just under the surface. The crime, the prostitution, the dirt.

Even now, with the area supposedly cleaned up, decent parents didn't let a girl go out after dark unless she was with other girls and boys, and then she was required to be home by nine.

The grime of London's smoke clung to everything. Washing never came up white, new bricks turned black within a year. Even faces had that grimed-in pallor. Stunted growth too. Cockneys were small people, small and tough. Mum and Dad were an exception, both above average height, passing it on to their girls, making them look ladylike.

Grime wasn't the only thing that clung to this place. Mum's kitchen smelled of Sunlight soap and Flit. The Flit was used on the walls and all corners and cracks – against the bugs. They came through the walls from the flats on either side of this one, even though the Solomons who had the corn chandler's next door kept their place spotless and Mr Jackman, a dapper little man who had the pet store on the other side, was just as particular. But nothing stopped the evil little insects.

It was always worse in summer after they'd been breeding in cracked brickwork. They came out in droves then. It was part of life in slum places and Mum swore they dated from when Arnold Circus had been the Nichol.

Running alive there they had been. In the maze of alleyways, the people hadn't even noticed them, let alone tried to get rid of them. Vice and lice, Letty remembered Mum saying. You don't get rid of things like that just by using a bit of Flit.

She could remember venturing into the place when she'd been about seven or eight. Some blousy women with straggly hair and scarlet lips had snarled at her to sling her bleedin' hook, but one had leered at her and beckoned. That one had frightened her more than the others.

When she got home she had asked Mum about the women and had got a smack instead of an answer. 'What were yer doin' down there?' Mum had railed. 'Ain't yer got no sense, goin' near ladies of the night?' She had never used the word 'prostitute'. It was a rude word. Letty aged eight would not have known what it meant anyway. She hadn't even understood what ladies of the night were except ever after to link the phrase to ugly and threatening women with scarlet lips and straggly hair.

The Nichol was gone now. Arnold Circus with its streets radiating like the spokes of a wheel from a central hub where now stood a raised bandstand where a band played each Sunday was clean even if the barrack-like blocks of flats shaded everything from the sunshine. Hordes of children played there now, and any passerby could go through it without fear of being robbed, kidnapped or corrupted.

If the original slum had been swept away, its bugs remained, and in summer marched down the walls in black fetid clusters. The flat would smell faintly but not pleasantly of almonds as Mum Flitted every nook and cranny against the invaders that might be breeding behind the wallpaper. To her the almond smell was one of shame and she waged constant war. Thanks to her they never had a full-scale infestation, but some people did.

With Mum ill now, it was Letty who wielded the Flit can as regularly as she used big square bars of Sunlight soap on the lino and the linen.

Mum and Dad had done their best to see their girls decently brought up, but it hadn't been enough, or at least seemed that way, seeing David's face after he'd fought his way through the screeching Sunday morning market to Dad's shop door.

'You know I love you,' she wanted to cry. 'Show me how much you love me, David.' Instead she said sullenly, 'I s'pose if I lived somewhere better than what I do, you'd have taken me to see your parents by now!' diction letting her down, proclaiming her for what she was.

David was glaring at her. 'To hell with where you live! You'll not have to live here forever. It's what you are that matters. It's me you will marry, not my parents!'

'But it's a different matter when it comes to meeting them!' She shot at him, then stopped.

'Marry?' she echoed faintly. 'Me? You . . . want to marry me?' But pride drew her up. 'You're only saying that.'

She saw him frown. 'What is wrong with you, Letitia? Of course I am saying that. How else can I say it?'

Knowing what she wanted from him but unable to put it into words, she shrugged, defeated. 'It don't . . . doesn't matter.'

'It does matter, Letitia.' He was pulling her to face him. 'Tell me what's wrong? You're not . . . not getting tired of me, are you?'

Tired of him? God help her! Her whole being trembled in case he was tiring of her. Was this how he was wriggling out of it, telling her she was getting tired of him? Oh, it was unfair!

'I don't know how to tell you,' she burst out, saw real fear come into his eyes at her outburst. 'I know I ain't . . . I'm not much ter run after. I know you could do better than me where you live. I haven't even seen where you live, but I bet it's posh and nice and you see all nice girls. But I . . .' She stopped, wanting to say, 'I love you.' 'I . . . well, I've tried, David. I have tried. I try to be ever so careful what I say, what I do – in case I say the wrong things, do the wrong things, and you'll see what I'm really like. I . . .'

She tailed off with another helpless shrug. He had let go of her shoulder, had gone quiet. She sank weakly back on the seat, staring at the cabby's back. The man was grinning, damn him! Facing front, his features unseen, she knew by the stiffness of his neck that he was grinning, amused by the lovers' tiff. She wanted to poke him in the back, ask what he thought he was laughing at, but that would have made her look more common than she was. And she had her pride. Why was David not saying anything?

When he did speak, his voice was low and hesitant. The driver wouldn't hear it above the rattle of the taxi. She could hardly hear it.

'Letitia, you shouldn't have to be careful – wary – with me. It's I who have been – am – wary of you. No, Letitia,' as she let out a small exclamation of surprise, 'I have been terrified you'll find me . . . stuck up, I think it is. I am constantly weighing what I say, how I say it, in case you see me as uppish, patronising, I don't know . . . I know it sounds ridiculous to you, Letitia. For one so young, so fresh, you are full of confidence. So worldly.'

'Me?' Inside her laughter bubbled, full of bitter disbelief. 'I've never been further than Southend, when you took me.'

'You are wrong, Letitia.' He was speaking unusually fast. 'All my life I have been protected by my parents, my mother especially. Even when I married . . .' He hesitated as though the word might offend. 'I'll not say it was arranged exactly, we were in love of course, but it had been rather expected by both our families that we would eventually wed. Then, when Ann and the baby . . .' Again he paused, this time the words catching in his throat.

'It took me a couple of years to pull myself together. Mother was a tower of strength to me. By the time I was able to face the world, her tower had become a prison, you might say. I felt I had to justify my every movement. The smallest show of merriment and she'd hark back to my loss, as though I was being disloyal. She couldn't believe I could still cherish my wife's memory and yet carve out a new life of my own. Letitia . . .'

She sat looking down at her hands in her lap, felt him turn to face her. 'I have never been able to tell her about us. Not because I am in any way ashamed of you. I admire you, wish I were as certain of myself as you are. But I dread my mother's inevitable reproach that I am casting aside my wife's memory. I've no wish to put you through that.'

He fell silent, gazing at Letty, but she couldn't meet his look although she felt its intensity. For some while she could find nothing to say. Though so much she wanted to say surged through her head, all of it would sound nonsensical if she did put it into words.

'I wonder what she'd think if she knew where I lived?'

'For God's sake, Letitia!' The sharpness of David's tone made her jump. 'Why do you put yourself down so? You're as fine as anyone I've ever met, and I love you! I love you, Letitia.'

In the dimness of the taxicab, he leaned forward and kissed her. It was long and lingering, full of passion. Almost stifled, Letty felt herself melt into it, closing her eyes at the delicious feel of it. David's breath was sweet and warm, and who cared what the driver thought of them?

Beyond the cab, Bethnal Green Road in full spate at ten o'clock at night reminded her that this wonder must end very soon.

'We're nearly home, David!' she just about managed.

His response was to call to the cabby to stop. 'We'll walk from here,' he said, paid the man his fare, then holding her arm through his walked with her the short distance to her road, passing the Knave of Clubs on the corner. In the glow from the pub windows, the frosted glass etched by advertisements for Nicholson's Matchless Dry Gin and Walker's Whisky, he slowed. Nearby, the hot chestnut stand wafted nutty smoke, the bearded vendor turning the roasting nuts on a blackened metal sheet, hands protected by scorched woollen gloves, his cheeks a fiery red from the heat of the brazier.

All around Letty, people surged by, the door to the Public pushed open time after time, emitting laughter, rushes of warm air into the chilly night, the potent smell of beer and tobacco and sawdust.

'I want you to come with me next Sunday to meet my parents,' David said abruptly. And now, after weeks of clamouring for that honour, Letty was caught by fear, by foreboding, wishing she'd kept quiet.

★　★　★

'I should have waited a bit longer,' she told Lucy, who could hardly wait to hear how she had got on. 'I should never have gone.'

'Was she horrible to you?' Lucy asked avidly over the teacups.

It was teatime, the table laid halfway across. There were only the two girls to have tea. Dad was downstairs, would be up as soon as he closed the shop, and Mum had gone to bed. She tired quickly these days. Lucy would take her a cup and a bit of cake later. She ate very little, as if the act itself tired her. At night Letty lay awake listening to Mum coughing, Dad getting up regularly to get her medicine for her. It was all so worrying.

'Horrible ain't the word,' she said acidly, putting the last of the Sunday fruitcake on the table next to the cheese dish. 'I've never felt so uncomfortable in all my life, and I was so sorry for David, he was so worried. And he behaved so different there than when he's with me – all stiff and starched, as though he was watching every word he said and everything he did – just like I was! And all the time I sat there I didn't know where to put me face or what to do with me hands, I was so nervous.'

As Lucy cut bread and buttered it, Letty told of the imposing double bay-windowed house with its large high-ceilinged rooms and its heavy Victorian furniture. 'They did have some lovely things,' she said. The way David's mother had received her. 'Her face all stiff, it was like looking at a white ship all posh, standing off from East India Docks – me being East India Docks. Come to think of it, she was in white – a sort of tea gown thing – all frills and froth and drapes, as if she was going to a royal ball or something instead of just meeting me. All I hope is I don't have to go there again, that's all.'

'What was his dad like?' Lucy said, spreading jam for herself on a piece of buttered bread.

'Oh, he wasn't so bad,' Letty said as she bit into her slice. She took a sip of tea to wash it down, Mum's thick sturdy everyday cups and saucers, painted with fern leaves, and thought of the fine china at the Baron home. Sunday luncheon it had been termed – set more like a banquet with so many knives and forks and things, she hadn't known which to use first, having to watch David before she dared to pick one up – all designed to intimidate her, she was sure. And a good job it had done too.

'I think he was a bit sorry for me. But he didn't approve of me either for all that. He kept looking at me as if he had a real low opinion of me. And all the time she kept referring to her poor David's sad loss. Made me feel proper awkward, it did. And how do they get their o's and a's to sound like they've got a plum in their mouth? Ours always sound flat, have you noticed, Lucy? I tried to make them rounder but it made it look like I was trying to show off. I wasn't half glad when me and David left. I ain't never going to go to meet them again, not if David goes on his bended knee to me.'

Outside in the early dark of the winter evening, a hand bell was ringing, a voice calling some undistinguishable word, but its message was understood well enough. Lucy jumped up and hurried to the mantelshelf where some coins were always kept in an ornate jar.

'Shall we get some for tea?' she asked, but didn't wait for an answer, was out of the parlour door and yelling down the stairs: 'Dad – I'm getting some muffins for tea!'

Letty had the parlour window open, the cold December air hitting her face like an icy hand as she called to the man immediately below, his face hidden by the large flat tray balanced on his head. All she could see was a foreshortened view of legs, one hand swinging the bell, the other hand gripping the tray's rim, and on the tray a cloth covering the delicious muffins, some of which she would soon be toasting by the fire.

Lucy had come out. The tray was put down on the pavement, showing the man's cloth cap white with flour. Six muffins were put in a paper bag from a bundle on a string around the man's waist, Lucy's coins received and dropped into the pocket of his apron. The tray hoisted adeptly back on to his head, the muffin man went on his way, energetically swinging his bell as Lucy came in and up the stairs, yelling to Dad: 'Tea's getting cold!'

Lovely to eat the muffins, dripping with butter, around the fire, Letty's face hot from the flames, then to go back to the table to pour another cup of tea for herself just as she fancied. No sitting on ceremony around a posh laid table, watching every word she said, every mouthful as if she was eating cotton wool.

Afterwards, David had taken her to see the house he still owned, the one he had bought for himself and his wife to live in. It had given her the creeps. Loss had seeped into the very walls, not because the poor woman and her baby had died there but because the house itself had died. For all his furniture there it felt so empty, desolate, a shudder had run through her and she knew nothing would induce her ever to enter the place again, much less go and live there when David proposed marriage to her – if he did.

'Most of the time,' he'd explained, 'I stay with my parents. I pay a woman to clean and dust it, open the windows to air the place. But I can't bring myself to live here on my own, if you see what I mean.'

She did see what he meant, that even now his sense of loss had not gone away, that she wasn't certain that it would ever go away, for all he said he loved her.

After the silent house, and the silent street where he lived, the busy thoroughfare of Bethnal Green Road had been a tonic. The people were vibrant, noisy, not afraid of life. Everywhere was full of bustle and urgency; groups meandering, talking, sharing jokes on street corners; girls in long lines, arms linked, swinging along, home sewn skirts brushing their ankles, second hand blouses and jackets concealing blossoming bosoms, straw hats embellished with wax cherries or a linen flower, boots clumping in unison on the pavement. The quips thrown by boys strolling in groups were readily flung back: 'Does yer muvver know yer out?' 'Does yours?' 'Wanna drink?' 'Not wivart me friend.' 'Oo's yer friend?' 'She's Alice, I'm Ethel!' Life was vital, death seldom thought of.

Dad gone to see how Mum was, Letty told her sister about the house David cherished like a mausoleum, its desolate atmosphere. Even as she spoke of it, she couldn't help a shudder.

'It's always the same when men live on their own,' Lucy said with the slow deliberation of someone who imagines they possess a world of wisdom. 'Look at old Mr Ford – he lived alone.'

What she meant was the two-roomed pigsty in which Mr Ford, for whom they'd run errands as children before he'd died, had lived alone. The place had stunk from neglect.

'I understand what you mean,' she said sagaciously. 'All that house needs is a woman's touch to make it all nice and cosy again. You're ever so lucky having a ready made home to go into and everything.'

But Lucy didn't understand at all.

CHAPTER 4

'I only hope I haven't caught it,' Vinny said.

She sat with her sisters in the parlour as Dad let the doctor out after he'd seen Mum. The doctor came to see her quite a lot now, his bills beginning to mount up.

'I hope none of us have.' Letty gave Vinny a look. Just like her to think of herself first! Though that was a bit unjust, Vinny had her condition to think of. Six months, and she was filling out well around the middle. 'Mum's always made sure she didn't give it to any of us. So long as Dad ain't got it, that's all.'

'It would have showed up by now if he had,' Lucy said, her pretty face puckered thoughtfully. 'Since you've shared with me, he's slept up in your old room so's he won't catch anything. Mum was always very insistent on that, and . . .'

She stopped on seeing her father standing in the door, his narrow face dark at her reference to Mum in the past tense. His tone as he reprimanded her was heavy with the fear that lurked inside them all.

'Was?' he queried. 'What d'yer mean, was? Yer mum looks a lot perkier than she's been fer a long time. Don't yer ever say "was" when yer talk about 'er.'

'No, of course not, Dad. I didn't mean . . .'

Crestfallen, Lucy watched her father move away from the door, going into Mum's room, closing the door softly behind him.

'I didn't mean it that way!' she burst out, her eyes brimming with sudden tears. 'I didn't.'

'Of course you didn't mean it,' Letty hurried to soothe her. 'Dad's full of worry, that's all. He knows you didn't mean it that way.'

Lucy's face was buried in Letty's shoulder, her body shaking with sobs. 'I don't want Mum to die . . . I don't want her to die.'

'She ain't going to. Mum's strong inside. Inside she's got a lot of willpower.'

'And people do get cured these days,' Vinny said, her voice steady and unemotional. Vinny who visited Mum as rarely as she decently could, saying one in her present condition couldn't be too careful, as brazen as you like, had the solution. 'You can go for a year or so somewhere like Switzerland, to a sanitorium. They say the clear air and the high altitude can cure.'

'If we'd got the money for it,' Letty said over her shoulder, still hugging Lucy whose tears were slowly abating. She almost yielded to an impulse to ask if Vinny, so ready with her solutions, might be as ready to help towards paying. Her Albert wasn't short of a bob or two by all accounts. Vinny boasted enough about how she could afford this, afford that. But she knew that even if Vinny were to offer, Dad would be too proud to start borrowing from anyone, though it would be nice to have had the opportunity of refusing.

'Dad ain't got that kind of money,' she said succinctly, hoping the hint would sink in. Vinny's reply, to her mind, was typical – simple and selfish.

'He would if he sold the shop.'

Vinny's insensitivity shook her. Letty bit back the obvious retort, and said instead, 'And what would him and Mum live on afterwards?'

'Well, it does stand to reason.' Vinny had no idea how she'd evoked Letty's contempt. 'Dad is getting on a bit. He won't want to have that shop round his neck forever. If he sold it, he and Mum could live comfortably once she's better.'

'It wouldn't bring in all that much,' Letty said. What she didn't say was that without the shop Dad himself would probably fade away. It was his life, the bits and pieces he surrounded himself with, always looking for that special piece. No one else would understand but she did, for she felt the same towards what others would call rubbish. Without his shop Dad would fall apart, go into a decline. Yet there was Mum to think of still. But there was no guarantee, was there?

Vinny was looking prim. 'You could work in another shop. You've always been clever at selling things. You've worked with Dad more than me and Lucy have.'

'He's never let any of us go out to work, Vinny.'

Vinny looked blank, shrugged evasively. 'It's Mum we must think of now.' She smoothed the modest bulge in her well-cut black crepe skirt with a careful hand. 'Beggars can't be choosers.'

Letty wanted to blurt out that Dad was no beggar and never would be. But Vinny was right. Anything that might help Mum get her health back had to be considered. Yet asking Dad to give up the shop he'd built up, spend the rest of his life in idleness or taking orders from someone else, wouldn't be easy. Though he'd do it, for Mum's sake.

With Lucy and Vinny unwilling to suggest it, and Vinny demurring at her Albert approaching him, it was left to Letty and she knew she could never bear to see the look on his face. She did speak to Doctor Rudd about it, and received the sad and sympathetic reply that things had gone too far for any good to be got from a sanitorium, and selling the shop for that purpose would be quite futile.

It was a miserable Christmas. David, compelled to spend it with his parents, managed to slip over late on Boxing Day, but Letty in turn felt obliged to stay in. Mum taking a bad turn and not getting out of her bed made her feel it wasn't right to go out to enjoy herself.

Conversation conducted in low tones, David talked to Jack when he came over for a few hours, and Uncle Will whose rude health only emphasised the wasted condition of his sister. The fun of last Christmas missing, the flat had a forlorn atmosphere despite being full of Uncle Will's family and Uncle Charlie's too, as if everyone was waiting for something, not daring to contemplate what.

Dad said little, and spent much of his time sitting with his wife. He ignored David almost to the point of rudeness which Letty chose to disregard, seeing he was almost the same towards Jack, no doubt feeling he could have done without outsiders at this time.

By January, Lucy had got to the point where she couldn't stop herself crying at the oddest times: setting the table, brushing the rugs, dusting, sometimes in the middle of reading a book. Once, washing herself at the kitchen sink, she burst into floods of tears so that Letty had to console her, dripping wet over the kitchen floor.

'Shush! Mum'll 'ear yer!' At such times, carefully nurtured vowels went to the wall. In grief she was Cockney through and through, and it didn't matter.

'I . . . can't 'elp it! I just . . . can't. Without Mum . . .' Words were broken by sobs.

'We ain't goin' ter be without Mum. Don't let 'er hear you talkin' like that. She needs all the strength she can get without you goin' on.'

She herself managed to keep on top of things during the day. At night it was a different matter, her head spinning with visions of Mum no longer being there; of Dad trying to cope – dreamy, dependent Dad. Then the tears would come. She'd clamp her pillow tight against her face and sink into a welter of smothered grief. But it didn't make any difference, except temporarily to relieve pent up feelings.

David was her strength now. 'Don't try to hold back,' he told her when, embarrassed, trying to stifle her tears, she suddenly gave way with such sobs in his arms that she thought she'd never stop. 'Let it all out, darling,' David, who had been through it, was far enough removed from her grief to be her comfort where family were too close to give it. Even Uncle Will had begun to break down whenever Mum's name was mentioned.

Dad had taken to ignoring David's presence completely. But then he ignored everyone now. He seldom went down to the shop and it was left to her to run it alone. At least it gave her something to occupy her mind through the day. As if by some sort of telepathy, Dad had spoken of selling up to get Mum away to a sanitorium and it had been left to her to tell him to see Doctor Rudd first. After he'd done so, he hadn't spoken of it again, but had become even more quiet and withdrawn.

'Dad worries me,' she said to David. He'd taken her to see a farce at the Whitehall Theatre, hoping it might take her out of herself for a while, concerned by her drawn features and loss of weight.

'You can't give in now, Letitia,' he'd said. 'Your father needs all your strength. Lord knows, he'll have little support from anyone else once Lucilla is married.'

Dad needed her strength, yes. And that strength she got from David. In the taximeter cab home, a transport David favoured, it being private, and hang the cost, she told him how Dad was behaving, apologised if he was being churlish.

'He's like it with all of us,' she excused, then went on to tell him about Vinny's idea of selling the shop to pay sanitorium fees. She heard David draw in an angry breath.

'That's preposterous!'

'That's what I thought,' she murmured glumly. 'But what else can we do? I couldn't face telling him. He loves his shop so much. I ended up getting him to see Mum's doctor. I think he must have explained how hopeless it all was, because Dad went all quiet and he hasn't said anything about it since.'

Dad's silence stemmed of course from being told of the hopelessness of Mum's condition. David took it as referring to the unlikelihood of selling property without profit, unthinkable in his circle.

He was quiet for a while, lost in thought, until Letty was sure she had said something to upset him.

'I wonder if perhaps I could help?' he said at last. 'I should have offered sooner but I felt I might be interfering in family concerns. Now, of course, it needs to be said. After all, I shall soon be one of the family, won't I? Once we're engaged.'

'Engaged!' Everything else flew out of her head. 'You're asking me to get engaged to you?'

'I'm asking you to marry me, my darling,' he said quietly.

'Oh, David! Oh, you can't be!' Her head was whirling, her throat dry. He was smiling at her confusion.

'But I am.' He was holding her to him, her tears dampening the collar of his overcoat in a flood of joyful disbelief.

Her excitement moderating, he held her a little from him, his face grown grave. 'Listen, my love. It wouldn't be wise to say too much to anyone just yet, to Lucy or Vinny or your father. Too many things to think about. We will be married, yes. In say a year's time. But listen,' he continued hastily as she made to interrupt. 'If I can help your mother . . . By help, I mean financially towards getting her abroad for a cure. I can do that, Letitia. I'm pretty well solvent. If your father feels he must pay me back at some time, that will be fine with me. Though that isn't a condition, you understand, darling.'

Her happiness slowly dissolving while he spoke, she said joylessly, 'I don't think he'd take it. Dad's never been a strong man except when it comes to his pride. He's never borrowed money off anyone.' This last she couldn't help saying with some pride.

'It's your mother's life we're talking about. He cannot refuse,' David said resolutely, and wouldn't listen to any argument.

He tackled her father one Sunday after Lucy and Jack had gone out for a walk, braving the cold damp breeze with its threat of snow.

Keeping out of the way, Letty waited in the kitchen. Sitting at the narrow baize-covered deal table, she stared aimlessly about: at the kitchen range, its coals blazing bright on this cold day – Mum used to cook delicious bread pudding in the oven above it, which Letty now did; at the cups hanging on hooks on the dresser in the recess beside the range; at the shelves, one above the other, where several durable iron saucepans stood upside down to stop the grease of cooking getting into them; to the heavy iron kettle, still warm from making tea, set on the gas stove; at the copper in the corner; at the sink where, besides dishes, the family washed themselves, a steamy mirror over it.

Beyond the coloured glass of the door was an open landing with an iron rail. It housed a wrought iron wringer, a tin bath that hung on the white-washed brick wall, and a lavatory in one corner screened by a wooden wall and a door.

Letty glanced again and again at the clock on its own small shelf. Two-thirty, twenty minutes to three, quarter to. David had been with Dad for half an hour – not only about helping Mum, but also she hoped about permission to marry. She knew with a surge of excitement that Dad would agree to the latter though she hoped he'd agree to both. She remembered how Jack had gone to see Dad and they'd both emerged beaming at the ecstatic Lucy. Letty waited for that wonderful moment to be hers, very soon now, straining her ears to catch what was being said, hearing Dad's low tones, David's just a little higher, but both too blurred behind the closed parlour door for her to make out.

Once she heard David raise his voice and her heart sank. Dad hardly ever raised his, never as far as she could remember. But he could be sullenly stubborn when he had a mind to be. Most likely he was being stubborn over the offer of money. As David's voice modulated, Letty's hopes rose again.

She sat on in a fever of impatience, jumping up with anticipation as David came back into the kitchen. Then she noticed he had come back alone and that his eyes were shadowed.

'Your father's a frightened man,' he told her after he'd made Letty sit back down on her chair. 'He said he appreciated what I was trying to do for your mother, but . . .'

He paused, and Letty watched him move towards the stained glass of the kitchen door to the white-washed balcony, to stand gazing out, his back to her.

'You do know,' he said, without turning round, 'that her illness has gone beyond any hope of a cure – beyond the help of money?'

She knew but had refused to believe. They'd all refused to believe. It had remained to Dad, dear, quiet-spoken, dependent Dad to convince them that they must accept that his wife, their mother, would not be with them for much longer, and nothing under God's heaven was going to alter that. Staring into David's dark eyes as he turned sharply to look at her, a suffocating weight descended to weigh upon Letty's chest so that it took a great effort to breathe properly. Her hands flew to her mouth as tears blurred her sight.

'How long?'

'The doctor told your father just before Christmas that it could be just a couple of months.'

'And he didn't say anything to us?'

'Perhaps he thought it better not to, or perhaps he couldn't bring himself to say it.'

'Oh, me poor dad! Whatever will he do?' She was on her feet, David coming forward to catch her as she staggered towards him. Her voice was muffled against his chest. 'David, I can't think of you and me – of marriage . . . It'd seem so . . .'

'That's why I didn't burden him with it,' he said as her voice died away. Letty straightened, looked at him through her tears.

'You never said nothing at all?'

His smile was wry. 'It wasn't quite the time.'

'But you do still want to marry me?' Immediately she wanted to bite back the words. 'Oh, David, I'm sorry. I don't know what made me say that. I didn't mean to sound so – so selfish at a time when . . .'

He had her tightly in his arms, his lips pressing down on hers, taking her by surprise.

He'd kissed her like this once before, in the taxi when she'd asked to meet his parents. At least there had been the driver present then to make it seem less abandoned. But here, the two of them alone together with the kitchen door practically closed, she should certainly not be allowing herself to be kissed like this, much less be returning it. Surely a decent girl didn't allow herself to be kissed in this way until she was married?

'We mustn't . . .' she tried to say, words muffled by his kisses.

Against her lips, David was murmuring, 'Because you love me, my darling. Because I love you. Because we will be married, my sweet precious darling.'

At that moment it didn't seem like her, Letty Bancroft, eighteen and a half years old, ignorant now of the strong passions that flow in the veins of lovers, making them oblivious to all else. At this moment she felt as old and wise as time itself, yet strangely buoyant and young, gasping against his lips, her body willing to be crushed against him, his to use as he would.

When suddenly David released her, she reeled slightly, with an effort regained her balance, stood blinking as the scruffy everyday appearance of the kitchen came back into focus. A laugh broke from her as her breath returned. 'Oh, David, I do love you so,' she gulped, amazed to see how glum his expression had become, knowing he was thinking of her mother.

★   ★   ★

In under a year Arthur Bancroft had seen his youngest daughter mature from a giggly girl who'd had all the local boys mooning after her, to a woman whose eyes held a faraway look. Letty was in love and love somehow had made her sad.

He too felt sad, a sad empty pit inside him. He didn't want to lose his little girl to any man, but that was the nature of things; there was nothing he could do about it.

He took her aside. 'I know you and your David are lookin' ter get engaged,' he said. 'I want ter see you 'appy, Letitia, but all I can think of right now is yer mum.'

Letty put her arms about his hunched shoulders as his voice faded disconsolately. 'I know, Dad. Don't worry yourself about us. You've got enough to worry about with Mum.'

'It's not that I don't want ter see you and 'im 'appy. I just feel there ain't nothing in life fer me any more. When . . .' He stopped sharply, then began again. 'If anythink was to 'appen to yer mum, there wouldn't be nothink left fer me.'

Letty's throat constricted. 'Don't talk like that, Dad. Mum'll be all right.'

'Lucilla getting married soon an' all,' he went on dolefully. 'I got no 'eart in it. 'Oo's to 'elp prepare fer it?'

Letty gave him a comforting squeeze. 'What d'you think I'm here for, Dad? I'll sort out all the necessaries, so long as Lucy pulls her weight too. That's if she wants a halfway decent wedding.'

It was good to see a small measure of relief creep into those grey eyes. 'Don't worry,' she said firmly, and just as firmly put aside all thoughts of David's proposal of marriage. That could wait for the time being. There were more pressing matters, and at least planning Lucy's wedding in April gave her something other to think about than Mum's fast dwindling health which was frightening them all.

There was little to do regarding Lucy and Jack's wedding after all, subdued affair that it was, accompanied by quietly flowing tears from almost all those who attended, hearts full of commiseration not only for their sad loss but the timing of it. Three weeks to the day Lucy was due to walk in joyful triumph up the aisle of Holy Trinity Church in Old Nichol Street, her mother's funeral service had been conducted in that same church, the coffin borne along that same aisle before being put into the ground in East London Cemetery at Manor Road.

Ill luck had followed upon ill luck. The day after Mabel Bancroft died, Vinny gave birth to a boy. The shock of not being at her mother's bedside as she passed quietly away made Vinny so ill she wasn't able to attend the funeral either, and weakened by grief of it all, she was still confined to her bed by the time Lucy's wedding arrived.

The absence seemed to heighten the loss of her mother and Lucy broke down in the middle of her vows and had to be given a seat for a little while to recover herself.

'We should have postponed the wedding,' Letty gulped, tears streaming down her cheeks as much from her own distress as Lucy's. She felt David's hand tighten almost painfully on hers, dabbed them from her cheeks and lifted her head bravely, her back long and straight, just like Mum's.

All around her, relatives were still in black in respect of a dear one recently gone from them, and as Lucy stoically got up from her seat to resume her vows in a small trembling voice, the church echoed to the sniffling of the women and the damp surreptitious blowing of noses into men's handkerchiefs.

Beside Letty in the front pew, her father made no sound at all, but she could see his tears running silently and steadily down his narrow cheeks. She had to admire the way he had conducted his daughter along the aisle, his stance upright as he gave her away to Jack. It was only when he finally eased into the pew that he sagged at all. Letty held his hand a great deal of the time, endeavouring to give him what small comfort she could find to give.

The guests returned to the flat for the wedding reception more from a sense of duty, it seemed, than to celebrate a marriage. The wedding breakfast was strangely far more subdued than the funeral lunch three weeks previously. Then even Dad had chuckled at Uncle Charlie's dry wit, the full impact of his loss having not quite hit him until later; not hit anyone until later, Mabel

Bancroft, a dear sister, aunt, mother, was gone from them forever.

Unfortunately for Lucy, it took her wedding to bring it home. Whatever had stimulated each to react so perversely to grief on the day of the funeral was missing on this day. Food hardly touched, they talked in whispers. There was no laughter, not even from Uncle Charlie. Congratulating Lucy and Jack on what should have been their happiest day, voices faltered, tears were sniffed back, words like 'Oh, my dears,' were uttered waveringly in place of 'So happy for you both'.

Lucy spent more of her time in her old bedroom being comforted by her new husband than in the parlour. By five o'clock they left very quietly for their new home, accompanied by tearful good wishes, Lucy again breaking down knowing her mother was not there to cry over her. The guests left as soon afterwards as politeness allowed.

The house gone suddenly silent, Dad went to the bedroom he had once shared with his wife, closing the door softly without saying a word.

Letty, taking him a cup of tea, a futile token of comfort but all she could think of, found him curled up under the coverlet, keeping to his own side of the double bed as though the half that had once been his wife's must forever remain sacrosanct.

He was asleep. Scant lashes lowered gently against his thin cheeks, his mouth beneath the droop of his moustache looked even more drawn down, full of sadness. Looking at him Letty felt fresh tears spring, felt she was intruding upon his sleeping grief. Gently she put the cup down on the little cane table beside the bed without waking him and retreated quietly back to the parlour.

'Oh, David,' was all she could say as she buried her face in his shoulder, seeking the comfort of his understanding arm.

The parlour with its empty chairs, its lonely ornaments, even its wall emanating a sense of something gone from the flat, seemed as if it would never again be filled with sound. It was as if the flat had died – the same impression she'd had in David's house – and now she understood. The place had absorbed love but was no longer able to give it back.

Even though Mum's old friend, Mrs Hall, was still busying herself clearing away the remains of the wedding feast – just as she had done the funeral lunch – energetically brushing crumbs off the parlour rug, her presence nowhere near compensated.

'Doin' me bit for yer poor mum, Gawd bless 'er,' she said in a low respectful whisper and nodded lugubriously towards Letty. 'You look just about done in, luv.' And then to David. 'You give good care ter that gel, son. She's worth every penny there is on Gawd's earth.'

'And I know it,' he said in a low firm tone.

Her obligation performed, Mrs Hall finally left. 'Yer've got a good man there, luv,' she said as

Letty went downstairs to show her out. 'Don't you ever let 'im slip through yer fingers.'

'I won't,' she said fervently. 'Thanks for all you've done.'

'Me pleasure, luv. Glad to of bin of 'elp to yer poor muvver, Gawd bless 'er.'

Letty, sitting in one corner of the sofa as the light faded from the room, watched David come back in with his hat from the hallstand in the passage, was very still as he came to stand in front of her, ready to leave and yet loath to go. In desperation, she took the initiative.

'David, stay here the night. I don't want to be on me own.'

'Your father is here,' he said, but he had read her expression; knew the empty aura of the place appalled her. Once it had been so full of life with her sisters moving busily about the flat, chattering, voices raised in laughter or argument; her mother restoring order.

'I'm being silly,' she pleaded. 'Me nineteen in a few weeks' time. But I ain't strong enough, all on me own, with Dad shut in his room and me . . .' She gazed up at him with imploring eyes, a child at this moment. 'Please stay, David. You can have Lucy's room. I can take my old one. At least I'll have you near me to call on.'

Sometime in the night Letty awoke and found herself crying. Her room full of morning light, Mum had come in to tell her off for still being in bed instead of up and ready for school. She'd been well again, that spring in her step Letty well remembered with the old zest for life that had given Dad impetus in making his shop the success it had once been.

She had sat up to defend herself against Mum's scolding, but she was already crying, something inside her telling her it was all a wishful dream; the room dark, empty and silent, full of bitterness of reality, and nothing she could do about it.

A gentle tap on her door stopped her in mid-sob. Holding her breath, she gulped back the rest, whispered huskily: 'Who is it?'

'David,' came the answer. 'I heard you crying.'

She hadn't realised she'd been overheard, the thin ceiling letting through every sound to Lucy's old room below; felt suddenly jealous of her private grief, nourished for a few indulgent moments of self pity. She didn't want even David to share them.

'I was only dreaming,' she said, amazed how terse she sounded.

His whisper came back, almost chastened. 'I thought you might need me. You seemed so distressed.' Then, after a small hesitation, 'May I come in Letitia?'

She hesitated. Dad didn't know David had stayed, would be horrified to know he'd come into her room. Anyway, it wouldn't be right, would it? But quite suddenly she didn't care.

Her face buried in her hands, less from misery than embarrassment at his entering her bedroom at her own invitation and her only in her night-dress, she mumbled her acquiescence, thankful the gas lamp in the street below sent only the weakest of glimmers to the room. All the same, she was being very improper and dared not look up.

She didn't hear his approach until the edge of her bed dipped under his weight. His hands touched hers, began easing them from her eyes, and, improper or not, it seemed most natural to cling to him, to lift her face to his, allow her lips to be kissed gently. No words; his body against hers gave its own comfort, shutting out the emptiness that had so frightened her. Yet an instinctive fear made her suddenly pull back.

'No . . . we can't. We mustn't!' And then, as he too moved back very slightly, confusion. She should never have allowed him to come into her room, but now he was here, how could she allow him to leave?

He held her lightly; the caresses that had threatened to overwhelm her had ceased. David's voice was low, a whisper.

'Go back to sleep now, my darling.' He was moving away, the edge of her bed rising back into place as his pressure on it lessened. 'It's best I go home. I shall come and see you tomorrow.'

But she couldn't let him go. 'I was being silly.'

'No, you weren't.' He was close to her again, his words halting. 'Letitia, my darling, I love you with all my heart. And because of that I could never be so selfish as to allow myself to . . . I want you for my wife, and until that time . . . Letitia, do you understand what I am trying to say, my darling?'

Yes, she did understand. Loving him, she did understand. His own past grief had made him compassionate rather than bitter, had not made him hard or selfish. A man to cherish. As he kissed her once more very tenderly before leaving, she knew she wouldn't cry again tonight.

CHAPTER 5

Arthur Bancroft's voice was thick with tears as he handed little Albert back to his mother.

''Er first grandson. It ain't fair . . .' he managed before his voice gave out and the tears washed over his blue eyes.

Vinny, still weakened from having little Albert under such a sad set of circumstances, held the baby to her like a shield, her face twisting with grief. 'Don't, Dad! You'll start me off again.'

'Never ever 'ad a chance ter see 'er first grandchild . . .'

'Dad!' Letty's voice was strong. 'Go and put the kettle on, love. I'll make tea when it boils.'

He went like a lamb, as he did these days. Whatever she said, he did; whatever command she gave, he obeyed as if his will had been sapped and he needed to obey to keep himself from falling apart.

Letty shook her head as Vinny's tears evaporated. 'He won't let himself get over it. I know it's only been six weeks, but we all have to try. I have to. For his sake. I suppose I'm being hard, and I feel it just as much as he does, but Dad just keeps dissolving. A dozen times a day. Like he did just now, seeing the baby.'

'We shouldn't have come,' Albert offered, but his round face held a partially offended look that immediately put her back up. She tried not to dislike him but his pomposity got right up her nose at times.

'Don't be silly.' She shrugged, vaguely angry. 'Dad would have been even more upset then. He's been fretting to see the baby. It's bound to upset him. Everything upsets him.'

She moved about the parlour as Vinny and Albert sat on the sofa. 'I can't believe she's gone, you know. It's like the funeral – it's got a sort of unreal feel to it when I look back. In fact,' she gave a small apologetic laugh, 'it does seem odd, but looking back, Lucy's wedding feels more like it was the funeral. Poor Lucy.'

She let her voice die away, the two watching her as she moved about aimlessly, hearing Dad filling the kettle in the kitchen, the dull metallic scrape as he put it on the stove. You could hear everything in this flat. Remembering, she let her voice fall. 'Every time I pass Mum's room, I think she's still there.'

It was Dad's room now. He kept it as neat as he kept himself; too neat – as if his own sanity depended upon it. He went round adjusting objects, picking them up, replacing them in different positions, then picking them up again, going through the same procedure. He drew Letty's attention to anything out of place in the flat, not content until she had put it right.

'I wish you'd leave things alone, Dad,' she said, a bit too sharply perhaps. Grief had made her sharp. 'I never know where anything is!' He'd look at her in a hurt fashion, retreating without a word.

He did little in the shop. When it came to facing customers his self-confidence would dissolve and he'd call up the stairs to her: 'Letitia – will yer? I'm occupied. Letitia?' his tone impatient, echoing the panic inside him.

Lately she was more down there than in the flat, Dad retreating to Mum's chair that he'd now made his own. He'd gaze vacantly out of the window for hours on end and it wrung her heart to see him, but she was doing everything now, seeing to the shop, looking after the flat, him, his washing, his mending, cooking, and she only had one pair of hands.

'If you could do something up here, Dad. Like the washing up, that'd be a help. There's not all that much with just us two . . .'

She could have bitten her tongue, seeing the bleak look on his face, and in mute misery they'd clasped each other so as not to be destroyed by their mutual loss.

Letty looked over at Vinny. 'You and Lucy are lucky, not living here any more. You don't know what it's like, Dad under your feet all the time. I do everything now Mum's gone. I can't even go

88

out with David without feeling guilty for leaving Dad on his own. You don't know what it's like. Thank God David understands.'

She shouldn't really have opened her heart to either of them. All it produced was uncomfortable looks that remained there until they left.

Thank God David did understand, behaved wonderfully about it all, because Dad didn't. Hardly speaking when David came on Sundays, he'd go off to his room as soon as dinner was over, and any Saturday evening David came, retreated – to 'lie down' as he put it. It left the two of them alone, true, but as Letty saw it Dad somehow resented David.

'Has he done anything to upset you, Dad?' she taxed him.

It was Monday. The weekend had been hot and sunny, ideal weather for a stroll. For Dad's sake she'd stayed in. And what had he done? Gone to bed, out of David's way, she was sure of it.

Dad was washing at the sink while she prepared breakfast. His reply was evasive as he reached for the towel from the hook beside him. 'Not as I know of.' But Letty wasn't prepared to leave it at that.

'When Jack and Albert were courting Lucy and Vinny . . .' She ignored the look he gave her at her use of her sisters' shortened names and ploughed on: 'You weren't ever funny with them.'

'I ain't ever been funny with no one,' he defended himself.

'Then why keep ignoring David? He's never done you any wrong, Dad.'

Arthur sat down at the narrow deal table where Letitia had placed a pile of toast and marmalade for him, his eyes averted from her face.

'Then what's so wrong about my David?' she persisted indignantly.

And now he did look up, his mouth beneath his moustache turned down by the bitterness of desolation, bitterness that suddenly overflowed before he could stop it.

'That's it – *your* David!' he muttered. 'I s'pose yer'll be the next one – goin' off an' leaving me? Not one of yer care a bloody toss 'ow I feel. Ain't seen Lucilla since 'er weddin' and the other one's come *once*. That's 'ow much they care fer me. An' now *you* want ter go off.'

'That's not fair, Dad!' she broke in, furious. 'All these weeks I've stayed in. I don't ever go out when David comes here, because I don't want to leave you alone. I try my best!' Anger caught the torrent of words in her throat. Gagging with rage and frustration, she slammed down the knife she'd been using to butter toast and fled from the kitchen.

Later that week she wrote a stinging letter to Vinny and Lucy. She suggested to Dad that he went with her to see them but it was trying to get a cat to swim; he refused point blank, saying he'd never been one for travelling and that Jack was capable enough of bringing Lucy to see him.

Vinny and Albert deigned to make another visit on the following Sunday, but Jack came alone, apologising for Lucy not being with him.

'She can't face coming here . . . well, at the moment, so soon after . . . you know,' he explained awkwardly, his smooth longish face concerned. 'Even at home she keeps bursting into tears, what with thinking of her mother . . . and the wedding and . . . all that.'

Dad was staring bleakly out of the window as Letty brought in tea and a bit of cake on a tray for them. Jack, sitting on the edge of the sofa, looked ill at ease, grateful for David's company next to him.

'It should have been postponed,' Letty said coldly, handing Jack his tea. 'Like I suggested.'

'She didn't want that,' said Jack, staring glumly into his cup. 'I think what upset her was not having her mother there at her wedding.'

'You're looking better now, Lavinia,' David was trying to change the subject, watching the way Arthur Bancroft's face was working. But Jack was as blind as a bat to everything but his absent Lucy.

'She keeps saying if only the wedding had been a few months earlier she'd have had her mother to see her married. It upsets her terribly.'

Yes, Letty thought, startled by a twinge of resentment, all Lucy thinks about is how *she* feels, not how Dad feels, or me. Seconds later she regretted the thought. Weren't they all thinking of themselves, of their grief, their pain? What of Mum, denied the sight of her first grandchild, cheated out of seeing her last two daughters wed? At the funeral the vicar said she had gone to a place of tranquillity and joy, was whole again and at rest, they should not be sad for her. In other words they were sad only for the gap she'd left in their lives, but at least they kept it to themselves as much as possible. It wouldn't hurt Lucy to think less of herself and more of Dad, and come to see him.

In August David took her completely by surprise, saying, 'I think it's time we got engaged.' That was it, no arguments, even if she had wanted to. He wasn't given to forcefulness, but when he was Letty's adoration knew no bounds. On the Sunday he took her, all flushed with excitement, up to Regent Street and bought her engagement ring, a band of five large diamonds, far finer than Vinny's or Lucy's.

'You can't afford that,' she gasped, having expected something much more modest. 'Not for me.'

'Who else for, if not for you?' he laughed as he slipped it lovingly on her finger.

She hadn't told Dad where they were going – hated the deception, but he'd only have said something to spoil it. By now she knew he had no fondness for David. He'd never actually said so, but she sensed he worried for her, perhaps thought David too high class for her, had her dangling on a bit of string. Well then, when she showed him the ring, perhaps he would see that David was serious after all.

He'd watched her with dull condemnation as she was getting herself ready to go, hardly able to contain her excitement, her cheeks aglow.

'Goin' out then, are yer?'

'For a little while.' She'd been unable to meet his gaze. 'Mrs Hall is coming in to keep you company.'

'While you go off gallivantin' with 'im.'

Today was too important to argue that she wasn't off gallivanting with 'him', as Dad lately referred to David.

'We won't be gone long, Dad.'

Even if it hadn't been for a special reason, it was good to escape, to get out of the flat, away from the shop. All week she lived for her weekends and David. He was her salvation; made the days between more bearable. She'd think of Sundays with David as she swept and dusted, mended Dad's socks and turned his collars. Lifting water-logged sheets from the copper to guide them sopping through the mangle's wooden rollers, turning the wrought iron wheel, seemed that less tiring. How much lighter her heart to think of Sunday as she pulled flat irons off the hob of the kitchen range to iron the dried linen, her arm sweeping tirelessly back and forth as she dreamed.

''Ow long?' Dad's eyes sought the ornate clock on the mantelshelf.

'An hour or two, that's all.'

Bound now to stick near enough to her promise, her afternoon with David would have been spoiled by fretting to be home before Dad noticed but for the ring encircling her engagement finger. She kept holding out her hand at arm's length to see the stones reflecting the sunlight with dazzling shafts of everchanging multi-coloured flashes, tilting her head this way and that for a better effect.

'I still can't believe it's mine,' she kept saying as they walked in Hyde Park in the time left to them. Everywhere, couples strolled in the sunshine, families picnicked on the grass, rowed on the Serpentine. She and David were feeding the ducks with buns he'd brought; she saw him glance at his pocket watch. A little of her happiness fled. 'I suppose we've got to go home. Show Dad my ring.'

She knew then that she couldn't – that it was a harbinger of his remaining daughter's intention to leave him on his own at the first opportunity. So strongly did she feel the emptiness that was soon to be his, that it squeezed out all the happiness she had been feeling.

On impulse she began twisting the ring off her finger, to David's surprised frown.

'What are you doing, darling?'

'I don't think me dad ought to see this yet.'

'But you said . . .' He looked hurt.

'Please, David, I've got to break it to him gently.' In a rush she explained, 'I can't spring it on him just out of hand. He's only got me. I miss Mum terribly, so Lord knows what he must feel like. And knowing he'll be losing me before long too.'

'He is going to have to know sooner or later.'

'Yes, but not so soon. Please, David, it'll only be for a little while, a few weeks longer, nearer the autumn. Then I promise I'll tell him. Let him have a few weeks.' She watched his expression relax.

'I suppose you're right,' he said, and sighed in disappointment.

By the time they reached home, her gorgeous ring hung on a narrow ribbon around her neck concealed by her blouse – black despite the fine weather, out of respect for her mother's memory.

Summer moved into autumn and with the ring still dangling immutably on its ribbon, David was becoming more and more restive.

'It isn't easy for your father, I know,' he told her. 'But your mother wouldn't thank him for all his pining for her. He has to pull himself together sooner or later. He can't depend on you forever, my love. No, you'll have to be firm with him, Letty, or you'll make a rod for your own back.'

They'd been to the Mogul Theatre that Saturday evening. Mrs Hall had agreed to keep an eye on Dad just for a few hours. These days there was no more going for supper afterwards but a rush home in time to relieve Mrs Hall. Even so, Letty had been happy, still giggling at the Harry Lauder jokes as they emerged to a rainy evening, the bilious gleam of gas lamps along Drury Lane reflecting the hurrying crowds unevenly upon the damp pavement. But David's reminder dulled her spirits.

At her door David kissed her. He very seldom came in, having long ago become aware of her father's inexplicable dislike of him. Now he gave her arm an encouraging squeeze. 'Remember, darling, you mustn't let him rule you. Be firm with him. Next week put that ring back on your finger and be damned to his reaction. You just cannot give up your whole life to him. He has to know about us at sometime or other.'

Letty nodded, lifted her head for his goodbye kiss and watched the taxi chug slowly along Club Row, deserted at eleven o'clock but for several drunks singing their heads off on the corner of Old Nichol Street. She closed the door despondently as the cab turned left into Bethnal Green Road and out of sight.

All very well for him to say 'be firm'. He didn't have to look into Dad's eyes and see the lost look that came all too often into them. David, who understood about grief, had only been on the receiving end. What he didn't know was what it was like to have to watch someone grieving and not know what to do for them; and she could not tell him, couldn't explain it to anyone.

Out of desperation she confided in Mrs Hall, one wet November afternoon as she mended some of Dad's shirts. Mrs Hall had popped in with a bit of fish for Dad. She'd taken to doing things like that. She was a bit startled by Letty's attitude, and somewhat severe.

'Well, it's only bin seven months, luv. Grief's a two-year disease an' I should know. When my Fred went, Gawd bless 'im, I was beside meself fer more'n two years, I can tell yer.'

'I know how he feels,' Letty said, practically imploring her to understand. 'But I can't sacrifice my life forever.'

'But yer wouldn't rush off and git wed so soon, would yer? I mean, seven months! Wiv'aht yer, yer dad ain't got a soul in the world. Them sisters of yours ain't no bloomin' consolation to 'im. Too wrapped up in their own lives, they are. You don't know what a great comfort you are to yer dad.'

Whatever Letty thought of her sisters, it didn't sit right to have an outsider criticise them, no matter how lacking they were.

'Vinny's got her baby to see to, Mrs Hall,' she defended tersely. 'And now that Lucy's expecting . . .'

Mrs Hall was instantly all avid interest. 'My, time do fly, don' it. 'Ow long do she 'ave ter go?'

'A good three months.' Letty's needle flew in and out of the twin holes of the button. She could almost see Mrs Hall counting the months on her fingers, wondering if conception could be calculated as having occurred before the nuptials proper.

Fastening the thread, Letty bit it off close to the button with strong teeth, laid the shirt aside, and glanced out of the window. It had stopped raining. She stood up, smiling politely into Mrs Hall's heavy face with its mottled cheeks.

'I've got to pop out for something for Sunday. I might get a bit of loin in the pork butcher's. My young man's coming for dinner.'

Mrs Hall chuckled good-humouredly as she followed Letty out of the parlour. 'Your dad don't seem to take to that young man of yours, do 'e? Well, that's the impression I get.'

She hovered in the passage while Letty took her black coat from the stand and secured her black tam o'shanter with a hat pin, putting on gloves and scarf for extra warmth against the wet November air.

'Mind you,' went on Mrs Hall, trailing her down the narrow stairs to where Dad was sitting in the shop, slouched on a stool, staring blankly at the busy street beyond. 'Mind you, I do fink that young man of yours is a bit too old fer you, if you ask me.'

'I'm not asking you, Mrs Hall!' Letty turned on her before she could stop herself, and saw the woman's face drop.

'Beg yer pardon fer me audacity, I'm sure. I'll say goodbye then, if yer don't mind. I'm sure I didn't mean ter intrude. Good day then, Mr Bancroft.' She bustled past him and the bell swung wildly, the wind catching it as the door was flung open to close with as near a crash as the incoming draught allowed.

'There was no cause ter be rude to 'er like that.' Arthur Bancroft straightened up with an angry gesture, and saw his chance to get all that had bothered him off his chest.

'She's been a good neighbour ter me, 'elped me in me time of need, when me own family was only thinkin' of nothink but themselves.'

He saw shock on her face. 'That's not true, Dad! I've stuck by you. I've done all I can for you, and you can't say I haven't!' But he gave her no chance to say more, the pent up feelings he himself could not completely understand pouring out in a torrent.

'Is that what yer fine young man's taught yer, ter go around being rude ter people who do their best er 'elp others in need?'

He advanced towards her, his face ravaged by as much anger as his normally placid nature allowed. 'Fine manners. Fine ways. But when it comes down ter the milk of human kindness, then all 'e wants is what 'e can get – takin' a daughter away from 'er father and ter hell with 'ow I feel, left all on me own, her mother 'ardly cold in 'er grave! That's what yer want, ain't it? Ter go off an' marry 'im? Forget all about me an' yer mother an' the 'ome yer was brought up in. People round 'ere ain't good enough for yer any more. Turnin' up yer snooty nose at decent lads like young Billy Beans oo's nearer yer age and could give yer as good an 'ome as *he'd* give yer, and ain't tarnished by bein' married before – making you second 'and. No 'e ain't good enough. None of us is good enough. You want ter go off, tryin' ter be what you ain't. And yer never will be, don't matter 'ow hard yer try.'

As he stood over her, she seemed to shrink. 'Well, you ain't goin' ter go off with yer fancy young man. This is yer 'ome, where yer belong, where yer was born. You ain't even proud ter be what you are, trying ter talk all la-di-da, fancyin' yer luck! Well, he ain't goin' ter take you away from me. You ain't twenty-one yet and you won't get no permission from me.'

His daughter's green eyes were blazing back at him from a mere few inches away. 'Then I shall wait until I'm twenty-one!' Even with her shoulders hunched forward, her chin thrust forward defiantly; even as she yelled at him like a fishwife, she sounded posh, the way she spoke in front of *him*, so practised that it had become second nature – as if she'd brushed her old life, like dirt, out of sight under the carpet. 'It's only two years away. I can wait that long. I won't need your consent then.'

'Yer won't get me blessings neither!'

The words, thrown at her in anger, hit back at him with their true import, sounded as though he was disowning her. He didn't want to disown her. He loved her, loved her dearly. Letitia's face, twisted and ugly with fury, swam before his eyes in a mist. He was crying, tears flowing down his cheeks, unchecked. 'Gawd 'elp me fer sayin' that!'

Letty felt his arms go around her. Her reaction was instinctive as she clutched him. But her eyes were dry, the comfort of tears forced back by what he had said, words that would always stay with her. Yet she couldn't blame him. They had come from a frightened man, a man made old by grief, though he was not old in years.

In the street she could hear the discordant confused jangle of the barrel organ that was nearly always drawn up outside the Knave of Clubs, jingling out a discordant tune: 'I live in Trafalgar Square'.

She could see people passing backwards and forwards beyond the shop window, going about their business as quickly as possible, huddled in their coats, scarves wrapped around the necks, heads down against the chill wind; could see them clearly because her eyes were as dry as the desert.

CHAPTER 6

Letty leaned forward and tapped little Albert's fat cheeks with a forefinger. 'Who's a darling chubby-cheeks then?' she cooed, evoking a smile from the nine month old sitting contentedly on his mother's lap, a small fist curled around the bit of buttered bread he was vigorously sucking.

Curtains closed against the winter's evening, everyone full up with Christmas pudding and cake, they sat around the parlour fire, pulling chestnuts out of the grate, muffins browned on toasting forks then being buttered and handed round. Nutshells littered the ash-strewn hearth; the men drank beer, the women sipped sherry. Letty gazed at each one.

Almost a year since losing Mum. It hardly seemed possible, for all Dad's face seemed to grow more lined with grief as the months grew. Vinny and Lucy had even put aside their black for something a bit more cheerful for Christmas. Vinny with baby Albert had proudly announced another on the way. Lucy too, her stomach in full bloom, looked so contented with her married state, Letty almost hurt with envy.

Lucy puffed her chest out over her bulge, leaning forward with an effort to retrieve a chestnut from the grate, and didn't quite make it.

'Jack, love, reach one out for me, there's a dear.'

Obligingly jiggling its charred blackness from one hand to the other until it was cool enough, he handed it to her. Lucy gingerly peeled off the husk. Nibbling the sweet floury flesh, her eyes sought Letty's.

'And when are you and David getting engaged?' She looked surprised when Letty, tightening her lips, didn't reply. 'Lord knows you've been walking out for long enough. Eighteen months, isn't it? Since Vinny got married.'

Letty caught David's look, sitting a little apart from the others, near the piano, read in his expression that now was probably the time to bring out her ring. She glanced quickly away. It definitely was *not* the time. At Lucy's enquiry Dad had got up. Shoulders hunched, he went out of the room, going past David with not one glance in his direction. Irritation immediately reared up in her. She almost called after him, 'It's Christmas! Goodwill to all men – that includes my David too.'

'Where's Dad off to?' Lucy, her blue-grey eyes wide with innocence, continued nibbling at the chestnut while Vinny prattled happily to little Albert, oblivious to everything but him.

Dad hates David, that's what, and you didn't help, Letty wanted to stand up and shout at them both. Your Jack and your Albert – the sun shines out of their backsides as far as Dad's concerned. So why in God's name is he so against David?

Instead, she shot her pregnant sister a sharp glance. 'You'll get indigestion eating all those nuts,' she said, and escaped Lucy's retort by getting swiftly up from the sofa to go and help herself to another muffin off the table.

She didn't really want it, put it back on the pile, sat at one of the upright chairs beside David.

'I can't show them the ring,' she hissed. 'Not yet.'

He said nothing, but his bowed head gave the impression of veiled disapproval, disappointment, a coolness towards her for lacking in courage, for letting him down perhaps in not boldly displaying the ring still hiding like a felon under her blouse.

'I'm sorry, David,' was all she could whisper, but again he said nothing, just stared sightlessly towards the fireplace, an apathetic half smile on his lips as though it was an effort to acknowledge her at all, though he did hold her hand when she touched his.

Her leaving had disrupted the pleasant stupor around the fire. Jack took a deep revitalising breath and turned towards Albert who had been lethargically smoking a pipe, the moustache he had been cultivating for some months now grown thicker, the fair bristles long enough to touch the pipestem.

'How about a game of cards?'

Albert took his pipe from his mouth. 'Don't mind if I do. How about you, David?'

'Couldn't we all play?' Lucy cried eagerly.

'I won't.' Vinny kissed little Albert's fat cheek. 'He's all nice and contented at the moment. If I put him down he'll cry.'

Dad came back into the room, adjusting his belt.

'We're going to have a game of cards, Father,' Jack informed him with respectful enthusiasm. 'Something the ladies can join in, if that's all right? What about you?'

Arthur shook his head, dropping into his chair.

'Oh, come on, Dad!' pleaded Lucy. 'Cheer you up.'

'I don't need cheering up,' he said glumly. 'I'll be going ter bed in a minute.'

'It's only ten o'clock!' Lucy exploded tactlessly, never glancing beyond her nose to see the obvious.

He's missing Mum more than ever on this day, thought Letty, as she had done several times over the past few hours. Last Christmas Mum was here, with us. As ill as she was, her presence filled this flat. And now all that was left was her memory, in every cup, every saucer, in the vases on the piano, in the humblest duster Letty used to polish the furniture with. Mum gazing out from the photograph Dad refused to put away, expression unsmiling as required by the camera though her eyes smiled, the pose military for the purpose of the photographer yet something behind it radiating warmth.

Emptiness surrounded Dad, even with his family about him, cloaked him in a sort of aura, and whatever irritation Letty had felt with him a moment ago disappeared completely. Like her sisters she was adjusting to her loss, it was in the nature of things. They were young. She had David, her sisters their husbands, each ready to challenge or enjoy what life had to offer. Dad had no such panacea, could only look back, live in the past, still living with the dead who had shaped his life.

The telegram came as Letty was closing for dinner. Guessing its contents, she gave the boy sixpence and raced upstairs, tearing open the flap as she went.

'It is!' she laughed, reading excitedly. 'Lucy's baby! A girl! Six-thirty this morning, seven pounds eight ounces. A whopper for a girl. She's called Elisabeth Lucilla. Oh, I'm so pleased for her!'

'Long as they don't call 'er Lizzy.' Taking the telegram from her, Dad read it for himself.

'She won't shorten it. Spelt with an "s" too,' Letty said with conviction. Nothing common for Lucy, living in posh Chingford.

'Be nice ter go over ter see 'er,' Arthur mused out of the blue as they finished the sausage and mash Letty had kept warm over the range.

Clearing the plates, she looked at him in amazement. 'You mean that, Dad? You'd travel all that way? The weather so cold and all?'

Unhooking the poker from its stand in the hearth, she vigorously raked at the moribund coals in the grate until the flames began to flicker grudgingly. 'We'd have to go by train. And we'd have to close the shop for the day.'

Arthur reached up, propped the telegram on the mantelshelf, sank into his chair before the now blazing fire.

'Can't afford ter lose money closing up. It'd 'ave ter be Sunday.'

Sunday? Letty's heart seemed to plummet. With an action that was slow and deliberate her father took his pipe from its rack, his tobacco pouch from a tin box beside his chair. The smooth age-blackened leather had so absorbed the taint of its contents over the years that the room was instantly filled with the pungent-sweet reek of Navy Cut which every evening he would cut from a plug with a penknife over a sheet of newspaper spread on the table, paring it into suitable slices and rubbing it between his palms into shag to fill the pouch for the next day.

The poker poised in her hand, halfway to its stand, Letty watched him fill the pipe, hands manipulating pouch and bowl together until the bowl was filled. Rewrapping the pouch over itself, he plucked a taper from the narrow wooden case hanging by the hearth and reached it into the coals, bringing the flame to his pipe, sucking at the stem, forefinger expertly tamping the tobacco, the flame plopping audibly with each suck.

Contented, he tapped the taper out against the grate, replaced it still gently smoking in its holder beside the rest, and sat back in his chair to puff a cloud of blue smoke into the air.

Wordlessly, Letty watched the ritual with cold anger growing inside her. Her whole being sensed the satisfaction with which he had made his statement. He knew well how precious her Sundays were to her. He'd been testing her, she was certain, in making the statement. Yet she knew few shop-owners would allow themselves to take any other day but that. And she was duty bound to go with him, could not let him travel all that way on his own. He was playing on it.

That evening she scribbled a note to David, dropping it in the post the same night hoping to be in time to save him a fruitless journey.

He would understand how heavily duty fell on her shoulders, but as the train steamed slowly out of Bethnal Green Station on the Sunday morning, she thought dismally of those precious hours lost to her.

Beyond the soot-grimed carriage window, her breath steaming up the inside of the square panes, the day had a cold grey look. Snow lay thin on the roads they passed, on roofs, in the bare patches of back yards, bleak empty flower beds poking through black and lumpy. A world that was black and white with leafless trees dotted here and there – like birchbrooms in a fit, as her mother used to say of anything that had a stark and standing up look to it.

'We're stupid going on a day like this,' she said morosely, leaning back on the hard leather seat. 'We should have waited for a better day.'

'There's ain't no better day than today,' she heard Dad mumble from within the heavy Chesterfield coat he was wearing.

In the freezing half empty carriage, he looked grey with cold. A thick scarf pulled up to his cap, hands thrust in woollen gloves, he looked like a bundle jerking stiffly from side to side to the sway of the train as he stared stolidly at the three sooty faded prints of watercolour landscapes above the seats opposite. In the first-class carriages there were mirrors as well as pictures, and nice lamps too, and blinds. Third class never had any cheeriness.

'Thought you'd be pleased ter 'ave me go out,' he went on. 'Been naggin' at me enough ter get meself out, ain't yer? Got yer way now.'

The bantering note surprised her and he even offered her a warm smile, the way she remembered from the past with such a flood of love, that her lips too parted in an equally warm smile.

Perhaps she was wrong thinking him unreasonable to want this day to see his new grand-daughter? Perhaps in most things he was not really being deliberately unreasonable? Perhaps it was she, grown so raw and touchy with wanting to be David's wife, who construed everything Dad did as solely to dig at her?

She settled back philosophically. Very well, this Sunday she would not be seeing David. There was always next Sunday to look forward to.

That wonderful prospect warming her soul,

Letty forgave her dad for whatever it was she ought to forgive him, magnanimously, totally, and looped both her arms about one of his for warmth in the cold comfort of the railway carriage.

His day out did Dad no good at all, a chill putting him to bed for over a week, and keeping her running up and down with medicine, menthol rub, bowls of broth – all on top of looking after the shop.

The housework going to pot, the flat looking a mess, she sent a frantic note to Vinny to come and help. After all, Vinny in Cambridge Heath Road was only a short tram ride away. Albert came over to say that Vinny wasn't feeling well herself, that little Albert had the start of a cold too – neither of which Letty in her frantic state of mind believed as she battled on alone.

It was several weeks before Dad was really well enough to get up. He sat crouched in front of the fire, complaining. Trying to do everything herself drew Letty right down and worried the life out of David.

'Get someone in to look after the flat,' he said decisively, taking charge.

'We can't afford it,' she said, swallowing pride with an effort.

'Don't be silly. I'll pay for it.'

But Dad would have taken this as charity. 'I'll ask if Mrs Hall might help me out with an odd day here and there,' she said.

Mrs Hall, pleased to be asked, was only too willing. In she came, shawl, straw boater, black boots, red face, gravel voice and all and took over. Despite her dictatorial manner, Letty could have kissed her.

But even when Mrs Hall finally withdrew her services, seeing Dad on the way to getting over the worst, he remained constantly under Letty's feet, creeping about the place as if he were an old man. She was never free of him. Only when shopping could she breathe easily, drawing in great gulps of the cold fresh air of approaching spring; then, and in the shop. She derived much pleasure from being in the shop, especial satisfaction in buying, haggling over things brought in, judging their quality, pricing them, the triumph when her price was met and she saw pleasure on her customer's face. And there was always Sunday afternoon to look forward to, when the shop closed and David came.

'Then when *are* you going to tell him?' David's voice trembled with barely concealed anger.

'I don't know!' she wailed back at him

They had been sitting, quite contented, on one of Victoria Park's benches in the weak April sunshine when the row had blown up out of nothing, some perfectly innocuous remark she couldn't even recall now. Something about going to see Mum's grave, she thought. And before they knew it they were at each other, David bringing up her lack of courage at Christmas in telling her father of their plans to marry, and threatening that if she wouldn't tell him, he would, and soon!

'I can't go on dangling on your string,' he'd said cruelly. 'When are you going to tell him?' Immediately provoking tears even as she snapped back at him spiritedly, 'I don't know!' a deep fear beginning to loom that she was in danger of losing David if she didn't look out.

Since Christmas when his impatience at her reluctance to display the ring had been all too evident, he had been decidedly distant, and she couldn't blame him. She had always thought herself a woman of spirit, but in this she had failed him; had failed herself. Of course he was disappointed, but it still wasn't fair to expect her to make choices, to make her decision and just go off and marry him, leaving Dad to fend for himself. Just thinking of Dad trying to cope on his own made her squirm inside.

'I can't see as our marriage could ever be happy under circumstances like that,' she fought to explain, through her tears. 'Me knowing I'd left him in the lurch as if I didn't even care, and feeling guilty about it for the rest of me life. And I would, you know. I'd be unhappy, and I'd make you unhappy because I was. I want to marry you, David. But it's not easy with Dad, feeling I can't leave him. And it's not fair, asking me to choose between you. I just can't. You've known what it's like living alone in a home that was once so happy. You still don't like being in your house on your own after . . . after . . .'

She trailed off, uncertain whether harking back to his own grief was a good thing. Then, to her surprise, he caught her, and hugged her to him. Even gave a low chuckle, bringing the row to an abrupt end.

'Hasn't it occurred to you,' he chided gently, as if what he had to say had occurred to him long ago, 'that if you wanted, he could come and live with us? I could look for a house with an extra room and he could be on his own or spend any time he wished with us.'

'But that's not fair to you!' Letty pulled away to gaze sceptically at him. 'It's not what most people starting married life would want to do. You don't really want to put up with having my dad with us?'

'I'd put up with anything to make you happy, my sweet darling,' he said with conviction.

'Oh, David,' she sighed, all her misery gone in a single sweep. She drank him in with her eyes. 'Why didn't we think of that before? It's the answer to everything.'

Such a simple solution! Before going down to open up the shop on the Monday morning, she screwed up all her courage and told her dad outright that David had asked her to marry him, would be coming as soon as she said yes to seek his permission formally. She said she wasn't prepared just to go off and leave her father all on his own and so David had thought of a way where Dad wouldn't be lonely. She said it all in the face of his stony silence and even stonier stare.

She told him what David so generously and selflessly proposed for him, and all the time her confidence dwindled little by little and prepared herself for argument. But she didn't expect such a bitter response.

'Yer askin' me to leave *'ere* – the 'ome yer mother died in? Yer askin' me ter forsake her memory so's your conscience is clear?'

She thrust that injustice behind her, keeping her voice level. 'Dad, it don't matter where we are, we'll never forget Mum. Never.'

'That's mighty good of yer.' Beneath the stiff moustache the lips curled bitterly. 'But I prefer ter stay 'ere, where she died.'

Fighting not to lose her temper, she brought out the alternative, rehearsed against the likelihood of refusal. 'If you like, Dad, we could live here.'

Thinking what David might say to that, her father's outburst caught her unprepared. He turned on her so sharply that she flinched.

'I don't bloody well want you bringin' anyone 'ere, soddin' well tellin' me what to do in me own bloody 'ome!'

'But he wouldn't . . .'

'I don't want to 'ear another bloody word about it!' he swore again venomously.

It wasn't the venom but Dad's swearing that shook Letty. He never swore at her, hadn't in her life as she could remember. Not even when she'd caused uproar from Mum by coming in with clothes torn from climbing railings or shinning up

114

lamp posts to hook a skipping rope over the bracket to swing on, or came home with hands filthy from popping tar bubbles in the road in summer. He had always stood by frowning but leaving Mum to do the shouting and walloping, had cuddled her afterwards when Mum wasn't looking, one hand around her shoulders pulling her briefly to him, helpless as she was before Mum's asperity. He'd never lost his temper with her, never sworn at her in his whole life.

She had often heard him, of course, come out with a mouthful down at the Knave of Clubs with his mates, good round cockney oaths, but he had always maintained a civil respect in front of women, said that swearing in any shape or form in women's company didn't make a man any more a man.

To hear him now tore at her like a verbal cudgel beating about her head, bruising, splitting the skin of her own self respect.

'You bloody well listen ter me fer a change! Time something was said about this. I ain't 'aving 'im and 'is fancy manners around me fer the rest of me life. Next thing yer know, I'll find meself bein' wheeled around in a bleedin' barf-chair, told what ter do, where ter go, 'ow ter think. I'll 'ave yer to know this is *my* 'ome. I do what I please in it.'

'It's mine too, Dad!' she shouted back, standing up to him because there was no alternative, defiance stiffening her spine. 'I loved Mum too. But I do have a life to lead, and me and David thought . . .'

'I don't want ter know what you and 'im thought!

If yer want the truth, I got no time fer 'im. As far as I'm concerned, he's a bloody snob. I don't like 'im, an' I don't intend tryin' to. But I tell yer this – I 'ope and pray 'e'll find 'imself some gel oo's a snob like 'imself and push off. I just 'ope 'e'll leave you standin' one day. Or die. It'd be a blessin' in disguise. P'raps then you'll find some bloke more your class. Someone like Billy Beans, 'oo can knock spots of 'im fer looks – could give yer as good an 'ome as anything that la-di-da bugger could. Even though yer've turned yer nose up at 'im more times than any bloke could take, he still fancies yer. P'raps it'd bring yer down a peg or two – give yer time ter think how I feel, being cast off like you're castin' me off, yer mum 'ardly dead and buried a year . . .'

He turned away, his face wet and twisted out of shape. Letty's appetite for argument gone, she turned and ran down the stairs headlong, blindly, almost falling. In her head was some vague thought, quite unconnected with what had been said upstairs, that she must open up for their customers, that someone must be there waiting impatiently to be let in.

How could Dad have wished such a terrible thing on David? Said in temper of course. Lots of people never mean what they say in temper, but to have been devastated himself by grief and still to wish it on her, his own daughter, even in temper, like a curse . . . Surely he hadn't realised what it was he was wishing on her?

Tears were flowing down her cheeks now, though she hadn't realised she was crying. Compelled by habit to open always at nine o'clock, she fumbled with the bolts, fingers trembling, refusing to obey her. But it didn't matter any more. Giving up, she let herself sag against the age-pitted frosted glass, stood leaning against it, sobbing out her anguish in great heaving, shuddering gasps.

CHAPTER 7

Arthur Bancroft watched his daughter narrowly as she came back into the parlour after letting David out, to set about preparing for bed.

He hated Sundays when David Baron came into the flat as if it was his right. Sundays the flat wasn't his any more. He felt in the way, the pair of them begrudging his even sitting well out of the way in the corner in Mabel's chair. And pride wouldn't allow him to skulk off into the kitchen to sit there on a wooden chair. Why should he? It was his home. His only escape was to go to bed. But then again, why should he?

As she took her David downstairs and through the shop to say their lingering goodbyes – and God knows what they got up to in the dark behind the door – he had sat in the parlour, too on edge now to go to bed. He had stared out at the last fading light of a miserable June evening, straining to catch the faint elusive murmur of voices. Every time they lapsed into silence he had held his breath, visualising the man holding the woman close. His thoughts had been bitter as always.

My Letitia in his arms. Damn him! Taking her from me . . .

'He's gone then?' he growled as she came back into the room.

'Yes. Of course.'

Her tone was sharp. It had been this way since that day when he'd lost his temper, voiced his opinion of David Baron. If only he could take back what he'd said. It drummed in his head at night, clamoured for release in apology, but he couldn't. Not now. It would only make it worse after all this time. His only escape was in surly sarcasm, meant to scourge himself rather than censure her.

'Good of yer to 'ave stayed in today.'

'Weather wasn't nice enough, was it?' she threw back at him, the inference that it, and not he, held the greater importance for her.

'I s'pose if it's nice next Sunday, you'll be off out?'

'Don't know yet, do I?'

Following her out to the kitchen, he watched her set the table ready for breakfast. She always did it the previous night to give herself time in the mornings to open up the shop. He had no interest in the shop any more; no interest in anything. Not even Lavinia's new baby, George, born three weeks ago, gave life any meaning with Mabel gone.

'If it rains as hard as today, I'll probably stay in and keep you company again, Dad. That'll be nice for you, won't it?'

He curled his lip at the sarcasm as he sank down

on one of the two kitchen chairs to stare into the unlit grate.

'Don't bother on my account.'

'If that's what you want, bugger the weather! We'll go out.'

She turned abruptly to get cutlery from the dresser drawer. She made a point of using swear words now and could feel his baleful gaze, like fingers on the back of her neck, knowing her reasons.

There was no triumph to hurting him. But he had hurt her. Let him know how it felt. Even so, there was no pleasure in it. If anything it hurt her the more to be this way towards him. Anyway, one week from today she would be twenty-one and he could do nothing about where she went or what she did. Next week she vowed she would put on her engagement ring, waggle it in front of him and dare him to stop her marrying David. Then again, could she bring herself to do that? Would natural love and emotion still rule, keep her as servile as ever?

The shop bell jangled sharply, making her jump as Billy Beans burst in, his wide bright blue eyes gleaming with excitement.

'There's somefink goin' on up Whitechapel Road. There's coppers all over the place. Crowds of people. On the corner of Sidney Street.'

He'd taken to popping in quite a lot since the girl he'd been walking out with had transferred her affections to another. Had been going out with her for some two years on and off, often more off than on, it seemed to Letty, until finally a more attractive face than his, so he said, had terminated their walking out together for good. Letty thought the girl, who came from somewhere the other side of Brick Lane, must have been barmy even to consider Billy, with his fair wavy hair and strong broad face, inferior in looks to this other lad.

A thick, well-cut moustache, which Letty strongly suspected he had grown for the girl's sole benefit, added to his strong good looks.

'Sidney Street?' she queried, turning back to what she'd been doing before he'd burst in, meticulously wiping the grime of ages off a gilt picture frame she'd just bought for ten and six.

'You know!' Billy was waving his arms about. 'Mile End Road and Cambridge Heaf Road. You know. The crossroads there.'

'Of course I know. By the London Hospital.'

'That's right. Just been seein' me bruvver in there. 'Ad operation on 'is 'pendix. But 'e's orright now.'

Letty went and closed the shop door which Billy had left wide open in his excitement, letting in the cold. Born in a field, Bill. Never seemed to feel the cold; always too animated, she supposed. And it was cold, only into the seventh day of the New Year, 1911.

Billy was going on. 'Someone said they got some bloke 'oled up there. 'Eard they've called out the army, and the 'Ome Secretary too. Someone said he saw him gittin' aht of a automobile wiv 'is top 'at and cigar an' everyfink. Wish I'd seen 'im. Aint never seen no one important. Someone said they'd cornered a Russian anarchist. I bet 'e was after our new king and 'im not bin on the frone a year yet.'

Letty, smiling obliquely, went on with what she was dong, losing interest in his tale, her mind wandering.

She liked Billy. Dad was right, if only he'd said it in a kinder way, that had she not met David, it could very well have been Billy she'd be going out with. He'll make someone a really good husband one day, she thought with a small pang of regret, not because she wasn't his wife but because at twenty-one she was still no one's wife.

Had she been told she must wait almost four years to marry David, she'd have deemed it a life-time. Had she been told she'd still be as far away as ever from marrying him, she'd never have believed it.

So many things got in the way. Dad's chill last winter had made him susceptible to bronchitis, her time constantly taken up soothing his rumbling cough with big spoonfuls of linctus and boosting his flagging spirits with big doses of encourage-ment that left her too drained to take much note of the passing of time, of events.

The death of Edward VII last year and the coro-nation of George V had taken second place to looking after Dad; the excitement of last year's general election had passed her by, with more things pressing upon her nearer home.

Last June Vinny had another baby, George; nearly lost him, Vinny herself ill for a long time, the baby having to have a nurse. Vinny seldom came to see Dad, Lucy even less now she had her daughter.

Hating to upset Dad further with talk of marriage, of leaving him, like her sisters, to pay him only occasional visits, she'd put off any talk of it time and time again. That she'd marry David no matter what she had no doubts, but in a while she kept telling herself; not just yet. She pleaded with David: a few more months, just a few more months. The months had stretched and stretched. Five more and she'd be twenty-two, and still no nearer being married.

'D'yer fancy comin' ter see what's goin' on?'

She brought her mind quickly back to Billy. 'Where?'

'Over ter Sidney Street. See what's goin' on.'

'They wouldn't let us anywhere near it. And I can't really leave the shop.'

'Yer could ask yer Dad ter give an eye.'

Billy, like most around here, was aware that her father was very seldom in the shop these days. People no longer asked for him. Under her hand it was thriving again, bringing in good money. The window displaying clean and well-displayed bric-a-brac enticed people in, especially the more well heeled who came to the Row out of curiosity.

'He's not at all well at the moment. I couldn't really come. Sorry, Billy,' she said, and watched his resigned shrug as he waved and left.

Upstairs after she closed she rubbed Dad's chest with winter green ointment, and put a few drops of Friars Balsam in a bowl of boiling water for him to breathe in to ease his tubes.

'Won't be long till you're rid of me,' he croaked as she told him about Billy asking her to pop down to Whitechapel. 'When I'm gorn yer can go orf and 'ave a good time with anyone you fancy.'

'Don't talk so silly, Dad!' She turned on him sharply in the midst of laying the table for supper. 'Anyone'd think you were at death's door. Anyway, I wouldn't have gone out with him.'

'Yer would 'ave if it 'ad been David Baron,' he muttered, watching her as she turned her attention to cutting the bread. 'Like a shot you would 'ave.'

'You know that's not true, Dad.' Letty sawed with angry energy at the loaf she was cutting. 'It's you who begrudge me the bit of time I do have for myself. I do all I can for you, willingly.' She heard him give a snort. 'Yes, Dad, willingly! You can't say I don't. All I ask for is a young man like other girls have, and . . . Oh, I'm sick of going over the same old ground with you!'

Dropping the slices of bread on to a plate, she turned to confront him. 'Why can't you find one good word for him? You're always going on about Albert and Jack, how well they're doing. David has just as good prospects as them. His dad's business will be his one day. But you don't want that for me, do you? You want me – all to yourself. I manage your shop for you. I manage it very well. I'm too valuable to lose. But don't be too sure of me, Dad. One day I might get so good I'll get me own shop, and whether he marries me or not, I'll be off, looking after me own business.'

He hadn't said a word. Seldom did these days, let her rant and rave and ignored her. Frustrated, she took the soup off the hearth where it was keeping warm, ladling some into a basin to slam it down on the table.

'There's your supper! Don't say I don't feed you!'

For a while longer he stared at her, then slowly lowered his eyes, his cough rumbling deep in his chest. 'Is that what yer think of me, Letitia? That I don't appreciate what yer do?'

Before the hurt tone, her anger softened, even though she knew he was manipulating her to suit himself. 'I don't think that at all, Dad.'

'Yer sisters don't care if I live or die, so long as they ain't affected. My deepest wish is ter see you 'appy. I just need a bit of time. Since I lost yer mum . . .'

'Dad!' Anger began to mount again. 'When are you going to get over it? How much more time do you want? And what happens to me in the meanwhile? I'm nearly twenty-two. How old will I be when you decide you can cope on your own? When I'm forty-two? When I'm too old to marry?

125

You've *been* married, Dad. I've not even had the chance!'

She fled, slamming the door of her bedroom behind her to throw herself across her bed, ignoring his gentle tap on her door, his concerned cajoling voice, until he gave up and went back to his supper, his rumbling cough plaguing her with guilt for her outburst.

Slowly she sat up, gazed at the closed door. If only he wasn't so afraid of life. How would she feel, frightened of being forsaken, no one else in the world to care about her? But he knew she cared. He'd refused point blank to live with her and David when they married, or have them come to live with him. The even-tempered, wouldn't-hurt-a-fly sort of person, who underneath was pure bloody-minded. How well she'd grown to know him since Mum had died. The father who had shone like a god in her child's eyes had proved to be clay through and through. And yet . . . poor Dad, full of fear. He must be feeling wretched, that cough tearing at him so. She ought to try and relieve it a bit for him . . .

She gave a deep resigned sigh, got up and opened the door, going to the kitchen to get the winter green jar from off the shelf.

The headlines stated SEIGE OF SIDNEY STREET, with beneath that lurid accounts of the whole drama, the Home Secretary Mr Churchill calling out the army to deal with a man suspected

126

of being involved in what were termed the Houndsditch Murders, the cornered villain said to be one Peter Piatkow alias Schtern, otherwise known as Peter the Painter. The paper described him as twenty-eight to thirty, five foot nine, sallow, with a black moustache. It painted a dramatic picture of exchanges of gunfire that ended when the house in which three 'anarchists' had been cornered had gone up in flames, only two bodies being later recovered, neither of them Peter the Painter's. The reporter already described him in the same vein as Jack the Ripper of legend.

'See what yer missed?' Billy said, showing her the paper. 'Should have gone wiv me, shouldn't yer?'

Letty smiled, putting down the paper to attend to a customer while Billy waited to one side.

'Could always come out wiv me another time,' he said as the woman left.

Letty laughed lightly. 'Cheeky devil! You know I'm spoken for.'

Billy did not laugh with her. His usually merry face was serious. 'Few years now, ain't it, Let – since yer was spoken for?'

Letty too grew serious, her faced pinched with a faint anger not commonly felt towards Billy.

'That's my business.'

His chin gave a sceptical jerk. 'Seems odd ter me, a couple goin' out wiv each other so long an' never gettin' 'itched. Seems ter me, either you don't love 'im, or 'e don't love you.'

'I *am* engaged, Billy,' she snapped. The ring lay on her finger at last, for all to see, for all the good it did; she realised she'd missed the boat for revelling in congratulatory cries of surprise and wonder. Everyone had already come to suspect she'd had her ring for some time, so there was not much point anyone making a great thing about it. 'And all in good time there'll be a gold band next to it. As soon as circumstances – which are none of your business, Billy Beans – permit.'

He put the paper aside slowly, got up from the table on which he'd been perching. 'Don't wait too long, Let,' he said, his tone low and heavy with meaning. 'See yer later, then.'

She'd grown used to remarks, snide or otherwise, over the length of time she and David had been going out together. No one even bothered to ask when she was getting married, and she somehow managed to ignore the fact that David too did not talk of it so much these days.

He was often as ardent as if they were married and she in turn had put aside that demureness she'd first displayed with him, her need of him was as strong as his need of her. In darkened corners they made no bones of it, though they always stopped before completing the act, both wary of the consequences. Only then did he beg her, his whole being trembling with wanting her and she almost in tears, to leave home, marry him, to hell with sense of duty – what about him?

She was angry with herself for letting Billy's simple remark evoke these memories. To relieve her anger she threw up her arms in a childishly dramatic gesture, pulled a face at the empty shop – and was immediately caught off guard by the couple coming in. Hastily smoothing her expression, dropping her hands to her side, she smiled at them. Could she help them at all? Looking for a wedding present, they told her, straight-faced.

'By all means, look around,' she said, as coolly as she could, and applied her mind to business.

No longer did she rely on the bits and pieces people down on their luck brought in to sell. She'd take short excursions to other second hand shops, pick out what might sell to the more opulent clientele lately coming to the Row.

'I have to make sure we've got what they want,' she told her father, and saw him smile, not unkindly, but with the derision of one who had been through all that and come out with damaged pockets.

'We ain't in bloody Oxford Street.'

'We could be, one day,' she told him, ignoring his caution.

Customers looking for quality stuff at reasonable prices, tasteful porcelain, well-made furniture, paintings – especially paintings which she was developing a feel for. She'd begun to know what would or would not sell, know what she was looking for, know how to knock down the prices when she bought, put them up when she sold

– not so little that they thought they were being sold rubbish, but not so high that they didn't think they were getting a bargain. In this she discovered she had her mother's people's blood in her, shrewd yet pleasant, tough yet charming. She wasn't being vain in thinking that, sensible enough to realise it was gift handed on to her by Mum, coupled with a love of beautiful things from Dad, and as such she was profoundly grateful and tried to remain humble about it. If only she could summon a little something out of her own self – a business head – who knows what she could achieve? Visions of a fine shop in London's West End filled her dreams. One day, she thought. One day . . .

The year slipped by; same old water under the same old bridge. Look after the shop all week, look after Dad, the flat; look forward to Sundays, Mrs Hall coming to keep an eye on Dad, Dad complaining he was sick of being looked after by Mrs Hall, always rattling on about her poor Fred and how he gave her everything when she was alive.

'Silly old bugger gave 'er a dog's life when 'e was alive,' he said.

Winter slid into a spring that turned swiftly into baking summer. Men sweated profusely in rolled up shirt sleeves. Women rolled theirs up too and fanned themselves with newspapers. Club Row's caged birds ceased singing, perched in cramped cages in full sunshine, their wings drooping, beaks agape, little feathered breasts panting. Lots of them died, found in the bottom of the tiny cages come Sunday evening, were dumped in dustbins for kids to fish out and hang on strings, whizzed round and round, aping the free flight they'd been denied in life.

The heavy air trapped between narrow streets and narrower alleys was a yellow haze. Unshod, kids jigged around the incessantly playing barrel organ, boys in hand-me-down breeches, girls with faded dresses hoisted high, showing holed black stockings, darned black drawers. Front doors stood wide open in side alleys to let what air there was flow through claustrophobic tenements. Chairs brought outside on to the pavement, neighbour sat chatting with neighbour, trying to ignore the stink of drains and outside lavatories.

David took Letty on a Sunday trip to Brighton. The sun beat upon a promenade crowded with trippers, bringing out colour whichever way she looked, giving everyone a look of wealth.

The grey tube-shaped dress that showed off her auburn hair Letty had made on her mum's old Singer, in cotton voile at sixpence three farthings a yard. She followed current fashion, the hem well clear of the ground to show her ankles. The wide straw hat with white daisies and pink rosebuds smothering the crown David had bought for her in Regent Street. It was terribly expensive. Though she'd protested furiously at the cost, now she glowed with pleasure to be wearing it, as posh as anyone.

On David's arm, his hand over hers, she gazed at the beach below, crowded with sunbathers in cloth caps and straw boaters. Beyond the lines of bathing machines drawn up at the water's edge, their big wooden wheels in the water, young men in bathing costumes were revelling in a refreshing dip while the ladies, well covered, paddled tentatively at the edge.

Her first sight of the sea had taken her breath away, the smooth shimmering expanse stretching away to the horizon. Overwhelmed, she'd gripped David's arm convulsively. 'Oh ain't it lovely!'

She drank in the sunshine, savoured the heat beating through the fine stuff of her dress, and as David squeezed her hand in reply, was glad to be alive, offering up a prayer of thanks for Mrs Hall who'd agreed to sit with Dad the whole day. Dad, who had complained of the heat getting at his chest, had also complained that he didn't need Mrs Hall fussing around him. What he really meant was that he wanted Letty to fuss around him rather than go off with David.

'I wish we could do it again,' she sighed on the train home.

'No reason why we shouldn't, is there?' David smiled at her as she sat close to him in the hot carriage crowded by weary passengers and their sticky children.

She didn't answer. Even now, David could never really understand what it was like to face those resentful glances, the long silences in the wake of her return. She saw a shadow pass over his face.

'Your father.' The defeat in his tone served to spoil the lovely day she'd had.

'No, it's not,' she said sharply, sitting upright away from him as far as the plump woman beside her allowed, and remaining that way for the rest of the journey, studying David's lean handsome face dark, eyebrows drawn down. They didn't speak again except for short terse directions when needed as the train steamed into Victoria Station and the tube took them on to Liverpool Street. Not until they were on the tram taking them the rest of the way home through the twilight, did David say anything positive.

'You worry too much over your father,' he said as they sat side by side on one long seat, shaken from side to side by the tram's shuddering. 'Hear me out!' he said firmly as she made to interrupt. 'I've tried to be patient and understand, but it's time you considered what you want from life. No – Letitia, please!'

He drew her arm through his, gripping her hand so tightly that she winced.

'You said by the time you were twenty-one your father would be well over his loss, and you would be free. But you're still nursemaiding him as though he were a helpless child.'

'He still needs me,' she hissed, her body rigid.

'*I* need you, Letitia! I need you for my wife. Now! After all this time I've a right. I want marriage and children, and I want it to be you who gives me that. No one else!'

He was right. Letty sank dolefully against him. David held her to him, his voice becoming low, persuasive.

'You know I can give you everything you ever wanted. But you must let go of him. I can't wait forever.'

'Oh, no!' Her body stiffened. 'You wouldn't leave me! You can't!'

All around, passengers half turned at her cry, looked and looked away in embarrassment.

'Don't say that, David,' she whispered with just enough presence of mind to lower her voice even though her heart was hitting against her ribs with sickening thuds.

'God – I couldn't!' His own voice was hoarse as though his throat had tightened enough to strangle him. He was holding her to him in a convulsive embrace. 'I don't know what made me say that. But what will happen to us if you don't leave him? If he refuses to let you . . . Darling, if you haven't the strength to break away now, when will you ever have it?'

'I do have the strength,' she hissed. 'But I can't be hard. He's all alone.'

'He is *not* alone. There's Vinny and Lucy. It's about time they gave some of their time to him, Letitia.'

'How? Vinny's got two children now. Lucy's expecting again. I'm the only one free to . . .'

'The only one enslaved, you mean,' he cut in. 'Both have domestic help. You're still a servant in your own home. I'm sure your Mrs Hall would be happy to earn a few pennies, employed on a permanent basis, instead of your begging her for help when you're finally too worn out to put one foot in front of the other.'

'The shop don't . . . doesn't pay enough for that.'

'To hell with the shop! You could get her for half the rate your sisters pay their domestics and she'd be happy. But that would be too easy for your father. It would mean losing you to me. Letitia, don't you see, it's sheer selfishness . . .'

'No, I won't have that!' Anger had replaced desolation. She broke away from his embrace. 'I won't have you both tugging at me like this. I won't be batted about like an old rubber ball . . .'

Everyone was staring at her but she didn't care. 'Can't you understand? I'd never be at peace with meself if I walked out on Dad. If I had everything in the world as you said I could, and saw me Dad left all on his own, I could never . . .'

'And what about me, Letitia?' David's raised voice took no account of those listening. 'What of me? Could you live in peace with yourself if you left me on my own?'

'I love you!' she wailed, distraught.

'Then marry me! Next month. Marry me!'

'What about Dad? I can't . . .'

'All right! Pander to him, be with him until he dies and leaves you on your own – an old maid no one will thank for all the sacrifices she made, least of all your sisters in their fine homes while you play the slave in yours. It doesn't matter to them or your father if you are happy or not, so long as you're always there.'

'That's not true!' she yelled desperately.

'It's God's own truth!' he yelled back, while some in the tram gave a gasp and others tittered, drawn in by this lovers' quarrel, and a spotty youth in the front called out. 'Go orn, marry 'im, ducks! Make 'im 'appy an' sod yer farver!'

CHAPTER 8

The heat had made corset and bodice stick to her skin beneath her muslin blouse, her narrow skirt hobbling her ankles most uncomfortably. David, however, looked so cool in a soft-collared shirt and grey-striped flannel trousers, his jacket over his arm. What it must be to be a man, unrestricted by tight clothing and fashion!

'I've got to sit down a minute,' Letty gasped, and was surprised by the relief on his face.

'I began to wonder if you'd ever tire,' he laughed, helping her down on to the beach, immediately to drop down on the stones himself. 'I thought you were going on walking to Land's End!'

She realised then he was as hot and tired as her. Only pride had prevented him from being first to complain. It made her feel better to know it, and laughing, she threw herself at him, pummelling him playfully.

What a lovely holiday it had been after all the problems she'd had just to be here! All that trouble with her father . . .

He'd been appalled when she had told him she

was going away with David for a few days; had become quite nasty about it.

'Plannin' ter get up ter no good with 'im, ain't yer?' he had accused, but she wasn't going to be drawn into an argument. She was going to Brighton with David and that was that.

She'd worked hard for it, planned, had somehow engineered Mrs Hall to look in on him, especially in the evenings. It hadn't been easy.

Mrs Hall had thought it not very seemly, a widow staying the whole evening in the same flat as a man. She deemed it all right during the day and if Letty was away only a few hours, but not for days on end and certainly not after dark. It took a lot of persuading, but Dad seemed less upset at being left on his own than at having his daughter going off for a week with her young man, and that was the hub of it, always had been. He wasn't so much troubled by her leaving him on his own as by leaving him for someone else, transferring her love. She was the affection he'd lost when Mum had gone and he couldn't bear losing it again, not for a minute.

'I know what yer up to,' he'd rumbled. 'Yer goin' ter let 'im 'ave yer. You're dirty. You're disgusting. If yer go, I don't want nothing more ter to do with yer. You 'ear?'

It was bluff. And it wasn't going to alter a thing. She was twenty-two, a grown woman. She'd do as she pleased.

Today in fact was her twenty-second birthday, a day as hot as any she could remember. It had perhaps been a mistake to have gone for such a long walk but they'd been here for three days and, other than visit the Pavilion and wander along one of the two piers, had done little so far but sit around, engrossed in each other all day.

They'd booked separate rooms of course. It wouldn't have been right otherwise. She hadn't enough face to pretend to the hotel manager that they were man and wife, though David being that much older than her would have carried it off, she didn't doubt. But doors had never been a barrier to people in love, and for the first time Letty knew the true pleasure of being gently coaxed to responding to a man's touch, so gently that she wondered what she had been afraid of all these years, except of course that it was supposed to be wrong, and nice girls didn't. And what would Dad say if he knew? He knew all right – had guessed what would happen, hadn't he? It was that which might have ruined everything made it sinful, but she couldn't help herself, it struck her as so entirely natural to give and be loved, and David was so considerate, that she felt entirely safe with him.

At twenty-two she was a mature woman but it was he who made her feel that more than any birthday. And now she felt as good as married, could hold her head up and say 'David loves me, he'll never leave me'. All that was needed was the blessing of a church wedding. Perhaps not all, for what she needed most was what she most feared she'd not get – Dad's blessings.

'We've seen nothing of the town yet,' she'd said as they emerged at last from their secluded world of the last two days. Her hand in his, they wandered through the charming maze of narrow streets, laughing when they got lost, having to ask directions of other visitors as lost as they, in the end seeking out a local with that look on her face of being sick of redirecting idiots from London.

Back on the promenade again, on the farthest outskirts of the town, faced with a long walk back to the hotel, they'd gone down on to the beach where David had collapsed gratefully on to the heavy shingle. As Letty threw herself on top of him, he yelped in brief pain, a flint as big as a boulder digging into the small of his back.

'That's it – kill me!' Grabbing her, he rolled with her, laughing, she squeaking in mock alarm; rolled until he was on top of her.

The beach here was deserted. No one had any idea of walking this far in the heat when there was more than enough fun to be had around the twin piers, the ice-cream vendors, the tea kiosks, the shops. The only figure to be seen was a fisherman bent over some lobster pots further along. Here was silence except for the surf flopping lazily on to the sloping shingle to suck the countless tiny stones hungrily back with a wet hollow rustling. Otherwise, the quiet was as near to tangible as it could possibly be, brushing Letty's face with an amorphous touch as the air wafted the salty tang of seaweed up from the water's edge.

She and David lay where they had come to a stop. His weight on her, he looking down into her eyes, his own a dark limpid brown, the laughter on both their lips dying simultaneously.

'I love you, Letitia,' she heard him say, breath hissing between his teeth.

Her hands behind his neck, she pulled him down to her, his lips pressing against hers in long gentle kisses. Suddenly lacking gentleness they began to explore her, fingers trembling as they unfastened each button of her blouse and bodice. Her breasts exposed momentarily to the hot sun, his lips shielded them and she could feel the heat of his tongue, heard her own voice begging, urging, 'Oh, yes, David!'

Awareness of the fisherman about his business, unsuspecting of the lovers further along the beach, any minute to stand up and observe by accident, gave a fine-edged pleasure to the risk, the danger of being seen. To be made love to in such a way on a deserted beach, to be frantically unclothed enough for David to find her, was something she had never ever dreamed of. Her body eager to be taken by him, careless of the consequences yet frightened, she welcomed him.

Some strange and wonderful tingle had leapt inside her, at once alarming and overwhelming. Yet he had not abused her trust in him, had left her safe. She knew it instinctively as, empty of thoughts, she lay gazing up in lingering contentment at the azure sky above.

Propped on one elbow, he gazed down at her. 'Marry me, Letitia.'

It was her birthday and she was twenty-two. She'd passed her twenty-first birthday as she'd passed all her others since Mum had died, with hardly anyone noticing it, except David who had taken her up West to a dinner and flowers and even a bottle of champagne, something she'd never tasted before and had found not as exciting as it was made out to be, apart from making her feel very expensive.

Had Mum been alive, she'd have organised a birthday party for Letty's twenty-first somehow. But Dad had been too wrapped up in himself to think about things like that, and Letty felt she could hardly organise it for herself. Twenty-first birthday parties were always arranged by someone else or it wouldn't be the same, and she had rather let it go unsung than draw it to others' attention that she'd had to do the whole thing herself.

David, however, had made it memorable. He had bought her a most beautiful gold locket and a tortoiseshell jewellery box inlaid with mother of pearl. They had gone to a studio to have their photos taken to put inside the locket. This year he had taken her away on holiday, brooking no refusal from her and no argument from Dad, had treated her like a lady, the Grand Hotel and everything. And he had loved her.

Four years he'd been with her. Sometimes she wondered where those years had gone to. All

142

through it he had remained loyal and patient. And now as he reclined beside her, propping himself up on an elbow to gaze down at her, he asked suddenly: 'Marry me, Letitia.'

It had been so long since he'd spoken to her of marriage, resigned to the state of things, that it startled her. Her spirits plunged instantly, knowing how it would end, as it always ended when he spoke of marriage, knowing what she would say. She said it now, hating it.

'David . . . I don't know. I know I should be saying yes, but . . .'

'But there's your father to think about,' he finished for her, she thought caustically, but he kissed her lightly before getting to his feet to brush bits of dried sea-weed from his trousers. Squinting against its reflection off the sea, he glanced toward the sun.

'Time's getting on. We've got quite a step to go back to town.'

It was as though nothing at all had been said; that this automatic acceptance of what her answer would be was more of a ritual. They might not have made love for all the difference it had made.

Letty said nothing, got up from the shingle, copied his actions in brushing herself down, replied simply, 'Yes, we must get going.'

They didn't talk much on the way back to the hotel, ate lunch in virtual silence, a few staccato observations perhaps; spent the afternoon quietly in the sun lounge, dined, took a stroll before retiring. David did not come to her room that evening, nor the next.

The remainder of the holiday was spent as friends might spend it: casually. When they returned home, he kissed her goodbye, casually, said how he had enjoyed their time together. There was a sense of hearing it as from a mere acquaintance.

Strangely fearful, she asked, 'I'll see you on Sunday?'

'Not this Sunday,' she was told. 'I'll be a bit busy stocktaking.'

She was disappointed. No, not disappointed – alarmed. 'I'll see you the Sunday after, David?' she questioned.

'Of course.' His tone was brightly brittle, unconvincing, and she wasn't at all surprised to receive a note saying he couldn't make it. He did visit from time to time, of course. But something had changed.

The last day of 1912 Lucy had her second baby, a girl, and Jack got his first automobile, a Ford Model T.

Lucy was thrilled with the Model T, but not quite so much with having produced another daughter. After a miscarriage the previous year, she had been doubly hoping for a boy.

'I really thought we'd have one this time,' she lamented, as she recovered finally from the trauma of the birth enough to comment on the sex of her new baby. 'All the suffering I've been through and all.'

'Well, I'm pleased.' Jack's bony face was rapturous as he beheld his second daughter, after Lucy, worn out from the twenty-eight hour ordeal, had been propped up by his mother and grandmother in order to make her appear as though she'd merely suffered a minor headache.

'I think she's perfectly beautiful,' he cooed. 'Worth all the trouble you've had. Don't you think, sweetheart?'

'If you'd gone through what I have, you wouldn't be saying that so happily, Jack Morecross. If you only knew what it's like to be a woman.'

Her face still dreadfully drawn, she lay in their big double bed, gazing dull-eyed and lethargic around the spacious master bedroom. Winter sunlight filtered weakly in through the large bay window that looked down on to the tree-lined avenue of similar bay-windowed, terraced houses. Beyond could be seen fields rising to Chingford Mount, all clean and bare until the new shoots of corn clothed them green again in the spring.

'And to find it's another girl, after all that effort. Oh, Jack, after all that suffering. It's not fair! And Vinny with them two boys she's always cooing over. And I bet all the tea in China that third one she's carrying will be a boy too.'

'We won't know until it's born, sweetheart.' Jack looked to his mother for support against Lucy's lamentations. She tilted her head in gentle sympathy while his grandmother clucked her tongue and looked at the wan thing lying in bed with the child in her arms. The old woman's tone was sharp when she spoke.

'You ought at least be thankful for the good fortune you have. A successful delivery, two healthy children now, a good husband, a nice and secure home.' Only with obvious effort did she refrain from remarking further on how that nice and secure home had been given to the couple by herself and her husband, and Lucy ought at least sometimes show gratitude for her generosity.

All she achieved was to produce fresh tears from the new mother, weakened by the birth, especially when Jack, without thinking as deeply as he should what he was saying, added: 'Perhaps next time it'll be a boy.'

The worst thing to have said to any woman just gone through the pangs of giving birth! Even worse with Lucy.

'Next time?' she echoed, wide blue-grey eyes swimming. 'Is that all you can think about? Don't you care about *me*? Don't you care one bit what I've gone through to bring your children into the world? As far as I'm concerned, I don't want any next time, going through all this again.'

There was another stern outburst of tutting from the most senior Mrs Morecross. 'Enough of that, Lucilla. That's what we women are here for. To bring forth children as the Good Book decrees. We must grit our teeth and do our duty.'

Chastened, Lucy tightened her lips. 'I've *done* my duty.'

'Two daughters? No, my lady, I don't think you have. I brought thirteen children into this world, eight of them boys. I am proud of my achievement, and after you've had a few sons so will you be. Now sit up and try to make yourself look cheerful for your husband's sake.'

Lucy felt anything but cheerful. Relieved that it was all over perhaps. But cheerful . . . There was Vinny with two boys to her credit and another on the way. If that did turn out to be a girl, she'd still have nothing to squawk about. But herself, she hadn't even got off the starting line yet.

'My mum had three girls on the trot,' she said in a small voice, as if half afraid her grandmother-in-law would hear.

Jack was feasting his earnest blue eyes on his newest daughter. 'She's perfectly lovely,' he repeated, yet again. 'What shall we call her?'

'Makes me sick,' Lucy mumbled against the tightly swaddled baby, deaf to Jack. 'The way Vinny purrs over them two boys of hers. As if she's the only one ever to have had boys. I'll be like my mum and have all girls, no matter how many I have.'

'What foolish talk!' admonished Mrs Morecross the elder. 'Jack told me that your mother had several boys.'

'Three,' Lucy dared to correct her. 'One still-born. The other two died when they were little.'

'But she had them. Jack's mother had four sons. Two still living. So rest assured, you will have *some*

147

sons out of those children you will bring into the world.'

Lucy felt it prudent to say no more, but it didn't stop thoughts running through her head. And those thoughts decreed that it would be a long while before she allowed herself to be subjected to the pain she had experienced in these last twenty-eight hours.

In such low spirits, her health took its time returning. It wasn't until April she found enough strength to take her first ride in Jack's pride and joy, his Model T.

With the children, they came in it to see Letty and Dad.

'Must be doin' well,' was Arthur Bancroft's first comment when he and Letty went down to view it.

Letty could share his sour sentiment, uncharitably suspecting that the visit was as much to show off the new motorcar and how well they were doing, as to show off their new baby.

'It was a snip, really,' Jack said proudly.

Driving coat and cap swamping his spare frame, he stood beside the vehicle, one gauntleted hand smoothing the shiny brown paintwork.

'Chap buying it changed his mind so the showroom let it go cheaper than I expected. Been thinking about getting one for a long time. It wasn't hard to learn to drive it. Just good co-ordination really.'

In the passenger seat, her hat well secured by a muslin veil, Lucy hugged baby Emmeline. She'd named her after Mrs Emmeline Pankhurst who also had two daughters and whom Lucy admired greatly. But if she admired from afar, being too taken up by matrimony and motherhood to be more active in women's suffrage, she could at least practise it on Jack. A perfect lamp, he hadn't touched her in bed at all since the birth of Emmeline.

She put one hand over her shoulder in an effort to stop two-year-old Elisabeth from bouncing up and down on the narrow rear seat.

Elisabeth merely went on bouncing, giving her mother hardly a second thought, and Lucy eventually let her hand drop.

'Fancy a spin in it, Dad?' Jack asked. He glanced up at the sky. In early-February, the weather was as clear and warm as if it had been June. 'Lovely day. We could run down to Southend for the afternoon or to our place for tea instead if you fancy? Bring you home tonight?'

Arthur shook his head. 'Ain't possible. Not with the shop ter look after.'

'What d'you mean?' Letty's tone was sharp with disappointment. To be done out of her first spin in a private car belonging to someone in her very own family, done out of the pleasure of being watched going off in it by all the neighbours. 'The shop's closed. It's Thursday afternoon.'

Since the Shops Act last year, he'd done little but grumble about being forced into early closing once a week; being done out of trying to make an honest living, he said, yet but for her he wouldn't have made a living at all, the way he'd lost interest.

Arthur shook his head again. 'Won't get me in one of them there contraptions for love nor money. Any rate, someone's got ter keep an eye on the shop. Don't want no one breakin' in while we ain't here.'

He was quite obviously out to spoil her enjoyment. Letty's lips compressed, her chin jutted.

'Then stay and look after your shop! The only time you do is when there's nothing to do.'

She saw Lucy and Jack squirm uncomfortably, saw the quick exchange of glances. Jack gave an extra wide smile, speaking hurriedly.

'Hadn't better be stationary too long.' He eyed the collection of grubby-faced urchins gathering to stare and touch, fingers already marking the paintwork. 'Take a run around the block in it with us. I can tell you, it's an experience. Nothing at all like a motor bus. You'll enjoy it. What d'you say?'

'*I'd* like to,' Letty said defiantly. 'You coming or not, Dad?'

But nothing would persuade him. Letty, with hat and coat and a set expression, clambered into the cramped rear seat, trying to calm an animated Elisabeth but giving up. She was never at ease with children, at a loss what to say to them, how to deal with sticky fingers, jerky limbs and penetrating stares. Her collar turned up, a travel blanket over her knees against a chill breeze, instead of an ambitious spin to Southend-on-Sea it was a mile or two around the turnings, she worrying herself sick at having had a go at Dad for no reason than that she was far too ready these days to react to his slightest remark, until she arrived back at the flat to get warmed up again around the parlour fire and get tea for them all.

For some time Vinny had been growing increasingly restive. Their house in Victoria Park Road no longer held the same attraction it once had for her. It had a cramped, ageing feel to it, wedged between similarly aging terraced houses. Even if it did look on to Victoria Park with quite a lot of greenery, the new motor buses and other motor vehicles passing the front door raised such a dust that nothing ever stayed clean for long.

Grimly she dusted, thought of Lucy with open countryside all round her; Lucy going on about her fine house, as if Jack had achieved something marvellous instead of having been practically given the house.

'She don't know which side her bread's buttered,' she told Albert after Lucy had her second girl. 'Two rooms downstairs. Three bedrooms upstairs. And her now with two girls. All that space. And what for?'

Finding herself expecting again definitely decided Vinny.

'We ought to be looking for something larger,' she said to Albert around her sixth month.

'Somewhere further out. The boys need fresh air. Look how rosy-cheeked Lucy's Elisabeth is. When this one arrives, the house will be so cramped, don't you think, Albert?'

Albert looking up from his evening paper took in the small front parlour with pompous self-satisfaction. 'Three boys sleep in one room just as easily as two. Three of us shared one room when I was young.'

Vinny's expression tightened over her knitting. 'And what if it's a girl? We'd have to have an extra room then.'

'Not for ten years at least.'

Vinny pulled a face which said ten more years here would be quite unendurable. 'And when the family gets even larger?' she queried.

Albert frowned. He liked it here, was very comfortable. A short walk each morning to the number 57 tram conveying him to Moorgate to his father's firm of accountants; moving would mean further to travel. He decided that now was not the time and left Vinny so tight-lipped and tearful for days afterwards that he almost regretted the decision.

Little Arthur William arrived on 4 August. Being Sunday, David and Letty went that very afternoon to see the baby.

'You must be ever so proud,' Letty said, feeling faintly envious as she gazed at the screwed up red little face vaguely resembling Uncle Will after a bit too much drink. 'Fancy that – three boys.'

'I hoped for a girl,' Vinny said morosely, still weak and drowsy from her ordeal. 'A girl's company. Lucy's so lucky having girls.'

Lucy felt nothing of the sort, or so Letty deduced from her most recent visit. Every time she visited her, she seemed to end up trying to placate a Lucy still far from resigned to not having had a boy.

'You'll probably have a boy next time,' she soothed when she went over to see her one hot August afternoon. 'You won't go on having girls.'

'I'm not sure about any next time,' Lucy said, pushing away the plate of biscuits on the tea table. She still had a remarkably slim waist, untouched by childbearing, and meant to keep it that way.

'At least not for a while,' she whispered discreetly, the men being occupied talking of things other than babies. She eyed Jack warily. 'We're being careful. Three pregnancies . . . I'm worn out. I told Jack. I said, if he can't be more careful with me he'd best sleep in another room. I do want more children, Let, but not as quick as it's been. If the other one had been born proper, I'd have had three now.'

Letty wanted to comment that had it gone to full-term she might not have had Emily but the boy she longed for, but she thought it better not to say so. As Lucy talked, she took in the plush furnishings, fine furniture, the expensive dress Lucy had on. Jack, like Albert, was doing very well, becoming very successful, yet Lucy took it for granted, didn't appear to appreciate any of it, spent

153

nearly all her time lamenting what she didn't have and what she ought to have.

'We've had a telephone installed,' she told everyone when they came to celebrate Dad's fifty-fifth birthday in October. Letty had it on the Sunday, two days after – thinking he'd appreciate his family all around him. She invited David too, daring Dad to make any objection. She had spent the best part of two days buying things for the party, cooking, making the cake, and if Dad so much as made a peep against David . . .

'You won't have to keep relying on telegrams,' Lucy said through a mouthful of birthday cake. 'You can telephone us instead.'

'I don't see how,' Letty said across the table. Her sister spoke as though having a telephone was the most normal thing in the world. 'Being as we don't have one.'

'You ought to, running a shop. Still, you can always use someone else's. Some shops around here are bound to have one.'

'Of course!' Letty's tone was brittle. 'We can always barge into someone's home to borrow their telephone, can't we?'

'You don't *borrow* it, you use it.' Lucy stopped cutting the rest of her cake into small pieces for Elisabeth to handle, to spoon some more trifle into little Emmeline, some of the pink blancmange dripping on to Letty's snow white table cloth.

Letty eyed the spots balefully. 'Telegrams work well enough to get a message to anyone the same day.'

'Yes, but you can't say *all* you want to say. You can have a chat on the telephone and get answers straight away. It's so convenient.'

'Not if the person you want to chat to don't have one.'

'We've been talking about having one installed,' Vinny pitched in, casting a warning glance at Albert who took the hint, nodded vigorously and turned a threatening glare upon his eldest son who was craftily prodding three-year-old George with a fork to make him grizzle.

'We've already made enquiries,' Vinny added, forking a dainty morsel of swiss roll into her mouth, managing to ignore Lucy's narrowed eyes, their message plain: If I have something new, you just have to have the same! Vinny and Albert had bought their automobile one month after Jack had, a new piano three weeks after theirs and were now looking to move again, to the suburbs with a bit of countryside around them, as Lucy and Jack had.

It was typical of the two sisters and Letty's glance met David's across the table, finding his dark eyes glowing with half suppressed amusement, obliging her to conceal an involuntary grin behind a large bite of ham sandwich.

But despite Lucy and Vinny constantly putting each other down, conversation flowed around the table, and in the kitchen as everyone helped with washing up when tea was over, and afterwards over bottles of beer, a bottle of Scotch – Jack's present to Dad – and a bottle of sherry. Nice to all be together. Nice to see Dad cheerful, to see him fractionally more friendly towards David. Letty thought she saw the merest twitch of a smile beneath his moustache as he met David's glance on one or two occasions.

She was glad, for David's sake. It couldn't be easy for him sometimes, Dad's peculiar attitude towards him. How he managed to survive it so philosophically always mystified her.

Following last year's holiday, Letty had suffered agonies of remorse, letting David make love to her like he had and then to throw his offer of marriage in his face! It was her fault that their Sundays together had become intermittent.

After a while things did right themselves, but knowing the effect it had had on them both, she avoided getting into that situation ever again, though she ached for that most wonderful of sensations that had touched her on that deserted pebble beach. What it was she didn't know and she wondered if it could be harmful? Whether it was or not, she knew she wanted to experience it again. The trouble was, it would only lead to David begging her to marry him, and being unable to let herself say yes would lead to another quarrel. Better not to let the situation arise in the first place.

David hadn't mentioned taking another holiday. Letty wasn't sure whether to be relieved or disappointed. At least she didn't have to go through the business of facing Dad's vituperations. Then again, she wouldn't have lovely memories to tide her over another winter with him. Last winter he'd had his bronchitis again, had kept her running around after him. The thought of facing the next made her spirits plummet. And then, in September, David pulled the rabbit out of the hat.

'I've booked us into a hotel in Brighton,' he told her. 'It's all arranged. Your Mrs Hall will do the honours by your father as she did last year. I've given her five pounds for herself and she's glad to oblige.'

I bet she is, Letty thought. 'I won't say anything about Brighton to Dad,' she said. 'I'll make up some excuse. I'll say I'm spending a few days with your parents.'

'You will not! You'll tell him exactly where you are going.' His brown eyes had become hard, obdurate. 'You're twenty-three. Old enough to do whatever you choose to do. And you're going on holiday with me.'

Letty melted. Whatever David said. And next time he asked her to marry him, she would say yes.

CHAPTER 9

'David – something's wrong!' Letty ripped open the flap of the telegram handed to her at the desk as they came in from a morning stroll along the prom. Feverishly she dragged out the single sheet and scanned it, the fresh colouring the sea air had given her draining from her face.

DAD BROKE LEG STOP COME HOME IMMEDIATELY STOP VINNY

Alarm widened her eyes. Her expression already filled with guilt, she handed it to David.

'I've got to go,' she said, beseeching him to understand.

'Of course you have to,' he said simply, immediately taking charge of her. 'Go up and start packing. I'll pay the bill and find out the time of the next train.' He put a comforting arm about her shoulder, pulled her briefly to him. 'Now don't worry.'

But she was frightened. 'I shouldn't have come. I should have stayed there with him. He wouldn't have fallen if I'd been with him.'

'Now that's silly. You couldn't have prevented it.'

'But I might have done. I might have altered the situation, just being there. He would have been in a different place and not gone and fallen if I'd been with him.'

'You don't know that!'

Letty glanced again at the telegram. 'She doesn't say how serious it is or if he's in danger. She's hiding something from me!' Panic began to grip her.

'It's a telegram, darling,' David soothed, his arm pressed tighter. 'It has to be short or it'll cost the earth to send.'

'But perhaps . . .'

'Look, darling, no more perhaps. Go and pack. In a couple of hours you'll know the worst – or the best. Now go on!'

'How could you be so selfish?' Vinny's tone was sharp, her lips tight. Letty could see she'd been crying.

There had been no welcome, but straight into accusations the moment she and David came into the flat.

'To leave him looking after the shop all on his own! He had to go running up and down those stairs to see to customers. No wonder he fell.'

'What, down the stairs!'

She could have protested at Vinny's attitude, defended herself that Dad had looked after the shop last year when she'd been away, and he wasn't exactly an invalid even if he behaved like one. But she was in too great a state of shock to argue.

'Of course down the stairs!' Vinny snapped back at her. 'Mrs Hall wasn't here and he laid like that at the bottom until a customer came in and found him. Think how embarrassed he must have been, being found like that. Half an hour he laid there, you know that? I think you ought to be ashamed of yourself, Letty, leaving Dad to go off to . . . to . . .' Her face coloured up and she glanced towards David standing quietly to one side. 'You know what I mean. Dad said you and . . . Well, I won't tell you what Dad said. But I'm really shocked, Letty. Really upset that . . .'

'He can speak then?' At last Letty gathered her wits, interrupted, slow fury filling her that Vinny was practically accusing her of indulging in indecency.

'Of course he can speak,' Vinny said tartly.

'Where is he?' With an effort Letty gained command of herself. Dad had broken his leg Vinny had said. He wasn't at death's door and was sufficiently himself to go leading off about her, able to vilify her enough to have incensed Vinny who now saw her as little more than a prostitute.

'Where do you think? In the London. They kept him in. I got there as quick as I could when Mrs Hall telephoned me from one of the shops. Pity you haven't got a telephone. It would have been so much easier. She had to run around all over the place to find one. Lucy is at the hospital now, but I thought I should wait here for you.'

To give me a piece of your mind, Letty thought

160

as Vinny went on. 'You'd best go there to see him – that's if you can spare the time.'

Anger blazed up inside Letty. 'Don't talk to me like that, Vinny! Anyone'd think I didn't care for Dad . . .'

Vinny's eyes blazed. 'The way you went off, enjoying yourself while Dad had to go and have a fall, what else can anything think?'

'I didn't know he was going to have a fall, did I?'

'But you shouldn't have gone off and left him all on his own while you went . . . well, enjoying yourself.'

'He wasn't on his own. He had Mrs Hall.'

'But she wasn't here!' Vinny's voice had risen to a shriek. 'You should have been here!'

'And what about you?' Letty's voice too was hitting the ceiling. 'It'd be nice if *you* could be here sometimes. You or Lucy. But, oh, no! You've both got your own lives to lead, haven't you? I mustn't have no life, must I? It wouldn't hurt one of you to come over now and again and keep an eye on Dad while I get a bit of rest from him.'

'Is that what it's called? Rest! I'd have called it something else!'

'Mind your own business!' Letty flared. 'It's because of Dad that me and David's not married yet. I've given up everything because no one else raised a finger to look after him. You and Lucy never wanted to know, did you? Until something like this happens, then it's: "Where was Letty? She

161

should have been here." I've been here, day and night, ever since Mum went, and not one word of thanks from either of you. Nor even Dad. All of you take it for granted. It's because of you two that I'm still here, still not married. You're all selfish! Every one of you!'

Vinny's response was a scream of outrage, but David, who had been doing his best to get between them, finally made himself heard.

'That's quite enough! Yelling at each other is not going to help. I think we should go and see your father. Don't you agree, Lavinia?'

Such was the authority in his tone that Vinny stared at him for a moment, her mouth opening and shutting, then with a last scowl towards Letty, nodded dumbly.

'So yer come 'ome then?' Propped up by pillows, the clinical white sheet and faded pink coverlet stretched board tight across his chest, his leg hidden beneath a cradle, Dad looked as uncomfortable as he possibly could be, and in pain. Despite the surly welcome, sympathy flooded through Letty at the sight of him at the mercy of nursing staff and the pervasive smell of anaesthetic and hospital carbolic.

'Lavinia let us . . . She let me know,' she stammered.

'Good job she could get 'ere, bein' as no one else could.'

She knew who he meant but wasn't prepared to

162

start up any argument with him in his present condition, even in her own defence.

'Good job she could,' she echoed limply, desperately hoping he'd keep off the subject now.

To her surprise, and in a way gratitude, he did, for the whole time he was in the London. In another way it put her all on edge. Had he made a great thing of blaming her, moaning as he usually did, she'd have defended herself to the utmost, but his silence had the effect of causing her to blame herself. It was silly and she was angry at herself, but there it was.

When Dad came home, his leg in plaster for weeks afterwards, to limp around, first on crutches, then with a cane right up to Christmas, it was guilt that made her drive herself twice as hard, doing for him, trying to make up for what she saw as her own error. He was so constantly and abjectly apologetic. 'Nothing but a burden to everyone,' he'd say almost to himself, his eyes seeking hers for confirmation as well as forgiveness. 'Of course you're not, Dad,' she would tell him, and eager to prove it, found herself taking her own sense of guilt upon her back much as a flagellant of the Middle Ages might have welcomed the self-inflicted wheals upon his willing flesh.

Yet it didn't quite manage to heal her soul or clear the air. She told him he wasn't a burden, wanted to add that if she'd been with him he would never have had that fall, convinced of it no matter what David said. But she didn't dare say that to

163

Dad in case that which she could feel smouldering just below the surface, erupted. Things would be said that might never heal. That was the last thing she wanted.

'For God's sake, Dad! I don't care if it's lunch or dinner, so long as you're back from the pub in time to eat it!'

By winter Dad was still using his stick but the leg was more or less back to normal. Everything was more or less back to normal. No more abject apologies; he was back to fault finding, her twinges of guilt back to a more healthy desire to retaliate, to want to go for long walks to get out of his way.

It was the sort of winter that made going out for any walk an effort. Far from being crisp and revitalising, the weather made the body ache from constant huddling inside a coat; made the inside of the coat feel damp to the skin after five minutes of being worn. Evenings came down like a blanket, fog cast yellow haloes around gaslamps and lingered well into the next day, smelling heavily of soot. The trouble was, Dad hadn't resumed his midday walk down to the Knave as he had done every now and again before his accident, and now the miserable winter weather was throwing them together until Letty felt like screaming.

'Go and take out your spite on your pals in the pub!' Taking her own spite out on the bread pudding she was making, she kneaded the soaked ends of last week's bread viciously into a soggy

164

mass with her knuckles. Dumping in sugar, marg, currants and sultanas, spice and egg, she pounded the stodge vigorously into a dish ready for the gas oven to get hot enough. It never turned out the same as Mum made it. She would use the oven over the range where, cooking slowly, it would fill the flat with a warm spicy aroma. But Mum always had plenty of time to cook. Letty had the shop to mind and no one else was going to do the cooking.

'Anyway what's it matter if it's called dinner or lunch?'

Suggesting he went to meet some of his pals for a drink, she'd said without thinking to make sure to be back in time for lunch. A slip of the tongue. David referred to a midday meal as that, and like a lot of things he said, it had rubbed off on her. Dad leapt on it straight away.

'I s'pose that's yer bloke talkin'? All la-di-da. In this part of the world it ain't lunch! We're 'avin' stew, ain't we? We're 'avin' bread an' jam an' cake tonight, ain't we? Yer can't call bread an' jam a dinner. That's tea as I've always known it ter be. Dinner's at dinner time.'

In trousers and wool combinations, braces dangling round his hips, Dad was washing off the residue of shaving soap at the kitchen sink. Gurgling like a drowning man, water cascaded from angular elbows on to the linoleum, darkening the bare patch around his feet. The brownish pattern had worn off into quite a few bare patches where there had been most activity, in front of the gas stove, the sink, around three sides under the kitchen table where years of feet had scuffed at breakfast time. The centre was still almost as new, having always been covered by a succession of kitchen mats, renewed as they wore out. Letty glanced at the water Dad was letting dribble, relaxed seeing it missing the most recent piece of kitchen carpet.

'So far as I know, the stew's fer dinner an' that's at one o'clock so 'ow yer can call it lunch when . . .'

'All right, Dad! We're having *dinner* at one o'clock. That suit you?' She thrust the bread pudding into the oven, closed the door forcefully, and, as the saucepan of milk began to rise to the rim, deftly removed it from the flame before it overflowed, turned off the gas and rushed it to the table to pour over slices of bread and butter layered in a bowl. One of dad's favourite breakfasts; and baked with sultanas, one of his favourite afters – bread and butter pudding. He loved it. Would have lived on it, but she, for the life of her, couldn't touch it no matter how well cooked it was. It made her feel sick, the way it slid down the throat.

'Your breakfast!' she stated shortly and, as he came to the table, braces still dangling, she went and fished up the floor cloth from under the sink to mop up the puddle he'd left.

It was eight-thirty, just time to run down to Beans for a loaf before opening her own shop.

'Shan't be long,' she said, leaving him to slurp up the milky slop, grabbed up a shopping basket and

166

hurried out. It was a relief to be out of the flat, if only for ten minutes, but by the time she reached Beans grocery just along the road, she wasn't so sure about being glad. Damp fog clung to her eyelashes, flattened her hair, crept inside the collar of her coat.

'I do hate winter!' she grumbled as she paid Billy for the loaf.

'I could have brought it ter you,' he offered, but she shrugged.

'My dad's really got the 'ump up to his eyebrows this morning. I just had ter get out for a break.'

Funny how she lapsed so easily into cockney with Billy, even if it wasn't quite so pronounced as his. Being with David had even rounded her vowels, but how thin the veneer was.

Billy grinned affably, didn't even notice the change in her accent. He still didn't have a girl, just the odd one occasionally but nothing serious ever came of it. It was surprising really, him being so easy to get on with, always so cheerful. If ever he was grave, it only seemed to improve those good looks of his.

His grin this morning was wide and cheerful as always. 'Never mind, Let. Thursday termorrer. Early closin's been a boon, ain't it?'

Still working for a father much younger than her own, who had years to go before he'd ever hand the shop over to his son, Billy had very little interest in it, living for Thursday afternoons when he could go and kick a ball around in a back alley with a couple of mates, like himself let off on the same afternoon.

'Thursday,' Letty said with a doleful smile, 'I'm usually stuck in the flat with me dad and four walls. With him moaning on about this and that, and me listening.'

'Never mind,' Billy said airily. 'Yer see yer bloke on Sunday, don't yer? That ought ter make yer cheery.'

'I suppose so,' she said absently, her mind on tomorrow. If the fog persisted, she and Dad would be virtually housebound.

Billy was grinning at her like a Cheshire cat. 'Yer suppose so?' he echoed. 'Anyone'd think seein' yer bloke was a chore. If yer that fed up wiv 'im, yer can always come aht wiv me.'

Letty's laugh died on her lips. Billy's smile was as broad as ever but it hadn't quite reached his eyes, brilliant blue and serious with meaning.

'I'm not fed up with him,' she said haughtily. 'We just don't see each other every week. People don't when they've been courting for so long . . .' She broke off sharply. She hadn't meant to say that.

Billy wasn't smiling now, was looking at her quizzically. 'It 'as been a long while, ain't it, Let?'

'That's nothing to do with you, Billy.'

'Of course not.'

He watched her thrust the loaf into her shopping bag, watched as she left, his bright blue eyes clouded, then shrugged off his thoughts as the shop door closed on her departing figure.

168

Letty couldn't get out of her mind the way Billy had looked at her. It brought up all those things that lurked deep inside her brain, like thieves in shadowy corners, ready to leap out when you weren't looking and steal that precious possession everyone cherished: the ability to deceive oneself. It had been months since David had made any mention of marriage. Their relationship had grown so casual that these days they saw each other out of habit. The ring on her finger that had once promised so much, seemed to be the only tenuous link holding her and David to each other. Even his kisses no longer had hunger in them.

Letty hoisted the handle of the shopping basket over her arm, held her coat collar tight against her throat against the creeping cold. In a narrow alleyway two girls on their way to school were bouncing a ball. One had a skimpy coat, the other none at all. The cold didn't seem to bother them, though Letty noticed the hands of the one bouncing the ball had a bluish tinge. She hurried on, anxious to cover the last few yards home as quickly as possible, her thoughts still on David.

It had taken Dad's accident to uncover the rift she'd pretended for a long time had not existed. The last time David had spoken of marriage had been after Dad had come out of hospital, and she'd said, 'David, I can't. Not now.' She'd meant to say 'not yet', meant to say 'let Dad get back on his feet'. She should have rectified the aberration then and there, but she hadn't. Had let it stand.

David had gone quiet, the glow in his soft brown eyes that of defeat. He had turned away, and had never asked her again. Somehow Letty felt she was losing him, steadily, surely, powerless to do anything about it.

Perhaps Billy was right. Perhaps she was losing interest . . .

No! Letty pulled herself up from the thought as she let herself into the shop. No – she loved David, ached with love for him; ached at the thought of never seeing him again. She wanted so much to be his wife and yet . . . and yet, there was always Dad. Always the same old argument, stretched like elastic between two loyalties, and Dad always the winner because she couldn't bear to think of him as being the loser.

Letty glanced at Dad ensconced in Mum's old wooden-armed chair. He was sitting one side of the hearth, feet in carpet slippers propped on the brass fender, she on the other side, darning a hole in one of his socks. In a wickerwork basket beside her several more pairs waited to be darned.

Despite it being April the fire was well banked up, the tar hissing and bubbling within the flames. Coal at near on a shilling a hundredweight wasn't cheap, but Dad was inclined to feel the cold a lot these days. He didn't seem to comprehend that money was tight, the shop only just ticking over. She had dreamed such wonderful dreams of expansion, of opening up in the West End, but it wasn't easy to make headway, a woman on her own. Those dreams gone, it was just ticking over as it always had, with Dad putting in his spoke at every turn to stop her doing what she thought best. Of course it was still his shop. He had the last say. Pity though he didn't put as much energy in doing something about it as he did in putting obstacles in the way. Letty still felt that, given a free hand, she'd have got somewhere with it.

'What we need is a telephone,' she said casually.

Even David's father, as old fashioned as David said he was in his business, had installed one in both his shops in March. David had told her it had proved a boon; goods ordered by telephone, the order on paper following more conventionally, so that as soon as it arrived the goods were waiting ready to be despatched. Everywhere the telephone was proving itself the best invention in years.

His parents were so pleased that they now had one in their own home. Letty's thoughts ran wild on a speculation that if Dad could only be persuaded to have one, she could use it to contact David at home. She'd be able to talk to him whenever she wanted, every day of the week. No more long days away from each other. It made her head spin to think about it.

'What d'you think, Dad?' she prompted, as he with his feet inches from the extravagant blaze, said nothing. Letty ignored the thought that one of these days those soles were going to catch light, waited for his reply.

'Well?' she urged.

His feet came off the fender so sharply she actually did think they had begun to smoulder. He leaned forward, reached for his pipe. 'What the 'ell for?'

'A lot of shops have a telephone now.'

She waited as he went through the lengthy ritual of lighting his pipe. 'I've managed fer nearly thirty years without one,' he rumbled at last.

'I know, but things are changing.' Her needle fairly flew in and out of the sock heel, jerky rapid movements. 'Look how much quicker we can order things.'

'What do *we* 'ave to order? Everythink we 'ave is what comes in by 'and. Don't need a telephone fer that.'

He was right there. They didn't really need a telephone. Letty bent her head over her darning, frowning, trying to find one reason Dad might accept. Beyond the drawn curtains, April lashed what sounded like its whole reserves of rain at the windowpanes. In the grate the coals slipped with a small crunching noise. In Letty's mind a single thought dominated – how close she and David could be by the simple expedient of just picking up a telephone earpiece and asking for a number; David's thoughts in her ear as though he stood beside her, their very thoughts exchanged through the wires.

'What about illness?' The idea came without any prompting. 'Say if you were taken ill, look how quick we could get in touch with Lucy or Vinny.'

'You expecting me ter be taken ill then?' The way he said it, he made it sound as if she was putting the wish to the thought.

For a moment Letty couldn't answer, with an effort quenched a spark of anger. Outside the wind buffeted the window. She eyed the small puffs of smoke billowing back down the chimney and into the room from the downdraught. The chimney needs cleaning, came the abstract thought in the midst of her cogent reply to Dad's unkind and totally uncalled for remark.

'Who'd have thought you'd go and break your leg last summer?' she countered manfully. 'If we'd had a telephone, Mrs Hall wouldn't have had to go running all round the place looking for one to call Vinny on.'

'Lavinia,' he corrected sharply, and this time Letty's anger rose unchecked.

'Fer God sake, Dad, I don't care! I'm trying to hold a conversation with you. It don't matter if I call her Lavinia or Vinny. Just stop treating me as if I was a kid!'

But Dad had effectively cut her argument short, which was what he had meant to do. And now his faded blue eyes swivelled towards her, a natural gesture much the same as she used, but where with her it was attractively provocative, from him it only appeared crafty and mean.

'We wouldn't 'ave needed any telephone,' he said slowly, 'if you'd have been 'ere, would we?'

So it was still there, under the surface, still

173

simmering. Letty's voice trembled beneath a wave of guilt she'd thought had healed along with Dad's leg.

'I'd still have had to go running around . . .'

The words died away. What was the point? Whatever she said was not going to subdue the sense that Dad's accident had somehow been her fault. Like an invisible chain, it still bound her to him; so invisible, there was no way to sever it without wounding herself.

Fastening off the darning wool, she twisted the repaired pair of socks into a ball and automatically picked up another, examining the threadbare heels with her finger.

CHAPTER 10

Nothing could have surprised Letty more than David drawing up, somewhat jerkily, outside the shop one Saturday afternoon in June in a splendid new Morris Oxford motor car. Dumbfounded, the dead litter of last Sunday's market going unnoticed underfoot, she stood staring at the black paintwork glittering in the late sunshine while David grinned up at her from the driving seat, impish as a schoolboy.

'My father has made me a partner in his business. This is to mark the event. £180 straight from the showroom. What d'you think of it?'

Touched by her wide-eyed amazement, the maturity of his thirty-four years sloughed from him like dead skin as he watched her green eyes dart and flicker, heard her exclamations, disjointed by excitement.

'Oh David, it's wonderful! You never said . . . about being made a partner. Or this. Oh my, it's wonderful. And a motorcar!' Goggle-eyed, she took in the vehicle, shaking her head in disbelief. 'Fancy now!'

'We could go for a spin,' he cut through her

incoherence. 'I could drive you over to Lavinia and Albert's and show it off to them.'

She looked at him, her expression dulling. 'Oh, but it's late.'

Vinny and Albert had moved out to Walthamstow, to a larger house, double-fronted, bay-windowed, with a garden; almost as good as Lucy's.

With three growing boys, little Arthur nearly two years old, they had certainly needed more room. But Walthamstow! Trust Vinny to go all posh. At least, with both sisters doing nicely thank you, Letty felt she could now hold her head up when she visited David's parents – not that she did very often if she could help it, their continuing so disapproving and distant towards her, no matter how properly she behaved.

Vinny's new home, large though it was, still gave as much an impression of lacking space as her old house had done, alive and noisy with three boisterous boys. So different to Lucy's with its air of never being truly lived in. Her two girls never romped, cried, got into mischief. If Elisabeth so much as spoke a quarrelsome word, Lucy would promptly get herself a headache. Nor did Letty reckon there'd be any likelihood of the family ever becoming larger.

Having abstained so long from allowing Jack anywhere near her, Lucy now seemed incapable of producing another child, girl or boy. Almost as though she'd put a curse on herself. Fret over it though she might, Letty couldn't imagine her

176

with any more children in her immaculate home. She'd probably have a breakdown if she had to put up with what Vinny put up with, and her expecting again in November.

Letty much preferred the chaotic upheaval of Vinny's home despite Albert's increasingly unbearable pomposity. She had never particularly liked Albert whose sleek youthfulness was fast fulfilling its promise of rotundness as he grew older. It would be fun to see his expression when David displayed this beautiful motor car to him.

Vinny's home was near to Epping Forest too. Letty's thoughts were already running on Epping Forest as she passed a hand appreciatively over the smooth bodywork. From now on they could drive there – drive anywhere – spend hours together without ever worrying about train and bus and tram timetables.

But so late in the afternoon, would they get to Vinny's and back before dark? Dad wouldn't be too pleased being left on his own at such short notice.

'We'd be ever so late getting home again,' she aired the thought, and David gave an explosive laugh.

Buying this had made him feel as light-headed as though he'd had a drink, could conquer the world. He flung one arm across its leather seat back, enticing her to get in beside him.

'It'll take only half an hour in this,' he said brightly as, unable to resist, Letty tentatively opened the door and slid into the seat. The devil inside David was brandishing its three-pronged fork and he laughed wickedly. 'Let's see Albert's expression when we show him.'

'It'll be dark before we get back.' Letty's face was sober now. Dare she say it? To rush off without any warning and leave Dad all that time. He'd go all ill-done-by. She'd feel guilty. For days afterwards life would be miserable. She hated those kind of days.

David was cheerfully unsuspecting. 'It's midsummer, darling. It won't get really dark for hours. It's only just seven o'clock now.'

'There's Dad's supper.' Letty knew instantly it had been the wrong thing to say, seeing David's face cloud briefly. But he brightened the very next second. Nothing was going to spoil his triumph.

'We could take him along if you like?' But a lack of enthusiasm had entered his exuberant tone. This evening he wanted Letty to himself. 'Obviously, if he doesn't want to, I'll make certain we're back before it's too dark. Half an hour to get there. An hour or so with them. Half an hour back. But if you'd prefer . . .'

Letty shot him a look. It was enough to tell her exactly what he was thinking. His joy in the new automobile was fast being dampened at the thought of asking her father along, knowing he'd refuse, knowing she'd be thrown into misery by his refusal. Her chin would go up, of course, determined not to let him spoil her few hours out of his sight but, as always, she'd be pulled apart, a mouse between two predators.

Letty could see David was doing his best to put on a brave face, and her chin did indeed go up. She came to an instant decision.

'It don't matter, David. He'll be fine on his own.' She was already out of the seat. 'Wait there. It'll only take me a tick to get me 'at on.'

Determination always gave her speech a hard aggressive cockney edge and David smiled, loving her for it, loving her resolve.

She found Dad in the kitchen, Braces dangling around his hips, his shirt collarless, he was trimming his moustache in front of the mirror over the sink. Scissors poised, he turned to see the twin spots of high colour in her cheeks, the glow in her eyes giving them an even greener hue that meant only one thing, but she voiced it for him.

'David's downstairs.'

She sounded breathless. The way she looked, as though on the point of taking off on new wings, told him her mind was already made up to go out with her precious David Baron.

Albert Bancroft's mind savoured its own bitterness. A wonder she even bothered coming up to tell him. His earlier good humour doused in a single swoop, tonight he'd be on his own, knowing all her attention would be given up to David Baron, and sod how he felt – up here all alone.

'And guess what he's done, Dad? He's gone and

bought a motor car. A proper motor car. Come and take a look. Oh, it's smashing!'

Arthur Bancroft grunted, turned back to snipping the stiff greying hairs on his upper lip. The small oval water-stained mirror reflected his faded blue eyes, baleful, full of possessive jealousy.

'I s'pose yer goin' out in it with 'im?'

'He's going to take me over to see Vinny and . . .'

'Lavinia!' he interrupted savagely without a pause in his snipping.

'Lavinia,' she echoed meekly. It wasn't the time to get on any high horse. 'David asked if you'd like to come with us. Be nice for you to see Vin . . . Lavinia. Make a change. Make the weekend nice for you.'

But all her coaxing fell on deaf ears. Nothing was going to suit Dad. He made a point of it now.

'I've said it before an' I'll say it again, no one's goin' ter get me in one of them there stinkin' rattlin' things!'

From the corner of his eye he saw her stiffen, her chin go up. He shrugged and continued to trim his moustache. 'Don't s'pose it matters ter you if I go or not. You're still goin', ain't yer? Out till all hours.'

'I'm never out till all hours.' Her tone was affronted. 'I'm always back before you go to bed. At least if you go to bed normal times. Well, are you coming or not?'

But she already knew his answer.

He stopped trimming to shake his head briefly.

'Can't see meself stuck in the back of that contraption, actin' the gooseberry. You don't want me with yer, anyway, you an' 'im, if truth's known.'

'Well . . .' Her words trail off, her lips tight. 'He only asked.'

Head up, she turned on her heel, went resolutely into her bedroom, the one that had once been her sisters'.

She returned moments later wearing a cream-coloured tam o'shanter that went well with her navy blue dress. David had bought it for her for her birthday. Very fashionable, the narrow hem of the three-tiered skirt high enough off the floor to show her slim ankles.

She'd been over the moon about her present, hardly even looked at the brooch he himself had bought her. He took second place to her bloody fine David in everything these days.

Arthur felt a force inside him endeavouring to make him ignore her, but she looked so attractive, her figure slim and shapely, her cheeks glowing, that a wave of affection constricted his chest.

'I'm going then, Dad.' Her obdurate tone cut through his momentary softness.

He grunted, kept his eyes on the mirror, conscious of her moving off, her footsteps an angry clatter on the stairs.

'And don't yer let 'im get up to no good with yer in that fancy machine of 'is!' he yelled after her departing footsteps, hearing the shop doorbell jangle fiercely and the door crash to.

'Don't let 'im,' he muttered, his voice like dead leaves rustling along the pavement. 'Don't let 'im take yer away from me. What'll I do if you go?'

For a moment longer he gazed at his reflection in the mirror, then moved away, dropping the scissors despondently on to the upturned wooden lid of the copper that served for a draining board.

In his thoughts he followed them; saw the glowing faces of two people in love; heard their secret laughter – his daughter no longer a girl but a woman who after six years being courted must know the man who courted her, every inch of him. And did he know every inch of her?

He forced that thought from him, but still he followed them. The man's face, as he drove the automobile, would be smiling, intent on the road ahead. The woman, head reclined on the seat back, hair blowing loose from under the tam o'shanter. She'd perhaps take it off, let her hair blow freely.

At Lavinia's they would laugh and talk around the tea table, play with the grandsons he himself seldom saw, for his eldest daughter rarely came to the flat. They'd talk about things that he sitting on his own in this flat would not be sharing in. Left out. No one to give a toss about him. Bloody families! Unspoken words raged in his head. You bring 'em up, care for them, work, sweat, so they'd be a bit better dressed, better fed than some around here. And what d'you get for it? They turn into bloody snobs who don't want to know where they were brought up. Too bloody stuck up to show their faces in the place where they were born and brought up.

Then, saying their goodbyes to Lavinia and Albert and their new posh house, the man and woman would climb back into the motor car, drive slowly through the dusk . . . Arthur pulled aside the heavy lace curtain at the parlour window, white from Letitia's recent washing and well starched. She did a good job of starching. The sky beyond, shot with thin lines of dark clouds, was tinged by dusk's last translucent shades of green and dull rose.

In the dusk the man and woman would drive slowly along the edge of the forest with its big quiet trees and its dark shadows. In one of those shadowy places, the man would bring the vehicle to a halt, would turn off the engine, would turn to the woman, his arm around her. He would pull her to him, kiss her, embrace her, fondle . . .

'Bleedin' bloody tyke! Them dirty 'ands of 'is all over 'er! My daughter! Means ter take 'er away, if 'e can. But I ain't goin' ter let 'im – by Christ I ain't goin' ter!'

In the darkening parlour, Albert, sitting in Mabel's wooden armchair beside the empty grate, pulled himself up sharp. Talking to himself now, was he? That's what old age did for a person. All the anger of a moment ago seeped out of him, left him as empty as the grate. His faded blue eyes roamed the shadows of the room.

'I'm gettin' on. Gettin' old. Fifty-six. Christ, what'll I do if 'e do take 'er away from me?'

With slow effort, like one suffering from arthritis, he heaved himself out of the chair, felt along the mantelshelf for matches, shook the box to ascertain its contents. The struck match filled his face with its yellow glow, touched the ornaments on the mantelshelf. He moved to the centre of the room, reached up, pulled the slender chain of the centre gas light. Escaping gas hissed quietly, then plopped as he applied the lighted match. The mantel spluttered, its light sickly green, then settled, hissed steadily, the light becoming incandescent.

In the darkness of the trees on the edge of Epping Forest, David leaned over, kissed her, a soft gentle kiss. Letty lay in his arms, trying not to think of Dad, wanting only to savour those soft, gentle kisses that said so much. But at the back of her mind she couldn't help thinking of Dad.

'It's getting late, David.'

'Not that late,' he murmured, oblivious to all else but her, lying in his arms for him to pour his love into her. The night breeze touching their faces, she returned his kisses. His hand kneading her breast through the navy blue dress made her sigh, want to rid herself of the heavy hampering clothes.

They were going to make love, here, in the shadows. She knew it, wanted him to love her, her hand behind his neck holding his lips to hers, her blood coursing. Yet, prodding the back of her mind, it's getting late. Dad'll be wondering . . .

Hardly aware why or that she had done so, her muscles tensed themselves.

'David, we should be getting back.' They came of their own volition those words, not at all as she had intended.

'Stop worrying, darling.' David's voice was hoarse with eagerness.

But her worrying only became stronger, made her even more rigid.

'David . . .'

'Stop worrying.' His breathing had become harsh, his hands had become urgent, seeking her. But they threatened too. Threatened to sweep aside all care, all conscience.

'No, David – don't.'

The habit of obligation, a cruel invader, without her realising it, dominated her. How she hated it, but like a helpless victim she had to surrender to it. One small compensation – there would be another time when she would be totally at liberty to forget everything and allow herself be made love to with all indulgence. One hour earlier she would have. But now . . .

'David, it's late!'

The sharpness in her voice brought him abruptly to himself. Leaning back from her he misread her anguish of indecision for rejection, was staggered for a moment, even as he realised it wasn't rejection of him but the influence of one who, for all he was miles away, might as well have been sitting behind her, frowning hostile disapproval. Someone against whom he could never hope to compete if he tried for a million years.

Sitting back to stare into the dusk, his lips tightened. 'Right! Let's get you back home to your father. That is what's worrying you, isn't it? Him. I take second place and always will. Then by all means let me get you home!'

The engine, still hot, roared into life without needing to be cranked.

On the verge of tears, Letty wanted to cry out, no, she didn't want to go home, wanted him to make love to her. But there'd be no mending what had just passed between them. David was beyond being consoled. He drove in brooding silence. She too sat silent, counting the interminable miles home, the drawn out creeping of the next forty minutes it took to reach there.

Outside the shop, he switched off the engine. His body sagged limp against the seat back. He didn't look at her.

'Letitia.' His tone, so grimly decisive, frightened her. 'I apologise for losing my temper. I have been thinking, bringing you home this evening . . . You and I – we are getting nowhere. All this waiting. We . . . I'm getting older. It has been six years, Letitia. A man can have only so much patience and mine is running out. I think it's time we made up our minds. You whether you really do want to marry me or whether you feel you must spend the

186

rest of your life looking after your father, and I must decide whether to wait for you for the rest of *my* life if you can't leave him. But in all truth, Letitia, it is asking too much of anyone. I've no idea what decision you will come to, but mine is that I can no longer consider having to wait indefinitely for you. It's up to you, Letitia, to say which course you will choose.'

He'd never spoken like this before, so stern, so solemn, so blunt. Letty's reaction, the threat of an empty future stretching ahead of her, was instant. Her voice echoed along the dim street.

'David, don't say things like that! You can't leave me – not after all these years . . .'

'Exactly.' He turned to her now, in the fitful glow of the sparsely set gaslamps, his face full of pain, tender love, fear. 'After all these years. For how many more do I stand in the background watching you give three-quarters of yourself to your father and the remaining quarter to me? Perhaps I'm not being fair to want you all to myself, but I don't feel you're being fair either. I'm not asking you to stop loving your father. I'm asking you to love me . . .'

'But I do!'

'Not as a woman should love a man, Letitia. It's ludicrous, the way you expect me to hang around. I can't take it much longer. I don't want to leave you, darling. I merely said, we must come to a decision soon. It can't go on as it is.'

'Oh, it won't David!' She clung to him now. 'I'll

sort something out about Dad. I'll tell him he's got to face facts. I'll tell him he can't have me round him forever. I want to be married and be like everyone else and have a husband and a family. I *will* do something, David. Please trust me. I will! I promise!'

'You've promised before.'

'But I will, this time I will. I prom –' She'd already said that, couldn't say it again. It meant nothing to him. 'Oh, David darling, don't frighten me like this. I don't know what I'd do without you.'

She knew she sounded dramatic, but desperation and wretchedness made her so. Her world was being demolished. Then, from deep inside, there came a feeling of defeat, a strange unwanted stillness that seemed to flow over her and through her, sapping all her will to fight, a sort of deadness, or was it pride instilling her with perverse stubbornness?

She sat still, head up, staring blankly in front of her, yielding herself up to that pride. She sensed him looking at her, but when she returned his look, he glanced away.

'I think it might be a good thing,' he said slowly as if to himself, 'if perhaps we don't see each other for a while.'

'Please don't say that, David.' Although she had interrupted him sharply, she was surprised at her own tone – low and even and without tremor, without any note of pleading even, as she said please.

'I was going to say, for a couple of weeks perhaps,' he finished. 'It might give both of us time to reflect on what is happening to us.'

'David . . .'

'I think you had better go in, Letitia,' he said abruptly. 'Your father's waiting up for you.' He glanced upwards and, following his eyes, Letty saw the dull glow of gaslight through the brown curtains.

Without waiting for her reply, he got out and came round to open the door on her side of the motor.

'Will I see you tomorrow?' Trying to smother the note of pleading, her voice sounded stiff, its tone flat. David was looking down at the pavement, avoiding her eyes.

'I'm not certain what I'll be doing. Next Sunday perhaps. I'll write to you in the week, let you know.'

Before she could argue he had kissed her briefly on the cheek and was making his way back around the vehicle.

Her earlier stubborn pride reared up instantly, whispered crazily: If that's the way he wants it. She felt she was choking. And someone was weeping in an empty room deep inside her own body. Beyond that she seemed incapable of thought. As if her mind and body belonged to someone else she walked to her door, fumbled for her latch key, pushed it into the keyhole and turned it, gently pushed the door. The bell jangled. You could never creep in without anyone inside being warned, no matter how carefully the door was opened.

Letty turned, looked back. The vehicle's engine had been ticking over all this time. She hadn't noticed. And now, without even looking at her, David released the brake, moved off slowly.

She watched it go towards Arnold Circus. He would most probably go through Calvert Street, coming out on to Shoreditch High Street to go diagonally northwards across London towards the elegant serenity of his nice home in Highgate. Another world, one which if she was really brutal with herself, didn't include her. Never had. Not in six years it hadn't. She felt strangely and unexpectedly deceived. All these years she'd been deceiving herself really.

Letty closed the door with exaggerated care, aware of a hard lump growing inside her chest, getting harder and tighter, filling the cavity, pressing against her ribs. She heard Dad's voice, 'That you, Letitia?' and automatically called back, 'Yes.' Who else did he think it would be?

The lump was suffocating her. By the time she'd got to the top of the stairs she could hardly breathe. Yet at the same time there was a voice inside her that was crying, 'You'll see him – next week, or the week after, you'll see him. You will!'

'That you, Letitia?' Dad called again from the parlour. She could hear him knocking out his pipe against the fender.

She couldn't face him. Not at the moment. Tomorrow perhaps, when she was more herself. The lump was strangling her.

'I'm going straight to bed, Dad,' she said, passing the parlour. Her voice sounded as if someone had their hands round her throat. 'I'm tired.'

'Too tired to come in 'ere an' see me after I waited up for yer?'

'Yes, Dad, sorry!'

She didn't care what he thought; wanted only to be on her own. She heard his muffled complaints as she closed the door to her bedroom; heard him come to her door, prayed, Please God, don't let him come in. Don't let him start on at me. I want to die . . .

Face in the pillow she listened, tensed, tears held back, bursting inside her; heard him move away and go into his own room, his voice low as he grumbled to himself about her not caring two hoots about his feelings.

His door closing quietly, the tears oozed on to the pillow, forming large damp patches where the outer corners of her eyes pressed. Never had she known a moment like this, when nothing, no amount of tears, could mend the hurt inside her. It was all over, everything. David was gone. He said he would write to her, let her know about next Sunday. But she knew he wouldn't. He would leave her behind, take up his life without her, doing things she'd never again share in.

It seemed incredible that six years could end so abruptly and so completely. She still couldn't believe it, clung to the belief that it wouldn't be so, yet knew that it was.

The worst hurt of all was the fact of being excluded from all he would do from now on in his life, sharing nothing of it. And it had been her fault. No – it had been Dad's fault. She hated Dad with all her being for what he had done to her with his selfishness, but more she hated the love she still had for David, exaggerated by separation, making her heart ache with nothing to be done to stop it.

CHAPTER 11

August Bank Holiday Monday was lovely after a sultry, changeable weekend.

Sitting quietly at home, Letty thought despondently of what she and David would have done with such a lot of things going on over this last official holiday before Christmas. The sun shining from a clear sparkling sky, almost as traditional as August Bank Holiday itself, shone only to mock her, it seemed.

Wrapped up in her own unhappiness, Letty was unaware of how it was mocking everyone. Families off for a day at the seaside, laden with buckets and spades, bags full of sandwiches and ginger beer, found trains cancelled, taken up by naval personnel and Reservists.

Moping over David, Letty thought only of how they might have been sharing in London's enjoyment of its August Bank Holiday: mingling with crowds in shirt sleeves or light summer dresses, strolling in its parks or packing into its zoo.

Together they might have gone to Madame Tussaud's waxwork museum where the likenesses of King George and Queen Mary were on display, or to the air display at Hendon, or Earls Court where there was a Spanish display. They might have hovered outside Buckingham Palace to see the changing of the guard, hoping for a glimpse of their Majesties in the flesh, or gone to the White City to see its Wild West show. Crowds there were, but an air of expectancy hung over everyone, even over Letty at home.

Days before, the usual quabbles in the Balkans had taken on a more sinister tone, Europe's mounting tension revealed in every newspaper.

'Yer read this?' Armed with a copy of the *Evening Standard*, Mrs Hall had come to park herself firmly on Dad's sofa. 'Them Austrians declarin' war on Serbia over that bloomin' Archduke. Them Balkans! All the same. Always squabbling over something or other.'

There was hardly need to read any of the account with Mrs Hall giving a blow by blow commentary on it ever since some young Serbian exile had assassinated the Austrian Archduke Ferdinand on a visit to Bosnia.

'The Black 'And,' Mrs Hall said darkly. 'That's what they call theirselves, so it says 'ere – them Serbians what shot 'im and 'is wife, poor thing.'

She had lately taken to coming to sit and read to Dad from the evening newspaper, more or less as bored with her lonely life as he was with his. He'd listen intently to her going into the last dot and comma of the smallest drama the paper had to offer.

194

Murder and bloody robbery now took back seat to events in Europe. More interesting all round, like the progress of some football match, they learned through her of the Austro-Hungarian foreign minister's suspicion of Serbia's having a hand in the shooting, his obtaining a promise from Germany of its support, demanding Austrian officials take part in the trials of the assassins, and that France and Russia were pledging to support Serbia in rejecting those demands.

'It'll put a cat amongst the pigeons,' Mrs Hall declared eruditely.

Within days she was in again, sitting in the old wooden chair Dad would normally use, a flat cap pinned to her untidily piled greying hair. The newspaper held as near to the evening light as possible, squinting closely at the print, she had read aloud in stilted syllables: 'It says 'ere – Austr-i-o-'ungary is rejectin' Sir Edward Gray's pro-posal for the dispute to be taken to arbi . . . arbi-tration at a inter-nation-al con-fer-ence. They're goin' ter cause trouble fer a lot of people, as I can see,' she added her own words.

Despite Mrs Hall's alarmist attitude, Letty, like most people, had taken the squabble between the two countries with a pinch of salt. The newspapers proclaiming Russia's mobilising, Germany's demanding they stop military preparations on its frontier, didn't truly touch her. It was, after all, a long way from home.

Nor did it bother her that Russia had ignored

Germany who promptly declared war on it, asking France to declare its neutrality. She had other things on her mind.

David had not contacted her at all since he had driven off into the darkness towards Arnold Circus three weeks ago. There had been a leaden weight in her chest as she'd waited for the following Sunday to arrive. When he hadn't arrived with it, vague panic had set in, then more anger than panic. By Monday, busy with the shop, she had pushed it aside. But the following weekend, preceded by that same dull leaden feeling, brought back the sense of panic, almost unbearable, far more acute than the previous week, as if some delayed reaction had accentuated it.

Any word spoken to her would have had her in a flood of tears. Yet she dared not cry in front of Dad. She had her pride. So she was sharp and unapproachable and had a blazing row with him over simply nothing at all, leaving him dazed and bewildered.

It was pride too that almost prevented her from asking Mr Solomons next door if she could use his newly installed telephone. Pride! To be first to give in, to beg David to see her. But she needed David more than she needed pride. And if it brought them together . . . She almost asked Mrs Hall for her advice, but in the end decided not to. Decisions were lonely things.

Dad had not once queried why David hadn't come for two Sundays running. When the third

Sunday passed without his appearing and Dad still hadn't queried it, Letty found herself wondering why she was being so loyal to Dad when he couldn't care less about her feelings.

Full of bitter anger, she made an excuse to him that third Sunday and crept next-door to the Solomons' shop, hoping her father upstairs in the flat, the window up this warm afternoon, wouldn't hear her.

Mr Solomons opened the door to her tentative knock, peered at her through thick lenses.

'Letty? What you vant, my dear?'

In spite of herself, she waved him to lower his voice.

'Vat iss it? Your father, is he unwell?'

'No, Mr Solomons. But I wondered if you'd mind if I could please use your telephone? I have to get in touch with my . . . fiancé.' It sounded oddly out of keeping now, but he had been – was – her fiancé. She still wore his ring.

The thin wrinkled face creased into a smile. He nodded. 'Your fiancé I know. Pleasant – always such a nice greeting he gives me when I see him Sundays.'

Four fingers scratched his lined, unshaven cheek. 'Come to think of it, lately I ain't seen him. He's ill, your fiancé?'

'No, he's very well, Mr Solomons.' Time was going on. Dad would be wondering where she was. 'But I need to telephone him – a bit urgent.'

'Of course! Of course!' He stepped back as his

wife called down asking who it was. 'It's the young daughter of Mr Bancroft, my dear,' he called back, and then to Letty. 'Come in! Come in! You'll find the telephone the end of the passage.'

'I've got tuppence for . . .'

'Oy, tuppence! Keep it! I should charge a neighbour vot hardly comes asking to use it ever? Not like some – they think I got it only for them. Of course use it. Vith my blessings. Let yourself out after. And give my regards to your father. I hope his chest is well with this nice veather we are havink. Such a nasty von he had this vinter. His coughing I could hear halfway down the street.'

Letty watched him mount the stairs out of sight. Grateful to him, she dropped her coins by the table all the same, took the earpiece off its hook, held it tentatively to her ear – the first time she had ever used one, private telephones being something of a rarity.

With five postal deliveries a day she would have got David's reply the next day, but she needed it now. Speaking louder than she needed to, she gave the telephone exchange David's number and waited.

The tinny nasal voice that answered was that of David's mother. Even distorted by distance, Letty could still recognise it.

'C-can I speak to David, please?' The sound of the woman's voice was enough to make her stammer.

'Who is it speaking?' came the refined tones.

198

'It-it's Letty . . . Letitia Bancroft.'

There was a silence so drawn out, she thought the woman had hung up. Then cold and sharp and imperious: 'What do you want?'

'Is David there, please? I'd like to talk to him.' Oh Lord, should she have said speak, not talk? She wasn't sure.

Mrs Baron's cool voice replied 'David is not here.'

'Can you give him a message then, please? Ask him if he could come and see me.' She hated the pleading in her own tone.

'David is not here,' Mrs Baron repeated as if they were the only words she knew, like a parrot.

'But can you give him my message?'

'I'm sorry, Miss . . . Bancroft.' Her own name sounded distasteful on the woman's lips. 'David is not here, nor do I think he would be much interested in your message.'

'But if you could . . .' She heard the click against her ear, the spurning silence of an empty wire. 'I only wanted to tell him I love him,' she said to the dead wires. 'I only wanted to say that.'

'You seen the morning papers, love?' Mrs Hall burst into the shop as Letty was opening up on Wednesday morning, her coarse voice all excited. She thrust the newspaper into Letty's hands. 'That bloomin' Germany! It says 'ere Britain's at war with Germany.'

It was difficult to read against Mrs Hall's account of Germany's having asked Belgium for permission to cross its territory with troops as the easiest route to Paris; that in spite of the King of Belgium's refusal, troops were already across its border.

Letty couldn't concentrate on reading anyway, still numbed by Mrs Baron's attitude toward her. The more she thought of it, the more it seemed to her that David had been hovering in the background, not lifting a finger in protest. Hurt pride ruled. She wouldn't have him now if he came crawling back on all fours.

'I said I could see trouble coming, didn't I?' gabbled Mrs Hall, and without pausing for breath, 'Yer Dad upstairs, luv?'

'Yes,' Letty answered woodenly. 'Having his breakfast.'

'All right if I go up an' see 'im?'

Not waiting for her sanction, the newspaper snatched from her hand, Ada Hall hurried up the stairs to relay the news to Dad, leaving Letty to shrug off Europe's current problems and return to her own, far more concerned by them than by the squabbling of nations.

Concerned or not, war bursting on to the streets of Bethnal Green as people woke up to go to work and thrust all personal problems aside.

Outside, paper boys on every corner were having a field day. Newspapers were ripped from their hands and people read avidly as they went off to work. Letty could see them through her shop window, their directions erratic, as if with no idea quite which way to go, work or home again.

Hurrying out, she bought a paper for herself, reading quickly with a tightening in her chest, which might have been excitement or might have been fear, that Britain had asked Germany to respect a treaty guaranteeing Belgian neutrality. The German Chancellor, Theobald von Bethmann-Hollweg, had disparagingly dismissed it as a scrap of paper. Consequently, in defence of Belgium, Britain had, as of eleven o'clock last night, 4 August, declared war with Germany.

Mr Solomons, beside himself, burst in on Letty standing dazed amid the bric-a-brac no one now showed any interest in looking at. Outside, people were beginning to go wild, cheering and hugging each other. Little paper Union Jacks had appeared magically, like rabbits pulled from magicians' hats, sober citizens of a few moments or so ago waving them dementedly in each other's faces.

'Your sister, Lucy!' Mr Solomons was yelling as though he were ten streets away. 'On my telephone. Vants urgent to speak to your father!'

Letty did not question him but yelled up the stairs: 'Dad! It's Lucy! On Mr Solomons' telephone next-door! It's Lucy!'

He didn't even correct the shortening of her sister's name, coming hurrying down, more nimble than she'd seen him in months, Mrs Hall puffing down behind him as he followed his neighbour out.

Automatically, Letty trailed out after them, waited as her father bawled down the mouthpiece:

'Yes, I 'eard! Don't get excited. We ain't goin' ter be slaughtered. Well, if it's upset yer that much, Jack can bring you and the girls over.'

'Don't vorry, Letty my dear.' Mr Solomons extended a thin hand to pat hers as she stood uselessly by, biting her lip. 'It is as your father says. No need for upsets. Ve are an island vith no borders. No soldiers coming to drag us out of our beds and throw us out of our homes and say to kill us if ve don't obey and leave.'

His sunken brown eyes held a faraway look, reliving that day he and his family, with hardly more than what they stood up in, had trundled a small rickety cart piled high with what belongings it would carry from their home in Galicia. But Letty saw only kindness in those eyes.

'I'm not worried, Mr Solomons. Lucy gets in such a state sometimes.'

Dad had hardly come off the phone when it rang again, tinnily. It was answered by Mr Solomons who hastily waved him back.

'It's your other daughter, Mr Bancroft. It's your Vinny.'

Letty hovered, listening to Dad repeat himself. Outside the corn chandler's clusters of grubby kids were whooping past, blowing whistles. War was exciting, a celebration, national pride on everyone's face.

By evening, Letty having rustled up some sort of tea for them all, the family sat together discussing war while she wondered what David was doing, what he was thinking. Surely he would send her a message now?

Nothing. No word – nothing. Everywhere men in an unprecedented flush of national solidarity were signing on in droves to fight the Boche.

Billy came to see her. His round blue eyes glowed with a fervour of excitement.

'I've joined up, Let!' he almost shouted at her as she stood in the middle of her shop, blinking at him in his rough khaki uniform, puttees anchoring his stance, peaked cap set at a jaunty angle.

'They took me on without a blinkin' second's hesitation. Passed me medical. A1 an' signed on the dotted line before yer could say 'ow's yer farver! So now I'm a soldier, Let. What d'yer fink? D'yer fancy me? I could take yer out tonight before I go off to join me regiment if yer like.' He saw her hesitate. 'Go on, Let. Fer old time's sake. Yer'll make me proud.'

What could she say but yes? Seeing Billy standing so debonair, so eager to get into the fray and fight for his country, be a hero, she felt a twinge of affection for him. Not love. Only one man had claim to that. If he hadn't had, she could have loved Billy with all her heart; kind, affable, his square face firm and cheery with cockney perkiness. Her heart almost began to ache for the chance she'd missed, almost verged on making her want to turn her back on the past, to let her feelings for Billy take her where they would, but some invisible thread held her and she hadn't the strength to throw it off.

Billy took her to the music hall, the Hackney Empire, and then to a little corner cafe for a slap up meal of pie and mash, saveloys and peas pudding for himself. He talked the whole evening, made her laugh, then took her home, kissed her on the cheek when she did not offer her lips, asked if she would write to him. She said yes, she would.

After he'd gone, she cried, missing him already, felt terribly sad. Beneath the banter of goodbye he had looked strangely lonely as he threw her that final wave, sort of lost. She had felt an urge to run after him, throw her arms about him and tell him it would be all right – it would all be over by Christmas. The newspapers that had gravely reported the retreat of the British Expeditionary Force from Mons at the end of August were now, by the beginning of September, gleefully reporting the Germans retreating back to the River Aisne.

But it wasn't leaving home to fight that had made Billy look so sad and lonely, she knew. All these years, for all his good looks, he had never stayed long with any girl and seeing his forlorn wave, even as he made it appear so nonchalant, she knew herself was the reason. Dear, sweet Billy. If . . . She swept aside sudden apprehension that was almost like a premonition. Of course he would be all right!

She thought again of the thousands of men

flocking to join up and then of David. Had he too joined that queue? Perhaps not so much in national outrage but in a rage against her? Thinking of David, thoughts of Billy all drifted away, her apprehension for him transferring itself to David. What if . . . She had to get in touch with David before he, like Billy, did something rash.

Swallowing her pride, Letty went next-door to Mr Solomons on Sunday and, with his kind permission, risked another telephone call to David's parents. To her intense delight, it was David who answered.

For a moment her throat seemed to close up, the words she wanted to say trapped there. When at last the tightness gave, they flowed from her in a torrent.

'David! Oh, darling, I'm so sorry. I didn't mean . . . I want to marry you, darling . . . if you'll still have me? I want to so much and I don't care who wants to stop me. I want . . . Oh, please, David, don't be angry at me. Come back . . . come and see me . . . come . . .'

She heard his voice, the strange quality of it, and knew exactly what he had done.

'Letitia. I'm leaving tomorrow.'

'You've not gone and enlisted?'

'I'm sorry, Letitia. I felt it my duty. They need officers. With my schooling and background, they jumped at me. Don't worry though, I shan't be going abroad, not yet. I'm to be trained to train recruits for the time being.'

Letty listened, stunned. His tone was so casual. After her frantic avowal of love, it was so casual.

'I see. That's it then, is it?' Her own voice sounded equally as formal as his. She'd made a fool of herself.

'David, I still feel the same about you.'

'I know,' came the voice over the wires.

'I mean what I said, about marrying you.'

'I know.'

There was only dull defeatism, resignation, in his voice. Her temper flared briefly. 'Is that all you can say – I know? David, I want to see you. I *have* to see you. Please! Just the once. To talk it out. Please come and see me. I promise I won't . . .'

She stopped abruptly. One couldn't go on pleading indefinitely.

She listened intently to the silence at the other end, her mind in a whirl to divine what he was thinking. All the time pride fought a battle with her need. 'Oh, David, answer me,' cried that need. 'Say you will. I need you. Oh, dearest God, how I need you. Don't go away. Don't hang up.' And pride rebuked her. 'Lowering yourself like the stupid worm you are! If he don't care, lowering yourself won't get him. You're just making yourself look cheap.' She had half begun to say his name, need winning the battle, when he spoke.

'I've got to leave tomorrow. But if you want us to talk, I could come over in half an hour. Will that suit you?'

Oh, yes, darling! 'That'll be fine,' she said quietly.

'See you in half an hour or so, then.'

The earpiece clicked into silence against her ear and she replaced it with exaggerated care, called thank you to Mr Solomons; heard his hoarse acknowledgement float down the stairs.

By the time David arrived, Letty's nervousness was unendurable. Tears persisted in welling up over her lower eyelids despite her repeatedly brushing them away with the back of her hand. She stood in the shop, Dad well into his Sunday afternoon nap upstairs, and as a precaution she had tied back the shop doorbell so as not to alert him when – if – David came.

She saw him pull up outside the shop, with an effort stopped herself from running out to meet him. She stood straight-backed as he came in, noted the exaggerated way he concentrated his attention to closing the door so he wouldn't have to look at her.

When he did, pity ran through her; his eyes looked so mournful, darker than she'd ever seen them, as if a lifetime of suffering was gathered there. He dropped his gaze immediately to his hands, making a careful exercise of dragging off his driving gloves.

'You wanted to talk, Letitia?'

Oh, how she wanted to talk; to throw herself at him, fall to her knees and clasp him beg . . .

'I thought we should,' she said evenly. Please, she prayed, don't let my eyes look red. 'We couldn't just end it like that, David. You going off in your car that Sunday. You didn't even wave . . .'

Her voice had begun to tremble. There was no controlling the tears that rose now over her lid to slide thickly down her cheek, and she couldn't properly brush them away without drawing his attention. 'Oh, David . . .'

The next second she was in his arms, not knowing if it was she who had run to him or he to her, or both of them together. All she knew was that they were standing together in the centre of the shop, each clasping the other, she sobbing on his shoulder fit to burst, David murmuring words of love and comfort in a voice that quivered with emotion.

'I want to marry you, David,' she heard herself sobbing. 'Please, I want to marry you.'

'When?' The word sounded drawn out, almost doubting.

'As soon as possible. It don't have to be special. But as soon as we can.'

'My parents won't like it, you know. They've never taken much to you.' There was quiet laughter in his voice, the laughter of relief. It surged through her too, in a flood of love and happiness.

'My dad won't like it either.' For a second reality buffeted her. Dad. All the old fears came rushing back. How could she stand there and tell him . . . No, she would not think of that. He had almost ruined their love, their future together. He would do so again if she allowed him. But not this time. Didn't David have as much a battle with his parents? He had never let them stand in his way. Nor would she let Dad.

She reached up, took David's lean face between her palms, stared up into his dark eyes – dancing now.

'It's us, David, not them what matters,' her tones sharp and emphatic, careless of flattened vowels, carried away with all that crowded her mind. 'They've been married, been happy. Now it's our turn. We've got to be. I don't care a bugger who's against who. I'm goin' ter marry you!'

Suddenly her throat clogged up, choked her into silence, and David kissed her as he had not kissed her in a very long while.

CHAPTER 12

Over the telephone Albert's normally superior voice sounded anguished. 'Vinny – she lost the baby!'

'Oh, Albert – no!' Letty's own throat constricted in shock and sorrow. 'Oh, that's a terrible thing. Is Vinny all right?'

'Not in danger, but . . . Letty, she's in a terrible state. I don't know what to do for her. I've been in touch with my parents but my father is caught up at work and Mother can't travel here on her own, certainly not in this weather. Vinny keeps saying she wants you and her father. Can you get over?'

'Yes, of course.' Letty's response was instant and automatic, yet in the same instant common sense prevailed. Eight in the morning, a November fog enveloping everything in a bilious yellow blanket. 'If I can get there,' she moderated. 'You can't see a hand before you over here. But if the 35 bus to Walthamstow is running, I'll try. But Dad won't be able to come. He's got a nasty cough coming on. And he's got to keep an eye on the shop.'

It sounded very reluctant and she didn't mean to be. 'I'll do my best,' she said.

'If you could.' Albert was obviously setting aside his normal self-esteem with an effort. 'I'd . . . she would be so relieved.'

By nine the fog had lifted fractionally, though it was still almost midday before she finally alighted in Walthamstow from a crawling bus, the suburban fog a little whiter and thinner with a colourless sun's disc breaking through.

It was sixty-thirty when she got back, fog coming down thick as pea soup, necessitating her feeling her way, virtually by hand, from the bus stop at the Shoreditch end of Bethnal Green Road. The world was eerie silent. An occasional figure, creeping like herself, would materialise out of the miasma to startle her momentarily and melt again into the fog as she passed. She counted the spectral haloes of street lamps to home.

'We've got to have a telephone,' she said to Dad as she warmed her hands gratefully by the fire after unwrapping herself from enshrouding yards of clothing. 'I should have stayed the night with Vinny. I could have if I'd telephoned you. It was murder having to come all this way home in this weather. I'm frozen to the marrow!'

She shivered as proof and continued her original theme. 'We can't expect Mr Solomons to keep running round here, or us begging to use his every time we have to get in touch with someone. Thank God Vinny's got one and I could tell Lucy about her. The fog's not so bad out of London. Jack's taking her to stay with her. We need to keep in touch.'

Her whole speech was a rebuke to him, one he managed to gloss over with a prolonged fit of coughing.

'Load of fuss,' he said, irritable at having been put out, expected to keep an eye to the shop, in his condition. 'Anyone'd think she's the only one to've ever lost a kid. Askin' yer ter run right over there, like it was next-door. They expect too much of yer. And you, yer silly easy-going cow, let 'em do it! Leavin' me stuck down there in that cold bloody shop. Me with me chest.'

Letty turned from warming her hands to throw him a look. 'Come on, Dad. You often go down, even in this weather. Wandering about, fingering this, fingering that.' She dearly wanted to add 'But come the hard graft of buying and selling, and you make sure of being well out of it'. But she thought it better to keep those thoughts to herself. She was too exhausted with the cold eaten right into her bones to have him start a row. To all intents and purposes, it had become her shop and she did not relish any interference from him at this stage in her life; making all the decisions herself now, hardly ever consulting him.

'Might as well not be 'ere at all fer all you tell me what's goin' on,' he would complain, but never took it any further, merely enjoyed making a business out of complaining, Letty thought uncharitably as she rubbed her hands together vigorously against

212

the last strands of chill in her bones and set her mind to getting him his tea.

'It was a girl,' she told him as she moved back and forth between the kitchen and the parlour. 'It's sad. She did so want a girl too.'

'She'll just 'ave to content 'erself waiting till next time.' Sitting up to the tea table, he bent his head to indulge in a long rumbling cough while Letty eyed him speculatively. With autumn well established, his cough promised to return full strength. With no notion how bad it would get, Letty just prayed it would remain as moderate as it had last year.

'Don't it worry you that Lavinia's all upset and miserable, losing her baby? She's really not herself, Dad. She's been longing for a girl.'

'So yer just said. Yer mother, God rest her soul, was always upset when she lost one, boy or gel. Yer poor mum, she . . .'

His voice faded, tears flooded his faded eyes at the memory and he stared sightlessly down at his plate, wiping the back of his thin hand against his eyes.

Letty, exasperated, went on sawing at the loaf, grasping it in an attitude of desperation against her aproned breast as she cut. Once she would have gone to him, put an arm on his shoulders, laid her head against his, trying to instil comfort. But it had gone on too many years. Now she was simply irritated by it.

Vinny had more need of Mum than did Dad.

'If only Mum was here,' she'd said. 'I want her to put her arms around me. I want it so much.'

It was pitiful. Letty had cried with her. Yet here was Dad all sorry for himself, hardly sparing a thought for anyone else. How then would he ever lay aside his own sense of loneliness enough to smile upon her marriage to David?

David had a whole week's furlough at the start of December. He came to see her on Saturday after the shop had closed.

He'd telephoned her the moment he had got home, Dad finally being convinced of its necessity for business and his own peace of mind, his cough steadily worsening with the onset of winter. He'd allowed it to be put in downstairs in the shop but refused perversely to answer its ring, as if this last gesture of stubbornness exonerated him utterly from any part in its installation.

So Letty had answered David's call, her father fortunately having a nap at the time so she had no need to tell him any white lies. David saying he would be there around seven, she had muffled the doorbell and waited downstairs in the darkened shop. She would let the doorbell tinkle after half an hour of privacy with David then bring him upstairs as though he had just arrived.

She waited with trepidation growing steadily, knowing full well the reason behind her secrecy. There was urgency in being in love these days, in snatching it wherever and whenever.

'And you *are* still willing to marry me?' David asked after she had welcomed him with a long eager kiss. In reply she drew him into the shadows of the back of the shop, lifted her lips to his again.

'Of course I am, darling.' It wasn't easy to make her voice sound utterly without reservation. Dad's winter cough had come on him early, had her running between the shop and his bedroom with linctus and winter green, fairly wearing her out. Hopefully he'd be better soon.

Not taking his eyes from her, David laid his officer's cap aside on a small rickety table. 'You are certain, aren't you, darling?'

'I am, David,' she answered resolutely. 'I am – really I am.'

As though testing her resolution, his lips came upon hers, bore her slowly lower until they were on their knees beside each other. He eased her down, with no resistance, unbuttoned her blouse front, her bodice, the cloth of his officer's uniform harsh and cold against her breasts.

Words raced through her mind. We mustn't be too long. Dad . . . But she dared not give substance to them in case David drew away in anger, or that resignation she knew so well. Besides, the blood was pounding in her ears, her head, her heart, and time was a precious commodity. How much of it did they have? In France men were dying – a war meant to end by Christmas showed no signs of ending. If David were to be called to the front. If she were never to see him again . . .

Fear made her clutch at him, receive him in a need to smother the visions flooding her mind's eye. Perhaps it was fear that made him savage with her, made him plunge into her as if more in lust than love, and she welcomed its sharp pain and the responsive welling up of that unbelievable, thrilling, frightening, joyous surge from the very depths of her; at that moment no one, nothing, mattered but the two of them.

David's dark eyes were glowing, those narrow features as animated as any boy's.

'I shall arrange everything, don't worry, darling. On my very next leave we'll be married. Fine with you, my love?'

She on his arm as they left the cinema, he cutting an adventurous, youthful figure in his lieutenant's dress uniform. Letty's glad heart pounded with eagerness, all reservation swept away.

'Your wife,' she murmured as she clung to him.

'My wife.' His arm, with hers threaded through it, tightened her hand against his side.

It had been a wonderful week. They hadn't ventured far – December didn't lend itself to jaunts down to Southend or walks in the park – but such diversions weren't needed. They had each other. And Dad had grudgingly warmed to David, a soldier on leave, a figure of respect. How could even Dad resent him?

More likely he had no alternative. Still in the grip of bronchitis and Ada Hall, who constantly popped in with remedies and hot broth, he was being spoiled rotten and seemed content enough to leave Letty free to be with David.

In the darkened seats of the cinema, they had hardly looked at the flickering screen; the phonograph music and laughter from the audience at the antics of a Knockabout Keystone comedy passed over their heads as David had laid tender and lingering kisses on her ready lips in the obliging semi-darkness.

His hand on her coat-enshrouded breast had been almost more than she could cope with and she had longed for the seclusion of her shop's back room, to have him all to herself.

As they emerged with the crowds into the clinging damp cold of the December evening, David spoke of marriage as he had done every day of his leave. It was Friday, he would be going back tomorrow, and still she hadn't found courage to confront Dad.

'I'd have liked you to have the most splendid wedding ever,' David breathed wistfully against her ear after they made love again, this for the last time before he would leave for his unit tomorrow morning.

'A wedding as your sister Lavinia had. I remember everyone was so convivial. But the way my parents feel, I don't think they'll ever be any different. But you must never worry. They're unmitigated snobs but it's me you're marrying, not them. And your father . . . I know he still hasn't reconciled himself to the fact that you must leave him eventually and make your own life . . .'

'Oh, David, please,' she began, with no wish to think about Dad, but he stopped her with a gentle hand to her mouth.

'I know, darling. It has never been easy for you. And I love you for your loyalty, your patience with your father, even to sacrificing all you want in this world. If I win only half that loyalty, I shall count myself the luckiest man alive.'

'You'll have it all, David. I promise you will.'

'I know, my sweet,' he said, and in the darkness his smile seemed to shine. 'You deserve so much that's good. We'll make our wedding as memorable as we can in the circumstances, and to blazes with other people. You'll have the finest wedding gown we can buy. I shall have to be in uniform, of course. We'll have a small wedding breakfast – not many guests, but it'll be the best. We'll spend our honeymoon in Brighton where I first took you to see the sea. Do you remember, darling?'

She remembered, recalled the dissension with Dad over it, recalled every argument they'd ever had over this one wish to marry David as clearly as if each one had occurred only yesterday.

She thought of the heartaches, the tears, the pain of wanting, glad to know it would soon end; she had prayed so long for this, and now it was almost here. All that she needed was the courage to tell Dad once and for all that she wasn't going to stand for any more of his argy-bargy, his sulking, his emotional blackmail. She would say it straight and to hell with what he'd reply!

One thing heartened her, gave her hope. Dad and Ada Hall had been getting together a lot more lately. Ada had been perking herself up, making herself look nice. No straggly bits of hair hanging around her neck these days; no tea-stained bodice, tatty shawl, and the man's cap she once wore was absent. She now wore a shiny black straw hat and her face positively shone from soap and water. Yet even now Letty dared not contemplate how Dad would take to her decision, solid though it was. She really ought to have broken it to him much sooner, but the longer she left it the harder it would become. She steeled herself to face him tomorrow morning without fail. No going back now. On David's next leave she would become his wife, and nothing Dad or anyone might say about it would make any difference.

Their final kiss as David left was the most poignant she'd ever known – wanting it to last and last, but aware of the impossibility; loathing to break off yet knowing she must. As if some thread still binding them dared them to break it at their peril, they held hands even as they moved apart as they knew they must, arms outstretched until only fingers were touching. Then they too lost contact.

'Take care of yourself, David,' she called as he moved off towards his waiting motor car.

'I will. Don't worry, darling.'

'I love you, David.'

She watched him get behind the wheel, draw his gloves over his fingers.

'I love you too.'

Don't go, David. Darling, don't go! She waved as he waved, stood with her hand still raised as he drew away, stood as the vehicle began to gather speed noisily, saw him half turn, his last wave through the misting of her eyes, waved back frantically.

Then he was gone. In a few short hours he would be making his way to his local station, the train to bear him back to his unit in the Midlands.

They would carry on their love in letters to each other, counting the days to his next leave and their wedding day. Meantime she must prepare Dad to accept her plans. Her fixed, immutable plans.

She stood a moment longer staring into the night; a dog was barking in another turning, a cat crossed the road, lithe, quick, body low and even, white paws going like the clappers, disappeared as quickly as it had appeared. Otherwise things were quiet. Quiet as once it never had been in this area.

Things were changing; no longer singing from the Knave of Clubs, people no longer going about in noisy groups. Fighting had been savage, little was left of the British Expeditionary Force, and already in the streets there was a distinct absence of men as more and more rallied to the call to arms. Already there were war widows in Bethnal Green and Shoreditch, Stepney and Hackney.

Carefully she closed the door on the night's quietness, released the bell on its spring as she always did these days, held it so it wouldn't jangle.

The stairs creaked faintly as she mounted them. Making as little noise as possible, she reached the top, hung up her hat and coat on the stand, smoothed a hand over her hair coiled low at the back.

In his bedroom Dad's cough was chesty, unrelenting.

'Letitia? That you?'

She paused by his half open door.

'Yes, Dad?'

'Where's me cough mixture?' His breathing wheezed.

'I'll get it.' There was no way in which she'd be able to break her news to him now, nor tomorrow morning, that was certain. But she would tell him, definitely, a little later. When he felt a bit better.

Christmas was quiet, if Dad's rumbling cough could be discounted; the first time Letty had been without David throughout the whole festival.

Lucy and Jack came over with the girls to spend Christmas Day, though Dad spent more time in bed coughing his heart up, keeping Letty on the run administering medicine, than with his visitors.

'It's not very nice for the girls,' Lucy said huffily, listening to the hawking and spitting in the other room. 'If they catch anything . . .'

221

'It's not catching,' Letty said.

'Of course it is.'

'Not Dad's type, it isn't. His is chronic – there inside him until the cold weather brings it out. Not like a cold or the 'flu.'

'Even so.'

Lucy picked at the chicken carcass lying on its dish on the dining table while Jack carefully pared himself an apple by the warm fire and the girls sat at his feet like fairy children and played quietly with their Christmas dolls.

'It's not nice for the girls, listening to all them nasty rumbly noises. Makes me feel quite sick, it does.'

Letty wanted to ask if she had as little control over that easily queasy stomach of hers if she'd ever had to clear up her children's sick – or were they, being her sweet little things, never prone to being sick like other kids? But it was Christmas and Lucy had been good enough to come over for Dad's sake, so she held her tongue.

Vinny, of course, was still upset by her loss and in no condition to travel, although Albert had telephoned to wish them all a Happy Christmas and hope Dad was feeling better.

Lucy wiped greasy finger tips daintily on a paper doily. 'When's your David coming home again on leave?'

'He's not long gone back,' Letty explained. She sipped her glass of sherry, keeping her eyes down. Lucy might be the one to tell, to pave the way in readiness for telling Dad.

'Lucy . . . David's asked me to marry him.'

Lucy gave her a sharp, half amused look. 'He's been asking you to marry him for years.'

'But this time I've accepted. This time I mean it. He's arranging it all, and we'll be married quietly when he comes home next time on leave.'

Lucy's eyes had hardened. 'And what about Dad? What's he going to do if you get married and leave here?'

Just what I'd have expected you to say, the thought pounded in a brief fit of anger through Letty's mind. But she kept her expression sweet, toying with her sherry glass, her eyes riveted on it.

'With David away, I'll stay on here. By the time the war ends and he comes home, Dad'll have to fall in with our plans, won't he? We can set up home here or sell up the shop and move somewhere else, Dad coming with us. He's lost all interest in the shop anyway and David's well set up – a partner in his dad's business now.'

Of course, there was always Ada Hall – her and Dad setting up together. What a lot of problems that would solve! There was still lots of time to tell Dad about her and David, well before his next furlough. However, it was best not to air any of those thoughts to Lucy. Not just yet.

'I take it you've told Dad all about it?' she said airily.

'No, not yet.' In the bedroom he was spitting audibly into his handkerchief – handkerchiefs she must soak in salt, boil in the copper, and scrub clean of phlegm after Boxing Day, a job she loathed.

'But I've got to tell someone or I'll burst! What d'you think, Lucy? I am right, aren't I? I'm as entitled as the next one to be married.'

Lucy shrugged dismissively.

'If everything goes well, darling,' David wrote in January, 'I'll be able to wangle seven days in April. We'll marry in your parish and I hope your father, Lucilla and Lavinia and their families, will honour us by attending. It's not certain if my parents will be there, but as I've said to you so many times, it is our life. We will live it together no matter what.'

Letty read with conflicting emotion – longing for April, dreading it too, with time growing shorter and shorter and still courage failing her in forewarning her father.

He had seemed to improve for a short while from that nasty bout of bronchitis over Christmas. That would have been the time to tell him, but she'd made the mistake of delaying too long, making certain he was completely ready to receive her news. Before she realised he had gone down again, so badly she had to call out the doctor who looked grave and said Dad should by rights be in hospital.

Ill as he felt, his eyes had brightened with fear.

'I ain't goin' inter no 'ospital, that's straight! Take yer there ter die, they do. Well, I ain't . . .' He'd fought a bout of coughing that left him sweating and continued wheezily, 'I ain't goin' ter no 'ospital. I'll die 'ere in me bed.'

'You're not going to die, Dad,' Letty said.

'What's 'e want to send me into 'ospital for, then?'

'Because you'll get better quicker there.'

'Well, I ain't goin', an' that's flat!'

'I wish you had gone,' she said peevishly after a fortnight of it. 'You're wearing me out, you know that? Honestly, Dad, you can be so selfish. You just don't care how I feel, so long as you're all right.'

She knew she was wrong blaming him. He couldn't help being ill.

She wrote to David saying how much she was looking forward to the day, said nothing about not forewarning Dad, received David's replies written in all innocence, talking of wedding plans.

Worn out she was indeed, her time as ever divided between running the shop, running after Dad, keeping the flat in order, cooking for him, shopping.

Even when Billy Beans came home on embarkation leave – destined for the front line, he said – asking her to go out and have a meal with him before he was due to go back, she only just managed to squeeze in an hour or so.

'You'll keep an eye on Dad for a couple of hours, won't you?' she begged Ada Hall, relieved that the woman expressed delight in doing that favour for her.

Billy looked grand in his corporal's uniform. 'I'll be a sergeant before long,' he boasted cheerily over pie and mash. 'When I've done active service, they said I'll get another stripe.'

'You should have bin an officer,' Letty told him. 'You might have stayed in England.'

'I should jolly well 'ope not. Why I joined, ain't it, ter fight? Ter see a bit of action. Gawd, what's the point bein' in the army if yer don't see action? No, old gel, I'm lookin' forward to it, I c'n tell yer.'

'But if you get hurt or . . . you know.'

His round blue eyes regarded her, his grin broad. 'Don't tell me yer'll be 'eartbroken? I didn't fink yer cared.'

'I do care, Billy. I care a lot.'

'An' you engaged to anuvver.'

Letty's cheeks flushed pink. She looked hastily down at her hands. 'I'm gettin' married in April, Billy.'

'Yer mean yer've accepted after all this time? Well, blow me down!'

'It's true.' Did she hear a tinge of betrayed hope beneath that lighthearted banter? 'I'm sorry,' she said inadequately, heard his laugh come a little sharply, with humour.

'What yer sorry for? Ain't nothin' ter do wiv me, is it?'

Letty caught at her lip with white even teeth. 'I

thought . . . Well, I thought you . . . I've always had a soft spot for you, y'know, Billy. We've bin good friends. At least, you've always bin a good friend ter me.'

She watched him nod contemplatively, almost wistfully. 'Yeah – a good friend.' The next instant he had brightened. 'Right then, eat up, old gel. It's me last meal wiv yer before I go ter meet me doom.'

'Don't say that!' she cried. 'Not like that.'

But Billy only laughed.

Letty lay in bed Sunday morning, counting. She counted with urgency and a deal of gnawing dismay.

It was 26 February. She'd not seen her period, hadn't seen it last month either. She'd never been strictly regular, that was true, her times never any bother – not like some girls who went through agonies of stomach pains and all that. Came and went and that was it.

But not to have taken note in January. What had she been thinking of? She should have been more concerned, she knew that now, yet had let it pass. Why, for heaven's sake? What brief amnesia had made her not make more of it? Stupid. And what was her excuse? That she'd been so busy with Dad's bronchitis, it had somehow not registered. But if it hadn't registered then, it was registering now, and realisation made her go cold beneath the warmth of the bedclothes.

A few minutes later she was chiding her silly imagination. It was fretting over David being away had made her edgy, and edgy nerves always made her irregular. Dad had been such a trial this winter too, no wonder nature was retaliating. By next Sunday she would be laughing at herself as she washed out the squares of towelling in salt water ready to boil and be used again.

From Dad's bedroom came a chesty spate of coughing.

'You awake?' she called, and heard his laboured reply. 'I'll be up in a minute, get breakfast.'

'All right if I lay 'ere a bit?' he called back.

'Lay there as long as you like,' she returned, extra brightly. But what if . . . What would Dad say? What would everyone say? Not something that could be hidden. God, what was she going to do if . . .

Now don't go jumping the gun, she told herself emphatically. You're just over reacting. It's nothing.

Springing out of bed, she dressed quickly, went into the kitchen and put on the kettle for her and Dad's morning cuppa.

Every day she waited. You can't be overdue two months running, she told herself. Any day now and you'll be laughing. The days strung themselves out towards Saturday. Sunday came and still nothing. Every time she thought about it – there were times when the day's toil did bless her with a degree of forgetfulness – her heart would thump with sickening thuds against her breastbone.

Monday morning, as she raced for the toilet on the landing beyond the kitchen, left her in no more doubt. Being sick into the pan, she heard Dad call. 'You orright, Letitia?'

'Yes, Dad.' She straightened up, wiping her mouth and moving back into the kitchen for a cup of water to rinse away the foul taste.

'You bein' sick or somethink?'

God, how sounds travelled in this blessed flat? 'I must have eaten something last night.'

Dad's cough rumbled towards her. 'Can't see 'ow. I 'ad the same as you an' I feel orright.'

'Things affect people different,' she said, heard acquiescence in the chesty clearing of his throat, and smiled slowly.

Odd how with the knowledge comes the will to face up to a thing and see it in perspective. She was marrying David in April. Why get all in a sweat about her condition? She'd be married before it ever showed, and to blazes with those who wanted to count on their fingers.

She would write to David and tell him. He'd be thrilled to bits. Might even arrange to get the wedding brought forward. She wrote the letter then went down to open up as the postman arrived with one from David.

CHAPTER 13

Letty put her own letter to one side, feverishly opened that from David, heart pounding excitedly. But as she read, all her joy faded, replaced by disbelief.

> Darling Letitia, my sweetheart, how can I tell you? Our division has been told just a moment ago that we are going overseas. We embark tomorrow morning. No idea where. Not much time to write with all that is going on here, except to say you cannot imagine how completely devastated I am . . .

How devastated *he* was! Letty felt she was about to collapse, the words seeming to swim off the page before eyes that refused to focus properly.

> I know you must feel the same, and I cannot be there to comfort you. But I pray to God to send me back to you as swiftly as possible. I pray you will be strong to face however long our parting will be with all the courage and fortitude I know you to possess, and I

pray fate will be kind to us and reunite us before we hardly know it. My love, I know I shall be in your arms again soon; that this war will not last much longer. Have to finish now. Being called away. Everything here is in turmoil. So for now, my love, please be strong. I love you. I love you.

The last words, written in haste, had become so virtually illegible that Letty could decipher them only with difficulty, except that she knew them instinctively, words of love, melting into the hasty kisses he had scrawled.

Vaguely she saw her own letter lying on a table where she had left it. The sight dragging her out of the state of shock that threatened to engulf her, one hand flew to her throat in panic. It had to reach him before he left!

Galvanised into sudden action she snatched it up, whirled round to yell up the stairs to her father still making his way through his breakfast: 'I've got to go out!' Her own voice sounded unfamiliar, high with urgency. 'To post a letter.'

'Post a letter? 'Oo's goin' ter look after the . . .'

Letty didn't wait for the end of his protest, was outside before he'd completed it, hurrying to the slim red postbox at the end of the street as fast as the narrow hemline of her skirt allowed.

If David didn't get this letter in time . . . Did they send letters on to troops going overseas? She didn't know. All she knew was that he must learn her news. Not that it helped her, left to face the pointing fingers of condemnation of others.

But she didn't think of that as she ran, breathless, to the pillar box, thrust the letter in and ran back; nor for some time afterwards, not until the shock had lessened some days later, though even then it seemed she was living in a dream, merely going through the motions of living from day to day, hardly aware of what she was doing while Dad looked on, frowning, that she might be going down with something.

By the following week he was looking at her critically, mystified by the listlessness that had now descended upon her. It was only a matter of time before he began to grow restive, began to take exception to his own peace of mind being affected by her attitude.

'What's up with you?' he demanded, eyeing her reproachfully as, with the shop closed for dinner, she dished up a lamb stew she had left simmering all morning. 'You ain't ailin' or somethink?'

'There's nothing wrong with me.' Swiftly she cut two thick slices of bread for him, cut a thin one for herself as he folded his together to dip into his stew.

'Don't tell me nothink's wrong with yer. Eatin' more like a sparrer lately. No wonder yer look all skinny. Look at yerself. Yer look like yer've found a penny an' lost a pound. Ain't yer not feelin' well or somethink?'

'There's nothing wrong with me, Dad,' she

repeated, sitting down at the table to nibble at her slice, toy with the tiny bowl of stew she had ladled out for herself. A week since David had gone. Where was he now? Was he lonely, unhappy? His health, was it good, bad? Was he . . .

'Yer could have fooled me!' Pushing aside his potatoes and dumplings Dad dunked his bread again, angrily. 'If yer not ill, then fer Gawd's sake cheer yerself up! Goin' around with that boat race of yours as long as a kite, sulking all over the place. I suppose that bloke of yours 'as bin sent abroad and won't be comin' 'ere any more. Well, it makes a change fer me, not 'aving you go out every weekend. Nice ter 'ave a bit of company now 'e's gorn. That's when yer face ain't as long as me arm. Gawd knows what I've done ter 'ave yer mopin' all around the place.'

Letty listened to him going on, closing her mind to it, tried not to react. That at least was easy enough. She no longer had the will nor the strength even to bother.

Dad having his usual afternoon nap, Letty took the opportunity to slip out for a walk to clear a muzzy head and a vague feeling of claustrophobia.

Drawing deep breaths of the fresh spring air, she moved through the leftover litter of Club Row, now quiet and deserted but for a few stragglers still clearing up after the hubbub of the morning's market. Reaching the end of the road she turned automatically into the Bethnal Green Road, continuing without much purpose in her direction.

Sunday afternoon. People sleeping off their Sunday dinners, the weather bright but a bit too chilly still for most to walk it off, made everything lovely and quiet. It smelt of Sunday too, cleaner, fresher than weekdays, a hint of roast Sunday dinner hanging in the air. Even the shabby Bethnal Green Road shops had a clean look today, being closed. Occasionally she glanced at them in passing; little food shops, their blinds down; larger shops that sold shoes, haberdashery, dresses, hats; shuttered greengrocers, fishmongers; the multiple windows of Wickhams with their fancy beige striped blinds.

Despite the chill, she walked slowly. May. Quite likely she'd have been married for two weeks now. David was somewhere in the Dardanelles where the Allies were fighting the Turks. She had received one letter from him, ages ago, dated several weeks before. He couldn't have received that first hastily posted letter of hers for he made no mention of his joy at her news. She'd written several times since, telling him of it, but hadn't had any letters from him for a few weeks now. Her time seemed to be spent these days waiting for the postman, hoping. Sometimes she couldn't bear the thoughts that raced through her head.

The papers reporting on the Turkish campaign had not given her much encouragement to feel easy. The Turks appeared to be a formidable and vicious foe by the accounts she'd read, avidly looking for hope as the allied advances were repelled. How was David? How would she know if he were wounded or worse? She wasn't his wife, wasn't entitled to be informed if anything had happened to him.

She ought to contact his parents. They'd have news, could relay it on to her – if they were sympathetic enough to her feelings to do so.

Lost in thought, she had walked the entire one mile length of the road, passing the empty stalls of Bethnal Green's market, the railway bridge with its painted advertisement for Frederick Causton & Sons Ltd, Joinery and Moulding Mills, throwing its shadow across her, before she realised how far she had come.

Pausing outside the Salmon and Ball pub on the corner of Cambridge Heath Road, she half turned to go back then changed her mind. She needed time to herself. The clock on the small cupolaed tower of St John's Church across Cambridge Heath Road showed ten to three. Ample time before going back to the aimlessness her life had become, to think, to wallow in a little self-pity without duty getting in the way.

The crossroads here were tremendously wide, gave space to breathe after the narrow streets around Club Row. Amazing how, amid the tatty confines of the East End, there could exist spacious gardens, pleasant buildings, a museum set amid trees, leafy walks. She felt suddenly if briefly free, and with new eagerness made her way across the wide road with its ornately railed off urinals in the middle and its double tramlines, silent on Sundays, through the wrought iron gates of the railinged enclosure to St John's Church.

It hadn't been all that long a walk, one she'd done many times in the past, happily, laughing with girlfriends as she went. Was it her condition or simply lassitude of mind, but she felt strangely exhausted as she sat down by the church steps, shivering as a cold light breeze found its way under her coat collar.

She glanced down at the shapeless garment. All her clothes these past few weeks were purposely loose, and shapeless, hiding the bulge, that was as yet mercifully small. Even so, she would eventually begin to show, and then what?

The sensible thing would have been to try to rid herself of it as soon as she'd discovered her plight, David no longer here to lend it respectability. She had thought of it but, fear of the deed apart, couldn't bring herself to destroy what was David's. Too late now.

Surreptitiously, as if even here in this quiet place the action might be seen, her hands traced the small bulge beneath her coat, noticeable to her exploring fingers. There was Dad to face yet. He'd be appalled, full of disgust, unable to believe what he saw, curse her for a whore. Sooner or later, though, it would have to be faced.

Wearily she got up as though prompted by the thought and began to retrace her steps homeward.

The sun had sunk appreciably lower, she'd been out much longer than she'd intended.

Bethnal Green Road seemed endless and she felt ready to drop as she turned into her own street. The traders had long since gone, leaving their debris to a street cleaner, stolidly wielding his broom in short sharp stabs at the gutter. He didn't look up as she passed, dispirited, negotiating the battered metal bins outside each shop door, their lids tilted, filled to the brim with rubbish.

Three doors from home a disturbance in one distracted her; a brief rustling, but enough to prick the curiosity.

It stopped as she glanced down, but almost immediately began again. Cautiously, Letty lifted the lid, holding her breath against any smell that might waft up to meet her. There, peeping out from under some crumpled newspaper, green feathers wet and ragged, a gaping brown beak, two dull little eyes, lids half closed.

Sickly birds and poorly kittens were often cast into the rubbish bins after the market closed. It was sad. It was cruel. But what good was protest? People had enough problems of their own to rush about raising Cain over a few dead birds. But somehow the sight of this tiny greenfinch struggling for life touched Letty's heart as it had not been touched in a long time.

Instantly alert, she pushed aside the newspapers and bits of soiled straw, lifting out the tiny bird. It lay cupped in the palm of her hand, warm, trembling, breast fluttering rapidly. Letty stared down at it. In her hands she held life. In her womb life also stirred. Covering this poor little body with her other hand, she hurried indoors hearing Dad's voice greeting her, asking where the hell she'd been and telling her he'd been worried sick, her not telling him where she'd gone, him left all on his own wondering what had happened to her . . .

He came and looked at the greenfinch as she laid it on a saucer in a hanky for warmth on the kitchen table.

'What yer bought that in 'ere fer? Stupid cow – the thing's on its last legs, yer can see that. Sling it out. Probably full of fleas.'

She didn't reply, went and got it a drip of water in a dish and a bit of bread. Watched for it to take interest, dip its fragile beak in the water, peck at the crumbs. It did neither, merely lay there, its head floppy, limp breast feathers fluttering erratically up and down.

'Go on, you silly thing,' she urged, feeling strangely desperate for it. 'Eat something. It'll make you better. It'll make you live.'

'Stupid cow,' Dad said again, and left her to it.

For half an hour she sat, still in her coat, eyes never leaving the scrap of life huddled in its handkerchief, its head all to one side, its beak half in and half out of the water to which she'd physically urged it. She watched the eyes close, the beak begin to open, but it still breathed and she dared to hope.

Her neck ached with watching. Her heart leapt as it made a struggle. It was reviving. She watched eagerly as it stretched its neck with an odd wriggling movement, then suddenly it was limp and still.

She'd seen only one other death. Mum's. This was like seeing it all over again. For an hour she sat by the stiffening little corpse, with tears running freely down her cheeks, a throat that hurt from the constriction of misery. It was only a bird, one of thousands that die in cages each week from ignorance and neglect when they should be flying freely, taking their chances against nature's dictates instead of man's. But she was crying for more than just a bird.

Silly, yet she couldn't stop; not as she wrapped it carefully in tissue paper used for wrapping her customer's purchases, not as she put it in among the rubbish in their own bin with all the semblance of a burial. And when she went to bed, she wept for the life in her womb lest that die too, knew she could never have rid herself of David's child; wept for David that he would come safely home. And she had wanted so very much to save the finch's life.

'I don't know what to do,' she said to her old friend, Ethel Bock.

Ethel had married two years earlier, going from brash girl to meek housewife hanging on every last word of her handsome husband who clearly fancied himself more than a bit as some sort of devil-may-care, swanking about the neighbourhood in grey suit and bowler hat. He'd enlisted, full of euphoria, and gone off to war already counting himself a hero, leaving Ethel pregnant and broke on a tiny army allowance.

She had, however, lost the baby. Having to get over it on her own had hardened her again. With her husband no longer around to tell her what she could or could not do, she had got herself a job as a tram conductress earning a good wage.

She and Letty had taken to going up West once a week, bolstering their spirits with tea and toasted teacakes in a Lyon's tea shop in Leicester Square. Airing their problems, they didn't always listen to each other but that didn't matter – talking about them was enough.

'Yer should have got rid of it, yer know,' Ethel said, and stopped abruptly as the waitress in black with white collar, cap and apron came with their order.

They watched mesmerised as she laid out the silvery metal pot of tea and one with hot water, a milk jug and sugar bowl, pretty flowered bone china crockery, a plate with four piping hot teacakes, a small pot of butter, another of jam, a knife each for spreading.

It was a bit pricey as always, but well worth it; the décor pleasant, the atmosphere opulent, the subdued murmur of conversation and the soothing clink of tea cups upon saucers never failing to envelope Letty's jaded nerves as warmly as a motherly embrace.

The tea shop was full of customers. Ladies sat in pairs, in groups, or with husbands or fiancés in uniform. London was a different city to a year ago: full of uniforms, of men in bandages or on crutches, of nurses in white, of women in men's jobs – hair bobbed, wearing wide skirts several inches off the ground, and loose jackets. Gone the inconvenience of the tightly swathed dress, the hobble skirt. For Letty in her present condition it was very fortunate, she said drily after the waitress had gone.

'Yer wouldn't have to be in this state if you'd done something about it earlier,' Ethel said, pouring tea.

'I couldn't,' Letty said as Ethel reached for a teacake.

'More fool you.' She vigorously buttered the hot cake, spread jam over that. 'What yer goin' ter do now?'

'Have it, I suppose,' Letty replied lamely.

'What's yer dad said about it?'

'I don't know.'

'Ain't yer told 'im yet?'

'No.'

'Best ought to.' She stirred her tea noisily. 'Break it to 'im as carefully as yer can and as soon as yer can. If yer don't, there'll be 'ell ter pay when he finds it out fer 'imself, 'cos he'll only think yer've bin under'anded with 'im. And that always puts fathers' backs up. I know one thing, I wouldn't fancy bein' in your shoes when yer do tell 'im.'

Sipping her tea, Letty didn't fancy being in them either, tried not to think of it.

'I've not had any letters from David,' she said, hastily changing the subject, though really it was one and the same thing.

Ethel looked up from her teacake. 'What, none at all?'

'Well, only the one I had from him in the beginning. He hadn't got mine then – the one I sent 'im telling 'im about meself.' Easy with Ethel to fall into the accents of her childhood. 'P'raps he got it later and got frightened, me telling him I was pregnant? Sometimes I think that's why he never wrote to me after that. Other times I get scared he might have come to some harm and I don't know about it.'

'Why don't yer contact 'is parents? They'd tell yer.' Ethel took a bite out of her teacake and a large gulp of tea to moisten it while Letty nibbled listlessly at hers.

'I'm not sure about them. They're proper toffee-nosed. Don't want to know me at all. I wouldn't lower meself askin' them.'

''Ow else yer goin' ter find out?' Ethel said simply and studied Letty with a critical eye. 'You've got a kid on the way – 'is kid. 'E's got ter know. At least got ter acknowledge it's 'is.'

'How can I make him if he don't answer my letters?'

Ethel thought a bit, rubbing her snub nose. 'I don't think 'e'd leave yer in the lurch, Let. Never struck me as that sort. You said 'e was out in the Dardanelles? According ter the papers, our blokes are gettin' a bashing out there. P'raps you ought to find out from the War Department if he's bin killed . . .'

'Oh, Eth, don't!'

Ethel looked a little crestfallen, then perked up again, took full command of the situation, forgetting her second teacake, her tongue going nineteen to the dozen.

'Yer've got ter face it, Let. 'E could have bin. I'm 'avin' ter face it, ain't I, with my George? Lots of us women are 'avin' ter face it. It ain't the war we thought it was goin' ter be. Them poor sods in the trenches are bein' killed right, left an' centre, an' it's just as bad with them fightin' them bloody Turks. An' honestly, Let, I'm as worried fer my George as you are fer your David. 'E could have been killed. Mind, I'm still gettin' George's letters.'

Ethel's face took on an earnest look. 'Or 'e could have bin taken prisoner – 'ave yer thought about that?'

She had thought about it, but hardly dared to linger on even that likelihood, fearing the contemplation of anything dire might become parent to the event.

But if David were a prisoner of war, it would at least be better than the ultimate dread that so often swept through her.

Taking Ethel Bock's advice, she wrote to David's parents – lacking the courage to telephone – and waited. Meanwhile her waistline was thickening steadily. She grew more pale and tired from worry, knowing she would not be able to ward off the fateful day of confession for much longer. And still there were no letters from David.

Vinny's eyes held a speculative look as she gazed out of the window upon a dull June Saturday afternoon, boredom – her fractious sons having been taken off her hands for an afternoon stroll by their nanny – brushed aside for a moment.

'Our Letty's pregnant,' she announced after a while.

Without looking round, she knew Albert had glanced up from reading his paper, his surprise conveying itself in the rustle of the newspaper, the sharp click of his pipe stem against his teeth as he removed it.

'She's what?' Then, more moderately, scathingly: 'How do you know?'

'I know.' Her tone was one of impatience. 'I've carried four times and lost one. I know when someone is in *that* sort of condition. And she is.'

Albert's newspaper rustled again as he laid it down, becoming interested. 'I've not seen anything different about her.'

Now she turned to him. 'You wouldn't would you? Men don't notice these things, but I have. She's putting weight on her stomach even though she tries to conceal it with those ridiculous dresses of hers. She looks like a sack. Pretends she's following the new fashion. Tsch! It's obvious what she's up to. She knows she'll be in disgrace when we find out and she thinks dressing like that we won't notice.'

'Could be she's just losing her trimness as she gets older?'

'I've not lost mine, nor has Lucy. Nor will she, except on certain occasions – like now. No, she's pregnant. How she can walk about with her head like it's on a stick like a blessed duchess, her knowing what she's carrying under those clothes of hers!'

Incensed with righteous indignation, Vinny got up from the window and wandered over to the occasional table in the centre of the parlour to pick out a cigarette from the fancy box on it.

She'd taken to the fashion for cigarettes. Girls everywhere were smoking them, not just society women but girls in munitions factories, on the land, conductresses on trams and buses, those who drove vans and did men's jobs while they were away fighting – nearly all smoked.

Vinny fitted it into a slim ivory holder, lit it from an ornate table lighter, blew smoke into the air in a thin stream to watch it wreath and curl.

'She didn't look the least bit ashamed when we saw her last week. It can't be anyone's but that David's, so she must be at least six months. He's been gone that long. And all that time she's been hiding it from us – no shame whatsoever! If it was me, I'd be mortified. I mean, what are Dad's neighbours going to say, her not married? Poor Dad, he'll never be able to hold his head up again. I'm sure he hasn't wheezed it yet. But when he does . . .'

She left the rest to Albert's imagination as she drew deeply and significantly on her cigarette.

Letty tore open the envelope the moment it arrived. She had waited in an agony of indecision for David's parents' reply for three weeks.

Frantically her eyes scanned Mrs Baron's small neat handwriting, the words so terse and cruel that she was incapable of reading behind them the woman's pain and misery as, for her, the room spun, what she read stabbing like a knife to her heart.

It was all she could do to understand what Dad was saying as she lay full length on her bed after the doctor had gone; Dad raging at the top of his voice enough for all the street to hear.

'. . . when yer feelin' better, yer can sod off! I don't want ever to bloody see yer again. Bringin' yer dirty trouble 'ome ter lay on my doorstep. I brought you up proper. Brought all me daughters up proper. An' this is what I get fer it?'

She listened, half listened, wondering vaguely what she would do, where she would go, even while never truly believing Dad would really throw her out.

Her head felt muzzy from the faint. She felt sick

and hot. All she could see was Mrs Baron's letter, the words floating in front of her, informing her that she had heard nothing of her son; that all her enquiries had unearthed was that he had been reported missing more or less from the first day of the Gallipoli landing; that it must be assumed he had been killed, for they would have heard by now were he a prisoner of war.

How tersely it had been put, with no emotion at all. How could she have written so calmly and so hard-heartedly? Even though she did not approve of Letty, how could she be so cruel as to have kept it from her all this time? Even her final words held no sympathy, trusting she would not be plagued by any more correspondence from Letty which would only grieve her more.

Grieve her? That woman wasn't capable of grief, or so Letty thought, submerged by the waves of her own grief.

Everything felt as though it wasn't really happening. Deep in her mind's memory she and David still ran hand in hand through the dappled light of Epping Forest, slowing, kissing, sitting side by side in a sea of fern fronds. Had all that actually happened once? Could a man who had been so alive now be dead, lying shot through the head or the chest on some parched sun-baked field of a strange land, or blown to bits on some dun-coloured beach? No, it couldn't happen, not to one so vibrant in life as he had been – not to the man she loved.

Inside her someone was crying, casting wildly about in distress, but her eyes stayed dry. There was Dad's dinner to prepare, the shop to be tended. Someone would have to do it. Dad wouldn't. She turned her head away and let his self-righteous rantings pass over her.

CHAPTER 14

From rage Dad turned sullen, his silence in a way more dreadful than his threats; didn't even grunt his thanks when, forcing herself, Letty got up, set about getting him his midday meal before going back down into the shop.

Bleak as granite, her heart ached physically, each beat a sickening thud against her ribs, her throat constricted from holding back tears.

Work – the cure for despair – was wrong of course in her condition and the shock she'd suffered, but with fierce energy, as though her life depended on it, she polished, swept, lifted things from here to there and back again, far heavier than she should have, manoeuvred unwieldy furniture, quite needlessly. At least it helped to distract the seething wretchedness inside her.

The afternoon passed, how she had no idea. There was still the night, and that she faced with the aid of several spoonfuls of Dad's cough mixture containing a decent amount of laudanum, the label stating not more than one spoonful every three hours.

This way she managed to get through two days.

But she should have known. A startling flow of blood on Friday morning brought Doctor Levy hurrying back to confine her to bed.

She watched him with huge eyes that implored him to confirm that everything was all right as he turned to Dad.

'She must stay in bed and not try for any reason to get up. A week at least.'

Twisting her gaze to Dad, Letty saw him frown. 'But what about the shop? The . . .'

For answer, Doctor Levy took Dad by the arm, practically propelled him towards the window, and away from her bed. The sibilant sound of his urgent whispering reached her but no clear words, though she saw Dad look at him, startled, then hang his head, nodding dumbly.

Doctor Levy came back to stand over Letty, his dark eyes intense, the smile on his lips professional. 'You, young lady, listen to me very carefully. I want you to relax, your body and your mind. Think of nothing if that is possible. Just the baby, that it must come into this world well and whole. Do not worry about the shop, about the cooking, about the housework, about your father. If you have any sharp pains, you will call me immediately. Otherwise I will see you in one week's time.'

He left then, taking up his black bag. Dad followed him downstairs to pay him his fee and let him out.

Whatever he'd said to Dad, it put a stop to the unbearable silence, at least for the time being.

250

Instead terror overlaid his anger, smoothed it, like oil upon water.

'Yer've got ter get well, Letitia. Yer all I've got. What would I do if somethink 'appened ter you?'

What had Doctor Levy said to him to put such fright into him? Not the loss of the baby, perhaps the loss of her? Anyway, she didn't much care.

'And the baby?' she asked wearily, mercilessly, from a sort of perverse compulsion to rekindle his anger, punish him, hurt him, though all she did was hurt herself.

Dad didn't reply, just mumbled something about staying in bed and went off down to supervise the shop himself – the first time in ages.

He continued in the shop even after all danger had passed, took the reins out of her hands, leaving her with no say at all in its running.

'*My* shop,' he corrected tersely when once she quite innocently and from habit referred to it as theirs. And venturing an equally innocent suggestion on its running, she received an acrimonious reply: 'Look, I don't need your interference if yer don't mind!'

It was how he spoke to her now. From being a man of gentle if complaining and at times sulky nature, he'd become sharp-tongued, bitter, most of all unforgiving, the cry for her safety he had offered up counting for nothing now, seldom addressing her without making his feelings for her very clear, casting her down – where she quite obviously belonged.

★　　★　　★

'She can't keep it. Can you imagine the neighbours?'

Lucy and Vinny were having a meeting over cups of tea at Lucy's house, while the children played in the garden – Lucy's two girls sitting on the grass playing nurses, Vinny's three boys played war, battles not always play, necessitating the meeting being interrupted four times on this one afternoon for Vinny to sort out her sons.

'I don't know how your Albert can stand the noise they make,' Lucy said, screwing up her face against the yells and subsequent fits of tears from an unluckily landed punch. 'Him so fastidious and . . .' She was going to say 'starchy', but thought better of it.

'He's hardly ever home to worry about it,' Vinny came back at her, her smile brittle, well aware what description her sister had in mind.

Lucy had always been jealous of her Albert, Jack being such a long streak of nothing for all he had money, and that only thanks to his parents' business after all. She was sorry for Lucy, of course, her Jack having been conscripted into the army two months ago. But it had taken Lucy down a peg or two, even if she was a little bitter now over Albert's continuing success, his ability to keep out of the war so far.

'So much work at the office these days, sometimes doesn't get home until the boys are in bed. Making money hand over fist.'

Lucy looked down at her hands, steeling herself

against another outburst of yelping as her own two angels, oblivious to the boys, went on bandaging their dolls in serene preoccupation.

'Is there all that much work in accountancy? What with the war and everything, I mean? Are there that many men left to want accounting done?'

She missed Jack terribly. Vinny could never begin to understand what it was like not having a man come home each evening, no matter how late. It had devastated her and she'd gone to Dad with her woes weeping bitter tears, but there had been nothing he could do. Jack's father's printing firm was hardly essential to the war, could afford to lose one of its members to its country. Lucy harboured a secret hope that before long Albert's job too would be found equally as unessential – there was some comfort from knowing he could soon be in the same boat for all his high and mighty success. Not that Jack was fighting for his country exactly, but printing booklets and pamphlets in Aldershot. Lucy prayed the job would last the duration.

She brought her thoughts back to the business in hand, was about to air her opinion of Letty's embarrassing indiscretion when there came yet another small interruption.

'Can I have some water, Mummy?' George, Vinny's middle son, a chubby little boy whose fifth birthday had been two months ago, stood in the parlour doorway, a bucket of dirt he'd dug up from the bottom of the garden dangling from one soiled little hand.

'What for?' Vinny anxious to get on with the meeting, twisted her head impatiently and noticed with a twinge of dismay the brimming bucket.

'I wanna make a pie.'

Vinny noticed the distaste on her sister's face.

'No, love. It'll make a mess all over your auntie's path.'

'I won't put it on the path.'

'I don't think so, Georgie. Just go and play with the others.'

'But Mummy!'

'No, Georgie! You're not at home. Now go and play.'

'But . . .'

'GO AND PLAY! No water!'

She ignored the crestfallen boy trudging out, the brimful bucket in danger of tipping dirt on the floor before he ever got to the garden door, and turned back to Lucy.

'What do you suggest then?' she asked as George, now on the garden path, stood looking back at the house, a determined set to his rounded jaws.

'What I suggest,' Lucy said, eyeing the child in case he came back for another go at his mother, 'is one of us takes it.'

For a second, Vinny's eyes brightened avidly. If it was a girl . . . She still grieved for the one she'd lost, wanted to try again, but Albert, with the fear of being called to war hanging over every man, had said they should be careful, at least for a year. He had hardly touched her in bed since then and Vinny was feeling spurned. Albert, however, usually so pliant at home if not at work, was having his say on this occasion, and she knew he was right.

If on the other hand Letty were to give birth to a boy, it would mean another one to look after. Yet, even if it was a boy, a new baby would fill a gnawing emptiness. Vinny realised she was one of those women who constantly needed babies around them, knew she wanted Letty's baby with all her heart.

'I'll take it!' she burst out impulsively. Albert couldn't object to that. Not like making a baby, bringing it into the present world of strife and danger. This one would be adopted and it wasn't as if it came from a stranger. Her sister's – almost like her own flesh and blood really.

Lucy gave her a straight look. 'Don't you think you've got enough with that lot?'

'One more won't make any difference to me. I'm used to all that shemozzle.'

'I was going to say, I would take it. After all, my two are never any bother . . .'

Vinny almost laughed. Lucy could make bother out of anything, certainly out of her two, without either of them lifting a finger to cause one. With Lucy everything was heavy going; her headaches, her so-called palpitations of which she'd complained this last year if the smallest thing went wrong, her overwhelming fear since Jack had been taken into the army.

'. . . and I haven't any boys,' continued Lucy, unaware of the way Vinny's lips twitched even though she tried to compress a smile. 'You know I've always wanted a boy. It has always been an upset to me that I couldn't really have any more children. I just suppose I'm not made for breeding, like you are.'

Vinny let the remark go by, stored it up for some future occasion, though one small dig as immediate deposit was to hand.

'And what makes you think *you* could manage? You found things hard going enough when Jack was here. How could you manage with a baby now he's not? You know you're not equipped to deal with extra worry. But I've always been able to cope with anything that comes along. I really do think I should take it.'

'I . . .' Lucy began, then her blue-grey eyes widened in horror as she glanced out of the window to the garden beyond. 'My God!'

Vinny too gave a gasp, following her glance with equal horror but hers laced with mortification.

At the end of the garden, George had solved the problem of lack of water to make his mud pie. He was piddling into his bucket of earth with all his might.

'GEORGE!' Vinny was up on her feet and making for the door, halfway up the garden before Lucy could rise.

'You little sod! I can't take you anywhere!'

The bucket clogged with nicely dampened mud,

went flying, landing with a dull thud on the pathway. Georgie caught a whack around the ear from his mother's hand, followed by two on the legs, and was dragged in and flung towards Lucy's elegant bathroom for a good scrubbing.

She hurried out to her girls who had witnessed that small winkle gushing out its contents – a sight not for little girls – and shooed them indoors, followed at a discreet distance by the two other boys. She prayed Vinny would soon depart, leaving her to restore her home to normal.

No more was said that day on the fate of Letty's baby, and she remained ignorant of any meeting, her time coming ever nearer.

She seldom went out now, had terminated her weekly visits up West with Elsie Bock, had certainly long ago ceased being down in the shop, Dad recruiting a willing Ada Hall to help him.

The shop had always been Letty's salvation and she missed not being there. Little was left for her now but to waddle about the flat, cumbersome and ungainly, her once slim figure no more. Nor would ever be again, she often thought. Not for her the loving compliments of an adoring husband and father to be, she looked as much a mess as she felt. What point caring for one's hair, brushing it for hours until it shone as glossy as a horse chestnut? She'd had it cut short last month, not because of the current fashion but for easier management. Its natural curl surprised her, ceasing to be pulled almost straight by its own weight.

Had she taken care of it, it would have flattered her oval face, now pale from staying indoors, but all it did was stand out from her face like the mane on the unkempt pony that drew the milk cart through the streets every morning, a jaded-looking creature in much need of care and attention, like herself.

If Ada Hall wasn't in the shop, she was upstairs, cleaning and tidying as if it was her own home.

'Don't want ter get yerself tired, love,' she'd say. 'Got ter think about that little 'un inside yer. Though Gawd knows what yer'll do with it once it's out. You unmarried an' all. Really upset yer dad, it 'as, the neighbours seein' yer in that condition. I do think 'e's taken it really well. Some would of turned yer out, yer know that.'

Vinny turned up on Sunday afternoon, her and Albert in their car, offering to take Dad off Letty's hands for a few hours.

Letty, with about a week to go before the baby was due, was only too glad to see the back of him for a while; a blessed relief from the strain of the atmosphere now existing between them.

Left to herself, she went down to the closed shop, took time to wander around it, savour its familiar mustiness, think of when not so long ago she'd had sole charge of its running, stocking it as she thought fit, selling at prices she had fixed.

It was Dad now who managed it once more, and with her not there to keep an eye on what he did, it had reverted to its old clutter, his customers

258

offered the junk while the choicer pieces were hidden out of sight for his own personal enjoyment. A business that no longer ran efficiently but limped along as it used to do.

She longed to be back at the helm, spent some time flicking dust from this piece and that, then weariness overcame her. Struggling back upstairs, a low throbbing in her back, the weight of a distended stomach no doubt dragging on it, she lay down exhausted on her bed to recover and wait for Dad's return.

'Dad, you'll have to decide.'

Between Vinny and Lucy there was stalemate on the question of who would take the baby, and Vinny was furious. There was no talking to Lucy who'd thrown a fit and, between floods of tears, told her she was the worst sister anyone in the world could wish for. 'How can someone with that sort of temperament have it?' Vinny asked Albert. 'She'd blurt out its background the very first time the poor thing played her up.'

She, Vinny, was definitely more suited. 'But I can hardly nominate myself over her,' she'd gone on to Albert. 'I don't want to cause any trouble between us. We should ask Dad for his opinion on it. She'd have to go along with what he suggested.'

For herself, Vinny was willing to abide by what Dad suggested, confident that he would choose her.

The only way to talk to him without Letty over-hearing was to get him out of the flat. He had protested at going out with them at first, his atti-tude towards motorised vehicles still as hidebound as ever, though not quite so rigorous as once it was now the motorcar seemed here to stay.

Somewhere beyond Ilford, where the country-side opened out, Albert stopped and took them all into a tea shop, and there Vinny explained the situation and asked Dad to act as arbitrator, peremptorily demanding, 'You'll have to decide, Dad.'

The following Saturday for Letty began with a small niggling pain low in her stomach that disap-peared within seconds, then came back stronger to disappear yet again.

After a third even sharper stab she knew a corres-ponding stab of fear and a sort of slow collapsing, a yielding to the inevitable.

No going back now – a thought foolish and trite, but one which dominated all others. She could not help but think of the stigma she had thrust upon her unborn child, her involvement in its future, sins of the mother . . . never realised until now. Around midday, pain exploded, making her cry out and half double up and forget all about irresponsibility.

From then on minutes felt like hours, hours condensed into minutes; time distorted. Ada Hall telling her to hold on, frantically phoning the midwife and doctor; Dad white as a sheet, praying, 'Look after 'er please, God! Don't take 'er from me! Yer took 'er mum – don't take 'er!' Loud enough for her to hear, as if she needed that just now.

The pains growing stronger made her arch her back, cry out, sweat beading on her brow. Dad, in a panic, had rushed out, down to the Knave of Clubs to wash away fear with several pints of black and tan.

Alone with Ada Hall, a midwife and Doctor Levy, who, aware of her situation, had sympathy enough to kindly be present, Letty wanted only to die – such a simple solution. She was so very tired of fighting alone, months of apprehension and misgivings, now this.

Those she really needed were not here. Mum, who would have held her and comforted her. David who should have been pacing the floor in the next room, given between concern for her and joy of new fatherhood; would have rushed to her side as the baby lay in her arms. All she had was Ada Hall, pinned up hair beginning to fall down, flowered apron all askew, clumsy hands trying to bestow some semblance of comfort.

The child arrived at ten to seven next morning. A boy of eight pounds who bellowed lustily.

Vinny and Lucy arrived at ten to nine, in response to a telephone call from Dad. They flooded into the small bedroom, filling it with their fidgety concern; Dad awkward and withdrawn standing by the brown-curtained window, Vinny leaning over the baby, cooing at it, lifting it from its crib, cradling it in her arms as though it were hers.

Lucy sat beside Letty on the bed, held her hand earnestly.

'Letty love, me and Vinny's been talking. We think it might be best if you do it as soon as possible. It'll make it easier.'

'Easier?' she repeated listlessly, hardly recovered enough to use her brain. What was Lucy talking about?

'The baby – you do realise it'll be awkward? We should have told you what we've been discussing, but really we didn't want to upset you, being so near your time. You hadn't planned to keep him, had you? I mean, Dad agreed that . . . Well, he agreed.'

'To what?' It was a job to concentrate. What had Dad agreed that he hadn't told her about?

'He agreed,' Lucy continued gently, 'that you'd never be able to cope here, with a baby, the shop to look after and everything else in the flat. Not properly. As things are. Well, you know . . .'

'Mum did.' Mum had brought up all of them in this small flat.

'But we weren't illegit –'

'Lucy!' Vinny's voice was sharp. The younger sister threw her an abashed glance, then turned back to make an effort to rectify the blunder.

'You see, it's the neighbours. Seeing you pushing

a pram and you . . . well, you know. You don't want everyone pointing a finger at you. But this way . . . what we've discussed, me and Vinny and Dad, people do soon forget. Afterwards you can go on just as you did before.'

'As I did before?' Comprehension of what Lucy was trying to say began slowly to take shape. She regarded Lucy with startled eyes.

'Well, it wouldn't be fair on you or the poor little thing,' Lucy blundered on. 'Giving it for adoption by some stranger. That's what me and Vinny were discussing. One of us would take it . . .'

'No!'

Worn out by the birth as she was, Letty managed to push herself up to a half sitting position, a mixture of fear and anger starting from the pit of her stomach to explode from her lips in that one violent word – an impassioned birth of its own.

She saw Lucy start back, was vaguely aware of Dad by the window, his faded blue eyes wide, his mouth beneath the bristly moustache open like an O, chin dropping. Vinny had hurriedly returned the baby to the modest little crib, she came forward.

'No!' Letty's second shriek took the strength out of her and she dropped back on the pillow with a moan.

'Leave him alone. He's mine!'

'But Letty.' Vinny's tone was patient. She came forward, easing her confused sister out of the way. 'Try to look at this sensibly. How on earth can you . . .'

'No!' Letty screamed again, too worn by her first outburst to rise again from her pillow, but her green eyes blazed in fear. 'He's mine. I won't let you have him. He belongs to me.'

Vinny looked momentarily helpless. Lucy intervened.

'Don't be silly, Let. How can you? You've already brought shame on all of us. You're being selfish and silly . . .'

Her last word ended in a squeal of surprise as Letty's arm came up, caught her with the flat of one hand across the cheek. Dad gasped and started forward.

'Look 'ere – I ain't 'avin' that!'

The look in Letty's eyes stopped him and he seemed to diminish in size before her gaze, a dejected confused figure, his eyes wandering to take in the corners of the room, looking anywhere but directly at her, though his lips tightened perversely.

Lucy's hand had flown to her cheek, already staining red, the white fingermarks standing out against the colour. Letty's hand had dropped back on to the bedcovers, weak from the exertion. In his crib, the baby had begun to cry, a thin little whimper that grew by the minute. To cover her pique, Lucy went and took the child up, rocking it as the cries died away.

Letty had turned her head away from the scene, staring despairingly at the wall.

'Go away,' she whispered. 'I'm keeping him – he

264

belongs to me and David. No one's going to take my David's baby from him.' Lying limp, she could say no more.

Lucy's voice came to her, resentful from the injustice of the slap. 'We'll see about that!'

Vinny's tone was gentle, persuasive. 'You're weak from what you've been through, so we'll leave you now. But think about it, Letty. Do you really want your baby to grow up being pointed out as . . . as a . . . I've got to say it, Letty. As a bastard? That's what he'll be called. Kids can be mean. Can be cruel. When they learn he hasn't got a father, that's what they'll call him. Is that what you want? If it is, then you're thinking only of yourself and not him.'

She had come very close, her voice soothing and so low that only Letty could hear the words.

'If I look after him for you, your own sister, it won't be like a stranger is taking him away from you, that you wouldn't see him again, would it? I could bring him up with the boys. He wouldn't be so much a cousin as a brother. They'd think of him as a brother. They're all too young to think anything else as time goes on. We could call him John or Christopher or . . .'

'He's got a name,' Letty murmured, distraught, audible enough for the others to hear. 'He's got a name. David.'

'Oh, I don't think . . .' Lucy's protest was quelled by a look from Vinny over her shoulder.

She turned back to the mother, her voice hardly

altering from its soothing quality. 'It's the best thing all round, Letty. Best for . . . David,' she added circumspectly. 'It's not as if you'd never be seeing him again, as happens to some unmarr – some people. I wouldn't stop you seeing him. You could see him as often as you like. But, you see, if I adopt him, he'd have a proper surname: Worth. No one'll ever need know he was born out of wedlock. He need never know.'

It was obvious Lucy had been listening. 'Worth?' she queried now. Putting the baby back into its crib, she came forward to do battle. 'Who said? I can bring him up as good as you. What's wrong with our name, Morecross?'

Vinny forgot momentarily to be circumspect and soothing, she swung round on her sister. 'And how d'you think you're going to cope, your Jack away in the army? You can't cope now with those you've got.'

'That's a lie!' Tears began to appear in Lucy's eyes. 'You just want him because you lost . . .'

'You shut up,' Vinny bellowed back. 'You should know what it's like, losing a child. You lost one!'

The screaming above her brought Letty out of her despair, replacing it with rage.

'Stop it, the pair of you! Stop it! Stop it!' She was very near to hysteria. Her voice poured out of its own accord, assaulting her own ears. 'Stop it! I can't take any more! He's mine!'

How many times had she said that now? She couldn't think beyond those two words. A claim, a plea. David was hers, would always be hers. His name was David. He'd have no other name but that.

'He's mine,' she said yet again, defiance melting into defeat from sheer exhaustion.

Vinny leaned over her, menacing, for all her tone had resumed its gentle, soothing note.

'And what will you give as a second name, Letty? What will show on his birth certificate? Your name? It can't be his father's. If he's adopted by . . . if he's adopted,' she corrected quickly as Lucy drew in a sharp breath, 'he has a name for life. It'll be his and he can hold up his head with the best. He'd never need to know you were his mother.'

'No,' Letty sobbed weakly.

'If you keep him, what're you going to say to him when he begins to ask questions? How are you going to face him when he looks at you accusingly?'

Vinny's voice went on and on, setting her head reeling. Someone had begun to sob – her – and she couldn't stop. Her whole body had begun to shake uncontrollably, great racking sobs coming from her.

She was in Vinny's arms, being held close to her as though Vinny was her mother. She didn't want to be held that way; wanted to sob until all the grief had died out of her, leaving just numbness – more than that – life extinguished with no anguish to tear at her; no more pain at losing her child, as something now told her she must lose him.

She lay limp in the arms of the sister about to rob her, loathing her even as she lay there, unresisting, because there was no alternative, no strength left to resist that Judas embrace.

'It'll be all right, you'll see,' Vinny said comfortingly, and laid her face upon Letty's head, one hand gently smoothing the short damp auburn hair.

I hate you! The words torn from her, yet she hadn't uttered them; only thought she had. I hate all of you. You, Lucy, Dad. Him most of all. I'd have been married but for him and David would be here because he wouldn't have been enlisted. (It didn't matter that he might just as easily have been killed in France or, as she still hoped, been taken prisoner.) David's parents too she hated with all her heart. Between them, they had all taken him away. Now Vinny wanted to take his baby. But Letty wouldn't let her. Yet how could she stop it? If she loved little David, she had to give in to their superior argument. One thing was certain David's parents must never know or they too would lay claim to him and that would be the worst thing of all. She'd never see him again. Whereas if Vinny took him . . .

'He's mine,' she whispered as if it was the last breath her body would ever gasp. She looked up into Vinny's face. 'He's mine,' she implored one last time. 'Look after him for me.'

'Yes, love. Of course I will,' Vinny said softly as she continued smoothing the short auburn hair.

CHAPTER 15

October in rural Chingford or in Walthamstow was golden, the leaves in mellow sunshine quietly turning from green to bronze and copper.

October in Bethnal Green was burnt sienna, the same sun reddening brick walls, adding a pearly blush to grey pavements and a jaundiced tinge to smoke-begrimed lace curtains.

October in Flanders held no colour at all, unless it was that of mud churned by shells and men's boots after an appalling summer, the sun leaden behind the fumes of cordite, smoke of gunfire and the thick, crawling, silent yellow-green cloud of chlorine gas.

At the warning whistles, the corporal dragged out his mask, stepped back, tripped over the body behind him and went sprawling, the mask dangling uselessly from its respirator.

Stumbling over him, a comrade grabbed the mask, managed to help him on with it, but the man's lungs were already burning, damaged. Corporal William Beans, having got himself a blighty one, was sent back to England to recover as best he could.

★ ★ ★

In October Arthur Bancroft had his fifty-ninth birthday; he'd had no intention of making much of it, but Lucy insisted.

'Cheer you up, Dad,' she said to him on the telephone. 'We all need cheering up – the way the war's dragging on. Three years! Me and Vinny thought we'd come over and make a day of it with you. Bring the children. You'd like that, wouldn't you, Dad? Seeing the children?'

'Lavinia, she won't . . . will she be bringin' . . . the other one?' he asked circuitously, his moustached lips close to the mouthpiece in case Letty overheard.

His other grandchildren he took on his knee and gently teased. 'K-A-T, cat.' He'd chuckle at the slighting way they looked at hm. 'No, Grandad, C-A-T!' He would regard them solemnly, say, 'No K-A-T, cat.' Until they either got off his knee in a huff or he would give in and have them hug him, relieved that he was wrong and they were right. His way of loving them was to tease.

But that one . . . From the very first, squalling and red-faced in its crib, he'd felt nothing for the baby Letty had given birth to; could not abide the boy if truth was known. Two years old now, the narrow delicate features framed by dark wavy hair, the dark eyes wary and uncertain. Not a bit like his mother, he was the image of his father, the man who'd had his fun with her and gone off to war and never come back – damn whether it was the war's fault or not!

270

'You mean Christopher?' Lucy's voice held total innocence, her father's fumbling for words utterly lost on her. 'She wouldn't leave him at home all on his own, now would she?'

'There's that woman who looks after 'er boys sometimes.' Silence at the other end denoted a shrug from Lucy. Arthur Bancroft went on purposefully, 'It ain't fair on Letitia, yer know. The circumstances regarding 'im bein' what they are.'

'It's about time she got over that.' Lucy's voice had gone huffy.

'Ain't fair on me neither, you don't 'ave ter live with 'er. 'Er goin' into a sulk for days after she's seen 'im. Lavinia knows 'er and me don't get on best of times. She should 'ave more sense.'

'I know, Dad.' Lucy's tone was stiff. 'But you and Letty ought to try, being as you've both got to live there. I can't tell Vinny to leave him behind. I couldn't upset her like that. Honestly, Dad, me and Vinny are trying to come and make your birthday nice for you, and all you do is make us feel as if you don't want us.'

She sounded petulant, ready for tears. Arthur quickly modified his own tone.

'No, it'll be nice to 'ave yer.'

He listened indifferently to Lucy, now placated, going on about her latest letter from Jack, still at the rear, safe, to her great relief; how she and the girls missed him, and oh, when would this war ever end? Automatically he answered her queries as to his own health, assured her that his chest wasn't troubling him as yet; finally said goodbye, and went to inform Letty, in the briefest possible terms, what her sisters had planned for his birthday.

It was immaterial to Letty how Dad celebrated it, except that she'd have to queue for hours for something to put in sandwiches; must make a cake too, if she could lay her hands on the ingredients.

In 1917 the war was in its third year, London bombed by Zeppelins then aeroplanes – the Allen & Hanbury's factory hardly half a mile away destroyed, bringing home how awful it must be for the lads at the front. Then the German naval blockade with merchant ships being sunk and everything in short supply. Letty would do her best with what she could get, of course, but as with everything these days, she felt little enthusiasm preparing for Dad's birthday, viewed it more with trepidation, knowing that Vinny bringing her boys meant bringing Christopher.

With fierce strokes, Letty spread the marge on the bread she'd cut thin and even for the sandwiches. A square of cheese and some slices of ham sat on the kitchen table by her elbow, the result of two hours of queuing outside Billy's dad's shop, for she couldn't be so underhand as to whisper in his ear, knowing how others must stand for hours for a small portion of this or that. Even so, Mr Beans had slid an extra slice of ham on top for her.

Laying the fillings on the marged bread, she covered each one with another slice automatically, her mind on Christopher, the name that had been given to her son.

To everyone he was Vinny's boy. Had always been. Dear God, how easily they kidded themselves into believing it, she thought bitterly as she cut the sandwiches across; thought that if they persevered long enough they could kid her into believing it too, didn't realise that to her he would always be her child, hers and David's.

An innocent to adult intrigue, the child had no knowledge she was other than he'd been told she was. To him she was Auntie, Aunt Letitia, Auntie Letty. How could she tell him otherwise?

Letty transferred the sandwiches on to two plates, not much caring how they looked, although her natural skill made the finished arrangement pleasing despite her embittered thoughts being elsewhere.

She ought never to have let Christopher go so easily. But then she had been powerless, weakened by the shame others had put on her, by her own grief and confusion. Today, she'd have made sure he wouldn't have been taken from her. But things had gone on too long. He'd never understand now. Would be confused and frightened if she took him away now, tried to explain. Knowing only Vinny as his mother, to be told she wasn't, that someone else was? A two year old boy? She couldn't.

'Goodbye, Auntie Letty.' His light child's voice,

his innocent eyes, so like David's, would tear her to pieces, having to resist the impulse to take him up in her arms, smother him with kisses. For that reason she never went to Vinny's if she could help. When he was brought here, she had no option but to endure the agony of seeing him; the wrench of parting, enduring his brief dutiful peck on her cheek as she held herself back from a natural reaction to hold him close, would leave her drained for days. But purposely to go there and suffer that torture, no.

Two years. Hard to believe David had been gone for longer than that. The pain, thinking of him, was as acute as ever it had been in the beginning. She had contacted his mother one final time last year, had received such a flood of abuse from the grieving woman that she had never dared contact her again, left now in no doubt that David had died in the Dardanelles.

In silence she and Dad had their Sunday dinner. Vinny and Lucy would be here around four. After she had washed up the dinner things while Dad had a lie down, Letty set about relaying the parlour table for his birthday tea, taking the ageing aspidistra off the table to put in the window temporarily, gazing at the leathery leaves. The plant had seen some dramas in this place, had seen grief, despair, love and hatred, and the silence of brooding animosity.

Dad had never got over her 'shame' as he called it if he referred to it; she endured his acrimony because to leave would have somehow confirmed that shame she still could not acknowledge to herself. Her son had sprang from a love that had been beautiful, tender, and would have been constant had David not been torn from her by war. It was others who had soiled it, who saw it as dirty and shameful.

The silence that had grown up between herself and Dad had come to rule them; at breakfast, throughout their day, Dad doing the books in silence, going off down the pub with never a goodbye; in the evenings, gazing out of the window in summer, morosely sucking on his pipe; in winter huddled by the fire; silence as she carried herself through the household chores, the washing – hers and Dad's hanging side by side across kitchen and balcony, stretched between the pegs like carcasses in an abattoir. And she was ready to give her soul to have him say one word to her that was not compounded of bitterness and enmity.

Relations did little to reduce the enmity, only adding fuel: 'Still goes around bold as brass then?'

How was she supposed to go around? Flog herself in public, shave her head, dash to the nearest convent to take the veil? What option was there but to face the world, hoping it would forget in time, which of course it didn't. Aunt Hetty and Aunt Mildred, when they came to see Dad, would still look sideways at her. Uncle Will, plainly embarrassed, kept his distance. Uncle Charlie was as jovial towards her as he'd ever been but regarding her now with a sly look as if he could hardly contain his imaginings of her with the man whose child she'd had. Her cousins, now at an age to know about love, sniggered.

She loathed them coming to visit Dad, usually made herself scarce. She hoped none of them would want to attend Dad's birthday and was relieved when none of them did, not even invited.

Lucy arrived with Vinny and Albert around four. Making excuses for Dad, Letty welcomed them in. She had woken him earlier but when he didn't respond had left him to get on with it; she took him a cup of tea while they ate sandwiches leaving him to make an appearance in his own time.

'You managed a cake then?' Lucy said, her mouth full.

Still warm from the oven because after even one day cake went stale without proper ingredients, its aroma filled the room despite its lack of fruit, was descended upon, not much left of it by the time they'd all had a piece.

'You really are a marvel, you really are.'

'Glad you like it,' Letty said, toying without appetite with her own piece.

'How did you manage to get the stuff for it? I can't get hold of anything over my way. So annoying getting to the head of a queue to be told they're sold out – no more goods expected today. That's what our grocer writes on his window. No apologies, nothing. So rude.'

Letty nodded, tried to rivet her attention on her

as Lucy prattled on, tried to stop her gaze straying towards Christopher, oblivious of her hunger as he played happily, trying to tie his 'brother' Albert's hands together with a piece of ribbon from her sewing basket.

Don't look at him, she told herself, watch the others. Albert's nine years old now. Sturdy and cheeky. George eight, Arthur six, both of them little demons. All three promise to be handsome. Lucy's girls, Elisabeth and Emmeline, also eight and six, were pretty, precocious and quietly confident of getting exactly what they wanted.

The room had grown hot. Despite the day being fine, Dad had a fire halfway up the chimney, and now sat staring into it as though he'd rather they all went home.

Lucy, fanning herself with a hankie, asked, 'Can we have the window open a bit?' And he, loath to deny her, nodded. Her girls went and sat by it, sedate as little nuns, gazing down into the street. Vinny's two older boys, bored by adult talk, were fretful, wanting only to go home or downstairs into the street to play with the local children.

'Can we, Mum? Can we go down?'

But Albert was having none of it. Removing his pipe from his mouth to regard them with an eye severe enough to meet his wife's approval, he declared it would not be good for them to mix with street urchins, his views bolstered by Vinny adding her own glares as she scooped two-year-old Christopher on to her lap to supervise his enjoyment of the last piece of cake. Letty, watching the action, said nothing.

'Why are you my aunt?' Emmeline turned from the window to give Letty a quizzical look.

Taken momentarily off guard, Letty fixed suspicious eyes on the girl. Had Lucy been taking carelessly in front of her? She wouldn't put it past her sister.

'Because I'm your mother's sister,' she said, even-toned.

'Mummy says you're a maiden aunt. What is a maiden aunt?'

Emmeline's questions were always direct, posed without thinking, her mother's daughter. Letty's reply was equally frank. Meet like with like whether it hurt or not, she'd learned that policy well.

'It's an aunt who's not married yet, Emmeline.'

'Mummy says you're too old to get married now?'

Lucy's voice cut sharply through the inquisition, for once being prudent. 'That's enough questions, Emmeline love. And just look at your hands – all filthy from that windowsill. The trouble with London, nothing stays clean.'

Through the narrow aperture the squeals of a dozen children playing under the window, rose up, shrill and excited. 'Gotcher! Gotcher!'

George had squeezed himself between his cousins and was staring down longingly. He risked another plea. 'Can I go down, Mum?'

Below him a ring of grubby kids were counting who'd be 'it'.

'Inky-pinky pen'n'ink, I smell a great big stink. It – must – be – you.' Repeated again and again as each dropped out until two were left. 'Inky-pinky pen'n'ink . . .'

'Can I, Mum? Please?'

The last one out had covered her eyes, the others scattering, into doorways, around corners, crouched behind dustbins.

'Ready! Comin'!' The sharp high cry, born of the East End, echoed along the street.

Cautiously the girl, skinny knees sticking like pale moons through holes in her black stockings, dress threadbare, pinafore grey from washing, hair tangled, uncombed for weeks, moved off from the battered tin can at her feet.

George held his breath, saw a boy's figure creeping out from behind a dustbin, wanted to yell to the girl, 'Look out!' But she had seen another hopeful and shrieked, 'See you! See you, Annie Wallace! See you. Come out!'

The discovered had stood up. The rest remained concealed, but the boy had crept nearer, eyeing the guardian of the tin can, hand out ready to grab it.

Too late she saw him, leapt back to defend the tin. The boy leaped too, his hands snatching it up before she could touch him.

'Tin Can Tommy!' At his triumphant bawl childish figures emerged from everywhere.

The girl was furious. 'I touched yer! I touched yer first!'

'No, yer didn't.' The boy gripped the tin posses-
sively. 'Didn't get nowhere near me.'

'I did. I touched yer. I bloody did!'

'No yer didn't.'

'Yer rotten cheat! I did. Yer bloody cheat!'

'Cow!'

'Don't yer call me a cow, yer boss-eyed bloody
cheat!'

'Cow! Silly cow!'

The abused stamped a foot, putting all her
energy into it. 'Tain't fair. I ain't playin' no more.
You cheat, Tommy 'Awkey.'

'An' you stink!'

A yelp as her hand flashed out, smacking the boy
full on the cheek. George from his vantage point
forgot about wanting to go down to join in, beside
himself with enjoyment of the entertainment.

The rest of the players watched wordlessly as the
can went flying, landed clattering along the pavement. The boy's hand came up but the girl was
already off. Apron flying like a flag in a high wind,
knees going up and down, flashing pale through
the threadbare stockings, she legged it down the
street, shrieking abuse behind her, the boy in
useless pursuit. As they disappeared, the watchers
reformed into a circle, beginning solemnly to count
out who next would be 'it'.

George's yearning to be there among them
returned. 'Can I go down and play, Mum?'

Emmeline had joined in. 'Can I too, Mummy?'

Lucy, in conversation with Vinny, threw the child

a look of extreme distaste. 'No, you can't. You're not mixing with toe rags like that. Whatever next?'

Letty, still stinging from Lucy's suspected reference to her as a maiden aunt, gave her a look. 'It was toe rags like that you used to play with once. Though I imagine you've forgotten – conveniently.' The last uttered with a curl to her lip. She saw Lucy redden.

'I hope I've moved on since then – tried to better myself.'

'Nice to have had the opportunity to move on,' Letty said acidly. 'Some of us aren't so lucky.'

'No one asked you to stay here.'

No, no one had. It had just been assumed hers would be the role of companion to Dad, condemned to be a spinster because he'd been too full of his own needs to let her pursue hers. And her reward? To have some precocious eight year old chirpily refer to her as an 'old maid'. She held Lucy in a steady look which her sister read clearly enough.

'Some of us had no choice,' she said slowly, 'but to end up as a maiden aunt out of duty to someone else. You're as selfish as him!'

Instantly she regretted the remark, saw her father stiffen, saw his head lift sharply; knew her words had bitten. But Lucy saw nothing but her own injured pride. Lines formed around her lips.

'I don't know how you can say such things! You had plenty of chance to get married. And now you've got no one. No wonder he went off and left you! Who'd want a person who cheapened herself like you did?'

'He didn't leave me. He was killed.'

How had she said it so coldly? How could she feel nothing from Lucy's remarks? Oh, but she did – the pain, the emptiness, the awful bitterness, not from what Lucy had said, but that Lucy had not the tiniest notion of the wounds she opened.

Dad was scooping tobacco from his pouch into his pipe, didn't look up, didn't look towards her though his face was tight. She saw his hand reach up, fumble for the matches on the mantelshelf above him.

'By the clock, Dad.'

Amazing she could be so matter-of-fact, amidst all that turmoil going on inside her. She wanted to throw the matches in his face, run screaming from the flat. Yet here she was being quietly practical, rebuking herself in silence for being so when he didn't acknowledge her, merely took up the box, extracted a match, struck it and applied the flame to the pipe bowl.

Vinny was looking anxiously from her to Lucy, holding Christopher defensively. But Lucy merely tossed her head, tutted, got up. Sweeping over to her daughters, she heaved the sash window closed with a sharp scrape, instantly muffling the cries of the children below.

'Trouble with autumn,' she said briskly, 'you do get a cold wind springing up suddenly. It's gone quite chilly. Here, Dad, I'll put a bit more coal on the fire, shall I?'

All attention, dripping honey over Dad, and he regarding her with fatherly love as he never now regarded Letty. It was sickening.

Billy had come home. Letty went to ask if she could pop up to see him, as a friendly gesture.

Billy's mother looked as though she had shrunk in size, and the expression in his father's eyes, not quite looking at her but somewhere beyond as he nodded his consent, made Letty hurry up the stairs to their parlour.

What she saw made her hand fly to her throat for all she tried to look natural as she approached him. In a civilian shirt, waistcoat and trousers that looked too large, Billy was sitting in a chair by the fire; the man hardly recognisable as the one who had so cheerfully gone to enlist that Saturday three years ago.

'You don't look half bad,' she said, over bright. 'Not half as bad as I thought you'd look.'

He looked as old as his father, except that his father's hair was white and his was still fair, but the gloss was gone and his moustache had a thin stiff spikiness. It was the eyes that looked old, and the mouth, tight in a crooked sort of way as if it would never again smile spontaneously; had lost the knack. The gas in his lungs had given his cheeks a pinched look, colourless now, and he breathed as though he were panting, shallow and spasmodic.

'You don't look half bad,' she said again, inadequately.

He managed to smile but the knack had gone.

'You 'ad ter – see me at me worst. Didn't cher?' he said, the quip weak. He seemed not to have enough power for sentences of any length. As he coughed, it was a dry wheezing that didn't ease him. 'Should have waited. A few weeks. The doctors say I'll improve. A few weeks – yer'd have seen me at me best. Could have swept yer – off yer feet. Then.'

Impulsively, Letty put her hand out to him, touched his arm. 'I know you're going to get better, Billy. Just give it time.'

His eyes travelled down to the hand, her left hand. She'd long ago placed her engagement ring back in its box, put the box into a drawer. To display the ring David had given her seemed a sort of sacrilege. Not so had it been a wedding ring.

'Yer didn't get married then?'

Letty edged the hand behind her back.

'He enlisted.' She hoped her eyes would stay dry. 'He was killed.'

There, she'd said it dry-eyed, her eyelids hadn't even flickered, she remained staring aridly at Billy.

It was he who lowered his eyes, once vivid blue, the whites now bloodshot. He began to cough, conquered it with an effort, cleared his throat ineffectually. It made her want to cough in sympathy.

'It was over two years ago – 1915.'

Billy's lips twisted into a travesty of a grin.

'Chance fer me then, except I ain't nobody's chance any more.'

'Oh, Billy, don't say that!' she blurted out, and the tears forced themselves slowly over her lower lids and slid down her cheeks.

Lonely tears – for herself; for a son to whom she was auntie; for a young man made old; for a man whose body lay unsung, bones bleached white on some sun-parched plain; for the waste of it all.

CHAPTER 16

'Ain't you 'aving nothing? Ain't feelin' off colour, are yer?'

The question was more peevish than concerned as Letty sank down in the armchair after dishing up Dad's supper, her own bowl of stew untouched.

Sighing, she laid her head back. 'Touch of the 'flu, I think. I don't know.'

These last few days she'd felt achey, but told herself she would work through it as she carried on down in the shop. The door opening and shutting, customers letting in gusts of cold damp February air while she hovered close to the oil stove as often as she could, she now felt feverish, her head as though it were full of cotton wool.

'Oughter see the quack,' he said as he finished supper and went to sit by the fire a moment, his own bronchial state rattling his chest. ''Ave a look at both of us while he's about it.'

The blazing fire uncomfortably affecting her already fiery cheeks while the rest of her remained shivery, Letty smiled.

'Fine pair we are.'

He didn't return her smile. 'If yer go down with the 'flu, I can't look after the shop in my state of 'ealth.'

The remark didn't anger her; didn't even hurt. Living under his unforgiving shadow so long, hurt and anger were more or less moribund.

'You can always get Ada Hall to come in,' she said listlessly.

It was an idea worth thinking about but he didn't bother saying so. She might be better by morning. With a rumbling cough, he heaved himself out of his chair, thinking of bed, neglecting to say goodnight.

Letty had been lucky, getting over it like she had. Three miserable weeks of 'flu had worn her out completely.

'People goin' down with it right, left an' centre,' said Ada Hall, who had volunteered to come in and nurse her. 'Needs a woman ter look after 'er,' she'd said and offered her services there and then, much to Dad's relief. He had kept himself as far away from Letty as possible.

Vinny's boys had all gone down with it, and Letty in her more coherent moments had been worried sick for Christopher, unable to do a thing about it, unable even to lift her thumping head much less stir herself to get over there. Vinny reported all her boys were recovering, but Lucy was keeping her girls strictly away and wouldn't have dreamed of coming over to nurse Letty, so it was Mrs Hall who had stepped in.

'It's really bad round 'ere,' she had supplied as she fed Letty the medicine the doctor had left, warmed her feet with stone hot water bottles, coaxed her to take hot soup from a spoon – 'Ter keep up yer strength,' she'd said, and stoked up the little bedroom fire.

'There's three or four from this turning 'as died of it,' she had regaled, an eager spreader of bad tidings. 'It's an epedemick. 'Undreds dying on the Continent, the papers say. That's where it's comin' from – the Continent. It's a killer. Even reached the United States of America, killin' people off there too.'

Letty, propped up on pillows reading the accounts, realised how virulent it was and thanked her lucky stars that she had recovered. But she had a strong constitution, she knew that. She wouldn't have survived the things she had if she hadn't been strong.

Still abysmally weak, she rested her head back on the pillows, letting the newspaper she'd been trying to read fall on to the pink counterpane, too heavy for her exhausted muscles to support, and watched Ada Hall bustling around her bedroom armed with polish rag and feather duster, picking up ornaments, her personal little treasures, to dust them one by one, putting them back none too gently.

'Best place for yer,' she said, making another circuit of the room. 'It's 'orrible out. Cold. Enough to freeze the cannon balls off a brass monkey. Bet

288

it's a picture where your sisters live, though. Nice an' white. 'Ere, it's just slush. Yer wouldn't credit the mess. Me boots is soaked through just coming down the road. No, love, yer in the best place.'

She gave Letty's dressing table another quick flick. 'My place's freezin'. Windows let in all the draughts. 'Ate that flat I do. All the noise in the bar downstairs. Keeps me awake at night. Smells of beer and tobaccer. Stinks it do. Gets inter yer mats an' yer curtains an' all yer clothes.'

Letty could have laughed had she felt stronger. Ada Hall worrying about her clothes smelling of beer – clothes that looked as though a good wash would have gone some way to help!

Ada gazed around the room that Letty had made very cosy over the years, a small fire burning in the little blackleaded grate, and picked up one of Letty's china ornaments to study it.

'I enjoy comin' here. Nice and warm. Wish my place was as warm. Still, while I can make meself useful 'ere, I ain't there, am I?'

Ada was still making herself useful weeks after Letty was up and about, back in the shop.

'She don't need to,' Letty assured Dad after another fortnight of her coming in 'to do for them' as she put it. 'I'm all right now.'

His amiability surprised her. 'Yer need a bit of 'elp still,' he said, the way she remembered as a child. 'And I ain't as young as I was.'

'But I feel better,' she insisted, keeping her voice down from the off key humming and the energetic clash of washing up in the kitchen. 'We don't' want to bother her more than we need to.'

Truth was, to her mind Ada Hall was being allowed too much access; would come into the shop and straight upstairs with a cheery 'mornin' love!' Not so much as, was it all right to go up?

'She's been good, I know, but really, we don't need her here every hour of the day.'

Dad's expression darkened faintly. 'She's been a good 'elp ter me. It's the least we can do after what she's done fer us – to let 'er come 'ere. She's very lonely. Besides she's company for me.'

There was a time, Letty thought dolefully, giving up and going down to open the shop for the afternoon, when he'd considered *her* company – at the expense of her own freedom. But she should, she supposed, be thankful that he had cheered since Ada had parked herself on them and become more talkative. Thankful too that his bronchitis was magically miles better. He'd become a different man with Ada now popping in most evenings as well as during the day as the weeks wore on into spring.

Thankful or not, she couldn't like Ada. Tolerate her, yes, but like her, no. Not when she would sit opposite Dad in the armchair, as if it were her right, Letty confined to the sofa – comfortable enough, but it was the principle of the thing that mattered. She noted too that Ada had begun sprucing herself as well, as she'd done once before, a few years back. Then it had come to nothing and she'd slipped back into her old ways. This time, there seemed to be more determination.

The scruffy hair had become tidier, her clothes smarter. She was changing her apron more often and those puffy cheeks with their broken veins were ruddy from more vigorous applications of soap and flannel than Letty suspected she had ever used before. Letty, remembering Mum with her smooth downy face, always neat, even when down on hands and knees scrubbing lino, resented Ada Hall's intrusion into her mother's domain – a role Letty herself amply filled as far as she was concerned.

Not that Ada wasn't hardworking – she busied herself with might and main, scrubbing lino and washing pots with the energy of a charity organiser, polishing fierce enough to break every last piece of Dad's precious porcelain, all but elbowing Letty aside to get at the weekly wash like a starving dog going after a bowl of scraps.

'I'll do yer ironin'. You just put yer feet up, workin' in that shop all day.' Shirts and vests tugged from her, fit to tear, she'd set to work, happy as a sandboy.

'I'll just have to start paying you something,' Letty suggested as Ada left one evening. It was April and no sign of her relinquishing her virtually self-appointed job, Letty's offer was made in the same vein as saying 'More tea?' to someone who'd outstayed her welcome.

Ada looked as though she'd been struck. 'No

need for that, love. The least I can do fer yer dad. Bin good ter me, 'e 'as.'

'But you should have some sort of wages.'

'No, thank you. Only too glad ter do it. Yer dad takin' me fer a drink some evenin's in the week is compensation enough – me an' 'im get on ever so well together. I wouldn't dream of takin' yer money.'

It wasn't only in the week he took her down the Knave, often weekends too. True they weren't out till all hours. Shorter opening times imposed by the Defence of the Realm Act to conserve dwindling stocks of hops, the beer weak and the prices high, ensured their return by eleven o'clock. But left to her own devices, feeling as if she were being thrust aside by him, Letty couldn't help recalling the fuss Dad would kick up when she and David had dared to go out.

'Thank God I've got you to come and see,' she said as she settled herself on Billy's sofa one Friday evening in mid May.

Almost as an act of defiance she'd made a point of going along to see him when Dad went out, her visits seen by Billy's parents as a chance for them to pop out for a much needed break.

Billy smiled, that difficult smile that pulled at her heartstrings. He sat by the window taking advantage of the warmer May sunshine that might relieve the chronic congestion on his chest.

'Glad I'm *some* good,' he said wryly, and embarrassed, she hurriedly tried to rectify it.

'What I meant was . . .' she began. But he only laughed, a sound that caught in his throat, throwing him forward in a fit of coughing while she watched helpless until he finally sank back, exhausted and fighting for breath.

She had thought that by now there would have been some improvement. At least, she consoled herself, he was out of the war – wouldn't be blown off the face of the earth as David had been.

The war dragging on, America coming into it in April hadn't made the difference people had anticipated. Men were still dying by their thousands in France with hardly any ground given by either side. In Turkey too they still died.

Letty thought often of David, knew the emptiness of those women who went about in black, faces bleak. Everywhere one saw window blinds drawn in mourning; the bluff envelope something to dread, the telegraph boy on his red Post Office bike no longer a cheeky lad who'd once held out his hand for a tip.

Conscription, long ago became compulsory, was being stepped up. All sorts of men were being taken, being trained to fight and die; so long as he had all his senses and could stand up, a man was fit for the front.

In June, Albert went. By July he was in France. Vinny, whom Letty could have sworn would cope, unlike Lucy, went completely to pieces.

'How I'm going to manage?' she pleaded, throwing herself into Dad's arms when Lucy brought her over on the tram that Sunday morning, Vinny saying she needed Dad, couldn't face being on her own that first day. 'If something was to happen to him . . .'

'Nothing's goin' ter 'appen to 'im,' Dad said inadequately as he patted her shoulder.

'I've the boys to cope with, and me all on my own.'

'You're not *all* on your own,' Letty told her. 'You've still got them for company.'

More than I ever had, came the thought, bitter and empty.

'I can't believe he's not at home any more,' Vinny wailed. 'All night I kept dreaming he was there beside me, and when I realised he wasn't . . . It's like having his ghost around. But I want *him*!'

Letty empathised with her. She sat by the open window reliving her own memories. The sounds of Sunday morning's market floating upward; David shouldering his way through that crowd, his tall lean figure, his bearing so upright, so noble – a man from another world to that seething below her.

Seething? It no longer seethed, becoming quiet with hardly any men in the crowd but for those pitiful sights, men invalided home – going about on crutches, with a leg missing; others with an empty sleeve pinned across the chest. So many of them. And that wasn't counting all those confined to their homes with nothing more to be done for them in hospital, both legs gone, blinded, or gassed like Billy. A lot of stalls missing, or manned by those too old to fight or women taking their men's places.

'Four boys to cope with single-handed,' Vinny was lamenting. Letty brought her attention back to her.

Poor Vinny had believed Albert would never be taken from her. It was hard for people like her who hadn't prepared themselves for the rotten deal life could throw at you. And her life had always been so easy.

Letty was sorry for her, dreadfully sorry, and annoyed with herself for an insidious hope that crept into her sympathy that Vinny might find Christopher too much of a handful now, what with her other three. Might decide to hand him back. Was it too much to hope for – that one day he might be hers again. Not yet three years old – not old enough to pine for long for the person he had called Mother. He would adjust, wouldn't he, to a new mother? In time he'd remember nothing of Vinny as his mother. As for the circumstances of his birth, those could be explained later. She'd tell him of their love, hers and his father's, the circumstances of David's death. Later in life he would understand.

Letty sipped her tea, gazed speculatively out of the window, gave herself up to her thoughts; sorrow for Vinny melting in a welter of hope.

'If anything was to happen to Albert,' Vinny was

saying, a tremor in her voice, 'I don't know what I'd do.'

'Thank God Jack's safe.' Lucy put her empty cup back on the table. 'He won't be sent to the fighting. What he's doing is too valuable. I don't really know what it is, mind. He's not allowed to say. But it's something very important. Decoding or something. He did drop a hint once. At least he won't be in the same danger as your Albert, thank God.'

A hollow look had come into Vinny's eyes. Letty would dearly have loved to have warned Lucy that anyone could be posted, no matter how valued, but decided to leave indiscretion to Lucy who did it so well. Bad enough to have Vinny on the edge of tears without Lucy as well.

Dad, however, wasn't so circumspect. 'Want ter be careful about crowin' too soon,' he said, knocking out his pipe against the empty fire grate. 'No one's indispensable, never 'as bin.'

It was Lucy's turn to look hollow-eyed.

'That's a cruel thing to say,' she burst out, tears threatening. 'Anyone'd think you wanted to see Jack in the thick of it.'

'No, he doesn't,' Letty appeased automatically.

Her mind was more on Christopher playing on the floor with a few spoons she'd let him have, making them into trains to push at each other. Every time the spoons clashed together he laughed, a giddy chuckle. She remembered David's had been like that, a low, private chuckle, as though what amused him was for his own personal pleasure. How she had loved that laugh. Her heart broke into silent tears, needing so much to hear the sound again from him.

'Yes he does,' her sister's peevish voice broke in, Lucy fishing agitatedly in her crocheted Dorothy bag for a handkerchief. 'How do you think I feel when Albert's already there, liable to be killed or wounded . . .'

'Lucy!'

At Vinny's ragged intake of breath, Letty broke free of her own thoughts, turned a warning glare on Lucy. 'Perhaps we ought to change the subject.'

'But it's true. Men are being killed . . .'

'For God's sake! This isn't the time!' Letty's voice had grown high, as much for the feeling of desolation her sister had conjured up in herself as for Vinny. 'Why can't you think before you say things?'

'I do think. I always do.'

Lucy's handkerchief was out, being frantically dug into the corners of her eyes. 'I've put myself out coming over here with Vinny, not to be ticked off by you. You're jealous because I've got Jack and you got no one. You're just a frustrated, sour old maid. Anyone'd think I wasn't sorry for Vinny. And what about her? When Jack went to France and your Albert was here at home, you crowed then, didn't you?'

She was on her feet, thoughts already on gathering up her coat from the hall.

'I really don't know what I've said to upset

everyone. It's best if I go home, and not come back here again for ages! Then you'll . . .'

'Oh, sit down!' Letty said angrily. 'Don't be so bloody stupid!'

Lucy's reference to her present plight had hurt more than she could ever imagine, but what was the point of causing even more of a row?

'What Vinny needs most at a time like this is a bit of comforting,' she said as evenly as she could. 'Just try not to upset her.'

'As if I would,' Lucy said, petulant, dabbing her eyes.

But she sat down, moody still but somewhat less ready to rush off in a huff, especially as Vinny showed no signs of wanting her to leave.

August was fine and sunny, so different from last year when rain had gone on right into the autumn and through the winter with hardly a break.

'It must be helping them in France,' she remarked to Bill. 'This lovely weather.'

It was Sunday afternoon. Dad had taken Ada Hall off for a wander around Bethnal Green Gardens finishing with a drink in the Salmon and Ball – that's if it was open, which it might not be with Government restrictions on opening hours. They hadn't asked her to go with them. She hadn't expected them to and probably wouldn't have wanted to go with them anyway, but she had felt left out and wandered down to see Billy. Well, it was something to do.

Nice to be welcomed by his mum and dad even though they had company – Billy's two married sisters and his sister-in-law, their husbands off in the armed forces. Nice, Billy's home, full of love, smelled cosy with a sense of caring. So much nicer than her flat; for all she had striven to make it cosy and comfortable, it felt lonely and unloved.

She sat now on the sofa, fanning herself with a copy of *News of the World* glancing from time to time at the headline: ALLIED ADVANCE ON A FORTY MILE FRONT – HUN ARMY FLYING.

It brought a twinge of hope, but there had been so many false hopes in the past.

'I 'ope we get somewhere this time,' she said, slipping easily into cockney as she always did with Billy. 'God knows when it'll end – 'alf way through 1918 and still draggin' on. If we get pushed back again like in March . . . It gets you down, don't it, all this?'

Billy's parents nodded agreement, but he merely gave her a crooked grin.

'That's it, Let,' he said whimsically. 'Be a Job's comforter, why don'tcher? Cheer us all up.'

Letty fanned herself vigorously, allowed herself a wry smile.

'I'm sorry. P'raps I'm feeling a bit down today. I don't know.'

But her mood had lifted a bit. A real tonic was Billy – a natural bouncer back. Made her ashamed of herself bemoaning her lot when she had her health and strength and he had . . . She saw the effort he had in breathing sometimes, the gas still in his lungs, but never a word of complaint.

He was somewhat improved these days, she thought with a lightening of her spirits, the dry weather good for his chest. Didn't look so thin as when he first came home, although the old broadness of chest was gone for good, she knew that.

He'd never mentioned his own experiences at the front, and Letty knew better than to ask, sensing that even his family had kept off the subject. What Billy truly felt about his war injury, he never let on to anyone.

Lifting the earpiece at the telephone's urgent tinkle, Letty heard an unfamiliar voice, well-spoken but somewhat agitated.

'It that Mrs Worth's sister?'

'Yes,' she said. Alarm sharpened her tone. Something was wrong. It had to be Christopher – something was wrong with him.

'Thank goodness I've got you.' The voice sounded full of relief. 'I'm Mrs Worth's next-door neighbour. I thought I ought to ring you. She has had a telegram. She's in a terrible state.'

Lucy felt a shock wave pass through her, directing the fear she'd had for her son on to a completely different path. Albert! Dear God, no!

'Is it her husband?' she heard herself asking.

'Yes, I'm afraid so. Killed in action, it said.'

The voice blurred behind a roaring in her ears. For an instant the floor of the shop began to sway, her knees to lose their strength, but there was no chair handy, only a small battered bureau beside her.

Hardly aware of all the woman was saying, Letty realised all at once that she was being asked a question. '. . . can you possibly come over? She needs someone, her family . . .'

Again the voice receded on a second shock wave, but now she was in control, said, 'Yes . . . yes, of course. I'll come.'

It was hard to think straight. What tram did she need to catch? How long did it take to get to Walthamstow? Had Lucy been told? If the neighbour hadn't, then she would have to. There was Dad to be told as well. The shop to be closed. Her mind in complete turmoil.

'I'll be there in half an hour . . . no, three-quarters of an hour,' she managed to say. Best not to underestimate the journey. Nothing ran on time these days. 'I'll bring my . . . father with me.'

She realised she had replaced the earpiece without saying goodbye or thank you; was already dialling the operator, giving Lucy's number. She waited in seething impatience, amazed that she could still remain dry-eyed.

'Lucy!' she shouted down the mouthpiece.

Another strange voice, less cultured, seeming an awfully long way from the mouthpiece, high with trepidation.

'Hu . . . hel-lo?' it queried hesitantly. 'Wh-who – is – it?'

'Is that Mrs Morecross's home?' Letty queried.

'Yes. I-I'm sorry . . . I'm not used to the telephone. I don't know how to use it.'

No time to bother with petty problems.

'Is she there?' Letty shouted down the phone, emphasising each word, slowly as though to someone with no command of the English language. 'Is – Mrs Morecross – there?'

'No.' There was a momentary hiatus, then, 'Uhm . . . She's out. She went to the new Women's Institute some time ago.'

'Then when will she be back?'

Letty felt her heart thumping heavy against her ribs, loathing the silly woman on the other end of the line, tears of frustration rising like a wave inside her.

'Uhm . . .' came the response to her sharp enquiry. 'Uhm . . . she's – been gone quite some time. She should be . . . oh, er, oh . . . Here she is – just come in.' Utter relief sounded in the voice. Another brief silence, then Lucy's voice, slightly out of breath.

'I've just this minute come in and . . .'

'Lucy . . .' she interrupted. 'We've had some bad news. Some dreadful news.'

There was a small squeak from the other end, then Lucy's voice. 'What?'

'It's about Vinny . . . Her Albert . . . he's been killed!'

She had meant to be tactful but her throat by now was awash with tears and she could hardly

302

get the words out, much less use tact. 'Oh, Lucy, what're we going to do?'

The phone went dead on a drawn out cry, cutting her off, leaving her hanging on unsure. What would Lucy do? Rush over here, go over to Vinny or merely stay indoors uncertain as Letty herself what to do – perhaps, like her, thinking what she'd heard had been unreal, that it was all a mistake? Would Lucy ring back? Should she ring again?

Taking a deep breath, Letty fought to gain control of herself. She must go and inform Dad. God, what a prospect. She was shaking deep inside her as she went to the shop door, turned the sign to read CLOSED, glancing out at the world beyond.

All was golden and warm, the sunshine mellow, the shadows delicate. A fine September afternoon. She noted it with an impartial eye, yet felt a vague anger that it should be so fine after such news; that it was wrong to be so fine.

Noiselessly she slipped the bolt and went slowly back through the shop and up the stairs to where Dad was sitting in his chair by the window, enjoying a nap.

Letty shook him gently by the shoulder. 'Dad.'

He came awake, irascible. 'What's the time?' His voice, hoarse from sleep, full of complaint.

'Dad – Vinny's neighbour has just telephoned. She's given us some terrible news.'

'News?' The irritation was still there. He hunched his shoulders, chilly from his sleep, peered at the clock registering half-two.

'What's up, waking me? Only just this minute nodded off, and yer . . .'

'It was Vinny's neighbour. Vinny's had a telegram – from the War Office.' How she managed to get the words out she had no idea.

Dad staring at her, fully awake but not comprehending, was looking at her lips, not her eyes, as she spoke. She saw the colour begin to drain slowly from his face and he seemed to diminish in stature in his chair, his gaze dropping slowly from her face, turned into the distance as though some answer, some miracle would be there to make what he was hearing untrue.

'My Lavinia? My little daughter . . .' Then, as the full force of realisation hit him: 'Oh God! Oh God! No!' His voice swelled to a roar as he lifted up his face. 'Yer can't! Yer can't take 'er 'usband from 'er!'

Letty took his hands. 'We've got to get a tram, Dad. We've got to go over there to her.'

For a moment he looked blankly at her, then snatched his hands from her grasp as though her touch had burnt him. 'I don't need you. I can go over there on me own. You can look after the shop.'

'No, I'm coming with you, Dad.'

'I don't need you!'

And now anger took hold – that he could still act out his rancour against her at a terrible moment like this, could hate her so that even Vinny's loss didn't diminish it.

'I don't care what you think,' she yelled at him.

'Think what you like of me. But I'm going to Vinny. There's nothing you can do apart from *you* staying here so you don't have to be near me. So do what you bloody like!'

She vowed then in an overwhelming rage that never again would she bow in shame before his condemnation of her.

CHAPTER 17

No Sunday market today. In Club Row people were dancing, jigging, laughing, clasping each other deliriously; flags were being waved, whistles blown. Everywhere church bells were being rung.

Letty standing at her shop door could hear those of St Leonard's in Shoreditch quite distinctly, all the others dissolving in the general cacophony of joy and relief.

The war was over. After four and a quarter years it was over.

There were those who wouldn't be kicking up their heels. Vinny, widowed just ten weeks before the last gun went silent; herself, the man she'd loved lost a few months after the first gun sounded.

Even while she smiled at the happy people, she let her tears flow quietly, steadily, unchecked. Lots of people were crying; some from relief at a loved one being saved by the signing of a piece of paper; some for one of their family, maybe more than one, for whom the Armistice had come too late. Who would notice her tears?

You're just one among millions, she formed the

306

words in her head. Millions of wives, mothers, sweethearts who'll never see their loved ones again. You ought to try instead to be pleased for the others and their good fortune.

What good did tears do? They wouldn't bring David back. You're only hurting yourself – he wouldn't have wanted that. You got to make your own life, that's what he'd have wanted. But it was hard not to cry.

She was crying for Christopher too. The child had lost one father whom he knew nothing about; had now lost another, the one he'd called Daddy. Oh, how badly she wanted Christopher at this minute. Three years old, he would forget that man in time. But could she dare tell him of his real father? Tell him he was a love child, born out of wedlock? A bastard? Her throat tightened at the thought. Not yet. Not for a long time yet. But one day . . . Dry her tears and think of that day. Plan for that day.

I will get him back, she vowed. He's mine, not hers.

Standing at the shop door, watching the throng flood by, she made her vow. I will, David – one day I will.

Upstairs Ada Hall and Dad were dancing, full to the eyeballs with beer and gin, doing a jig. The ceiling above Letty's head was vibrating to it.

Bert Wilkins, now married to Clara Wilson that was, from a few doors away, came past in uniform, Clara clinging to him. He'd been wounded in his foot and been sent home to recover, was to have returned to the front next week. They really did have something to celebrate and Bert was beaming all over his face. So was his wife.

Letty lifted her hand, waved to them, watched them disappear in the crowd.

'Come on, Let! Comin' wiv us!' Ethel Bock was waving a little flag in Letty's face. Was clinging on to a Canadian soldier, one arm about his neck, him slobbering over her, his kisses missing most of the time as they were jostled this way and that.

'Orf up West ter see the celebrations in Trafalgar Square. Comin'?'

Letty shook her head and, without pausing to coax her any further, Ethel and her soldier took off. Ethel's widowhood hadn't torn her apart as it had others, she was making the most of it.

Behind her Dad's voice was slurred by beer and excitement.

'Me'n Ada's poppin' down the Knave fer a couple. You stayin' 'ere?'

Without waiting for her to reply, they thrust past her, Ada directing a silly smile towards Letty as she shoved her way through the throng in the wake of Arthur.

Ada had practically taken up abode in Dad's flat; came in as soon as the shop opened, left just before the pub closed, him seeing her home, with a pint in the Public before returning.

Letty turned on her heel, closing the door behind her, shutting out the noise of celebration.

Upstairs, she sat on the edge of her bed. How silent the room was against the muffled noise outside. Isolated, a small corner for a hunted creature to hide in. Letty smiled at the notion, looked down at her hands, the fingers of one massaging those of the other. Becoming roughened by housework, hardly the hands of a proprietress of a West End shop, were they? Where were those dreams she'd once had of that?

She let the smile die, too hard to maintain, gave a sigh and slowly straightened her back; after a while she stood up and went to the top drawer of her chest of drawers and drew out the small dark blue heart-shaped box. Taking the ring from its bed of padded grey silk, she replaced the box and slid the ring on to her finger.

'Will you marry me, darling?'

She should have said yes that first time. How could she have been so stupid? She had pushed happiness aside for Dad's sake. Why? He had never once bothered to wonder what it had cost her – had never once expressed gratitude, had never felt any; only condemnation of the outcome of the love she had sacrificed for him.

'Yes, David,' she said aloud to the flowery wallpaper. 'I'll marry you.'

The words sounded dead to her ears. The ring heavy on her flesh, unaccustomed as she was to it. She felt suddenly frightened of wearing it, twisted it off and thrust it back into the box, closing the drawer sharply.

'David! Come back! Let me marry you!'

She stood very still, trying not to acknowledge the stupidity of what she'd said. Instead, she made a silent vow. I shall never put on your ring again, David, until I get your son back. When I do get him back, then I'll wear it, and I'll never take it off again.

By midnight much of the jollifications had died away. Here and there singing still floated on the misty November air. A burst beneath her window startled Letty out of a light sleep. A chorus of 'Goodnight, sleep tight, see yer termorrer!' assaulted her as the revellers parted company to go their separate ways. A dustbin someone accidentally stumbled against rattled madly. A startled curse, then uncontrollable giggles followed by noisy shushing while an alarmed dog somewhere nearby barked fit to wake every drunk out of his bed.

Letty heard the harsh jingle of the bell as the shop door was eased open, ceasing abruptly as it was held in check by someone's hand. She didn't hear the door close but the stairs creaked as someone began easing their way up them. There came a smothered laugh, cut off as abruptly as the bell had sounded. Dad wasn't alone.

Incensed at the notion of what caper he was up to, she was in half a mind to go and confront him. But why should she care what he did?

There was no further sound after his door closed quietly. Perhaps she had been mistaken? He could

310

have been giggling to himself – drunk from celebrating.

Letty lay thinking of Lucy, of Vinny, of Billy. The war over, Billy one of its casualties, condemned for years to an invalid life – how must he feel? She should have gone along to see him but had been too wrapped up in her own sense of loss.

There'd been no word from Lucy. She had Jack's grandmother nearby – his grandfather had died two years ago – Jack's parents, her girls. Didn't need Letty and Dad.

Vinny hadn't been in touch either. Perhaps, like herself, she'd sat indoors nursing her loss. But she had Albert's family to comfort her, and her boys about her, didn't she? Even David's son.

From Dad's bedroom a muffled cry, hurriedly stifled, brought her mind scurrying back to the present. Instantly suspicious, Letty lay rigid, listening for the least sound from that room, hating Dad for his lack of consideration.

Listening, she fell asleep, not realising it until she awoke to a bright fresh Monday morning – a world with no war, no more news of fighting to be scanned in the morning paper, only stories of how everyone had celebrated its end.

Letty was in the kitchen getting breakfast for herself and Dad when he emerged from his bedroom, half dressed and needing a shave.

'How'd yer sleep?' he asked as he moved past her to the sink for his razor. An odd question to ask, he who seldom asked her anything.

'All right,' she said abruptly, hearing him begin to strop the blade into fresh sharpness.

'Didn't 'ear me come in?'

'I heard something. I took it to be you. Wouldn't be anyone else.'

'Didn't make too much noise then?'

'No.'

She stirred the porridge in its saucepan. Behind her she could hear him frothing his shaving brush in its mug, after a while heard the scrape of the razor across his chin. The porridge was done. She spooned it into two plates and went to lay a cloth halfway across the parlour table for the two of them; preferring breakfast in the parlour rather than have Dad splashing around at the sink, water dripping off his elbows, while she tried to eat.

His bedroom door was slightly ajar as she crossed the passage; not enough to see into, but a movement caught her eye, a shadow passing across his room.

Letty hesitated, ears pricked, but there was no sound. As if someone was, like her listening. She let her breath out, realising she'd been holding it, and continued on into the parlour, trying not to put words to thoughts.

She was laying the table when she heard a rustling, someone moving hurriedly from the bedroom to the kitchen. Bent over the table in the process of smoothing the folds of the cloth, Letty froze. From the kitchen came whispering. She crept to the door, eavesdropping.

312

'D'yer think she 'eard us?'

'I ain't sure. We didn't make no noise, far as I know.'

'I'd better go, before she comes out.'

Letty took the passage in one catlike leap, made oddly out of breath by the suddenness of her move, and stood looking at them from the kitchen door.

She could have laughed at their expressions, gazing at her like a couple of kids caught with their hands in the sweet jar.

'Enjoyed it, did yer?' she said slowly, her chin lifted, tilted, her green eyes gazing sideways upon her father.

'Letty . . .' Arthur stopped, not quite sure of what he should say. For the first time that she could remember shortening her name. 'Listen . . . me an' Ada . . . we've got something ter tell yer.'

'I bet you 'ave.' She'd lapsed into his way of speaking, hardly realising it. 'I bet you've got a lot ter tell me!'

'We'd have told yer last night if you 'adn't been asleep,' he said awkwardly. 'We didn't want ter wake yer. But p'raps we ought ter tell yer now. Yer see, me an' Ada, we've decided ter get married.'

Letty gazed full at him now, her chin lowered, no idea what she was supposed to feel, apart from the shock of surprise. It had never once dawned on her that Dad would ever contemplate marrying again; had always imagined Mum's memory to be as sacred to him as it was to her. Yet here he was, calmly announcing plans to marry Ada Hall of all people – scruffy Ada Hall! After neat and quietly proud Mum, it was unthinkable, sacrilege. How could he?

'We thought we'd make it as quick as possible,' he was saying. 'I mean, neither of us is getting any younger. Don't want ter wait around too long. So we thought we'd make it next month.'

There was nothing Letty could find to say for the bitter confusion going on inside her. The man who had denied her marriage to David, having the audacity to announce his own – to that slovenly cow! The more Letty stared at the red-faced woman, bleary-eyed from sleep, smelling all fusty from Dad's bed, from what Dad had done, the more she wanted to be sick.

She felt the bile rise in her throat, knew she could never touch Dad again as long as she lived, that it would defile her. Dad, once so fastidious when Mum was alive, doing what he had done last night to that unsavoury creature. It didn't bear thinking about!

She turned away.

'Do what yer like,' she yelled over her shoulder as she went down into the shop.

Outside, the door swinging shut behind her, the November air hit her like a slap in the face. She was without a coat, hatless, running along the street, forced by the realisation that she'd have to go back or catch her death. She could go to Billy, but she had her pride. It was all she could do to turn back, ring the shop doorbell, to have Ada of all people to let her in.

Dad and Ada were married the Saturday prior to Christmas. It was a noisy affair. Ada had a regiment of relations as well as two married sons and their spouses, and two married daughters and theirs. There was Dad's brother, Letty's cousins on his side, none of Mum's she was glad to note, Dad's drinking companions from the Knave of Clubs, a few of his regular customers, a few neighbours. They crammed into the parlour, down the stairs, through the shop, the kitchen bursting at the seams with well-wishers. A friend of Ada's had supplied the sandwiches, the drink had been brought in from the Knave.

Ada was in a nice grey suit, a fox fur stole, for once looking really neat and tidy, hair nicely brushed under a grey toque hat. At least, Letty thought, she ain't in white!

Lucy, as shocked as Letty, didn't come. 'Showing off,' Dad said, briefly vexed, then forgot about it, being too besotted by Ada.

Vinny too stayed away, using mourning as her excuse. That Dad accepted as right and proper and thought no more of it.

Letty kept to her room as much as possible, to stop guests using it as much as anything else; glad when everyone left but detesting the knowledge that across the passage tonight, her father and Ada, now Ada Bancroft, would be enjoying their conjugal rights.

The next morning he took Ada off to Margate for a week's honeymoon leaving Letty mercifully on her own. The flat felt empty, with Dad not there the first time ever, but Letty used the time to busy herself in the shop, dusting, tidying, re-arranging; rather enjoyed it really, felt happy, light, as if released from a dead weight. She began to regret that they must ever come back home.

Over the small round mahogany table she'd been moving to a more likely spot, Letty glared at Ada. Anger rose up inside her like a small explosion as the table's polished edge scraped the side of a brass fender with a horrid grating sound.

'Look what you've done! Can't you leave things alone?'

'I was tryin' to 'elp.' Ada's florid face had gone even more red as Letty swept her angrily aside. 'I thought it was 'eavy.'

It was April. Dad and Ada had been married four months. To Letty it seemed like four years.

Ada, certainly of herself, had slipped back into her customary ways, the flat becoming a mess which it was left to Letty to tidy up. True, Dad was far more sociable than he had been, but it didn't compensate for the way he condoned Ada's sloppiness. He himself was still meticulous with his own stuff, but besotted with Ada's easy-going good humour, he didn't see that her cleanliness had been but temporary, done to impress.

316

It was true, leopards never changed their spots, Letty decided. Merely camouflaged them when it suited. And there is none so blind as them that won't see, she decided too, directing that one at Dad.

'You're not helping,' Letty spat at her as she tried to smooth the minute scratch with a finger tip. 'You're interfering. The shop's my concern, not yours!'

'That's enough of that!' Dad came hurrying down the stairs, full of indignation. 'You wouldn't have talked like that ter yer mother.'

'But she ain't my mother, is she?' Letty turned on him suddenly, startling him.

Four months of bickering was all but destroying her. It was such a silly thing. One tiny scratch – the table needed restoring anyway – but all her grievances against Ada compounded themselves into that single scratch.

'And I tell you this for nothing, Dad – I wouldn't have her for a mother if you roasted me alive. I can't for the life of me understand what you can see in her.'

Dad's face was livid. His blue eyes wide and staring, frightened her a little, his moustache standing out like a walrus's.

'I ain't havin' yer talk to my wife like that. You 'ave a bit of respect for 'er. You apologise to her.'

'Your wife?' Letty stood her ground. 'Mum was your wife. You've forgotten her, but I ain't. You've pushed her aside like you did me.'

'And what d'you know about it?' he retaliated. 'About marriage? An old maid like you? Look at yer – nearly thirty. Yer act like forty.'

'And whose fault's that?' she blazed at him, Ada thrust aside.

'Yer got yerself ter blame,' he shouted. 'Ruined yer life fer that bloke. Left yer with a kid. Yer sister takin' it ter give it a name.'

'I don't want to talk about it . . .'

'Twelve years of yer life wasted 'cause of 'im,' he ranted, hearing nothing but what he wanted to say. 'Yer could have been married proper ter someone by now . . . 'ad kids . . .'

'I have a kid.'

He didn't even pause for breath. 'Instead, Lavinia 'ad ter do what was best for yer – put 'erself out, she did, and no word of thanks from you, ever. Yer should have married someone from round 'ere. Someone of yer own sort.'

'And you think you'd have let me marry anyone at all?' She bent towards him, her pretty features now matured to a striking beauty, at this moment twisted with hate, hardly two inches from his.

She could see every line of his sixty-one years etched on his face, twisted like hers into bitterness and hatred.

'You wanted my company so's *you* wouldn't be lonely. Your property that's what I was, like your blessed ornaments – worse, because I had feelings, and you didn't care. So long as you had someone to keep you company. Now you've got her, you

318

say I should have got married! You act like I don't count any more.'

'You ain't counted for a long time, miss,' he railed at her.

He swung away from her, making for the stairs, but he paused as he reached them and swung back to her, his hand spread in appeal.

'I'd have wanted ter see yer marry, Letitia . . .'

'Oh, don't come the old soldier with me, Dad!' Letty gave a burst of bitter laughter. 'You couldn't care less. Now you've got her, I could walk out of that door and it wouldn't bother you.'

She saw his expression alter – the trace of appeal turn instantly sour.

'Why don't yer then?' he challenged from the stairs.

'Not until I'm ready,' she said, her lips tight.

It was always like this, row after row, starting from a small incident, a remark, blossoming into warfare, smouldering resentment. It would blow over, like all their rows, but one day it would go too far, she was sure of it.

It was June, the first Sunday after her birthday. She was twenty-nine, nearing the thirtieth year when a spinster's state can be truly confirmed, at least by Dad's estimation during that row they'd had in the shop in April.

There hadn't been any tiffs for weeks, everyone being amicable. Ada even making a big thing of her birthday, had excelled herself and made some sort of a cake for her, with everyone being convivial, Dad truly sociable. She should have known something was in the wind.

Something was. Letty had washed up and Dad had put his head down for a snooze in their room. Ada came up close as she was replacing the aspidistra on the table and put an arm lightly on her shoulder. Letty caught the faint stale whiff of underarm sweat, and tried to ignore it.

'All right, love?' Ada asked amiably.

Letty, feeling generous enough to forgive the odour, nodded, glad when Ada took her arm away and moved over to the dining chairs now back in their place along the wall each side of the piano.

'We've bin thinking,' Ada said, her tone cautious. 'We've bin thinkin' of settin' up an 'ome on our own, Letty.'

Letty stared at her, dumbfounded. Ada was making a play of putting the chairs straight. They were already straight.

'Me an' yer dad, well, we need what all married couples need. You know – a place of our own. You know 'ow it is . . .'

No, she didn't know how it was. Had never had the chance to set up home with a husband. She continued to stare at Ada who went rattling on.

'Well, yer see, me brother's got this 'ouse in Stratford. Wants ter sell it and move right out of London. Not that Stratford's all that much London, you know – it's a nice part of it – nice 'ouses some of 'em. But 'e wants ter move out to Essex. He's

320

willin' ter let us 'ave 'is place, cheaper, being family. Well, yer can't miss up on a thing like that, now can yer?'

Couldn't they?

'What's Dad think about it?' Letty said tonelessly.

'Oh, 'e thinks it's a good idea. But 'e'd like ter know what you feel about it.'

'I wouldn't have thought it mattered to him what I feel about it,' she said, watching Ada still buggering about with the chairs.

'He thinks it do.'

'Can't he ask me himself?'

''E reckoned I might make a better job of it.'

He would, Letty thought, always did leave others to do things for him. Mum used to do everything for him, think for him, do his business for him while he played fine art collector with all those bits and bobs that might have kept them in a bit more luxury if he'd sold them in the proper manner.

'Well . . .' She shrugged. 'Whatever he wants to do is up to him. It's his life.'

She was being hugged by Ada, the stale odour smothering her.

'I knew you'd see it that way,' Ada was saying. 'Things'll be better fer yer with us not 'ere. You'll be able ter do whatever yer want. Yer won't have yer dad treadin' on yer toes all the time. Yer dad said 'e thought it might be a good idea fer you ter carry on managing the shop.'

Enthusiasm poured out of her. 'We could get

papers drawn up proper. You'd 'ave charge of the shop, all the profits yours an' you payin' yer dad rent fer it and the flat. What d'yer say ter that then?'

Letty was hardly listening. It was what she'd wanted, if the truth be known, wasn't it? To be her own mistress? Yet underlying it was a pang of apprehension at being on her own for the first time; stronger still, her father's betrayal. She hated him, wanted him to go as soon as possible, yet she needed him to stay here – needed him desperately to stay.

'What d'yer say to it then, Letty?' Ada was prompting.

'Hope you and Dad'll be happy then,' she said obediently, hardly realising she had said anything at all.

CHAPTER 18

Such a silly thing to get upset about, the sugar bowl slipping through her fingers, sugar and glass all over the kitchen floor.

For a moment Letty stared at it, unwarranted despair running through her whole body. In seconds it had turned into frustration and for no real reason she burst into tears, swung away from the mess confronting her, unable to bear the thought of clearing it up; unable to think of anything but that she needed suddenly to weep, to beat hysterically at the kitchen door with her fist, her forehead, wanted tears to engulf her.

This quite everyday accident was as good an excuse as any, she leaned with her face against the door and let herself be convulsed by great gulping sobs. She knew what she was doing yet could not – did not – want to stop, all the loneliness of these three months culminating in the fit of insane, ungovernable weeping.

Her eyes red and sore, she finally ceased from sheer exhaustion, becoming rational again, and turning her face to survey the mess. It would have to be cleared up.

Going into the parlour, she sat in Mum's old wooden-armed chair, turned her eyes from the drizzly December morning outside the window to gaze about the room. The faded flowery wallpaper, the ornaments no loving hands tended any more, the shabby furniture.

Fancy breaking down like that, bursting into tears. As if the mere sound of crying could take away the quiet. Crying to fill up something that had gone so deep inside her she no longer acknowledged it. She hadn't realised just how lonely these last four months had been.

'You should be accustomed to your own company by now,' she said to the walls. She could go out whenever she fancied, couldn't she? With Ethel Bock to the pictures – that was, when Ethel wasn't out with some bloke or other. Having a good laugh at Charlie Chaplin, Charlie Chase, or being thrilled by handsome William S Hart. She saw Billy a lot. There was the shop too, the satisfaction of knocking it into shape without Dad or Ada to interfere. They'd hardly come near since they'd left. It didn't matter.

Dad had been generous really, turning over the shop, taking only rent from her. Not that it had pleased Vinny or Lucy, still smouldering at what they saw as favouritism, unable to see further than their own noses. Would they fancy a swap then? Would they really prefer her life to theirs? Lonely. She was lonely. Oh, she was . . . But no more tears.

She really must control herself. All very well crying, but what did it achieve with no one to listen but herself?

Lucy, handing Letty a cup of tea, the bone china pretty with flowers, regarded her critically.

'What *are* you doing to yourself lately? You look so dowdy!'

It was March 1920, a new era. Lucy had plunged into it, golden hair now cut short. Her slim apricot dress showing a deal of calf was light and pretty, like herself, and hid a bust brassiered flat as a pancake.

Jack was doing well in the printing business. His grandparents were both dead now having left him a substantial sum. Lucy and he were living on the fat of the land, making the most of it. The house was beautifully furnished, redecorated and repainted, the stone stanchions of the Victorian bay windows impressively white. Lucy employed a man to do the garden. Her girls at private school now, spoke with plums in their mouths, not even trying to disguise their contempt of Letty's cockney vowels.

'Really, Letty,' said Lucy, offering her a plate of sweet biscuits as they sat by a little table looking out on to budding daffodils in neat beds, 'you've let yourself go since Dad left. You used to dress so well. You've lost weight too. You ought to eat proper, you know.'

'I do,' Letty said, munching her biscuit.

'I don't expect you even bothered to have a proper Christmas dinner all on your own like that. We did ask you. I really can't understand you staying away like you did. Being so standoffish. It really mystified us all.'

It hadn't been a case of being standoffish. More a case of after none of them had come nigh or by for months, she'd been expected to go trailing off round to see them, and didn't see why she should. It went deeper than that of course. The lonelier she was becoming, the less she wanted to drag herself out of it. Months on her own had steadily accentuated a yearning for Christopher, one she fought against daily; telling herself that it was just as well Vinny hadn't come visiting. To see him would have destroyed all the self-control she'd built up.

'Dad was a bit put out, you know,' Lucy said, reaching for another bourbon. 'After what he did for you and all, last year.'

Letty knew what was coming, braced herself not to get angry.

'It really surprised me,' Lucy said, sipping tea to make her remark appear less pointed. 'It really did, him giving you the shop.'

'He didn't exactly *give* it to me,' Letty said. 'You know I pay him rent for it, and the flat as well.'

'But you take all the profits.'

'What profits?' Letty gave a disparaging chuckle. 'It just about keeps me in shoe leather.'

'So it appears.' Lucy eyed her outdated fawn

voile blouse and dark brown skirt. 'It's positively Edwardian. You look about fifty in that. But then you hardly go anywhere to get dressed up. I suppose you're putting every penny you make in that shop in the bank, eh? For a rainy day!'

She gave a tinkling laugh that had a caustic edge to it and quickly changed the subject.

Jealous! Letty thought, as she came away. How can either of them be jealous of me? Lucy with her money and Vinny comfortable enough with her father-in-law giving her a substantial allowance – eight pounds a week, Lucy said it was – in memory of his dead son; that on top of her widow's allowance. And he paid for her boys' educations.

How dare they begrudge her, having worked in the shop for Dad most all of her life, this small compensation for what he'd done to her?

The thing she dreaded most happened in August, Christopher's fifth birthday – Vinny visiting that Sunday afternoon, tormenting her with the five year old, so handsome it hurt to watch him.

'He'll be starting school next month,' she said blithely.

As if she didn't know how much it hurt – or was it deliberate? For again came the insinuations about the shop. Amazing how Dad could favour Letty above herself and Lucy, he should have divided the place. Letty wouldn't have been put out, would still have been managing and living in it.

Holding back fury, Letty smiled sweetly.

'We *could* still share it,' she suggested evenly. 'The three of us. You come over to run it one week, Lucy the next, me the next, and so on. We'd share the profits equally, so long as we each work a week.'

Just as she'd expected, Vinny looked as though she'd been hit with a brick.

'I couldn't do that! I couldn't leave the boys. They have to go to school. I have to be here when they come home.'

'You've got someone who looks after them sometimes, haven't you?'

The shock hadn't left Vinny's face. 'Not on a permanent basis. I couldn't leave them a whole week at a time every three weeks.'

Letty, knowing a similar excuse would be issued by Lucy, almost laughed. Except that the laugh would have been acrid with contempt. The shop was hers. Would remain hers. It had been done legally with a proper solicitor and everything. And if Dad or anyone tried to get funny, she'd fight it into court.

She vowed with renewed energy after Vinny left that she'd make it pay if it killed her. Would do what she'd always dreamed of – move to her own shop in the West End. That would show them! And then, when she was rich enough, she would demand Christopher back.

The next few months were busy ones for Letty, trying to put her plans into action. Out went the rubbish she'd lived with so long, most of it put up in the top room out of the way. She shopped around with care for good objets d'art to replace it. With an eye to what the well off would buy, she searched wisely, bargained sensibly and thriftily, arranged what she bought to look more presentable than it really was, everything at modest prices. She put a large sign on the door and in the window: Treasures to Cherish.

By the New Year she had thought of a name for her new shop if the day ever came when she could afford it: The Treasure Chest. Her hopes began slowly to grow. A brave new world, a post-war boom, most men in work – after four years' slaughter there weren't enough of them to go round.

By now Letty was accustomed to being on her own, managing her own affairs. She felt she did it very well. With Club Row always crowded on Sunday mornings, her shop had become more busy. Paying Dad his rent on the dot, it had begun showing more profit than she had at first hoped and her dream of branching out looked more like becoming reality some day.

Then with the spring of 1921, suddenly the Treasury coffers were revealed to be empty. Two million thrown out of work as summer came, their dreams of a land fit for heroes diminishing fast, Letty's dreams of success faded along with them as her till fell unnervingly quiet.

'I don't understand politics,' Letty complained to Billy. She saw a lot of him, spending most of her evenings with him and his family.

'How can things go so quickly from being rosy to

everyone being out of work?' she asked, looking towards his father for an answer.

Mr Beans drew reflectively on a cigarette; he would have chain smoked but that too much smoke in the room tended to affect Billy's chest.

'The economy,' he said sagaciously, his cockney richer even than Billy's, ''an' strikes. Them that's still in work. Wantin' 'igher wages an' shorter hours, an' sod everyone else! A bloody daft government – that Lloyd George and 'is National Insurance Act. Wiv less comin' in from National Insurance because so many's aht of work, it's costin' the government even more!'

Letty, more interested in her own problems than politics – she'd have to be thirty to vote – saw her own hopes going down the drain.

'Scrimping and scraping fer me future,' she told Billy later as they took a slow stroll in the summer sunshine. They never went very far, because of Billy's health. 'The shop's just one up-hill struggle, with nothing to show for it in the end. And I had such high hopes earlier this year!' Strange how things could change between last December and now. All her clothes came secondhand from The Lane – Petticoat Lane as the Wentworth Street Market was known. She saved on food, and now no longer went to the pictures as she used to with Ethel Bock. Anyway Ethel Bock was now Ethel Baker – had married in April – with a baby on the way and Letty saw little of her.

'The only ones doing any good are pawnbrokers,'

she scoffed. It wasn't nice to think that she was a single step from that trade; that were she to lower her principles, she'd thrive.

'I ain't out ter make money on other people's troubles like that,' she said firmly, her cockney surfacing as always in Billy's company. 'I wouldn't want ter score off other poor devils, just ter make money.'

The fine porcelain she had spent out on, the bright ormolu and highly polished furniture had gradually crept to the rear of the shop, giving way to more ready sellers: sturdy crockery, second hand dinner services, chipped at the edges, serviceable brown tea pots, jugs, slop basins, heavy glass sugar bowls – the stuff Dad always used to make his money on. Letty was well aware that she had fallen into the same trap as he had.

'I don't know why I bother,' she told Billy. 'Certainly not for Christopher, because sometimes I think I'll never get him back. He'll soon be six.'

He knew about Christopher. She had told him some time ago how David had been killed in Gallipoli, and how she'd been made to feel the shame of her condition, her child taken from her for his own good when she'd been too weak to resist. Afterwards, it had been too late to get him back. Billy hadn't made any comment, just nodded understandingly.

Letty sat with Billy in the parlour over his father's shop. The room redolent of steak and kidney pudding from dinner time, was bright with an early evening May sun. She had been seeing a lot more of Billy this past year, these days confided in him much more. She confided in him now – about Christopher.

She sat on the sofa as usual. Billy, in the armchair by the window, wore a grey flannel jacket and a brown and fawn Fair Isle pullover in spite of the sun's slanting warmth. He hadn't improved as much this year as last. It had been a bad winter for him and he hadn't properly recovered. His illness was like that – one season good, the next bad.

'Time for me to get Christopher back,' she said. 'Hard to believe he'll be seven this August. If I ever do, he'll be old enough not to want to leave me sister. Won't be doing him any favours, will I, telling 'im about himself? He'll probably hate me. Not as if I was married. I don't suppose I'll ever be that. Too many surplus women younger than me won't find husbands, with so many gone in the war. It would have been nice to have been married, though.'

'It ain't too late,' he said, so quietly that she didn't at first catch what he'd said but went on thinking of what might have been, how a life could be so wasted and not through anyone's fault. Perhaps Dad's fault in the beginning, but not now. Time had dulled the pain anyway.

She felt only sadness for Dad now. At nearly sixty-three, he wasn't the man he'd once been. In the pub every night, drinking away the rent money with Ada's help. She was a dirty old drab; her brother's nice house a tip now. Letty had been there once. Never again. She thought sadly of the dad she'd known as a child – the fastidious dreamer, the collector of beautiful things.

She still had his paintings on the wall, those lovelorn maidens with the sea foaming about their loins, the wallpaper behind them lighter than the rest of the room. Still had a lot of Dad's treasures up in the top room too. Poor Dad. He didn't care any more.

It wouldn't have hurt Vinny or Lucy to see him more often. Perhaps she should have made more of an effort, but it was hard to forget how different her life could have been if he'd been kinder to David . . .

She broke off abruptly from her reverie, looking at Billy.

'Sorry, what was that you said?' she asked quickly.

'Oh, . . . nothin' much.' He smiled at her, his breathing laboured.

Now she felt guilty. 'No, what was it? Tell me!'

'I said it ain't too late. I do remember you once sayin' yer wondered what yer was doin' it all for. Why not do it for yerself?'

'Myself?' she queried, lips twisting into a sneer. 'What a laugh!'

'Fer me then?'

Letty stared at him and saw him shrug, grinning self-consciously, suddenly embarrassed.

'Just a thought,' he said quietly.

Letty felt emotion rise inside her, making her want to cry. There was no nicer person than Billy. He hadn't deserved what he'd got and she was so very fond of him. But had she heard him right? Surely he hadn't been trying to propose?

She dropped her eyes, fiddling with the frill of her dress, a sky blue one she'd bought in a proper shop. She might not care for dressing up these days, but one thing she always did when going to see Billy was to dress nicely, brush her bobbed auburn hair until it shone like finely polished mahogany, put on a dab of Californian Poppy and a bit of pink lipstick. Why this compulsion to look good for him, she wasn't sure – just that she felt she had to.

Billy's grin had faded when she looked up again. His bright blue eyes, wide and honest and unsmiling, were fixed on her. He seemed eager yet fearful.

'Let, I know I ain't much of a catch, but I wouldn't be a burden to yer. I won't be offended if yer say no. I expect yer to really. But I just 'ave ter ask, just this once. If yer say no, I won't ever ask yer again.'

She didn't know what to say now; what to think. She *was* fond of him – but to marry him, if that's what he was asking . . .

'I've always loved yer,' he said, speaking fast. 'From years back. But yer looked as if yer never 'ad eyes fer me, an' when yer started goin' out wiv

334

that bloke – 'e was such a toff, I fought, well, she's got a decent one, an' I couldn't 'ave 'alfway given yer what 'e could. So I backed off.'

He gave a dry chuckle. 'Never did get meself a steady gel after that. I suppose none of 'em ever came up ter you in me estimation. But now, when p'raps I could 'ave yer fer me own, the war goes an' 'ands me this bloody dose of crap in me lungs! I can't even 'elp me dad lift a couple of boxes of soapflakes wivout coughin' me lungs up and bein' as out of breaf as if I'd been running a thousand yards race. Me, what was strong as an ox before I went into the bloody army . . .'

He stopped suddenly, realising he'd been going off the track, giving her no chance to get a word in. He shook his head in confusion.

'What I've bin tryin' ter say, Let, is I'm not askin' yer ter fall in love wiv me. That's too much to expect. But a sort of partnership. What they call a marriage of convenience. But yer can say no.'

At last, Letty found her voice.

'Oh, Billy, I can't.'

There were visions of David running through her head as though he were still there, still alive. For an instant it was as if she was betraying him by even listening to what Billy was saying.

It was like a dart going through her to see the eagerness disappear and be replaced by a bleak but stoic expression.

'Just thought I'd ask – get it off me chest.'

He said it so simply that thoughts of David fled.

'Oh, Billy, I didn't mean to say that. I mean, I'll . . .'

There was more to accepting than just saying yes. So much to be explained, to be understood, by him and by her. She felt such affection for Billy, such a tenderness, but it wasn't love – not the sort she'd known. It would never be like that. There was only one love of that sort and it was unfair to accept him as second best. She'd have to explain.

'How could you think of taking me on, after . . .'

'How could I take *you* on?' His laugh was self-deprecating. 'Good God, Let! I've been scared stiff all this time 'ow yer could dream of takin' *me* on! In my state of 'ealth!'

But he was grinning all over his face, suddenly exhilarated, and with a small shock Letty realised he was assuming she'd accepted, that she'd said yes.

She hadn't said yes at all, but how could she say she hadn't? How could she hurt him like that? She sat there, wondering how all this had happened as Billy went on, his face positively shining, telling her how she'd be able to get back her son, legal like; that her sister couldn't stop her having back once she was married.

Within minutes, the hope Letty had clung to all these years seemed to be within her grasp. She felt a fleeting sadness for Vinny, soon to know the agony that she herself had seven years ago, suffering every day of her life since then. But she recalled that Vinny hadn't turned a hair at inflicting that agony upon her, and brushed aside her sadness for her sister.

'But is that possible? I could get him back, just like that?' She had been leaning forward eagerly. Now she quickly stood up and strode about the room, turning back to him suddenly.

'She couldn't use the law to stop me, could she?'

Billy was grinning from ear to ear. ''E's yours. If yer want 'im back, she'd 'ave no say in the matter. Not once yer married.'

'What if she won't give 'im back?' Fear consumed her.

If it had been possible, Billy's grin would have grown still wider.

'She'd 'ave ter. She couldn't refuse. She never legally adopted 'im as I recall you sayin'!'

Yes, she did recall saying that – quite some while ago. Letty was on her knees beside his chair, gazing up at him. 'No, she couldn't, could she? Oh, it'll be wonderful to have him back!'

There came the slow realisation that this was being discussed as if the marriage had already been arranged: that without her actually having said yes, she had consented to marry Billy.

CHAPTER 19

They were married on 7 December, a Thursday – early closing. Letty didn't expect her marriage to be a grand or romantic occasion. Not the way it would have been with David.

Billy had treated her with tenderness on their first night; had told her he loved her but didn't make love to her. Did she mind? He asked, then told her of his terror of reducing it to a mockery by dissolving into a fit of ludicrous coughing. He asked her forgiveness with such dignity that Letty gave it readily, feeling strangely fulfilled, spiritually if not physically, accepting that they shared a gentle caring love that was without lust or selfishness.

Her respect for Billy rose even higher the next morning as she lay beside him in their new double bed, over her shop, their own furniture around them. Then he told her in quiet tones that his father had recently been diagnosed by the doctor as having a touch of heart trouble.

'Oh, 'e's all right,' he said, staring up at the ceiling from his pillow as Letty murmured her concern at the news. 'But 'e's bin a bit under the weather for a while lately. 'Im and me mum talked it over and they decided that this year they'll sell the shop, get themselves a little retirement place. I didn't tell yer when I asked yer ter marry me, Let.'

He turned towards her, propping his head up on one arm, his vivid blue eyes taking her in.

'What I didn't tell yer was . . . they made a decision ter take only half of what they get from selling. They said it'll be enough ter see them out. The rest they're givin' ter me. That's what I didn't tell yer – in case yer fought I was bribing yer inter marryin' me. That's what I meant when I made reference ter a marriage of convenience. I could see by yer expression yer fought I was bein' funny. An' then I fought yer wouldn't take me in marriage because I might assume yer was after me money . . .'

'Oh, Billy!' Letty burst out, but he gave a quiet chuckle, one that set him off coughing. He managed to regain control of himself, returned to being serious again.

'I wouldn't have wanted ter embarrass yer, so I didn't say nothin'. But now I'm tellin' yer, Let. My intention is ter put that money towards what yer've always wanted – yer shop up West.'

Letty sat upright in shock. 'Oh, Billy – I couldn't! I couldn't take your money.'

'Of course yer can. What's the point of me 'avin' it if it can't be of 'elp ter yer in gettin' yer dearest wish? It's what I married her for. Ter make her 'appy.'

'But I wouldn't take . . .'

'I know yer wouldn't.' He sat up now, putting an arm about her and drawing her close. 'But I want yer to. Mind you, it'll be a few more months yet, yer know. But come summer, yer can start lookin' fer yer premises. I'll be a lot better then an' can 'elp a bit.'

'What d'you mean, a lot better?' Letty queried, pulling away. 'Anyone'd think you was ill.'

This time Billy's chuckle was bitter. 'We ain't reached the 'ard part of winter yet. Yer know what it does to me, Let. The worse months is yet ter come. I wonder at yer takin' me on like yer did, Let, wivout questioning what yer was in for. I wonder at meself fer lettin' yer. Lovin' yer made me selfish. You was a proper nurse ter yer dad what was always very bronchial – a proper 'andful as I recall, yer sayin' many a time. I reasoned that if I made a point of never moanin' yer'd find me less of an 'andful. But I shouldn't have asked yer ter take me on, Let. Even though I love yer.'

'Oh, you are a chump, Billy!' she cried, throwing her arms about him. 'All these years we've known each other. I'd have married you years ago if you'd persisted. Except that when . . .'

She let the words fade away, not wanting to think of the past, of David, which would have made her nostalgic and spoiled this morning. The past ought not to be dwelled on and worried at like a sore place not allowed to heal.

'I know,' she heard Billy say in a low voice.

'You don't know at all, Billy Beans!' she blurted, her mind searching for some alternative excuse. 'If you must know, it was your name. I'd have let you propose to me years ago if . . .'

'My name?' He was looking at her, puzzled, demanding an explanation. Letty gave in.

'I didn't fancy being called Letty Beans.'

For a moment longer he stared, then laughter exploded from him. She had to thump him before he would stop and the pair of them were in stitches.

It was a bad winter for Billy. Letty was kept on her feet looking after him. It was just like Dad's winter bronchitis, but Billy she nursed willingly, with love, respect and admiration that grew daily for the stoicism with which he behaved – with never a whine, never a cross word, more often than not with wry humour.

If she could come to love a man totally without once experiencing sexual fulfilment with him, Billy was that man. As March blew itself out and he began to gain ground, inch by inch, as an army determined on victory might, Letty knew she loved him with all her heart, that if anything should happen to him, she would be devastated, she spent the moments before dropping off to sleep in frantic prayer that he would live to a ripe old age, despite his gas-torn lungs.

'Fer you!' Pleased as punch, Billy watched Letty's expression change from surprise to delight as she came into the room.

'Lor, it's not me birthday! What on earth made you get that?'

She stared at the polished rosewood box, the turntable, the dark shiny disc ready for playing, the horn soaring above like a great wing.

'I fought yer wanted one. Yer did, didn't yer?'

'Oh, Billy – a gramophone!' she cried rapturously. 'Oh, it's lovely! You do think of some lovely things!'

He'd thought of something else too. 'Easter in a couple of weeks,' he said. 'Your boy breaks up from 'is school. Might be a good time fer us to ask fer 'im back.'

In the midst of her delight, a chill of foreboding clutched at Letty; a fear she'd always had lurking somewhere at the back of her mind, that to ask would be to ask in vain, that it was better not to rather than suffer failure and be destroyed by it. And now she was terrified.

'Better write to yer sister first,' Billy advised as she made to protest. 'It's not fair ter break it to 'er sudden. Best ter 'ave a word wiv a solicitor first, ter be sure of yer rights.'

She thanked God for Billy. She'd never have had the courage, would have been lost before she'd started. He was her strength. She would put it to Vinny delicately, of course, but she'd do it.

In the end there was no way to put it delicately as she stood in Vinny's living room, her body so taut she feared it would snap were she to move.

'He's mine, Vinny. I've explained it all. By law

you were only minding him until I was able to have him back. I was told that.'

She'd consulted a solicitor who'd told her with the air of one who considered she was wasting his time with so petty a matter that she could get her son back quite legally whenever she pleased. There had never been any formal adoption. Letty had not been able to bring herself to sign anything when Vinny had approached her about it some years ago, and Vinny had shelved the request for the time being. When Albert had been killed in France, she had forgotten it altogether in the shock of becoming a widow.

'*Loco Parentis*,' the solicitor had said in a weary tone. 'In place of a parent.' The small matter settled as far as he was concerned, he had charged Letty his fee – pretty hefty she thought for such a short appointment – promising she should have no legal problems whatsoever getting back her son. He'd said nothing about the emotional side.

'You must have known this could happen. You should have realised.'

It was awful to see Vinny's face so distraught, but Letty had prepared herself. She wondered if this was how she'd looked when Vinny had taken the baby from her, and with that thought hardened herself against those wide staring grey-green eyes.

Vinny only had herself to blame, had put the final nail in her coffin as mother to Christopher by not coming to Letty's wedding to Billy. Nor had she visited them since.

343

Vinny faced her now, desperately challenging.

'And what will you tell him? That he's illegitimate? That's really giving him a good start to living with you!'

'I shan't tell him anything as yet,' Letty said. 'Anyway, he'll learn from his birth certificate one day. You can't hide that. I'll tell him for the time being that he's coming to me as a sort of holiday.'

'My – that's rich, that is!'

Vinny, striding about her fine living room that smelled of lavender furniture polish and cigarette smoke, pretending she wasn't wringing her hands in anguish, turned on Letty.

'How long d'you think you can keep that up?' she asked, agitatedly lighting up yet another cigarette, far too distressed to bother with a holder. A cloud of scented smoke was blown through her pursed pallid lips as she exhaled sharply like someone trying to blow up a balloon.

'Sooner or later he's going to want to come back,' she said between nervous puffs. 'He'll want me – his mummy. For heaven's sake, the child's not yet eight years old. He's bound to want his mummy.'

'He'll have her,' Letty said, keeping calm with a great effort. 'Me.'

'You're going to tell him that, are you?' Vinny said with a terse and bitter laugh. 'Going to tell a nearly eight year old that his mummy isn't really his mummy – that his aunt is? Oh, yes, he'll swallow that won't he? You'll have him in tears. You'll end up with him ill, needing medicine from the doctor, to make him quiet. Oh, you're going to have a terrific time, Letty!'

The truth of what Vinny was saying began to make Letty unsure. But she clung on. Nothing, no one, was going to make her give up now.

'I'll take care of that when it comes,' she said. 'I can make him happy with me. He'll get used to being with me in time, and when I think the time's right, I'll explain things to him. I shall be all right, don't worry.'

'Oh, I'm not worrying,' said Vinny, who looked as if she might fall down on to the floor. 'I'm not worried at all.'

'Then if you'll kindly pack some things for him,' Letty said, all businesslike, seeing despair in her sister's face.

'I never realised just how cruel you can be, Letty.'

She smiled sweetly. 'As cruel as you were when you took him off my hands, and me too weak to do anything to stop you.'

'I did it for the best. What was best for him. And this is all the thanks I get.' Vinny, her voice almost a wail, stabbed her cigarette out in the glass ashtray on a fireside table and stood gazing down at the thin blue trail of smoke. But Letty wasn't done.

'You robbed me of the only thing I had left,' she said stonily.

Nothing, no amount of weeping and wailing, would pierce the armour she had built up over the years in preparation for just this moment. She needed to be as unemotional as possible so as not to be undermined by the terrible look Vinny directed at her – that hatred, that appeal for pity, that devastation. She wondered if she'd ever be able to forget the look on Vinny's face.

'And now I'm claiming him back,' Letty said, tonelessly.

Facing Vinny had been the easy part. Her predictions proved to be alarmingly correct.

'Will I be going back home soon, Aunt Letty?' Christopher had only been with her three days so far. His dark eyes so like David's, that they tugged at her heart, had gazed questioningly at her.

She had tried to smile. 'Don't you like it here with me and Uncle Billy?'

'Oh, yes. I'd like to see the zoo again, but . . .'

'Then I'll take you again tomorrow.'

Easter holidays finished next week. There were still so many explanations – why he would be going to a different school; why he was to remain with his Aunt Letty and not go home to 'Mummy'.

She could stall him, she was sure, but there would come a time when he became suspicious, resentful at being kept here. The fun of all the things there were to do in London would pall eventually. Then what?

Letty felt sick at the mere prospect. How was she going to combat his bewilderment, the tantrums when they came, perhaps even having to face final admission of defeat and allow him to go back? His happiness had to come before hers. What was her love worth if all it considered was her own selfish need?

There were other worries too. Her time nowadays was taken up with escorting him here and there, keeping his mind occupied, keeping him happy. The shop would go to pot even though Billy was ready to stand in for her.

'S'long as I don't lift nothin' too 'eavy, too quick,' he told her, laughing, shamed by the admission, 'it's no trouble ter me.'

It was painful to see how hard he fought not to be a burden. Cheerful even if she herself was down – her mood not always at its best in the morning – he inevitably managed to cheer her up with his crooked grin.

'That's what I like ter see,' he'd banter in the face of her scowls. 'An angel poppin' out of me bed first thing!'

How could she be grumpy with him? She'd put her fluctuating mood behind her, for his sake: his stoic disregard of his own pain, his ready grin, his wonderfully gentle consideration of her, working so hard to put her back on an even keel. Letty said prayers of thanks to the Almighty for Billy.

Three days of Christopher, an energetic child she discovered, used to boisterous brothers and feeling the loss of them for all they saw less of each other going to school, had already frayed her nerves; she wondered how on earth she was going to persuade him into a different school, rehearsed every other second how to break it to him.

Then at the end of his first week came a godsend in the form of the boy who'd come to live in the flat next-door some months ago.

Mr Solomons had retired the previous summer, he and his wife going to live with relatives elsewhere. The shop had lain empty for months, boarded up frontage stacked with itinerant market traders' bird cages. Eventually in November it was bought and turned into a pet shop that, as well as birds, sold mice, rabbits, kittens, puppies, even goldfish in glass tanks.

It was a source of fascination to Christopher – in fact, the whole Sunday market with its birdsong as well as the yapping of dogs and cooing of pigeons intrigued him. Pigeons had become popular with East End men with little to do but stand around in apathetic groups outside the labour exchanges, though things had improved a bit lately.

Pigeons obsessed Christopher from the first day.

'Can I have one?' he begged at the end of his first week.

'Let 'im 'ave one,' Billy said indulgently.

'Where are we going to keep it?' Letty asked, not daring to say no.

'Out back in the yard.'

The yard was a short expanse of concrete, divided from others just like it by a three-foot wall, each a refuse dump for the shop to which it belonged.

'We'd have to build a hutch of some sort,' Letty said.

'A loft.'

'A what?'

'It's a loft. An 'utch is fer rabbits. Yer need a pigeon loft.'

'You can't build one . . .'

She broke off, knowing she'd touched a sensitive spot, but Billy's grin didn't diminish though she knew he'd felt it.

'I'll ask me dad if 'e'd 'elp,' he said.

Mr Beans still seemed healthy enough despite his heart condition, and with the shop being taken over in a month's time by new owners, he did very little in it now. Yes of course he'd help Billy. Work was not a problem, worry was. A bit of activity such as woodwork didn't entail worry.

By Easter weekend Christopher had his pigeon loft and two pigeons to put in it. A book out of the library which Letty sat and read to him showed how to take care of them. Christopher was in raptures.

It was then he discovered Danny, while watching Grandfather Beans up the ladder securing the small slatted box with its perches and sleeping box to the wall several feet up on uprights to keep it out of reach of cats. The boy next-door dangled over the wall.

'Watchyer doin' mister?' When told he said, 'We've got pigeons. 'Omin' pigeons. Dad keeps 'em at me uncle's 'ouse over 'Ackney way. No room 'ere ter train 'omin' pigeons.' An authority on them, the boy next-door.

'I'm having mine as pets,' Christopher said readily.

'Mind the cats round 'ere don't 'ave 'em fer Sunday dinner,' said the boy. 'Wot's yer name?'

'Christopher Worth. I'm staying with my aunt. What's yours?'

'Danny Carter. Wanna see me mouse? Got it downstairs. Me dad gave it me.'

Over the low wall they hung, with heads together. From that moment sprang a friendship, so intense, so miraculous, Letty could hardly contain her joy. When St Nicholas's School resumed after the Easter holidays and Christopher discovered that his newfound friend went there, almost a new boy himself, he looked less keen to go home just yet to the clean Walthamstow air where older boys said swear words with nicer accents, tormenting the swift-growing Christopher as a skinny squit. Here he'd be described as 'skinny as a sparrer's kneecap', which Danny had already called him, and which seemed more preferable.

Letty jumped on the opportunity as it presented itself.

'Would you like to stay here for a while then?' she suggested. 'I can ask your . . . ask my sister to let you. You can go to school for a while here with Daniel. What do you think, Christopher?'

He nodded absently, his mind more on his friend's new mouse snuggling in his pocket, on temporary loan.

'He's really called Danny by his friends, and he

350

says I'm Chris 'cos Christopher's too long for anyone ter say.'

Letty noted the slip in speech, felt a little sad that some of the advantages of his upbringing were already in jeopardy, at the same time considering it a small sacrifice to win the love of her son one day.

CHAPTER 20

Letty spent the rest of her morning after the shopfitters had gone adding her own little touches. When she had done all she could for the time being, pangs of nervous hunger prompting thoughts of getting home, she let herself out, locked the door behind her with an air of satisfaction, and returned the key to her handbag.

A scruffy handbag for one who'd just taken a lease on Oxford Street premises! Her clothes could have been more fashionable too – serviceable plain green autumn coat and brown tam-o'shanter. Not what you'd call the height of fashion. That would come later, would have to if she wanted to show herself off as proprietress of this place. Until then, money wasn't to be wasted on high fashion; not after taking on such an exorbitant lease.

The money Billy's parents had given him would help, but for how long if profits didn't justify the rent of the place? It was taking a heck of a gamble branching out into the West End like this.

Letty still felt guilty at taking Billy's money, even though he'd said it was as much hers as his. She felt more guilty because he hadn't wanted a penny

352

for himself. But she'd dreamed of this moment for so long that when these premises came up she couldn't help but yield to his urging, and Billy had been genuinely delighted for her.

Even so, she had still to stock the place with what the better class of shopper was looking for. No money from Dad's shop, of course. It was his and he wanted to keep it, to continue living on the rent it would bring in. She couldn't blame him for that, though she had hoped he might have offered his daughter some help.

There had been his pictures though – his two lovelorn maidens. She could keep them, he'd said, for old time's sake. But a need for cash overriding sentiment, Letty found herself offered fifty pounds each for them by an art dealer who claimed there was no interest in Victorian art. No interest – at fifty pounds each! She took them to another art dealer and got half as much again, enough to pay for the décor, lighting and furnishing of her new premises.

There still remained the need to stock the place. Full of optimism, she'd secured a loan from the bank, repayable at four per cent per annum. How it would be repaid if her shop didn't realise her hopes, heaven only knew, but Letty's optimism knew no bounds. Last November's elections had given the Conservatives a clear victory, Lloyd George abandoned for Bonar Law. Groups of young boys had paraded the streets prior to the results, chanting 'Vote! Vote! Vote for Bonar Law.

Punch ole Lloyd George in the eye . . .' People were more hopeful for the future than they'd been since 1921. Parliament had its first ever woman MP, so why shouldn't a woman like Letty Beans make a fist of her own venture?

Snapping shut her handbag, she walked briskly off along Oxford Street, head erect, carriage upright, exactly as her mother's had been at thirty-three, unaware how like Mabel she was, strong-minded and proud.

At Tottenham Court Road bus stop she caught a number 22 back to Shoreditch. It ought to have been a taxi the way she felt, but until she'd made some money in this new, almost crazy, venture a bus home was good enough.

She sat on her seat, taking in the other passengers, exhilarated. She kept thinking, What if they knew I have a gallery in Oxford Street? Mustn't say shop. Narrow enough to be called a gallery. At least she hoped it would be worthy of that title. It *was* a crazy undertaking. But if she hadn't done it now, she never would have.

'Now it's done out, it's smaller than I'd have liked,' she said when she and Billy and Christopher went back in the afternoon.

Her speech had improved since Christopher had come to live with them. It was for his benefit as much as her own; if she set a good example he might not lose that nice way he'd had of speaking.

'But it does have an attractive display window,' she went on.

The window consisted of small square panes surrounded by highly polished dark wood frames, the door very much the same design.

They stood gazing around. The interior décor of a tasteful Wedgewood blue with a touch of oatmeal gave a feeling of tranquillity, Letty said. Glass shelving to throw back the new electric lighting. The floor was carpeted in a darker blue.

All her life Letty's feet had touched unyielding linoleum. Ironic to think that this shop was far cosier than the flat she lived in.

'It's got a very select look about it, don't you think?'

Billy readily agreed. Christopher stood saying nothing, his narrow face sullen.

'True the premises either side are small,' Letty continued, trying not to look at her son. 'But that adds to the charm, don't you think? Small things and places look expensive.'

Billy was being entirely supportive, but Chris – as she now called him, like his school chums did – clung to his sullen and withdrawn expression, showing no interest. Tall for eight years, even after eighteen months with her, he was still reproachful, had not forgiven her.

She'd been forced to explain everything to him much sooner than she'd really wanted to in the face of his fretting for Vinny. She had thought he would understand; had thought that because he was her and David's son, he would feel about it the way she did. He hadn't.

Looking back on it, Letty hoped she'd never have another experience like it, felt sick every time she thought about it.

'I don't believe you!' he'd yelled at her. 'You're telling lies! I know who my mother is, I want to go back home!'

How she persuaded him that she wasn't telling lies, that she was his mother, she could hardly recall, but somehow she managed to tell him about David, about her shame, about how he'd been taken from her and brought up by her sister.

Chris had gone into himself after that, grew silent and brooding, sat for hours on his own, spoke only when compelled to, and then only the tersest of replies. But he didn't ask again to go back to Vinny. As the months progressed he did seem to say more, but there was no spontaneity in anything he said, except when he was with his friends in the street. It hurt Letty to see him so natural with them and so stiff and formal with her.

His school reports had been disastrous every term, his teachers demanding to see her over him. She had spoken with Chris about it, had tried to be philosophical and patient. He had listened silently, his eyes dull, his obedience a barrier she couldn't pierce.

His features were narrow like David's had been, so heartrendingly handsome. It raked her soul to see them so sullen, so unforgiving. Letty wasn't sure he'd truly understood the real significance of what she'd told him, but to discover that she and not Vinny was his mother had thrown him into confusion. Letty knew how hard it must be for him. She was painfully aware that he still used all sorts of means to avoid having to call her 'Mum' or 'Mother'.

'It'll be a great asset,' she went on purposefully. 'Having nice premises each side of us like this.'

One sold rather expensive gowns – nothing under five pounds a go. The other was a book shop. She hoped some of their air of graciousness would rub off on hers, bring in people with money to spend.

'Lucky we came across it when we did,' she said to Billy as they came away, reluctant to leave. 'October's just perfect to open up. I mean, Christmas round the corner. People with money will be looking for good quality gifts at not too exorbitant prices. But not so inexpensive that they'll walk on with their noses in the air.'

She went on talking too fast, far too much, as they made their way to the bus stop. Excited, yes, but she always spoke too much these days when Chris was present, trying to fill in every second of those long silences he seemed to specialise in.

'Yes, October's definitely the right time to start,' she said, her voice firm and decisive, as they walked slowly for Billy's benefit.

It took another week to open. In a new green wool tunic dress, straight and simple with a low belt and a hem of fashionable length, just below the knees, Letty stood ready to open at nine o'clock on Monday, having spent nearly her whole weekend there, leaving Billy at home as his chest was beginning to play him up again.

The October mist took longer to lift each morning as the last week of the month passed, heavy and smelly with coal smoke, tending to yellowness. Billy's chest was already suffering and his breathing wasn't at all good, his cough beginning to carry the wet rumble she dreaded to hear.

At the back of Letty's mind was the problem of nursing him as well as going all the way to Oxford Street each day. It had been all right when she'd merely gone downstairs to the old shop. She hadn't expected to be able to do that with the new shop – not in an area like Oxford Street where rents could be as high as rent on several houses put together in the East End. It was going to be hard work looking after this place and Billy. Her only consolation was that as much as Chris appeared to shun her, he was totally under Billy's spell. But Chris didn't have anything against *him*, did he? And Billy was the kind of person everyone could get on with, ill as he was.

At thirty-six Billy was looking far older than he should, lines radiating around his mouth, across his brow; his cheeks hollow, no longer full and firm, though his good humour was undiminished.

Last year he had shaved off his moustache. 'Gives a more up-to-the-minute image,' he'd said, grinning, but Letty suspected his aim had been to try and make himself look younger. If that was so, it

358

hadn't worked, only revealed the lines of suffering his moustache had hither-to concealed. 'I don't like you without your moustache,' she had told him, but though he said he'd grow it again, he hadn't.

Turning her mind back to the job in hand, wishing Billy had been well enough to be with her to enjoy this first day, she took a last look round before she went to turn the CLOSED sign to OPEN.

All around her were the results of all that scrimping and scraping. The fact that her shop wasn't cluttered with stock was because she couldn't have quality *and* quantity, and so plumped for quality.

Four glass shelves, one above the other, along one pale blue wall held half a dozen – no more – fine opaline glass vases, subtle shades varying from pink through to blue, green to grey. On other shelves were cheaper versions (she couldn't yet afford the real thing) of Gallé glassware, heavy Marinot, Tiffany type, the iridescent hues not as deep or as rich in variation as the original, but good nevertheless.

There was glass and crystal from Austria, Sweden, Germany, Italy. Other shorter shelves held sculptures of animals in softly glowing alabaster, smooth ivory, carved ebony, tinted marbles; willowy figurines in porcelain and silvery metal.

A girl in bronze, arms outstretched, balanced delicately on one leg on a white marble pedestal, the other leg high up behind her, her dress billowed in an unseen breeze. On a suspended shelf were displayed a small jade Buddha and a lacquered chest, beneath it some ivory cats. One long low shelf held fine china.

Letty regarded it all thoughtfully. Was there time to rearrange it to look even better? It certainly looked very tasteful, the electric chandelier she'd invested in making everything glitter. She hadn't lost the gift of displaying things to their best advantage and today she had the satisfaction of knowing her stock did her credit, not the other way around.

No more thick crockery tea sets or dinner services, scratched tables and chipped vases. Now she offered Worcester and Derby and Chelsea, a little delicate Dresden and some Copenhagen. She had decided against going in for furniture of any sort. With so little room, it was better to have none at all than spoil the effect with one isolated piece that would detract from what she was trying to achieve.

She had, however, stretched to pictures. Not many, but all modern originals – expressionistic, abstract, geometrical; some art photography, stark and striking, not everyone's cup of tea, but Letty's business sense told her they would sell, were what the fashionable and well off wanted. None of them were by well-known artists, of course. But one day . . . one day when she had a proper art gallery . . .

One dream had been fulfilled; another was blossoming within her. Letty's eyes were already on the future, and she hadn't even opened the door to her first customer yet!

Tired but hopeful, she went and opened up for her first day in Oxford Street, wishing she had some champagne to drink in celebration and someone to drink it with; she thought then of Billy at home, a pang of fear for him submerging some of her joy.

'You wouldn't believe how wonderful it is to have you here, my dear.' Vinny's eyes feasted themselves on Christopher. She'd been overcome seeing him standing on her doorstep this Tuesday afternoon, had drawn him into the house, folded her arms around him in the ecstasy of reunion. In concern too – a nine year old coming all this way alone.

She had told him so several times already, still caught up in the marvellous shock of seeing him. 'They'll be wondering where you are.'

'No, they won't.' Chris sat drinking lemonade while his aunt sipped tea, gazing about the sunny room he had once known – every corner, every stick of furniture once taken for granted. It looked so strange now, unfamiliar, yet little had been altered, except perhaps for different wallpaper and curtains. 'I said I was going to the park and I would be 'ome five o'clock.'

Vinny winced at the tinge of cockney. 'So long since you were here. It's been two years, Christopher. I still miss you so very much.'

He brought his eyes back to the person he'd

once called 'Mum', wanting suddenly to burst into tears, but boys of nine didn't do that. All his mates at home would laugh at him.

Calling it home, was he? The streets he'd played in these last two years. Soon they wouldn't be home either. After the summer holidays they were moving out of Club Row. It seemed the shop in Oxford Street had done so well, they were to move into the flat above it. 'All or nothing' his mother had said. Three rooms and a kitchen, with high ceilings and wide Victorian doors but nowhere to play. He'd be going to a new school nearby, saying goodbye to Danny, the boy next-door, to the schoolmates he'd become used to. Change, nothing but change.

He wished he was back here where life had been orderly, where there was space to play – a long garden, the woods. He'd played in those woods with his brothers . . . he must call them cousins now . . . Albert and George and Arthur. Though probably they wouldn't play with him any more if he *was* here now. They were pretty well grown up. Albert at fifteen was going on to college soon. The other two were at high school. To them he was still a kid, although he was tall for his age, tall and skinny. Christopher swallowed hard.

'I mustn't stay long,' he mumbled into his glass, his voice echoing into it. 'Them not knowing I'm here.'

He'd said he and a mate were going to Victoria Park for the day. It was a gorgeous August day and he'd been given cheese sandwiches in a paper bag, an apple and a bottle of fizz, and warned to behave himself.

He had felt very deceitful going off like that using two shillings from his savings box to pay for the bus fare to Walthamstow where Aunt Vinny lived. He had planned for months, to sneak over here and have it out with her – the one he used to call Mum and must now call Aunt Vinny – why she had allowed him to be taken away and made to feel so confused.

Grown ups were so two-faced and underhanded. He hated their lies and double dealings. If he did something underhand or lied, he'd be in hot water before you could say Jack Robinson. Grown ups weren't nice, except perhaps for Billy. Chris called him that. He'd said to do so, being a mere stepfather. Chris liked and respected him for that.

'But you must stay for something to eat,' Vinny pressed him.

She gnawed anxiously at her lower lip, her mind on how she could entice him to stay longer, stay the night. Perhaps two nights. She had a Women's Institute meeting tonight, but she could soon cancel it.

'I'll get in touch with your . . . your mother. Explain to her . . .'

'No, don't do that!' Chris hurriedly put down his glass and got to his feet. 'She mustn't know I'm here. She thinks I went over to the park for the day. I've got to be back by five. I don't want her ever to know I've been here.'

Vinny put her cup and saucer back on the small white-clothed table.

'Then why *did* you come?'

'Because I wanted to know if you really did love me?'

Tears began to gather in Vinny's eyes. She saw the boy mistily – the narrow face, the dark hair. The sensitive mouth swam before her.

'Of course I loved you, Christopher.'

'Even though you weren't really my mum?'

'I loved you as though you were my very own.'

Chris stood very still. 'Then why did you let me go?'

'I had no option, dear.' Quickly Vinny explained her oversight about the adoption formalities, how they hadn't seemed all that urgent, how after her husband was killed in the war, she forgot in her grief to do the things she ought to have done. Then it was too late. His real mother had married – to that awful cockney Billy Beans, and the man so sickly! No doubt she'd only married him to get her son back, though how she could stoop so low to gain what she wanted . . .

Vinny's face began to twist as she spoke, eyes narrowing with venom, lips beginning to work.

'I mean, who'd want to marry a type like that out of choice? With his "finks" and his "foughts" and his "ahts" and "abarts"? The lowest of the low!'

'He ain't low, Aunty Vinny!' Chris burst out in defence of the man who had stolen his affection. 'He's the nicest . . .'

'There, you see?' Vinny gazed up at him. '"He ain't". Is that the way for a young boy to speak who once went to a good school?'

Chris ignored that. 'You mustn't talk about him like that, I . . .'

He was about to say 'I love him', stopped himself in time. It would have sounded disloyal, though to whom he wasn't sure. But Aunt Vinny wasn't listening.

'And your mother's no better than she ought to be! Carrying on like she did, then getting all upset because she got herself into trouble.'

Vinny retrieved her cup, took a swift sip of the cold dregs, hardly pausing before she ploughed on: 'Anyone would have thought it was our fault . . . my fault. The way she went off at me. And me offering to take you off her hands so she wouldn't have to face the shame of it! She had none of the trouble, the problems I had bringing you up. Kept awake half the night with your crying, trying to feed you with a bottle, and me half dead from lack of sleep. And then when you're growing up, along she comes. Wants you back, after the hardest part of it has been done.'

The cup clattered abruptly back on to its saucer, the sharp sound assaulting Christopher's eardrums like a rifle shot.

'She didn't deserve my help, your mother,' Vinny said harshly. 'A trollop, that's what she is. That man – your nature father – heaven knows how many times they did . . . well, the things they did.

You wouldn't understand. But you were the result. And all I can say is, she never was any good. Oh, she was upset when he left her, but only because she didn't have him to marry her and make a decent woman of her. She was no better than a common tart!'

'That's not true!' Chris found his tongue at last. 'Don't say that about my mother!'

'Your mother?' Vinny looked at him in amazement. 'Did she have any part in bringing you up? No. I had all the hard work on my shoulders bringing you up. I'm more mother to you than she ever was, than she'll ever be . . .'

'Don't say that!' He was hopping from one foot to the other. 'You're not to say that about her! She cries. I've seen 'er. She talks to my dad when she's on her own and thinks no one else is listening, and talks to 'im as if he's there. And then she cries.'

Suddenly the need to protect Letty flooded over him. The quiet kind way she had treated him while he'd been with her. Her and Billy, being so nice to him. And here was Aunt Vinny who had behaved as a mother to him, with a mother's hard hand on his legs when he'd misbehaved, now telling him what a trial he had been to her. She wasn't his mother. Had never been his mother. And now she was making out his own mother was a horrid person. Well, he wasn't having that.

'She's my mother!' he yelled, making Vinny wince. 'She's my mother!' he shouted again, hardly realising he was making a declaration that would now bind him to Letty forever. 'And I won't let you talk about her like that. I've got to go home.'

'But you can't . . .' Vinny's cry was desperate as she stood up, her hand outstretched trying ineffectually to stop him, Christopher backing away.

'I've got to go. I won't tell Mum what you said about her.' It was the first time he had ever referred to her spontaneously as 'Mum'; he didn't even realise it then, but the pattern was at last established.

'Goodbye, Aunty Vinny,' he yelled, and turned from the cosy house he had once called home, the woman he had once known as his mother, out into the bright August sunshine, running the whole long way to the bus stop.

CHAPTER 21

The flat echoing to her footsteps across the boards, Letty paused a moment at the parlour door and looked back into the room. There were dents in the lino where the piano had stood. Mum used to play so nicely on it, the family gathered round to sing at Christmas and New Year and birthdays.

Dents too where the large, round, polished mahogany table had been, and the sofa with its sagging seat. That was where Dad's old armchair used to be, Dad sitting by the fire, suffering his three young daughters' bickering, his two boisterous sons pushing each other about. Terrible thing, the boys dying so young. Dad had never been the same after that, not in all these years.

And there was Mum's wooden-armed chair, the one she always claimed had given her a nice upright posture. There she'd sat, a duchess in her castle . . . Letty switched her eyes away and looked again into the empty room, the dents in the lino a record of her family, there for all time until someone chose to replace the linoleum with a different one.

She'd got rid of most of the stuff, sentimentality put firmly aside – the piano to Lucy, the sofa and Dad's old chair to a family along the road in need of a few sticks and too poor to buy any. The old Victorian ornaments had been bought up by a man with a stall.

Dad had the dining table and chairs. She had kept the photographs, her own ornaments and Mum's old chair. It would look a bit out of place in the new flat with its modern furniture, but that was just too bad. She would never part with Mum's old chair, not as long as she lived. Everything else had been sold to raise a bit more for the rent on the new flat.

In the kitchen the wall dresser stood empty; the deal table gone, the old gas oven and copper looked forlorn. The bedrooms were deserted, the age-darkened wallpaper showing pale rectangles where pictures had hung.

Nothing left of a home that once vibrated to the comings and goings of a family; its dramas, joy, sadness, its overcrowding, the slow emptying as her sisters married and left. Love too had gone eventually, and returned in part with her marriage to Billy but was never as it once had been. Where had the years flown?

Now it even smelled empty. Slowly Letty closed the door, her throat tight, and went down the stairs and out through the back into a dull September afternoon. The family had seldom if ever used the back door, usually going through the shop to get out. The shop belonged to someone else now. The flat would too, soon.

'Everythin' oright, ol' gel?' Billy stood waiting for her. His cheery voice put the smile back on her face, took the tightness from her throat. She looked at him with fond affection, feeling suddenly better.

'Fine,' she said brightly, turning her eyes to Chris, who was standing a little way off.

'You said goodbye to Danny?' she asked, and saw him nod dejectedly. 'We're not going to the other end of the earth,' she said brightly. 'You'll still be able to come back here to see him at weekends.'

Christopher nodded, giving her a little smile. He had changed. It was hard to believe he'd been so sullen until a few weeks ago; then, quite suddenly, he was easier to speak to, more ready to respond, though she didn't dare question what had occasioned the change.

'Yes, I will . . . Mum,' he said, the last a mumbled afterthought, but it was there, she was sure.

It was some seconds before it actually sank in, that he'd addressed her by name. She gave him another look, smiled again, and received one in return. In that instant, life became bliss for Letty. She needed nothing more to fulfil her beyond the fact that her son had smiled at her quite spontaneously and called her 'Mum'.

In just one year her shop started paying for itself. Never in her wildest dreams had Letty imagined she'd have paid back the money owed to the bank in that short time, plus interest, and still been able to afford the first floor flat above the shop – two bedrooms, bathroom, kitchen, and a huge living room with a lovely high ceiling, its long narrow windows overlooking busy Oxford Street.

Lucy came to inspect it, of course, breaking a year of silence, having sided with Vinny over Christopher. Vinny stayed away – had never forgiven Letty for taking the boy from her.

Dad and Ada came, warned her she was biting off more than she could chew, had tea and departed early. Dad at sixty-six was beginning to stoop; he walked heavily on a stick, already coughing in readiness for winter. With him and Billy the flat had resembled a sanitorium.

'I hope you'll come often,' Letty said as Dad and Ada left. She doubted they would.

With Christmas six weeks away, Letty had taken on an assistant. A widow in her thirties, Mrs Nelly Warnes had a quiet self-assurance that pleased the customers. Letty could leave the shop in her hands much of the time allowing herself the chance to see to Billy.

Thick yellow November fog muffled the sounds of the world outside. Car and omnibus headlights peered through it like myopic old men. Billy gone downhill lately, the smoke-laden air attacking his lungs in full force. It was a setback after a decent summer, but as Letty told herself, you can never have things too good for too long.

Now it was heartrending to see him propped up in bed by three or four pillows, discreetly covered spittoon at his side, each breath laboured, each cough racking his thin body. Letty was beginning to grow frightened about him and plagued Doctor Cavarolli, their new doctor, for reassurance. She worried every minute of the day she was downstairs, though smiling sweetly persuasively at her customers.

'You ain't . . . doin' yerself . . . no good neither,' said Billy between gasps for breath. 'Doin' two jobs at once. Yer mustn't overdo it.'

'And you mustn't talk so much,' Letty said as she straightened his pillows to make him more comfortable. 'I'm fine. I'm an old soldier at doing two jobs at once – three sometimes.'

She reminded him of when she had nursed Dad through winters like this ('And him still going strong at sixty-six, which goes to show,' she said significantly), *and* had held down their old shop *and* did all the housework, *and* without an assistant to help her in those days.

'So you stop worrying,' she said sternly, pouring his cough mixture.

The place was filled with Christmas shoppers. In back streets behind the glittering façade of London's affluent West End, and in the East End, there was still the grinding poverty of those with not enough to buy decent food, much less Christmas presents. But in Letty's shop the better off browsed, found a bargain and went away happy, even though she had raised her prices and her sights with confidence in her ability to sell.

Moving through the thriving gallery, she knew she was seen as a woman very much in control. Poised, tastefully dressed in the slim loose style of the day, she smiled pleasantly at the more opulent of her customers. It wasn't a façade – she really did feel confident; felt that life was settling down at last. Chris was no longer the sullen boy who had first come to live with her. He had settled well into his new school, and he now called her Mum, without reservation. Nor did it worry her that Vinny was still not speaking to her. According to Lucy, she had met a gentleman, a widower. Letty privately wished her luck and hoped it might rid her sister of some of her bitterness.

Above the jostling sea of heads, she watched the door opening and shutting, letting in even more people as well as the cold afternoon air. It was already dark at four o'clock. Letty thought with gratitude how crowds tended to attract crowds; that had the shop been empty no one would have ventured in. She hoped that nothing would get broken.

A tallish man with a fine pencil slim moustache, well dressed in an expensive topcoat and trilby – the type of customer she welcomed – was holding the door open for a handsome sharp-faced woman, no doubt his wife, in a fur coat and a fur-trimmed cloche hat. Letty noticed how bad-tempered the woman looked. Her eyes moved casually on, only to turn back instantly in shock and disbelief.

'Do you have any jade things?' A voice at her elbow forced Letty to switch her gaze to an elderly speaker, hardly seeing her for the thoughts racing through her head.

'Yes, certainly, madam. One of my assistants . . .' Already she was signalling to Violet, the temporary assistant, her own mind elsewhere.

The couple were inside the shop now, their backs to her, looking at the porcelain. For the next few minutes, while answering customers' enquiries and attending to their demands, Letty's eyes were on the couple, willing them to turn round. When at last they did, she felt dizzy. Take away the moustache and the man was the image of David.

He was beckoning to Mrs Warnes. Letty watched as he indicated a Sevres porcelain figurine, saw her assistant hurry away to get the box for it, return, and guide the couple through the throng towards the till beside which Letty stood.

She had already taken control of her emotions, annoyed that she had let herself get all breathless like some film-struck flapper over someone who merely reminded her of David. She forced her eyes down to the purchase and began writing the receipt 'One Sevres Figurine – Man with Hunting Dog'.

'What name?' she asked.

'D. R. Baron.'

The voice was deep and well-remembered.

Letty's pencil froze. She raised her eyes in disbelief. The face looking back at her held a similar expression of shock, deep brown eyes staring, brows drawn together above a long straight nose. It was David. He hadn't been killed. He was alive . . .

Letty's mouth had gone dry. She was vaguely aware of the woman looking impatiently at her, the silly person gaping at her husband instead of doing what she was supposed to. Coming quickly to her senses, Letty realised she must not betray herself. Hardly able to credit it wasn't overwork and worry over Billy that was playing tricks on her, she bent her head swiftly to the receipt she had been writing, trying to combat the tightness in her chest. It was like being suffocated.

When she looked up, David's expression had changed to a blank stare. He was married then. Letty saw the large diamond and the chased wedding ring on his haughty wife's finger – Letty herself was his past, was nothing more than an embarrassment. He needn't have feared, she wasn't about to humiliate him. Affecting serenity, she handed him his purchase and his receipt, nodded her thanks, and watched him go without appearing to.

At the door, his wife preceded him. David turned briefly, saw Letty otherwise occupied, making towards the rear of the shop, and went out, following his wife into the cold breezy December evening.

Fleeing to the little office behind the shop, Letty

did not see the desolate look he cast after her retreating figure. She hurried on up the carpeted stairs to the flat above with some vague notion of seeing how Billy was. If she tended to him, the suffocating feeling inside her chest might be forced away. It was a long time before she felt it recede.

Two days later the phone rang in the little office behind the shop. Letty answered it, trying to focus her mind on the fact that she must reorder. Stock was dwindling fast. Not having enough to meet demand, especially at this time of year, was as bad as a lack of demand. But it had been hard to think of anything but David these last two days.

Day and night, his face haunted her. The nights were worst. His face was older, of course – he would be forty-five now. Her heart groaned under the burden of re-awakened love, at the waste of it all, with nothing to be done about it now. All far too late.

She felt angry as well. With fate. With her own stupidity in believing his mother whose grieving voice had rung so sincere all that time ago; for not having made more enquiries, accepted what she had thought was the gospel truth. Her rage against the woman had robbed her of sleep and of the ability to work calmly. And she had been short-tempered with Billy for the first time ever.

Most of all she was bitter against David himself. Never to come seeking her, to have married and forgotten her! Coming face to face with her, his expression of dismay had betrayed him.

Damn him! How dare he awaken her heart when he had never bothered to look for her? Why should he come back now – just when her life had become orderly and contented? And then to look through her like that as if she was nothing. He didn't even know he had a son . . .

She lifted the telephone. 'Letitia Beans, The Treasure Chest.'

'Letitia?'

Letty caught her breath. Only one man other than Dad had ever called her by her full name.

'David?' She was hardly able to believe she was uttering his name after all these years. She made herself businesslike.

'Was your purchase to your satisfaction?'

'Letitia.' His voice sounded tight, strangled. 'I don't know what to say. I felt I'd been hit with a hammer when I saw you.'

Me too, she thought, but said: 'All these years, David. I was given to understand you'd been killed. Your mother said you had been and I believed her . . .'

She stopped in confusion. The line was quiet for a time, then he replied: 'She too was given to believe it. I was a prisoner of war but not listed for a long time.' With a lame attempt at humour, he added, 'I'm afraid the Turks weren't terribly efficient in that direction.'

There was another long pause, then, his voice

flat, all humour dissipated, he said: 'My mother told me that you had married.'

'Yes,' she began, then it dawned on her that there was something not quite right in what he had said.

'But she couldn't have known!' she cried. 'I wasn't married when I spoke to her in 1916. I never contacted her again.'

'But she said you *told* her you had married?' David sounded bewildered.

'I never did no such thing!' Letty cried hotly, forgetting her grammar. There was a time he'd have laughed at her for it. He didn't laugh now and nor was she ready for him to. 'She lied to you!'

'She must have misheard you.'

'She never misheard anything!' Letty blurted out. 'She knew what she was doing all right. She never thought I was good enough for you. Never wanted us to marry. Well, she's got her wish, hasn't she? It was a wicked thing to do, saying that to you . . .'

'Letitia,' he broke in sharply, 'my mother died two years ago.'

'Oh.' She should have bitten out her tongue. 'Oh, David – I'm sorry. I didn't know.'

'You weren't expected to.' His tone had become formal. 'I rang you because seeing you – the shock – I suppose you were shocked as well, imagining I was . . . I felt I should get in touch and apologise.'

She too became formal for all her heart ached. 'No need. But it was nice of you to ring me. Nice to know you're happy and settled now. Nice . . .' Stupid word! Letting her down. Showing her upbringing.

'Letitia.' Emotion trembled in his voice. 'To see you after all these years . . . I don't know how to say it. Letitia . . . I have to talk to you. Can I meet you somewhere?'

She heard herself saying, 'I don't think that would be right, do you, David? You and me – both of us married. No, I don't think so.'

But she did want to see him, wanted so desperately to see him, was suddenly asking where, agreeing as he gave the name of a restaurant in Oxford Circus not far away, limply agreeing to lunch tomorrow and replacing the telephone on its hook, not able to believe she was soon to see David again.

Bright with holly and Christmas baubles, the place was crowded. Half of London was unemployed and lived hand to mouth; the other half ate in cafes and restaurants like this at midday.

David had found a table in the far corner. Letty, with little appetite, ordered coffee and a Chelsea bun which she found herself unable to eat anyway. David had only coffee, also in no mood for eating. Around them all was chatter and clatter.

'Well then?' Letty asked as she stirred her coffee almost to lukewarm. 'What was it you wanted to see me for?'

He'd been there already when she came in. In a neat grey suit, his face drawn with anxiety that she would not turn up. His large dark eyes had brightened at her appearance. He'd risen, taken her hand while she sat down. She withdrew it quickly and the pair of them sat down opposite each other, David's expression apprehensive again.

He leaned forward now, hands on the table to either side of his cup.

'Letitia, darling . . .'

She stiffened. 'Look, David, I'm not your darling.'

'I'm sorry,' he said quickly, looking down into his cup. 'I just thought . . .'

'That you could pick up where you left off?' she finished for him, hating herself for saying it like that as he looked up sharply. But she ploughed on, pouring out her feelings.

'You took everything your mother said about me as gospel truth,' she said, refusing to spare him. 'But I'm telling you, she didn't misunderstand or mishear anything. She told you a pack of lies, David. Oh, I know she's dead. And I *am* sorry. But I've got to speak as I find. She lied to you, David. I loved you. I loved you all those years I thought you'd been killed. I've never stopped loving you. And I . . .'

She stopped herself, took a deep breath. He had to be told.

'I had a baby. Your baby. His name's Christopher. He's nine now.'

'Oh, Christ!' His face was white, his eyes tightly closed. 'She never told me that.'

'She didn't know.' Hate his mother though she had, Letty had to be fair. 'I never told your parents because I thought they might take him away from me. Then I'd have lost the only thing I had left of you.'

Quietly but resolutely she told him how Vinny had taken Chris and brought him up; she obdurately evaded David's interruptions, asking what his son was like, if he knew about his father, how he'd taken it, if he could see the boy? He must see him!

She went on doggedly, her coffee growing cold, seeing the pain behind his gaze as she told of how she had claimed her son back after so many years and eventually married Billy, a victim of gas during the war; how, married, she could better reclaim her son.

'He's a wonderful man – Billy,' she said. 'I owe a lot to him. I'm very fond on him.'

David looked worn. 'Fond?' he queried bleakly. 'Not in love with him then?'

'I don't know what you'd call love, David,' she said tonelessly. 'I don't know if love is what we had, or if it's the respect I feel for Billy. All I know is that he's been a wonderful husband to me and a good father to Christopher, despite being so ill. He never complains and does all he can to make things lighter for me. It's an honour to look after him.'

'You nurse both him and your father?' David questioned.

'No – Dad got married again. To Ada Hall who used to help in the flat. They live in Stratford now. I suppose that was another reason I married Billy. I was so lonely after Dad left.'

David was frowning at her in pitying amazement. 'Is that how he thanked you for all you sacrificed for him? He went off and left you on your own! And yet he stopped us time after time from marrying. Jesus Christ!'

'I was all right,' Letty said quickly. She didn't want his sympathy. 'I had the shop. When I married Billy, we pooled our resources and I bought the one we have now. I'm doing very well, thank you.'

'And I no longer figure in your life,' he said half to himself.

Letty wanted in that moment to cry: 'You do, David. Yes, you do!' But she held herself in check and saw his shoulders slump.

'Perhaps it's for the best,' she went on, needing to touch him, to know again what his skin felt like. 'Billy is a wonderful man and I respect him so very much.'

David was looking beyond her into the distance. 'I envy you. What I wouldn't give to be able to say the same of my marriage.'

It sounded so terribly bitter that Letty felt tears sting her eyes. She put out her hand then and touched his briefly.

'Oh, David, I didn't know,' she said, seeing him shrug.

'We tolerate each other,' he told her. 'We've no children. She's frightened of having any. I respected her wishes but that wasn't enough. Now she despises me. She never says so, but I can see it there in the way she looks at me. She considers me weak. Perhaps I am. I suppose I gave up after the war. All those years in captivity, then coming home, finding you . . . thinking you'd married, forgotten me. I felt let down. Angry. Hurt. God, I felt so bloody hurt! After all that – to come home and . . . There was this girl. My father had gone into partnership with her father. They have a large department store now in north London – Baron & Lampton's. You may have heard of it?'

Hardly waiting for her to shake her head, she having little to do with north London departmental stores, he went on, his fingers toying with the coffee spoon: 'They thought it might be an idea for me and their daughter to marry. Make the business more of a family concern. We married in 1920.'

He let his voice die away. Letty thought that, yes, she could see how the sharp-faced woman she'd met would regard him as weak. She forced her mind back to the day Lucy had first introduced David to her, when she had learned that he'd been married before. That marriage too had been arranged by his family rather than him. Letty recalled how she herself had fended him off time and time again because of her father – David resigned to it without any of the arguments and anger some men would have displayed. Only once had he been really angry. But instead of claiming her, he had gone away and enlisted.

It came to her that David had never really possessed a will of his own – at least not one he'd impose on others; he was by no means a weak character, merely easy going, vulnerable to the pressure exerted by others. It was monstrous that any woman could take advantage of that and with the realisation of her sympathy for him, Letty felt love for him again.

Her hand reached out, touched his, tightened on it. She felt love flow from her to him, saw him look up, saw his expression and knew that what had been between them had not died but merely lain dormant, was now reawakened beyond anyone's capacity to stem it.

For a moment Letty thought of Billy with an overwhelming sadness; she wanted to run away from here, run to him and comfort him with a sort of need to do penance. She could never desert him, but she also knew she would deceive him, unable to control herself as she held tightly to David's hand across the restaurant table.

CHAPTER 22

'Give me time,' she'd said. 'It's Christmas the day after tomorrow. I can't do anything – *think* of anything – until that's over. He'll need me over the holiday, perhaps for weeks to come. His chest's so bad in winter. I must give some time to him.'

January was almost over now and she'd heard nothing from David. She was on the edge and unable to sleep. She resisted the temptation to find his home telephone number; almost rang Baron & Lampton's, but hadn't the nerve to.

When at the end of January David rang her while she was in the office, her heart leapt and thumped so much she felt physically sick, having to breathe deeply to calm herself down.

'I thought I ought not to get in touch too soon,' he said, his voice clipped and rapid, though he tried to sound nonchalant. 'Do you think we could meet for lunch – same place as before?'

Her words tumbled out with equal haste. 'That'd be nice – yes, I suppose I could.'

'Saturday? This Saturday? Or if you like dinner in the evening? Whichever.'

'No,' she said, immediately alarmed. 'It had better be for lunch.'

An evening together – it was begging for trouble. That's what frightened her – the upheaval that seeing David again threatened. Her life in its safe little rut, just looking after Billy, a wall built high and strong around them. Frightening to realise how easily that wall was in danger of being breached. She didn't want to see any intrusion from the world beyond her own. The shop door closed, shutting outside the day's dealings, the curtains drawn, she and Billy could be safe together. No, she wanted nothing to invade her world. And yet . . .

'Lunch then,' he said. He didn't sound too disappointed. 'Say one-thirty – the same place as last time?'

Even this, as she agreed, was one step through the breach he had made. Could she, ought she, take another, then another, until on turning round she found the wall closed up behind her?

Christopher came in from school as she hurried upstairs and followed her into the flat.

'Been out, Mum?' His wide dark eyes scanned her. 'Gosh! You look jolly flushed. Sort of out of breath.'

His own face was bright from the biting January wind after coming just fifty yards from the bus stop at Tottenham Court Road. Cap askew, his satchel hanging haphazardly halfway down his arm, socks down his calves, knees rosy from the cold and hair all tousled, he was a typical schoolboy. Ten this year and he'd adjusted marvellously, hardly ever mentioning his years with Vinny who might as well have left the face of the earth for all he spoke of her – in fact, for all she ever contacted him or Letty.

'I've had a busy day,' she excused herself.

'How's Billy?' Chris's mind flitted from one thing to another with the randomness of a moth. In that he was like his Aunt Lucy.

'Not too well.' She was glad to talk of Billy. It made her feel more normal, stopped that sickening beating against her rib cage. 'The doctor will be in tomorrow to take another look at him. Not much can be done until the weather gets warmer and drier, though.'

'I think he must be jolly sick of staying indoors all the time,' said Chris as he dropped his satchel on to the striped moquette settee and clambered out of his coat and scarf. The blue blazer had small dark pear-shaped stains on the lapel. Letty leaped on them, glad of something domestic and safe to tune in to.

'Oh, look at that, Christopher!'

He drew in his chin, staring down his nose to where she'd indicated.

'It's ink.'

'I know it's ink. I'm going to have to try and get that out before tomorrow. Why are you so careless?'

'Wasn't me,' said Christopher. 'Anthony Lovett flicked his pen at me – the nib was full of ink. He did it on purpose.'

'You're all the same at that school – no regard for how much your uniforms cost. A poor family could feed itself for a week on what that blazer's worth.'

She stopped short, a little guilty at making the comparison as Chris hung his head sullenly. Letty altered her tone. 'I can't afford to keep buying new uniforms. Give it to me. I'll have to sponge it out right now.'

Sponging energetically, she tried not to think of Saturday. She hadn't told Chris about his father yet. He'd have to be told at some time, but that meant telling Billy who wasn't well enough for any shocks. A month or two more wouldn't hurt. In the meantime, she must keep David at bay. After all, she told herself as she dabbed at the uniform, one Saturday each month couldn't really hurt. What was so sinful anyway, about having lunch with a friend?

In fact David behaved like a perfect gentleman, speaking of his wife, Madge, and Letty of her life with Billy and Christopher. It was all quite innocent.

As February moved into March, Billy slowly improved though each passing winter debilitated him that bit more. He had grown so thin and haggard, Letty hardly recognised the young man she'd know in 1914; would have walked right by had she met him for the first time since then. Yet she knew every inch of his face. It was her job to shave him, wash and dress him, help him to the toilet, so weak had he become during the winter.

Dr Cavarolli said with doleful expression that there was little of his lungs that wasn't congested with fluid. She could almost see him mentally predicting the time Billy had left to him. Letty refused to acknowledge the gloomy prediction. Billy had years in him yet. Had to have. Life without him was unthinkable.

'You're lots better,' she told him one day when he was at last able to get to his chair by the living-room window.

'Till – next time.' He grinned. It was hard for him to maintain that old humour of his these days, yet he could still grin at her, making light of his breathlessness as he fell gratefully into the chair. 'God – I don't 'arf fancy – a cuppa! I'd make it – meself – but I wouldn't – want ter do you – out of the job.'

March slid into April, then May, June, David reluctantly bowing to her wish not to tell Christopher about him just yet though she could see how he longed to meet him. He honoured too her wish to keep their meetings to once a month, but in June insisted on dinner together, her birthday being the previous Monday, and refused to take no for an answer.

'Birthday treat,' he said, and as she finally agreed, 'I've tickets for the Wyndham Theatre afterwards.'

'Oh, no!' she hissed into the telephone mouthpiece, hoping no one would come into the office at that moment. 'That's going too far, David. I can't possibly. Where's it going to end? I'm making enough excuses now to Billy. I can't overdo it.'

All the signs were pointing to this relationship becoming too deep, despite her good intentions. She'd even declined his suggestion of a stroll in Hyde Park, the weather growing warm and heady.

'And there's your wife,' she reminded.

'I can handle her.'

He sounded so confident that for a moment there was a certain seediness to it all, to what was supposed to be lovely and romantic.

'Oh, I forgot,' she said haughtily, forgetting to lower her voice. 'She doesn't care where you are, so long as she's got her own friends and her bridge parties. Well, Billy's a different matter. He cares for me and he's so damned unsuspecting it makes me feel rotten. He thinks I'm attending business meetings, and I detest lying to him like this – he's so good-natured about my going and leaving him.'

'Darling, there's no harm to anyone,' David said hastily, but she couldn't subdue the feeling of deceitfulness that had come over her.

'I can't start telling him I'm going to even more meetings, and then stay out half the night. I can't! Not that he'd guess anything but I would know it was wrong. I'm already ashamed of what I'm doing to him. No, I can't come, David, I'm sorry.'

'Have you thought what it's doing to me?' he asked slowly after a long pause.

'I know, David,' she said bleakly. 'I'm sorry.'

He too sounded bleak. 'You're saying you'd rather not see me at all?'

'I didn't say that!' she cried, lowering her voice instantly to a whisper as Mrs Warnes looked up at the glass of the office window. 'I didn't say that. I want to go on seeing you, David. I don't know what I'd do if . . .'

Her voice was dying away. She hated to think what she would feel if he put the phone down on her. So far she'd been astute, allowing no chance to be alone with him; he hadn't even kissed her yet, merely allowed his hand to touch hers over the table, and, oh, how she wanted him to kiss her!

'If?' he prompted quietly.

'What?'

'You said you don't know what you'd do if . . .'

'I meant – I don't know what I meant.'

'You meant if we were never to see each other again?'

'No.' She was confused. Then suddenly she wasn't. 'I couldn't bear losing you again. Yes, I'll come. I'll make some excuse.'

She was almost panting now, with relief and anticipation. 'Where do I meet you?'

David sounded equally urgent. 'Take a taxi to Leicester Square – I'll be waiting.'

The two of them made their furtive plan – it *was* seedy. Yet as she thought of David, Letty felt elated.

'Go off orright, did it?'

For a moment Letty stared at Billy. He had been

waiting up for her, sitting in the armchair, looked tired. She felt her face grow warm.

'Did what go off all right?'

'The lady yer said yer was meetin'. What did she say?'

'Oh, I said I'd go and see the paintings,' she lied. 'Next Saturday at her studio. It's across London – in Middlesex. I think they'd be worth looking at. I'll have to stay overnight. She was very nice. I met her husband . . .'

Embroidering, as those who lie very often do, to sustain the story, to convince listeners of its authenticity with more bits of information than need be. And Billy sat listening, smiling, believing every word. God forgive her!

David had held her hand through the play; had kissed her in the taxi bringing her home; had held her urgently, one hand on her breast.

'No, David, you mustn't!' But her willpower had melted. She had lain in his arms while the taxi driver concentrated on steering his vehicle through the streets, having seen it all before – the couples who rode in his cab to kiss and cuddle and giggle. So long as he got paid well for it, why should he care? He'd smiled broadly at the good tip David gave him, the cab pulling up some yards from Letty's home.

'I must see you next week,' David had begged. 'I can't go on like this. Come away with me for the weekend. We'll go to Oxford. Spend Saturday afternoon and Sunday there.'

'I can't.' Fear and love were stifling her. 'What excuse can I make?'

'Say you've got some business to attend to.'

'I can't!'

'I'll say the same to Madge. She won't even miss me.'

'My Billy would. There's the gallery too – I have to be there.'

'You have your assistant. Darling, I need you! Say you will?'

And here she was, lying in her teeth to the most trusting man God had ever put breath into. It was sickening, yet what could she do?

Oxford bowled her over – or was it that she was with David? In the hotel, calling themselves husband and wife, that night she *was* his wife. But daylight re-awakened conscience. Anxious to appease it, she insisted on returning home immediately. But what a wonderful night it had been. Not to be repeated though without asking to be found out.

Not since her early days with David had she gone out and about so much. Thinking back, from the time David had first disappeared from her life, hers had been a narrow world in a way, apart from those few years going up West with Ethel.

Now she was rubbing shoulders in Piccadilly, in Leicester Square or the Strand, with flappers, those bright young things with not a care in the world; Letty at thirty-five was mature, her taste fashionable but conservative against the beaded and fringed hemlines flapping around the girls' rouged knees. With vaselined eyes and Max Factor lips for a Vamp look, shingled hair concealed under shimmering sequined helmets, their escorts dapper in dinner jackets, they hurried on to clubs and dance halls to do the Charleston, the tango, the foxtrot, the shimmy. But none of them was happier than Letty.

David looked so handsome in a double breasted dinner jacket as he took her to the theatre, dinner, or seats at the classier cinemas. At forty-five was still good-looking, a strand of silver here and there amid the dark wavy hair but the dark eyes as fine as ever they'd been. One arm looped through his, Letty felt she was where she belonged, dressed to the nines and feeling a million dollars.

The year was passing like a dream. They still met just one Saturday in four, sometimes in five so as not to arouse suspicion, the odd snatched evening midweek came very seldom, but what joy those evenings were. Beyond help, needing David's love as she needed air to breathe, Letty tried not to think about Billy; she fretted for David every moment she was away from him. In the intervals between she immersed herself in her business.

'Yer 'alf killin' yerself,' Billy told her, much re-covered after a good summer but aware there was still next winter to face.

'I'm fine,' she sang. 'I've got hidden strength.' She tried not to dwell on the underlying truth that her strength came from David's love.

Many people would remember 1925 as the year

Madame Tussaud's Waxwork Exhibition burnt to the ground, the year Mr Winston Churchill lowered income tax by sixpence and gave widows a ten-shilling pension as well as the elderly insured at sixty-five, the year Amundsen flew over the North Pole and Oxford sank in the Boat Race.

Letty would remember it quite differently. She would recall sitting in the circle seats at the Tivoli in the Strand, David's arm about her shoulders as he smiled down at her, she hastily wiping away her tears at the overwhelming climax to King Vidor's stupendous war film, *The Great Parade*. She watched it without shuddering, knowing David was with her, was alive. Nevertheless she was embarrassed as the pitiless cinema lights went up at the end to reveal her reddened eyes.

She'd remember it too as a year of torment, of longing, of furtive meetings. David was asking more and more to see his son, despite the photos she gave him. David would kiss her hungrily in darkened taxis as she hurried home to Billy, thinking the world of her husband while aching for those stolen minutes with David, minutes that had become her very life's blood.

Billy no longer smiled so readily.

'I didn't fink yer'd need ter go ter so many meetin's.'

'Nor me,' she lied, becoming adept at it. 'Goes with the job, I'm afraid.'

''Oo are they, the people you 'ave ter see?'

'Oh . . . just people.'

'Same ones every time?'

'No, different ones.'

'What sort of people?'

'Well, you know.' She could feel herself growing irritable with him. 'Art people. Dealers. Collectors. You know. I do have to do a lot of negotiating for some of the things I sell. There are auctions. Important auctions. You don't like going to them. You get bored.'

He had never been that interested, art going over his head, so she had never browned him off by including him or showing to him all that came in. Which was just as well as, although she hadn't planned it, it did serve as an excuse. That was, so long as he didn't start delving as he was doing now.

She watched him shrug, not entirely convinced, hoped he wouldn't ask any more questions, detested the way she was having to lie, with no idea how to make it all right for him without lying. A year of scheming was beginning to get her down, making her feel vaguely ill. The Sunday before Christmas, Billy as expected having gone down with his chest, she decided she must have some respite from deception, at least for a couple of months, or go out of her mind.

Billy in bed listening to his beloved wireless set, Christopher out somewhere with friends, Letty sat at the table in the living room, pen in hand, a sheet of writing paper before her, reading what she had written so far.

Darling,

I've been thinking about us and I feel angry with myself, tormented by every second we're apart. But I have to have a little time to do some thinking. I know it's going to be awful for you, darling, but I must try to give myself a little time to recoup from the misery we are causing to ourselves. I really do feel I have to be with Billy over Christmas and give my whole attention to him – that's if I can possibly tear it away from you whom I love so much I could die. But I do need to try not to think only of myself. A few weeks, that's all. I owe him that. His chest trouble has started up again – it always does in winter. I shall have to watch him, be with him all the time in case it gets any worse. I wish I knew how to tell you how I feel about him. I can't understand how I can be so devoted to him and yet love you as I do; how I can want to nurse him yet can be so unfaithful to him. How can I make you understand how I feel when I don't really know myself?

Please understand, darling. It probably appears terribly selfish to you but don't telephone me. I'll let you know when circumstances allow me to see you again. If you want me to, that is. But never forget, David, I love you very much.

She stared at the letter, re-reading before going any further. It sounded so awful, so pathetic. How could she write such drivel to him? If it didn't make him laugh, it would hurt him.

'Letty!'

Billy called from the bedroom. Immediately she was on alert, knowing the sounds. He'd been struggling with his lungs on and off for nearly a week. It had started up, as it usually did, as the year grew damper in late-October. The ever present bronchial cough, at first slight but becoming more persistent. Then, as the fluid built up, the damaged air passages unable to cope, these full-blown attacks.

'Letty!'

'Coming!'

It was awful to watch him struggle for breath, nostrils dilated, lips blowing in and out with the effort, eyes turned to the ceiling, and that terrible fluid rattling.

'Hang on, Billy!'

Running to the narrow kitchen, she poured boiling water from the kettle kept gently steaming for this emergency up to the air-hole of the inhaler, added a teaspoonful of friar's balsam, averting her face from the pungent steam she had come to loathe.

A towel wrapped around the inhaler to keep the temperature up, she hurried back with it to Billy. It would ease him. She'd had all this with Dad, though never to this extent; his affliction stemming from natural causes, rather than the wilful warring of men, had never seemed so cruel, so heartless.

Slowly the steaming balsam took effect. The wheezing of Billy's clogged lungs reducing, his breathing growing easier, Letty relaxed a little as he recovered enough to grin up at her, half in loving gratitude, half apologetic.

'I'll be – orright now. Yer can – take this – away.'

Busy with him, she didn't hear Christopher come in.

'Keep it by you in case you tighten up again,' she instructed. 'As soon as it begins to cool, call me and I'll put some more hot water in it. Will you be all right for a moment? I'm in the middle of writing a letter.'

'Didn't mean – ter disturb yer, Let.' His apology wrung her heart.

'You didn't disturb me, Billy. I was only putting pen to paper for something to do.'

'Who're yer writing to?'

'Oh, just a business letter.'

'Well . . .' He smiled wanly at her. 'You get back to it.'

She was reluctant to leave him. All the time she'd been tending him, half her mind had been on tearing the letter up, perhaps telephoning David instead. On the phone she could better argue her case, be more adamant, gauge his reaction easier.

She'd made up her mind as she reached the living-room door across the tiny hall. She opened it and immediately froze, all resolution swept from her.

Christopher stood in the centre of the room, a ten year old with the expression of one twice his age, dark eyes narrowed, young face twisted.

In his hand, creased and distorted where he'd screwed it furiously into a ball then opened it again to confront her with, was the letter she had left on the table.

Letty's eyes were fixed on the letter. Heat flooded through her, exploded in a welter of fear-borne anger.

'Christopher! Who gave you permission to . . . What've you been doing?'

'Reading,' he said expressionlessly.

'You've no right to.'

'It was open on the table. I couldn't help seeing it.'

She stood petrified, wanting to snatch it from him, not daring to. It would only emphasise her guilt. Perhaps he didn't truly understand the significance of it. He was only ten years old. She made herself smile. Her mouth felt stiff. She held out her hand, came forward.

'It's only a silly bit of writing, darling. I was making something up . . . out of boredom,' she added quickly. 'We can throw it away now. I've done with it.'

His expression hadn't altered. 'Who's David?' he demanded.

'Just a name, darling.'

'It's somebody's name. You wrote that you love him.'

'A silly game I was having, that's all. Something to do.'

'Does Billy know? About your silly game, Mum?'

'Don't be ridiculous, Chris!' she blustered, reaching out again for the letter. 'Give it to me and we'll throw it away.'

'He *is* a real man, isn't he?' Chris sounded as though he was being strangled, his voice husky and tight. 'You said you loved him lots of times in it. He's someone you've met, isn't he, Mum?'

'He's nothing of the sort.'

'But you do know him – this David, don't you? He's not pretend.'

'Chris . . .' She reached out both hands to him, but he backed off.

'Are you going to leave me and Billy?'

The plea was of sheer desolation. A boy confused for half his life by the subterfuge of adults was now being confronted by a new deceit that he seemed to imagine would touch him in the most cruel way: leaving him cast aside completely. She had to tell him. Had to explain.

'It's not what you think,' she began. 'Christopher, that letter – it was to your father. I was told he was killed in the war but he wasn't. Last year I met him again and I still love him. I can't help it. But I wouldn't leave you and Billy. David's married now, you see . . .'

Her voice faltered at the expression on his face,

the anger turning to hatred, lips curling away from his white teeth in a snarl. But there were tears in his voice.

'A whole year you've known about my father? And you never told me, you kept him a secret from *me* . . .'

Suddenly he stopped, his gaze directed beyond her. Instinctively she swung round, the sounds of Billy's distressed breathing reaching her as she saw him standing in the doorway, leaning heavily against the doorjamb.

Grey-faced, he stared back at her before he turned, using the wall for support as he staggered back to his room without a word, the door closing gently behind him.

CHAPTER 23

Billy was coughing. Throwing Christopher a last appealing glance, Letty hurried to her husband's aid.

His strength gone, he was kneeling beside the bed, collapsed across it. She quickly helped him get into it, propping the pillows behind him. Now wasn't the time to start vindicating herself, but she tried.

'Billy . . .'

Feebly, he waved towards the inhaler. Letty felt it. It had cooled. No use to him.

Grabbing it, she hurried to the kitchen, glimpsing Christopher where she'd left him, the letter still in his hand.

'Billy's not well!' she snapped at him. 'Go down to the office and phone the doctor.' She saw him leap into action, anger for the moment driven out by fear.

There was no need for the doctor. Letty could cope. But she needed anchorage – someone to bring some stability to a world cast adrift. At least it would give her time to compose herself, explain things more rationally; time for others better to understand the circumstances.

The inhaler filled, she hurried back to Billy, folded his hands around it, brought the tube to his labouring mouth. He didn't look at her as he breathed in the soothing fumes; didn't look at her as, recovering, he finally laid the inhaler on the bedside cabinet.

'Billy . . .' she began again, but again he stopped her.

'Not now,' he said, his voice a whisper. Closing his eyes, thus avoiding any need to look at her, he lay back on the pillows.

Letty knew he would not open them until eventually she was obliged to leave him; knew too that behind the closed eyes his mind was going like a treadmill, rejecting what he'd heard, rejecting any explanation from her. There'd be little sleep for him that night. Little sleep for her either.

Going through the motions of a busy pre-Christmas week was almost unendurable, the longest week Letty could ever remember, even though there were only four working days in it, Christmas being Friday.

Billy lay immobile in his bed as though all the stuffing had been knocked out of him. Letty, awake half the night, the small cabinet between her bed and Billy's feeling as wide as the Sahara, blamed herself for everything. There seemed nothing she could say to narrow the rift she had caused. Her mind churned endlessly, futilely, until exhaustion finally rescued her from her milling thoughts and she slept.

Billy's parents came to share Christmas Day with them, and looked worried.

'I've never seen him so bad,' Mrs Beans said as between them they laid the table for the Christmas dinner. Billy would be having a little on a tray if he felt like eating at all, which didn't seem likely. 'He ought to have a doctor to him.'

'He's had a doctor,' Letty told her. 'He's been here on and off this past week.'

'He ought to be in hospital,' said Billy's father, himself quite robust despite the heart condition.

'The doctor says that too,' Letty said. 'If Billy's not improved after Christmas, he'll make arrangements for it.'

She had done her best this past week to persuade Billy that a spell in hospital would do him a power of good, but he had merely shaken his head, saying all he needed was to stay in bed. It was all he ever said. If she tried unloading her conscience on to him, he'd turn away, say he was tired, needed to sleep, the ready smile absent for once. It broke her heart.

Christopher avoided her like the plague; his school broken up for the holiday, he spent his spare time in his room or seeing this or that chum. Over Christmas he spoke hardly two words to Letty, ate his meals in silence, barely acknowledged the Meccano and Hornby train sets she'd got for him. He at least put on a brave cheerful face for Billy's parents who saw nothing untoward, but several times Letty caught him staring in her direction and looked quickly away from what she saw in his face. His model behaviour was unnatural, the healthy naughtiness of a ten year old absent, and Letty could find nothing to say to him.

She did write to David on Boxing Day, after her in-laws had gone home – a terse, uncompromising letter, explaining that Billy's illness would prevent her from seeing him for some time. Would he please bear with her until she next contacted him?

Love for him still burned inside her, a desperate longing love, but there was no way she could have put it into words just then. It would have been best for them all if she could have terminated their association right now, but she knew that would have been an impossible condition; so better not to see him for a while – in itself a penitent's scourge.

It was four days before Billy said anything directly to her. Giving him his medicines, she tried another attempt at reconciliation, making her tone cheerful as though nothing was at all wrong.

'My, you take this stuff without turning a hair. It smells vile.'

He was looking unsmilingly at her. Something inside her seemed to break, like a twig snapping, only it was soundless. All at once there were tears flowing and words pouring out.

'Billy . . . I can't stand this! You not looking at me. Chris all sullen. I know what you overheard and I've got to explain. Please let me explain. Please!'

On her knees beside him like one seeking absolution, she let out her misery in a torrent. She hadn't wanted to deceive him, hadn't intended to hurt him. What else she said she had little idea beyond trying to convince herself as well as him that it had been out of her control, that she loved Billy, would always love him.

He was talking to her, his tone low and despondent. 'I ain't blamin' yer, Let. I ain't much of a catch.'

'Oh, Billy . . . don't!' It was rubbing salt into her wounds.

'I just feel – let down,' he went on. 'For Chris especially. It's 'is father, Let. If yer'd just told 'im. Yer should 'ave, yer know.'

'I wanted to, Billy,' she mumbled against the coverlet. 'But he'd have told you. You'd have been so hurt. I didn't want to hurt you.'

'Yer think – findin' out this way ain't 'urt me? I've always known yer – never loved me, not really . . .'

'No!' She looked up, face tearstained. 'That's not true. I did . . . I *do* love you.'

He gave a wry grin but said nothing, and seeing the truth, Letty bent her head again to the coverlet.

'Oh, Billy.' No point in trying to convince him of a love that would never compare to that which she bore for David. Billy's voice was low.

'A few months, Let. Stay wiv me – a few months. Give me that. I'll try not ter – prolong it.'

Letty looked up in terror. 'What're you saying?'

But she already guessed. He was smiling at her, the old smile.

'I'm tired, Let.'

She remained kneeling beside him as he turned away wearily, his breathing laboured. On impulse she placed a tender kiss against the tousled confusion of his hair, her tears falling upon it.

'I love you, Billy,' she whispered hoarsely, and getting up, left the room, leaving, she hoped, to sleep.

1926 came in with torrential rain, though to hear revellers along Oxford Street yelling Happy New Year to one another, blowing their party whistles and singing, no one would have guessed it was coming down in stair rods. Partygoers caroused outside the flat, soaked to the skin, beads and feathers dripping cascades, furs drenched, shoes and stockings waterlogged, the brims of men's boaters and homburgs making waterfalls down their coat collars. Most were too drunk to care.

Curtains drawn, the gas fire turned full on, Letty kept an anxious vigil over Billy.

Since yesterday he'd complained of pain upon breathing and this morning had developed a fever that had become steadily worse as the day wore on. Doctor Cavarolli had urged getting him to hospital, but Billy had put up a fight.

Doctor Cavarolli had puffed out his fat cheeks, fiddled with his stethoscope and said he couldn't force Billy, but to keep him as warm as possible, keep an eye on him, and inform the surgery if there was any change.

There had been a change about midnight and now, at three o'clock, revellers and drunks dispersed and London at last quiet, Letty was in two minds whether to get Doctor Cavarolli out at this time of the morning in such weather.

But by four-thirty when Billy began to toss and turn, his breathing becoming rapid and shallow, she knew it was a hospital job – out of her hands.

Outside rain lashed the bedroom window. Torrential rain and floods were reported all over Europe. It sounded as if they had all arrived in London in one go. But Letty was past caring about the doctor's discomfort.

Hurrying down to the office, she lifted the phone off its hook and put it to her ear. A crackling like rustling paper made her stare at it angrily. Rain was interfering with the wires. Furiously she depressed the receiver. No response at all.

Letty ran back upstairs, grabbed coat and brolly and rammed a hat over her ears, going to shake Christopher awake before she left.

'Phone's out of order!' she called. 'I'm going for the doctor!'

Head down, umbrella held firm against a driving wind that had got up in the last hour or so, the waterlogged pavement splashing water into her shoes, she cast about futilely for a taxi as she ran towards Great Titchfield Street where Dr Cavarolli lived.

It was no great distance, usually she would not have needed a taxi, but in this weather, the umbrella was turned inside out twice, forcing her to struggle with it. By the time she reached the surgery, her expensive coat and hat bedraggled, she looked more like a vagrant than a successful owner of an art gallery as she staggered, panting, up the four steps and rang frantically at the doorbell.

She pressed it several times. It seemed a lifetime before the door opened, the light in the hall flickering on, and a woman in a pink dressing gown stood looking askance at her.

'My husband's ill!' Letty gasped. 'The telephone's not working. I had to run all the way . . .'

She wasn't making sense. The woman stepped back.

'Come inside out of the rain,' she instructed briskly, leading her into the waiting room and switching on the light. 'Wait here, Mrs . . .?'

'Beans – Letitia Beans. My husband's William Beans, Dr Cavarolli's patient. It's his chest. It sounds awful. I'm sure it's pneumonia . . .'

'Wait here, Mrs Beans. I'll wake the doctor.'

The door reopened admitting the portly figure of Billy's doctor, dressed and ready in outdoor clothes, clutching his medical bag, a morning stubble on his chin. Letty made towards him in a welter of relief.

'Oh, you must come. I tried to phone you but the phone was . . .'

'Was out of order,' he finished gently. 'My wife told me. We'll take my car. But first I will telephone the Middlesex Hospital from here. Fortunately mine is working.'

'He won't go into hospital.'

'He has no choice,' came the reply. The doctor had already turned from her to the telephone on the desk, and was speaking to someone on the other end.

Chris sat by Billy in the white-painted ward, seven beds spaced out along either side. His mother was with Billy's parents in the sister's office, discussing him.

For two long weeks the hospital had fought Billy's pneumonia, this third week announcing they were winning through. Except that Billy looked as if he'd been buried alive and dug up again so he hadn't really won, it seemed to Chris.

The hospital doctor had had a long talk with Chris's mother. He didn't know what about except that she'd listened with bent head, had wiped tears from her eyes with a handkerchief and had given the doctor a brave smile.

Full of fear, Chris would have liked to ask her what had been said but couldn't bring himself to speak to her even now, after all that had happened with Billy being ill. In his mind she'd been the cause of it all. He wanted to cry with rage at her.

'Are you all right, Billy?' he whispered, gazing

intently at the pallid face before him, propped up on pillows.

Billy nodded. His colourless lips shaped a travesty of a grin. His breathing sounded awful, sort of rattling. Chris touched his hand as it rested on the harsh white bedcover, felt the fingers close over his in response.

'You're going to get better now, aren't you, Billy?'

The thought that he might die terrified Chris beyond description. Billy was his shield against the father he had never seen; whom he disliked without ever having seen him. All he prayed for now was for Billy to live for years and years to keep the faceless man at bay – the man his mother had written to. The words she'd written had made him feel strangely uncomfortable, sort of embarrassed, though he wasn't sure why.

'You won't die, will you, Billy?'

His fingers tightened a fraction. 'Yer mustn't be frightened.'

'But I am frightened. If anything happened to you, Billy, I don't know what I'd do. That man Mum wrote to – my father. He don't care about me or he'd have asked to see me. If Mum went off with him and he didn't want me, I'd be left all on my own. Oh, Billy, don't die. Promise!'

Chris saw Billy bite his lip and knew then that all his begging was a waste of time.

The boy's eyes were beginning to sting. There was no one left but Billy with his round blue eyes and his ready smile. Mum didn't really love him.

She had taken him away from Aunt Vinny where he'd been happy. It occurred to him that he hardly saw anything of his own family now, except perhaps for Aunt Lucy and Uncle Jack. Hardly ever saw his grandfather and that awful frowsy woman who called herself grandmother but wasn't. Mum was always too taken up with her gallery to visit her father and he was too old and doddery to come and see her.

As for Aunt Vinny, the last he'd seen of her was when he'd sneaked off to visit her. She and Mum didn't speak.

It was a strange family. A strange life. An aunt he'd once thought his mother; a mother he'd once called aunt. An uncle he'd called his father had died, and a father he had never known was alive and trying to take Mum away from him and Billy. Now the only person he really loved, who had been as wonderful as any true father could have been, might leave him too. Tears welled over.

'I hate Mum! She doesn't love me. I hate her! And I hate *him*!'

Billy's grip strengthened. 'You mustn't – you mustn't say that. They're yer parents – true parents. Yer mum – she loves yer. She gave yer up – sacrificed all 'er love so's you'd 'ave a better chance in life than – than she thought she could give yer. And it was – was 'er love that made 'er get yer back . . .'

It was painful to hear his laboured intake of

breath, the effort it cost him to talk, the words hardly more than a hoarse whisper.

'An' yer father – she loves 'im too. Yer see, yer can't stop someone lovin' someone when it's as strong as yer mum loves yer father. It sort of takes over. Yer mum can't love me as she loved 'im. And I can't go blamin' 'er fer what's only natural. You mustn't either.'

'But I don't love her!' he burst out, bewildered by the words.

'Listen ter me, Chris!' Billy fought to regulate his breathing, and talking taking it out of him. 'I ain't goin' ter be 'ere . . . well, that's as it maybe. But you've got yer 'ole life in front of yer. And yer'll 'ave ter grow up wiv what yer've got.'

'But you don't know how I feel, Billy.'

'Yes, I do. But what's done is done. Yer'll 'ave ter learn that – as yer go along – or go under and stay there – all bitter and 'ating and never comin' ter terms wiv anyfink. I want ter see yer prop'ly adjusted ter what's 'appened to yer.'

He lifted a hand as Chris again made to interrupt.

'Yer can't go blamin' people for what 'appens to 'em. No one's ter blame. It 'appened, that's all. When yer grow up an' meet someone – a gel – and yer fall in love wiv 'er, yer'll want 'er to be 'appy. That's 'ow it is. When yer love, yer give. Yer give yerself – even yer own 'appiness, for 'er. Your mum – she gave up 'er own 'appiness fer you. She wan't married when she 'ad you. Yer do know what that means do yer?'

Christopher nodded vaguely. He understood that people had to be married to have children and his mother hadn't been. She'd explained it a little to him but it had gone over his head then. He understood a little better now but still could not entirely accept that it wasn't a nice thing to be, what he was.

'Yer see . . .' Billy was having terrible difficulty, breath wheezing with each intake, rumbling and rattling with each exhalation. 'She thought – yer dad was dead – and she wasn't 'avin' you 'urt – by other people pointin' at yer – callin' yer names. So she let your aunt – let 'er take yer ter bring yer up. It broke 'er heart.'

He seemed to be rambling, his eyes closed, his lips distressed.

'Now she's met yer father again. I ain't goin' ter stand in the way of 'er 'appiness. Nor should you. She's yer mum who gave up all 'er 'appiness fer you. So if yer've any kind of understandin', yer mustn't blame 'er fer – wanting the man she's loved all 'er life and 'as found again. Yer'll bide wiv 'er. Be 'er son – 'er friend. You'll be that to 'er won't yer?'

His voice had grown fainter and fainter while he spoke, as though the effort had drained away all his strength.

Christopher, his face creased up, his eyes stinging with tears, not looking at Billy, felt him pat his hand,

415

heard his breath coming in racked gasps, audible enough for a nurse to pause in passing, double back in her tracks to take a closer look at him.

'Go an' find yer mum,' Billy managed as the nurse hurried off. He laid his head feebly against the pillow. 'And tell 'er yer love 'er. An' mean it!'

Christopher found himself being hustled from the ward by the nurse who had come back with the sister and another nurse. His mother and Billy's parents were staring past him as screens were put up around Billy's bed, a trolley with odd-looking bottles and things hurried behind it. A doctor in a white coat, a stethoscope hanging around his neck, had arrived too.

'Go and sit in the sister's office,' ordered the nurse, and left Chris to go on alone as she confronted the bewildered adults and began talking to them.

Chris, being rejoined by the grown ups, looked at them one by one, wanted to ask what was happening but dared not, each face registering gnawing fear. Something awful was happening, he was sure of it.

'What's the matter?' he finally asked Billy's dad, saw the man's face pucker as he patted Chris's shoulder. Billy's mum looked tense. So did his own mum.

'Is Billy going to die?' he whispered, hoping someone would answer, but all that happened was that Billy's mother started crying softly into a handkerchief.

'Mum . . .'

'Not now, Chris.'

He had never heard her voice so strangled, so pain-racked; suddenly he realised how much his mother loved Billy. She loved another man too, but loved Billy enough to be suffering terribly.

The sullen hatred that had hung within him like some dark amorphous cloud melted away. All he wanted to do now was to comfort. But who'd listen to him?

Standing by his mother, tall enough to be past her shoulder now, he slid his hand into hers.

'I love you, Mum,' he said quietly.

CHAPTER 24

What she really wanted was to cry on David's shoulder, to have him take away the guilt that comes with losing someone dear; all those words left unsaid, all those that might have been better left unsaid.

Instead she wrote asking that he not see her until she'd been able to collect herself.

'I have to think of Christopher,' she wrote.

It was an excuse, a clinging to duty that was no longer relevant. There was nothing to keep her from doing exactly what she wanted to do, yet duty had become a habit, a second skin after a lifetime of laying aside her own freedom for someone else. She felt almost as though she'd be guilty of desertion if she saw him, but to whom and to what she no longer knew.

She received a letter from him in return, reminding her: 'He's my son too. He needs us both at a time like this.' Also that he had hoped she'd turn to him in her hour of need, was disappointed and hurt that she hadn't.

But she couldn't – longed to, but couldn't. The pain she must have caused Billy at the end was haunting her. Going running off to David now would have accentuated that even more.

Chris didn't need his father – he needed Billy. He had grown closer to her with Billy's death. Having time off from school, he was constantly by her side.

'I'll look after you, Mum,' he said, with the grave over-emphasis of a child that made her heart fill as she hugged him, grateful to have him with her in this now lifeless flat.

Billy was buried in East London Cemetery not far from her mother's plot. Letty went through the funeral in a daze, unable to cry, unable to think, giving the impression of being fully in possession of herself. She drew some admiring glances, though others frowned disapprovingly. If they knew the numbness that produced this unemotional exterior!

Afterwards the family gathered in her flat. Billy's family, his brothers and sisters; her family, except of course for Vinny whom she hadn't expected to come anyway, animosity still present. Her sister didn't even send a letter of condolence. Letty, past caring, felt nothing.

'How're yer goin', Letitia?'

A warming glass of sherry in her hand, Letty turned to her father. She saw an old man, the once dark wavy hair thin and limp now and completely grey, the blue eyes rheumy, only the moustache healthy-looking.

Ada, plump and comfortable and blowsy, stood

beside him, holding him by the arm. Letty, still unable to like her, admitted that Dad would probably have departed this life long ago but for this frowsy woman.

Dad's hand touched Letty's. 'We don't see much of yer these days. Wasn't easy to get 'ere today but I felt I 'ad to. If there's anything we can do – anything yer need – let us know, Letitia. We oughter see more of yer, yer know.'

'I know, Dad.' Feeling a twinge of her old love for him, she smiled down at him, realising how age shrank a person. 'I'll be all right. I shall try to come and see you and Ada more often. The gallery takes up so much of my time.'

'Gallery – fancy!' Ada put in, sipping her glass of Mackeson's stout. 'We called 'em shops in our time. Yer'll 'ave to show me downstairs, love. I'd love to see 'ow that gallery of yours is comin' along.'

'I'll take you down later,' Letty offered. 'It's still small.'

There were a lot of people to talk to – art dealers, collectors who had come to know Billy through her and had come to pay their respects to him. The flat full of subdued conversation, she circulated, longing for them all to go, dreading the emptiness they'd leave behind, when she must start to think again.

She never did take Dad and Ada downstairs to show them around.

★   ★   ★

It was the little things she missed: not listening out for Billy's cough, hurrying upstairs every now and again to see how he did; not having to thump his back or to fill the inhaler, now three months later stacked away in the top of the kitchen cupboard. She missed someone to speak her thoughts aloud to, longed for four-thirty when Chris came home from school, Mrs Warnes in charge while she prepared him a meal. He never went out after coming home although she assured him she was fine on her own; wished he would for his own good. He would eventually, she imagined, as her own sense of loss eased.

David telephoned twice a week; couldn't quite understand why she was still not ready to see him, but it was hard to explain how she felt. She did want to see him yet couldn't feel easy about it. How could she explain the persistent sense of disloyalty? Worse since her loss.

David's call to her yesterday had been fraught with impatience. 'This is stupid,' he'd said, tetchy but pleading. 'I've tried to understand how you feel, but it can't go on.'

'I'm sorry, David.' What more could she say? She dared not tell him how she ached to see him. Her love for Billy had been gentle and giving and she had an abiding fear her memory of it was being soiled by the tingling desire inside her every time she so much as heard David's voice.

'I'm still not over losing Billy,' she fought to

explain. 'I can't help how I feel. You must try and understand, David.'

'I do,' he told her. 'But you have to stop eventually. You have to get over it.'

'There's Christopher . . .'

'Yes – Christopher,' he echoed. 'How much longer can I be kept away from my son? I think I've been remarkably patient, but this is driving me insane. What is there to hold us apart now?'

'There's your wife,' she replied feebly.

'Damn my wife! It's you I want, Letitia!'

She couldn't hold off any longer, had agreed to see him. But not here. She wouldn't have him come into the flat. Not yet. He could meet her a few yards away – take her to the cinema if she liked?

Now she must break it gently to Chris, hoping he wouldn't see it adversely, that after three months he might not think straight away that she was being disloyal to Billy's memory. She wasn't.

She waited in a fever of anxiety for him to come home from school, waited until he had eaten, was twiddling the knobs of the wireless set until distant music came crackling through, absorbed as always in the novelty of it.

'Chris,' she said, and as he looked up: 'I suppose you know that I – that your father and I have been – well, he has telephoned me on quite a few occasions and I – well, I've decided to let him take me out this evening – to the cinema. I know it's a little soon since . . . I just thought I had better explain things to you. You see, Chris . . .'

Battling to explain things to a boy hardly yet eleven in words he would understand, unable to see how she was going to accomplish it, she faltered to a halt. He cut in smoothly, without animosity, and with a child's forthrightness.

'There's no need to explain, Mum. I understand.'

He turned momentarily back to the wireless set as she stared in surprised relief, then looked at her again.

'When *am* I going to meet him?' he asked, suddenly earnest.

Quickly Letty gathered her wits. 'Do you want to, Chris?'

'Of course I want to.'

'Then we'll go to the cinema together – the three of us.'

The wireless set forgotten, Chris leapt up, his dark eyes brilliant. 'Gosh! D'you think it'll be all right – me going along? What a surprise! What's he like?'

'He's very like you.' Happiness was flooding through Letty. 'In looks, that is. He's much calmer than you. You're more like your Aunt Lucy in temperament. That's the only thing wrong with Dav . . . with your father – he's rather a little reserved and sedate. I'm glad you're not reserved, Chris . . . Oh, Chris! I'm so glad!'

She caught him to her and hugged him convulsively, all the dull years fading behind her, all the wonderful ones stretching out before her, going on and on, into the distance.

David was waiting further down Oxford Street as he'd promised, was sitting at the wheel of his car as she and Chris came out of the door next to the gallery used in common with the apartments above her.

At the sight of two figures, Letty saw him get hurriedly out of the vehicle, the bright Oxford Street lighting illuminating the tension in his face.

'Is that him?' Chris whispered urgently.

He'd dressed himself up in his best blazer and short grey trousers, his thick school scarf wound around his neck against the biting April evening. Socks for once pulled up to full height rather than sagging around the ankles, he'd spent over ten minutes polishing his shoes.

David was coming swiftly towards them, surprise and delight now lighting his lean handsome face.

'David,' Letty began as he stopped just short of them, 'this is Chris.'

She could find nothing else to say, stood by foolishly inadequate, her whole being in a sudden turmoil. She needn't have worried. David stretched out a hand to the lad who took it solemnly, then as if it were the most natural thing to do, David pulled his son towards him, his other arm looping about the boy's neck in an embrace.

With tears in her eyes, Letty stood to one side, watching the thing she had dreamed of all these years come to pass. Christopher and his father meeting in loving embrace. It was beyond her wildest dreams; she knew she could never be as happy again as she was at this very moment.

'We're going to be so happy together – the three of us!' her heart sang impetuously, forgetting in her happiness that there was still one obstacle to the completeness she visualised: David's wife.

Letty and David were standing together swaying, mesmerised by the strains of Al Jolson's poignant ballad, 'Sonny Boy'; a gramophone record she had bought after seeing *The Jazz Singer*, the first ever talkie. Letty, moved to tears by the song's words during the film last week, could hardly wait to buy it. Now she was made dreamy by Jolson's compelling voice.

Chris had been packed off to bed, leaving them to a brief nightcap before David made for his home and wife. The music turned down low, they'd danced slower and slower. And now he kissed her, asked why he needed to go home at all tonight?

Letty's reaction was to press her face to his shoulder, suddenly guarded. 'Not with Chris asleep in the next room,' she said hastily. 'It wouldn't be right,' she finished, knowing how silly it sounded.

It was always the same excuse, even after all this time; it had taken her these two years to get over the feeling of still being married. Ada had once said bereavement was a two-year disease. She had been right.

David had asked before, but only when Chris's holidays took him to stay with friends. An outgoing twelve year old, popular with his school chums and liked by their parents, Chris was often invited to spend time with this one and that – sometimes for a weekend, sometimes a week in the longer breaks, even going on holiday with them.

She had consented to let David stay on two occasions but each had been a disaster with Letty breaking down, unable to shake off the notion of betraying Billy. David had understood, been so patient with her. But now he was asking again, lifting her face with a gentle hand, kissing her again tenderly. 'We are his mother and father, you know, darling.'

'But not married,' she reminded softly, regretfully, wishing so much that it was otherwise. 'It makes a difference.'

'You never used to be so prudish.' He smiled down at her. 'Do you remember those years we first knew each other? The beach at Brighton?'

'I was young and silly then,' she said.

'I wasn't. I was in deadly earnest – loved you with every ounce of my being. I've never ceased to love you, Letitia.'

The music forgotten, David held her and kissed her closed eyes. 'You're even more beautiful than you were then. These glorious green eyes, the flame in your hair. You've gained such poise these past years, I can hardly . . . Letitia, let me stay tonight.'

He was becoming insistent and she was being

persuaded. Chris wouldn't need to know. And she wanted David's strength at this moment – wanted him so urgently. 'Oh, darling. Oh, David . . .'

The music faded; the needle, caught in the central groove, began to circle with a jarring repetitious grating. It brought her back to her senses. She wanted David so much. But it would only be the same as before. Her half responding as she fought with her conscience, ending in tears; he frustrated, trying to make out that it didn't matter.

'It's no use.' Better to say it now than in the middle of his lovemaking. It could be perfect, anywhere else but in this flat. 'It's no use. I just can't – especially with Chris here. Please try to understand, David.'

His expression told her that he was beginning not to.

'I'll go then,' he said abruptly, to which she could only nod bleak assent.

David's father died in the spring of 1929. In his will he left David a partnership in Baron & Lampton's, with the full approval of course of his father-in-law, Henry Lampton.

The news left Letty unhappy. This past year she had been dreaming of the day when he would be hers alone.

'How can I refuse it without giving any reason?' David asked when she summoned the courage to express her thoughts, hating to see him even more troubled than he already was.

They sat on a bench beside the Serpentine on the Sunday following the funeral, the weather almost as overcast as Letty's spirits.

'I've always dreaded this day,' David went on glumly. He missed the lack of sympathy in Letty's eyes.

'You mean you knew what was in this will?' she queried, gazing at the ducks feeding at the edge of the water on bread she had been so happily throwing to them before David had dismayed her with his news.

'He told me when I married Madge,' he said. 'Before I met you again, so I never thought it would affect me except to better my life.'

Letty took her eyes away from the ducks. 'And you've never said anything about it to me?'

He turned his head to look at her. 'I've never known how.'

'You knew there was no chance of ever leaving your wife?' she said, astounded, anger building up inside her. 'All those times I talked of us being married one day, you let me go on believing that you'd be free? And all the time you knew that what was in your father's will would tie you down forever!'

'It won't be forever,' he protested, attempting to take her hand which she snatched away immediately. 'I'll find a way, darling.'

Letty's heart was beginning to race, a sense of betrayal making her feel slightly sick. 'You knew you couldn't ask her for a divorce *and* happily stay a partner with her father.'

She saw his mouth beneath the thin moustache tremble as he lowered his gaze, but couldn't stop her outburst, made sarcastic by bitterness.

'Why, all you've worked for, schemed for, sacrificed – just to marry me! So you let me go on believing. You never did intend to leave her, did you, David? Not with the security your marriage gave you, while you could come and get what you wanted from me without any risk to you!'

His eyes darkened with her injustice. 'That's not true, Letitia!'

'It is true! You've known all along you couldn't marry me.'

'You're saying I've used you?' He was angry now.

'What else would you call it?' Near to tears now, she rushed on: 'I don't dispute that you love me, David. But I never thought you could be so selfish with it. You've never, ever contemplated giving up your comfortable life for me, have you? Because if you'd loved me as I thought you did, you'd have thrown it all aside for me. It wasn't as if you were walking into poverty. Lord knows, I'm not penniless. We could have made a wonderful team together in the gallery . . .'

'I've no intention of living off you, Letitia,' he protested. 'It's yours. Your business.'

'It could have been ours,' she wailed.

'I do have my pride . . .' he began, but she cut in angrily.

'Oh, of course – a man's pride mustn't be damaged! What sort of pride is it to lead me along these three years, quite happy to make love to me every now and again, then going home to your well-ordered life with your well-ordered wife and your well-ordered business. You have the cheek to ask me to go to bed with you, thinking that one day we'd be married, when all the time . . .'

Words failing her, she got up, spilling the bread she'd brought for the ducks on to the path, and hurried off almost at a run and hardly able to see for a mist of tears. She could hear David running up behind her, felt his grip on her arm, turning her round to face him.

'Is that what you think of me?' he demanded. 'After all we've been to each other? After . . .'

'I don't know what I've been to you, David!' she hissed viciously.

'You've been my life, Letitia,' he cried, still gripping her arm. 'I couldn't live without you. If you knew what my life is – at home. Home! It's no home. It's a mausoleum where I sit or stand or lie, like one of her precious pekinese. Did I tell you? She has three of 'em.'

He sounded breathless. 'They sleep on our bed at night. They eat at our table. She speaks to them before she speaks to me – when she's not out and about or entertaining her fashionable friends. And I am expected to take a back seat and smile. She's her father's darling, and so long as I toe the line, I am his partner by approval. Upset her and I hear hints of some larger concern's interest in our direction – of shareholders voting to sell out. I'd let

430

him, Letitia, but it was my father's business. I can't let him down, let it all go to some huge concern like Selfridge's. I want it to be as big as them, not part of them – in his memory. I loved my father, Letitia!'

'More than you loved me?' she challenged hotly.

He gazed levelly at her. 'I've tried not to talk of our future because I could see no way out of my marriage. But if I could be free, I would. I dream of it night and day. You are my very life!'

She gazed at him through her tears, her love for him draining out of her. 'We'll never be married, will we?'

He was growing calmer. The well-ordered man in charge of himself once more. His hand slipped down from her arm to her wrist, held it gently. 'Be patient. I've been careful. Madge suspects nothing. But I will tell her about us as soon as I see a way clear, I swear. Come hell or high water, I'll tell her that she has to let me go. It could mean I'll be asked to resign from the board, the business my father built . . . But for you, I promise, we'll be married one day.'

'When?' Letty asked. Her tears were drying on her cheeks but they lay in the tremor of her voice still. And a coldness had taken hold of her as she tested him. 'How long?' she questioned.

'When?' she repeated, feeling now like a spur of granite, brittle and cruelly sculpted by the remorseless buffeting of some ice laden wind.

'I don't know,' he said again. 'But we will.'

Determination had put an edge to his tone but it still wasn't enough. Something inside her wanted him to say: 'I'll abandon everything I have for you, Letitia.' But he hadn't. And now her own pride took upper hand.

'Then I think it best you go back to her,' she said haughtily, amazed at her own coldness. 'Because there's no point us going on.'

CHAPTER 25

Lucy had a satisfied look on her face.

'That told him!' she burst out, and leaned back on Letty's immaculate brown-striped sofa to add emphasis to it. 'I really think he's treated you like a dish rag. I wouldn't have let him go on this long. Good for you, Letty!'

She nodded acknowledgement and went on sipping her coffee, thought of David, smiled, and tried to ignore the heavy weight inside her chest.

It was autumn – a whole summer wasted cutting off her nose to spite her face. David had telephoned her every week consistently these past months, begging her to see him. She in turn had given a firm denial each time he had craved her patience a while longer until he could find a way to confront his wife. But worse, Chris was constantly asking after him. What could she say?

On two occasions she had seen David's green Talbot ticking over across the road from her gallery, and had almost been tempted to run out and across the road to him. So far she'd managed to distract herself in serving customers, learned to ignore the ache in her heart on glancing out later to find the car gone. A good thing perhaps that her gallery was always so busy, helping to keep her mind occupied.

The business was doing well – not just well, was going from strength to strength. The book shop next-door had become vacant that autumn, a victim of the financial waves being felt in England from a disastrous Wall Street crash in the America. Letty's first thought was to get in and enlarge her own premises.

'I'm taking the lease on,' she told Dad when she went to see him.

Confined to bed with his old illness, now more complicated by what the doctor had called emphysema, his breathing was horribly laboured. The doctor had advised getting him into hospital but Dad had become a stubborn frightened old man with strange ideas. 'I ain't goin' ter no 'ospital,' he'd said obdurately. 'Damn dangerous places, 'spitals. Only take yer there ter die. Look at your Billy – 'e died there, didn't 'e? Well then. If I'm goin' ter die, I'll die 'ere in me own bed!'

Letty, sitting beside him in the cluttered bedroom speaking of her plans – more for something to say than for his opinion – remembered how she'd felt with Billy, saw Dad's grey face crease with anxiety as she voiced her decision to take a lease on another shop.

'D'yer think it's the right time? Jobs goin' ter the wall – all the unemployment.'

She wasn't to be deterred. Why should men be

434

the only ones expected to succeed in business? Besides she had a premonition about it. 'Expand while others are being careful' had become her edict. She was becoming well known enough to take the risk. She would invest in good modern paintings – something she'd always wanted to do.

'I *am* doing the right thing,' she said adamantly.

Dad still wasn't convinced. 'I don't know why yer want ter go on tearing yerself inside out over this ambition to go all arty-crafty! Yer've still got yer Chris ter think of. School fees. Clothes. Them 'olidays that posh school of 'is sends 'im on. If yer ask me, you've got too big fer yer boots.'

Chris at fourteen was hardly home these days. 'All right if I stay the night with Leslie Allington?' or 'Richard Martin says I can spend the weekend at his house?' Or handing her a letter from his school near King's Cross, to which he had won a scholarship at eleven, to say a holiday in Switzerland was planned over the Christmas Break and could she send a deposit within the next two weeks? How could she deny him? Popular and outgoing, unlike his father, Chris was never still for a moment. And so once again, Letty was facing lonely evenings and weekends, this year a lonely Christmas unless she made herself go to spend it with Lucy and Jack. As with most ruts, it was hard to drag herself out of it – looking over the rim with envy yet unable to achieve the impetus necessary to climb up into the open.

★   ★   ★

435

David put the phone down with a feeling of complete despondency. There was no escaping that Letitia meant what she said and no cajoling, no pleading, no show of anger, was going to shift her resolution.

From the pink and gilded master bedroom, came Madge's voice, high and querulous.

'Who on earth can you be phoning on Christmas Day, darling? People will be arriving any minute now and all you can do is chat on the telephone. Who was it?'

'No one you'd know,' he called back.

He heard her give vent to a high-pitched, derisive 'Huh!' And then: 'Not one of your fancy women, darling, is it?' Her idea of a joke.

For a moment he was so tempted. To walk back into the bedroom, stand behind her as she sat at the ornate white dressing table with its gilt scroll-work, stare at her mocking reflection in the mirror and say, 'As a matter of fact, *darling*, it is. We love each other. Have done for years. And I want a divorce!'

'I said,' Madge called again when he didn't respond, 'not one of your fancy women, is it?'

He walked into the bedroom, stared at her reflection gazing back at him just as he'd anticipated, and said quizzically, 'As a matter of fact, it was.'

His reward was a high rippling laugh, the sort of penetrating yet infectious sound that made her so popular with her set. A woman of striking looks, when she laughed Madge could look positively beautiful.

'Dear God, darling! How deliciously funny!'

It was only when humour failed her, which was often in his company though seldom in others', that the sour lines showed. Her high spirits had given her a certain allure that he'd mistaken for beauty when he'd first known her.

Now as the laughter left her face she peered once more at herself in the mirror and dabbed a touch more powder around her firm jawline and chin.

Madge was proud of her looks; she was tall, slender still at forty, with a graceful neck many a fashion model would have envied. Her short expertly waved hair was dark and glossy and she meticulously shaped her eyebrows to a fine arch, giving herself a perpetually surprised look. With cleverly rouged cheekbones and wide mouth painted deep red to present a more rosebud line, she could look quite ravishing.

'If you could be as witty as that in front of our friends,' she went on mockingly, 'you'd be far more popular than you are!'

Something in David snapped.

'Yes, have your laugh!' he grated, seeing her look up at the tone of his voice. 'But it's true. I do have another woman.'

She was peering at him from the mirror. She gave a little nervous laugh, started to look away, but something in his tone arrested her gaze. She turned on the pink-upholstered dressing stool to confront him.

'Look, darling, you're going just a wee bit too far.' A pause, then a frown that took away her beauty. 'You are joking?'

'No,' he said firmly, his voice low. 'No, Madge, I'm not.'

She gazed at him, angry now. 'Don't be so utterly ridiculous! Who on earth . . .'

'I've been seeing her every weekend for four years,' he said evenly.

'But you've been *here*! Every weekend! At least these six or . . .'

Her expression changed as her voice conveyed recollection of the months before.

'That's right, Madge,' David confirmed. 'I've not seen her for some seven months, but now I intend to start seeing her again.'

'You won't!' The amber-coloured eyes began to blaze. 'Not if you value this marriage.'

'I don't, Madge. It's been a farce for years, and you know it. I don't count in your life. I have no standing with your friends. You go your way just as you please and damn what I say – how I feel. If I walked out this very evening, you wouldn't miss me, physically or financially, and Daddy would take care of the latter detail for you.'

'I don't doubt he would. Except that I'm not prepared to *have* you walk out on me, darling! Who is she, anyway? I don't suppose for one minute she's some little shop girl. You're too fastidious for that. Is she well up in society? I bet she is. Wouldn't want her good name smeared about to all and sundry. Do I know her?'

'No. She's not in your class,' he countered caustically.

'Fortunate for you, darling!' she sneered. 'But I'll tell you this for nothing, David – you can go on seeing her until hell freezes, but if you think I'm letting you go, you are very much mistaken. Now go and get ready. We've people coming any minute. And you know most of them, don't you, our friends – Daddy's friends? One's a JP and one is that prominent banker Daddy deals with – I can't remember his name off hand. And Archie Bannister. His father is head of that newspaper – now what is it called? The big one?'

'I can give you grounds for divorce,' David cut in, ignoring the overt threat, his thoughts on Chris, his son. But it wasn't to be.

Madge gave another of her bubbling laughs, only just disguising its cynical tone, managed to adopt an air of flippancy. 'Don't be idiotic, darling! Why on earth would I go out of my way to have my name bandied about? On everyone's lips? Pointed out as the wounded wife? Dear God – what a thought! I'm sorry, David. Just can't do! Now, do hurry yourself. Everyone will be here in a few ticks and I'm not having our party spoiled. Polly!'

Her voice rose sharply. 'Where is that girl? These silly waves aren't setting right. Polly!'

As a flustered maid came hurrying in, David

retired silently to get ready, not sure even now whether Madge had believed him or not.

Throughout Christmas he wondered where Letitia would be celebrating, how she was faring, whether she was thinking of him? She had to be thinking of him. The love they'd had couldn't all go for nothing. She had to care.

It was nigh impossible to phone her until the New Year. The house, large as it was, constantly overflowed with guests. Madge threw a huge New Year's Eve party. Smoking elegant Turkish cigarettes, behaving like a young thing, sipping champagne with delight, dancing with every man there as though he were the only one . . . On New Year's day took her guests to the pantomime – *Mother Goose* at the Palladium – to throw bits of screwed up programmes at the performers from the front stalls and generally join in the fun and singing.

David, obliged to go along, sat back in his seat amid the rich and reckless, longing for the serenity of Letitia's flat. Almost as much, he longed for his son. He had missed virtually all of the boy's growing years; did not want to miss the rest.

Next week, Madge at her hairdresser's, he telephoned Letty like a little boy playing truant – told her what he had told Madge, asked if he was reprieved and was consumed with relief as Letty, voice betraying her own eagerness, agreed to his coming over on Saturday.

★　　★　　★

This Letty was far more in charge than the Letty he had once known. Perhaps she had always been, even in their most passionate moments, concerned where everything was leading, how she'd cope with it, always feeling answerable to someone. She no longer had anyone to answer to, not even Christopher, sixteen and a half and broadening out across the shoulders, yet still insisted on being answerable to herself.

'You're no nearer being free of her than you were two years ago,' she badgered him when he told her of Madge's reaction. 'Two years, David! How much longer does this go on?'

'Have some sense, Letitia?' he retaliated, sharp with her, taking out his chagrin over Madge on her. 'I can't *make* her divorce me if she refuses to. She's done nothing to merit my divorcing her. There have to be grounds, Letitia.'

'*She's* had ample grounds, hasn't she? You've made it plain enough to her about us. Ample grounds for *two years*!'

'If she chooses not to exercise her prerogative, what can I do?'

Bickering, hurting each other, making up in a welter of mutual passionate forgiveness, they might almost have been married. But they weren't!

The new Letty fended him off – or was she so new?

'No, David, you're not moving in. Not until you're free.'

They had made love the night before. Again this

morning. Christopher as usual was away for the weekend. It was always wonderful having the place to themselves. Lying in David's arms, naked and fulfilled, her head on his bare shoulder, Letty gazed up at him. He still had a wonderful lean body, a firm jawline for all he was fifty-two. He had got rid of that ridiculous moustache and looked much younger for it. She, at forty-two, looked good as well, felt like a young girl in his arms.

He stared hard at her. 'And what's the difference, making love with you on Saturday night and moving in lock, stock and barrel?'

'The difference,' she said, lowering her eyes, 'is that you still have your wife and I have a business to run. But let's not worry about that now.'

She snuggled closer under the bedclothes, the bedroom chilly. It was February 1932. A lot had happened in the two years since David had come back.

Dad had been in hospital twice with fluid on the lungs, was still hanging on like a wind-buffeted spider with a broken web, but had had a stroke in the autumn, leaving his left side useless, and was now confined to home.

Vinny had remarried, to a gentleman friend. Lucy and family had been invited but not Letty and Chris.

Lucy's eldest, Elisabeth, had married a stock-broker's son last year. Vinny, knowing Letty would be at the wedding, had declined to go. It still hurt, Vinny's attitude towards her. 'Nine years,' she'd remarked to David. 'You'd have thought she'd have got over it by now.'

Her gallery's expansion meant travelling more: to auctions, to fine houses, even across the Channel, conversing with buyers, with dealers, developing an expert and discerning eye for value.

Letty was now worth a bit more than a few bob, as she put it with an old touch of cockney understatement. Elegantly dressed, outwardly self-assured, she could have owned a fine piece of property by now but still felt more at home, safe, in her flat after a day with affected but hard-nosed art dealers. At times she was so mentally tired, all she wanted to do was to lock herself away from everything. Sometimes she wondered why she had done it all, remembered Dad's words about getting too big for her boots. Dad whose words were little more than a slur these days.

David was her solace, her rock to cling to. Looking back over these two years, for all the change in her fortunes, very little had changed between her and David. They still only saw each other at weekends. Perhaps one evening in the week to go to the theatre or a cinema if something special was on. Always aware that he must go back to his wife, his office. Henry Lampton had long known of his son-in-law's affair but, Madge preferring to keep it from her smart little circle of friends who loved nothing better than a scandal, he had been compelled to turn a blind eye.

For that reason, Letty spent Christmas entirely

alone while David stayed with his wife in a pretence of married bliss. She didn't go to Lucy's, knowing her sister would have been all advice, making her Christmas even more miserable. Chris, seventeen and going on to college next year, was full of understanding and spent the day with her, even declining to go out for a walk with a friend. Together they listened to King George's Christmas message on the wireless; the first ever broadcast by any monarch, Letty listening with special attention.

Last summer Queen Mary, passing through Oxford Street, had paused to come into Letty's gallery, had spoken a dignified word with her and departed; the visit was so brief, so unobtrusive, that Letty had been left with a sensation of its almost being a dream. But she had felt a personal tie to royalty ever since and listened, avid as any relative, to the king's speech, crying at the end of it because he had moved her so and because she longed for David here beside her, though she didn't tell Chris that. He assumed she'd just been overcome by the uniqueness of the moment and her feelings towards the royal family.

In the office the telephone on the desk before Letty began to ring. It was lunchtime – she often worked through it, taking a sandwich and a cup of tea while her twenty-four-year-old secretary, Ann Hopper, went off to lunch. Absently, she answered its summons.

'Bancroft Galleries. Letitia Beans speaking.'

She had changed the name to Bancroft Galleries on acquiring the lease of the bookshop next door. The Treasure Chest had been trite, not worthy of one who now dealt in original paintings and fine art. Beans Galleries didn't have the right impact either.

She'd have liked to change her own name from Beans back to Bancroft as well, but still felt an allegiance to Billy for all he'd been gone seven years.

It seemed like yesterday – as if her life had been stuck in limbo ever since. She still went to the cemetery once every month and laid flowers, dividing them between two green metal containers and arranging them with great care. Afterwards she stood awhile reading the inscriptions on the fast discolouring headstone: 'William Beans, beloved husband, cherished son. Born 1889, died 22 January 1926. Now at Peace'. She tried to wash away the sacrilegious smears of sparrow droppings and the stubborn circles of grey lichen, gave up, gazed a moment at the crack appearing at one side of the limestone, then came away sad but satisfied.

She was sad, not for herself any more but for Billy, a strong young man reduced to a human wreck by war. She prayed to God that such a conflict would never recur and thought of Christopher especially, praying he'd never go through what Billy had, or David, or any of those

445

young men who had grown old in a few hours of gas and bombardment.

But, of course, there was no likelihood of a war like that ever happening again – it had been too terrible ever to be repeated. And with this world-wide depression, so much unemployment, Germany was in such a state it would never again raise its head as a great power. True someone called Hitler had taken up the reins, being hailed as the country's saviour, but it would never again try to test its strength against others – thank God.

There was another reason Letty had not changed her name back to Bancroft – always the hope that one day David's wife would agree to divorce him. Madge couldn't go on clinging to him forever. She didn't love him, she had no need of him, wouldn't miss him. She was just hanging on out of spite. In time she would have to tire of his continual pleas for divorce and give up. And then . . . wonderful day . . . Letty's name would become Baron.

The voice at the other end of the telephone was Ada's, gasping as if she was crying. 'Letty! Oh, Letty – yer dad's died! One minute 'e was 'ere with us – the next 'e'd gone all funny. They took 'im to the London 'Ospital but 'e died on the way. 'E never even said goodbye ter me!'

CHAPTER 26

The front room of the house in Stratford held a paltry gathering. Most of Arthur Bancroft's own contemporaries, his several brothers and sisters, had gone ahead of him, or were no longer in any state of health to attend a funeral. Their offspring grown away from his generation had their own families, and hardly knew Arthur much less had come along to mourn him.

Lucy was already there when Letty, David and Chris arrived. Lucy looked very attractive in a trim black linen suit and white blouse.

Jack was still the same long thin streak she'd brought home to be introduced to Dad twenty-five years ago, a little round-shouldered now, otherwise looking very prosperous in a well-cut black worsted suit.

Twenty-one-year-old Emmeline, with her mother's shade of golden hair, had come. So had Elisabeth, Lucy's other daughter; tall, slim and fair despite her early pregnancy. Her husband was a well-built young man with a handsome if rather flexible face.

A sister of Ada's, a woman just as dowdy,

shadowed her continually, asking if she was all right. Ada gave perfunctory nods. She looked care-worn from nursing her late husband. Seeing her, Letty realised how much the woman must have loved him; recalled and regretted her own uncharitable feelings towards her and Dad when they'd first, as she'd seen it then, deserted her to take up their own lives together.

A neighbour or two completed the gathering but of Vinny there was no sign. Letty felt bitterness, even hatred, flood over her. Not even to attend her own father's funeral – because Letty was there! How deep could it go?

'No Vinny?' she asked Lucy as casually as she could as Ada's sister handed her a glass of sherry before they were called to depart for the East London Cemetery where Dad was being buried near to Mum.

'Your father's upstairs in the front bedroom if you want to go and look at 'im,' Ada's sister imparted before going on with the tray of tiny glasses containing their thimbleful of wine.

Letty nodded, forgetting Vinny at the idea of gazing at Dad for the last time.

'Coming up there with me?' she begged.

David had already shaken his head, declining the invitation. He hardly had any reason to see the old man. Chris had turned faintly long-faced and looked appealingly at his mother. He was young, had not looked upon death yet, was obviously not inclined to begin now.

Lucy inclined her head at Letty's plea in rather reluctant agreement.

'I have been up to see him once, though.'

'Don't matter then,' Letty said.

'No – it's all right,' said Lucy quickly. 'I don't mind.' And with Letty going ahead, they went with suitably solemn steps up to the front bedroom where the coffin lay, its lid slewed to one side to allow a view of the deceased.

'He looks very peaceful,' Lucy said in a whisper.

'Old,' Letty said.

'They've done him up well.'

'I don't like all that make up they use. Don't look natural.' Her old childhood way of talking came through. She suddenly felt a child again – wanted to cry out, 'Dad, can I go down to play?'

She took a deep breath. She was forty-three years old next month. Far away from childhood. But she felt like a child, saw herself skipping down the street in Club Row, saw again Dad looking out of his shop door, his strong moustache bristling, blue eyes vivid and alive but kind. His voice was kind too. 'Letitia! Come in now – yer mum wants some 'elp.'

Tears for those days, for what could never be again, filled her eyes. The moustache was sparse now, had been darkened by the undertaker's brush, looking ludicrous against the papery skin, its pallor tinted a strange shade of pink. Dad was lying straight in his coffin, his eyes closed. She'd never hear him call her Letitia again. But oh, dear God, how she wanted the past back again!

Lucy's arm was around her shoulders. 'Come on, Let, don't cry. We can't do a lot here. Let's go back downstairs.'

There was subdued talking, a quiet murmuring, around the room. The two sisters joined it, melting into it unnoticed. The front door had been opened and remained ajar for a brief while. Letty felt the draught of chill April air come into the room from the hallway, taking the heat from the low fire, then cease as the front door closed. She momentarily thought it might be the undertakers but there was no stir of expectancy from the people around her.

They joined David and Chris. Lucy, now talking to Chris, her head tilted up to his six foot, glanced towards the door and her eyes lit up in welcome. Automatically Letty turned to see Vinny with her new husband and boys, now grown men, standing in the doorway.

Vinny's grey-green eyes had roamed the room uneasily. They came to rest on her youngest sister and she blanched, mouth tightening. Held by the other's stare, Letty saw the woman she had not set eyes on for ten years and was stunned.

Where Lucy had aged gently, keeping her figure, ample bosom redeeming her slimness, Vinny had grown gaunt. Sunken cheeks, the jaw bone a sharp line above a thin neck, she had hardly any figure, the new shapely fashion doing nothing for her. She was, after all, forty-six now. But Letty had expected her to wear her age well, as Lucy did – she'd been so beautiful as a young girl.

Still Letty and Vinny stared at one another. Indecision churned inside Letty. Should she keep up the stare until Vinny was forced to turn away, or give way herself, pretend she had not seen her? But that was silly. She gave a nervous smile – it felt more like a grimace. Vinny's lips never even twitched, remaining a thin scarlet gash. It almost took Letty by surprise when her sister turned away abruptly, seeking Ada to offer her condolences.

Letty clutched at David. 'I don't think I can stand this.'

'It's all right.' His hand squeezed hers, firm and reassuring.

'It's going to be horrible these next few hours. In the same room together and she acts as if I don't exist!'

Chris was looking worried. 'Take no notice, Mum.'

'Probably a bit of a shock to her, your being here,' Lucy put in.

'She must have known I'd be here. Our own father. Obviously I'd be here. You'd think that after all this time . . .'

A faint stir rippled through the gathering. Again a draught swept through the front room making the fire flicker. Dark-suited men in black-ribboned top hats moved past the door, going up the stairs. Conversation ceased, the air was still, then past the door came the long shape, hoisted on the shoulders of the coffin bearers, heads bowed, hands held low and crossed, as expertly they balanced the coffin on shoulders.

There was a subdued shuffling in the room as the gathering sorted itself into an order of precedence, Ada supported by a brother going ahead, handkerchief to her nose, sniffing softly; the deceased's three daughters following behind, Vinny on the farthest side from Letty with Lucy a barrier between them. The rest moved out of the house into the chill April air, a silent double file, to find their places in the waiting limousines.

Lucy sat between her sisters on the back seat, very aware of her role as intermediary, saying nothing to either of them, which was unusual for her, while Ada, comforted by her brother, sat in front.

After a sad service, which was expected, and words of quiet encouragement from the vicar, they returned frozen to the marrow from standing at the graveside in a stiff April breeze. There was whisky and brandy and warming cups of steaming tea poured by a neighbour who had done the funeral fare of ham and tinned salmon sandwiches and small iced cakes and Swiss roll.

As whisky began to warm the mourners, conversation livened up. Stories of when Arthur did this or when Arthur did that brought reminiscent laughter and Ada was smiling again.

Lucy was talking with Vinny, Jack with David as if he were a true brother-in-law; Letty went and sat by the window, gazing out at the large double-fronted bay-windowed houses opposite. Here the blinds had been lifted and a weak sunlight filtered into the room with its high ceilings and heavy furniture.

A small brandy in her hand, a sandwich on a plate on the table beside her, she tried to ignore Vinny's presence, thought of Dad then found it best not to as nostalgia descended. She and Dad had grown apart too long ago for her to feel any deep grief but she suffered keenly from a persistent sense of something lost. The past perhaps? Seeing everyone swapping anecdotes, she felt very isolated yet had no wish to join in; she still felt Vinny's presence like a ton weight, fighting an urge to get up and run out of the house.

'Are you all right, Letitia?'

Letty jumped, momentarily thought of Dad always calling her by her full name, looked up, and smiled at David.

'Yes, I'm fine.'

'You looked very down.' He drew up a chair. 'You mustn't sit here all alone mourning him, you know. You won't do yourself any good.'

She suddenly wanted to throw all the weight of her burden on to him.

'It's not that!' she burst out. 'It's Vinny. Deliberately ignoring me. I think she just came to make me squirm . . .'

'No, that's silly,' he interrupted gently. 'She came out of love and respect for her father. As you did.'

She *was* being silly. She let her shoulders slump a little. 'I suppose so. If only she didn't make me feel that I'm to blame. Chris was my child, not hers. But she's my sister and I love her, in spite of everything. I don't want her to hate me . . .'

'Letitia!' He leaned close. 'Give it a chance. And don't sit here by yourself. Go and talk to everyone while I . . .'

'But how can I?'

'Don't worry.' He got up, patted her cheek lovingly. 'Just trust me, Letitia. Now go and talk to someone!'

Wondering, she stood up as he left her, going to seek Lucy once more. Vinny's boys were standing around, bored. Young men now, they hung about their mother as though she were a lodestone. None of them, Lucy said, had girls, even though they were all good-looking.

'She's always mothered them,' Lucy said. 'Made big babies of them.'

Letty smiled wryly, sipping her brandy. She felt proud of Chris – the way he spoke with everyone, interested in what was being said. He was very much in command of himself and in September he would be going on to Cambridge. This past year he'd discovered girls and made no bones about it. In her opinion he knocked his cousins into a cocked hat.

She noticed David talking to Edwin Nicholson, Vinny's husband, more like long lost friends than men having met for the first time today. The next moment he had moved over to her, taken hold of her arm and was guiding her back to Vinny's new husband.

'Edwin, I don't believe you have met Letitia, Lavinia's sister? Letitia, this is Edwin, Lavinia's husband.'

Letty tilted her head solemnly. Vinny was standing behind Edwin with her back to him, talking to someone. He turned and attracted her attention.

'Vinny – here's your sister.'

The men had a look of conspiracy about them, Letty noticed as Vinny glanced round. Her expression was a picture, finding herself suddenly at arm's length from Letty. She guessed hers was only fractionally less guarded.

She heard herself saying, 'I'm sorry, Vinny – it wasn't me,' while her sister assumed the look of a cornered cat, bristling and wide-eyed.

'Aren't you going to say hello to your sister?' David, very much in command of the situation, was refusing to allow them any escape.

What else could Vinny do? 'Hullo, Letty,' she said stiffly.

'Hullo,' she returned, stifling an urgent need to giggle. But if she had she'd have dissolved into tears. She swallowed hard, gazing in silent appeal at her sister.

'We'll leave you two alone to have a chat,' David was saying, his tone blithe. 'I expect you've a lot to talk about.'

You can say that again, Letty thought as the two men moved off. She sensed Vinny about to turn away too, predicted the move, and put a restraining hand on her arm.

'Vinny! Don't let's go on like this. We have to talk sometime.'

She saw Vinny stiffen, felt suddenly dreadfully sorry for her.

'Please – can't we make it up?'

Vinny remained stiff-faced. 'I don't know what you mean,' she said, almost viciously.

'Yes, you do. You've blamed me all these years. And perhaps you have a right.'

She wanted to say more. Say: 'I was his mother. I had a right too.' But it would have driven a wedge back into the gap she could see had started to close, ever so slightly. She stood gazing at Vinny, all that was in her mind visible in her glistening green eyes. Then the words began to flow of their own accord.

'Think about Dad,' she said slowly. 'He wouldn't want us to keep all this animosity between us. It don't matter who was wrong, or who was right. We each had our claim, Vinny. We each felt so terribly hurt. But I didn't mean to hurt you.'

Her eyes were swimming. Vinny's as well.

'Let's make it up to Dad, by making up. He'd have wanted that. And I still love you, Vinny.'

For a moment, her sister's tears threatened to spill over. Embarrassed, Vinny switched her gaze to the tall figure of Chris with her sons who were laughing at something he'd said; George, who'd inherited his father's pomposity at times, was laughing the heartiest.

'He's grown tall, your Christopher,' she observed huskily.

456

Letty half turned, followed her gaze, and nodded. 'Like Dad was.'

'No, he's like your David.' Vinny's tone made her turn back. Vinny's face had softened unexpectedly.

'But he's got Lucy's nature,' Letty said with new heart.

'He's totally different to the child I was bringing up. So self-assured, I wouldn't have recognised him. He's your boy, Let, through and through. I've been clinging to memories of a little boy but he's a man now. He's yours – yours and David's.'

She couldn't believe it was Vinny saying this – the Vinny who had ignored her all these years, who had borne such a terrifying grudge against her.

She wanted to hug her but still felt wary; instead said quietly, 'Let's be friends again, Vinny. Let's forget . . . things, shall we?'

For a moment Vinny regarded her unsmiling. She hadn't smiled in all this time, but Letty could forgive her that.

'I was sorry to hear about your Billy. I know how it feels, having lost . . .' She hesitated then went on, 'But you've got David now.'

'It's nice of you to say that,' Letty began warmly, immediately to realise something was not quite right as, attempting to take Vinny's hand in a gesture of sisterly affection, she felt it instantly drawn away, as though her touch had burned.

Vinny's tone had become frigid.

'I do agree, Letty, it is rather negative to carry

on being nasty to each other. For Dad's sake, I suppose. But I can't ever forgive you for the pain you caused me when you took Christopher away from me. I just hope you never have to suffer the sort of misery I did. But, as you say, we should bury the past. If only for Dad's sake.'

With that she moved off to where her husband stood talking to Jack, leaving Letty utterly confused by the change of mood; she knew that for as long as she lived, she and Vinny would never again be real friends, that she would be better off erasing the whole business from her thoughts.

She moved away through the gathering that was beginning to thin as some turned their thoughts to going home and went to look for David, to suggest they too should leave, wanting never to see Vinny again.

Letty received a frantic phone call from Lucy a few days later. Dad had made a will leaving everything to Ada, including the shop and the rent from it.

'I always thought it would be divided between us girls,' she said, enraged. 'But it's all going to her! All of it. Not a penny piece for any of us! You know what she'll do. She'll drink it up the wall, that's what. Well, we're going to contest it,' she added resolutely, as if that would magically solve everything.

For her part, Letty felt a little glad nothing of Dad's was coming to her. She wasn't sure why.

'He couldn't very well leave Ada without a penny,' she soothed.

'But *everything*!' Lucy paused. When she began again, her tone was far less friendly, having detected Letty's lack of enthusiasm for any fight.

'Of course,' she went on in a knowing tone, 'I suppose Vinny's right. It wouldn't affect you. You don't need any of Dad's money. I mean, like Vinny said when she heard about the will, you've already had your share, long before he died. He always favoured you.'

Taken aback, Letty frowned into the phone. 'I don't understand.'

'You should, Letty,' Lucy's reply came volleying back. 'You moving out of Dad's shop into Oxford Street! You don't do that on peanuts.'

Anger rose up inside her. Her fingers whitened around the receiver. 'Are you insinuating I used Dad's money?'

'I'm not,' Lucy said hurriedly. 'Vinny said . . .'

'Ah, Vinny!'

'I wouldn't have given it a thought. But she said . . . Well, you must admit, it does look odd when you add it all up.'

'Add what up?' Her anger against Vinny grew. She'd tried to befriend her again, and had found her hand viciously bitten.

'You couldn't have saved up on your own,' Lucy said. 'You couldn't have afforded the place you've got without some help from Dad.'

'I had no help!' Letty asserted. 'I wouldn't have his money – not after the way he and Ada walked out on me, after all the years I gave him. This place has come from *my* savings. And from what Billy's father gave him.'

'Yes, you did well out of Billy, didn't you?'

It sounded nasty. 'That's not your business!' Letty burst out in fury. But it was Vinny she could hear talking. Vinny's words put into Lucy's silly mouth. Bullets from her to fire and she stupid enough to fire them, realising nothing of the damage she was doing.

'I saved every penny myself!' A small lie but resentment had boiled over at the insinuations. 'And from bits and pieces I sold . . .'

'Dad's bits and pieces?'

'I beg your pardon?' She couldn't believe she was hearing this.

'Dad's pictures,' Lucy reminded harshly. 'They hung on the wall in the parlour. Where did they go? Dad never had them. We never. You've not got them any more. I bet they were worth a good few bob or two.'

'Dad didn't want them. I asked him.'

Why was she trying to justify her past actions in this way, to Lucy and Vinny, just because they were both incensed about Dad's will?

'Don't include me in your squabbles, Lucy,' she burst out suddenly, and put the phone down so abruptly her sister's ear must have tingled.

'Don't take it to heart so,' David told her when, near to tears with anger, she related it to him. 'Leave them to it. You've got me.'

And she knew he was right.

CHAPTER 27

'There's nothing they can do about it,' Christopher observed with amusement. 'Honestly, Mum, I've never heard anything like this family. Always squabbling. They're sniffing around the wrong tree this time. When you remarry, everything goes automatically to the spouse when you pop off, unless you specifically make a new will to include issue from a previous marriage.'

He had a feeling for law, and in September went off to study it at Cambridge. Letty felt so very proud of him – and missed him dreadfully.

It might not have been so bad if she and David had been married, but her days dragged. For all the gallery took up her time, her thoughts were geared to weekends when David came, those two days of bliss.

In the New Year, from a pure need to occupy herself, she arranged an exhibition of a young Italian painter's work. Her very first attempt at exhibiting a single artist, her reward was a succession of sleepless nights, telling herself she had overstepped the mark into a world she was not

461

yet fully conversant with. But there had to be a first time. The exhibition turned out to be a success well beyond what she'd expected.

David came to the opening, congratulated her, told her he was proud of her, praised her courage. But she hadn't done it for that, wished she hadn't done it at all.

In late-spring she was persuaded to try another exhibition by an English newcomer whose work included wonderful industrial landscapes. A large manufacturing company pounced on him and commissioned a vast painting for the foyer of each of its many branches around the country.

For Letty, the financial rewards of both launchings were of less consequence than the prestige they brought. Ironic really. All her life she had dreamed of becoming someone of note. Now that it was knocking on her door, all she wanted was to push it away, longing only to be on her own with David, quietly and simply married.

Evenings were the worst, when she sat alone wondering what he was doing, if all he had told her about his wife was true; that she was a cold bitch, that she had no love, no care for him, wanted only to enjoy herself with those of her own sort. Those long solitary evenings added weight to her suspicion with nothing to allay it. Sitting at the table balancing books or checking diaries, a cup of coffee growing cold beside her, meagre meal uneaten, she would look up to stare meditatively at the wall and her lips would tighten at thoughts of David.

By the weekend, all her frustration at his not being beside her, and suspicion that he was having a gay old time without her, spoiled their time together. She a fury, he standing meek and browbeaten, uncertain what had caused the furore.

'You know what the cause is!' she yelled at him. It was August – holiday time. Families thronged main railway stations, loaded down by suitcases; sturdy young men with rucksacks were bound for the Lake and Peak Districts; groups of office and shop girls were all flowered dresses and giggles looking to find a likely lad on some crowded south coast beach. Letty could only sit in her flat, waiting for David.

They would have a meal together, take in a theatre, would make love in her bed, would awaken on Sunday morning and she'd prepare breakfast. Sunday would be spent taking in the sunshine in one of London's parks. The day drawing to a close, they would make hurried love and he'd go back to his large house in Barnet and to Madge, leaving Letty to her lonely bed.

Today they'd taken advantage of the lingering August evening, and had sat quite contented by the river at Richmond. They'd driven back to the flat in the purple dusk. They'd had coffee, been laughing at a joke – she couldn't remember what it had been. Then for no reason it had all boiled up again. It always did.

'You know what the cause is!' she hurled at him again, striding around the room. 'It's her! And you! How many more years do I sit here waiting for you to come and favour me with your presence once a week? Have you told her about Christopher yet? No! Your son, and you're ashamed to reveal him to anyone.'

'You're talking rubbish, Letitia.'

'Don't Letitia me!' she blared, hating him. But it would end the same way. She would rant and rave, slay him with her tongue, reduce herself to a quivering heap of misery, cry on his shoulder, apologise for having been so horrible to him, would let him take her to bed and make love to her. But as yet she had not reached that stage.

'How long do you expect me to go on like this?' she ranted. 'Years ago you accused me of delaying things, not wanting to marry you. The boot's on the other foot now, isn't it? It's you expecting me to wait until you've enough courage to make the break. But I'm not prepared to wait forever. If you don't tell her about Chris soon . . . If you don't force her to divorce you, then we might as well part.'

How many times before had she said that? How many times had she seen him looking at her, his face pale with concern, seen him gnaw his lip, helpless, because Madge refused to give him his freedom and she herself refused to live with him until he was free. Why did she and Madge lead this gentle man a dog's life? Was it because he *was* so gentle? And what was really so bad about David living here, though still married to another?

His face was pale. Not pale . . . grey. Breathing as if his chest hurt, he was rubbing one hand hard along his left arm.

Letty stopped ranting and looked at him. 'What's the matter?'

'Nothing.' He winced. 'Just an odd pain. I get it now and again.'

'Where?' It hit her that he wasn't young any more – was fifty-four.

'Nowhere in particular.' He was massaging a region near the centre of his chest.

Alarm spread over Letty, fear gathering. 'Have you seen a doctor?'

He was smiling at her, straightening up, glad that her temper had receded. 'It's a touch of indigestion, I expect.'

'How long have you had it?' She was all attention now, voice full of love and concern.

David shrugged dismissively. 'A few weeks. It'll go.'

'I think you should see a doctor,' she stated flatly, knowing she wouldn't feel easy until a doctor had indeed confirmed it to be just a touch of indigestion. For that was all it was, she was sure of it, she told herself firmly.

'What d'you expect me to do about it?'

Madge fitted a cigarette into an ivory holder. Holders were going out of fashion. Filter-tipped cigarettes were used straight from the packet or box, extracted with exaggerated sophistication by film stars like Katherine Hepburn and Ginger

Rogers. But Madge had reached an age when unconsciously she clung to some of the elegant mannerisms of an earlier era, and still preferred a holder. Blowing the perfumed smoke of a Passing Cloud from her pursed lips, she turned to look at David.

'If you're thinking of playing on my sympathy, you can think again. I'm not at all impressed.'

David regarded her from where he stood by the art deco fireplace Madge had just had put in; she was always having something done to the house.

'It wasn't said to impress you. I merely thought you should know.'

'And how long did the doctor give you?' Her attitude was indifferent, and David grimaced.

'You are a fantastic bitch, Madge. It wouldn't bother you if he gave me just six months, would it?'

'And did he?' She bent to flick over a page of sheet music from *Bitter Sweet*, propped up on the grand piano she had also recently had installed on a whim. She hadn't learned to play it, of course.

'He said I have every likelihood of making it into a ripe old age.'

'Pity!' Madge smiled and wandered away from the piano. 'Pity for you, I mean. Good try, darling. But I've no intention of divorcing you if you fell at my feet gasping out your last but one breath.'

David spread his hands in appeal. 'What do you get out of this, Madge? You don't want me. I make no difference to your life. I'm never seen with you.

You go your own way. I go mine. You have friends who have divorced. It's no longer a stigma.'

She turned on him, her tone light. 'Let's just say I don't like playing second fiddle to anyone, least of all your mistress. Runs an art gallery, doesn't she, your Letitia? One of those odd sort, is she, all trailing scarves and Bohemian skirts? Oh, come, David, you don't expect me to relinquish you to someone like that.'

He gave her a level stare. 'There is one thing I have never told you. Perhaps I should have. It's that I have a son by her.'

'My God!' Madge executed a shocked look, as false as her eyelashes, one hand spread dramatically across her breast. 'Don't tell me you can still do it! A bit of a surprise for you, wasn't it? Her too, I should imagine!'

David suffered the bubbling laughter. 'His name is Christopher. He'll be twenty this year.'

'So long ago? Oh, I can forgive you then, darling. How you must have suffered. So that bit of information is supposed to shock me into a fit of fury strong enough for me to fling divorce papers in your face? Wrong again, darling. I'm sorry to be such a bore, David. But the truth is I am having a quite wonderful time with my friends and don't intend to go all gloomy on them in a sordid divorce.'

Quite suddenly the laughter left her. Twin lines appeared each side of her mouth and between the finely arched eyebrows. She looked down and stubbed out the cigarette in a pink marble ashtray. 'As far as I am concerned, David, you can die my husband, but you'll never die my ex-husband. Is that clear?'

'Clear enough, Madge.' He moved away from the fireplace. 'And I shall make something clear to you. You can do what you like about it. The house – everything – is yours. I shall live elsewhere.'

'Everything?' Her mirthless laugh followed him as he left. 'Daddy will be pleased!' As if that too was a threat.

Henry Lampton was seventy-eight. Madge was his only child after he had lost a son and a daughter from childhood illnesses and his last surviving son, who would have taken over his business, had been killed early in the Great War. Since then, Madge had been his life's blood – as he had often told David.

Confined now to a wheelchair, Henry Lampton hadn't been near the boardroom for years, not since his wife had died four years ago. In his large house in rural South Mimms, he was cared for by a resident nurse, housekeeper and gardener.

Thin and shaky, wrapped in a thick tartan shawl this cold January morning, he hugged the blazing fire in the drawing room where he sat. His rheumy eyes nevertheless held the dark ones of his son-in-law as David sat opposite. Henry's quavering voice held a bitterly sarcastic tone.

'Thought you'd come and put your case before Madge did? She's already telephoned me, before you arrived. Got in first, you see.'

David returned the glare. 'I thought it only right to come here and tell you myself. As from today I shall no longer be living in Barnet. I can't go on living there and . . .'

'Yes, yes.' The gnarled and protruding from the folds of the shawl waved abruptly, an almost comical movement except that the eyes held a smouldering animosity. 'You don't have to repeat everything to me. I might be at death's portals but I'm not senile.'

He shifted irascibly in the wheelchair, rang a small bronze handbell on the table beside him. At the sound, a middle-aged woman with straight iron grey hair and flat colourless cheeks came into the room, a starched wrapover nurse's dress rustling with each swift step. Henry Lampton turned irritably towards her.

'Sort out this cushion behind me, will you? It's crumpled again. Damned bloody thing! We'll have to find something more substantial than this. It gives me back ache. Damned thing!'

As if in one smooth movement she leaned him forward, plumped the cushion, leaned him back and moved out of the room. Left once more to themselves, Lampton fixed David with a harsh stare.

'So you thought you'd get your say in first, eh?'

'I thought it only good manners to tell you that we've separated.'

469

'You mean *you've* separated.' He leaned forward, cursed roundly as the cushion slipped again, but this time didn't reach for his bell. He remained leaning forward, eyes full of dislike of the man opposite.

'My daughter says she has no interest in any separation. Has no interest in divorcing you either. Never will.'

'I understand that,' David said quietly. 'It still doesn't mean I have to live with her. So she has two causes for divorce if she wants them. Desertion and adultery.'

'And a child by your mistress,' Lampton finished. 'You and Madge were happy enough until you met this woman. You are the sole cause of the break up of your marriage and I agree with Madge that if she wants to hold you to it she is perfectly entitled to do so. So we could say you are a prisoner of her wishes. How do you like that?' He paused for effect and, thwarted, raised his tone. 'I said, how do you like that?'

'It makes no difference,' David supplied.

'You realise you'll never be allowed to marry this person?'

'Certainly,' he admitted truthfully. 'Nor have I any intention of remaining in a marriage which is nothing more than a farce.'

'A farce, eh?' The pale lips sneered. 'In other words, you share little in common with my daughter's circle of friends. Until this all came about, you were content enough. So – you're prepared to break up a marriage, using any excuse.'

'It broke up long ago.' David's expression almost matched the old man's but Lampton's glare was hard and protracted. 'Your father was my dear and trusted friend when you were but a boy. Hard for me to believe you are his son – a man of your years behaving like a fool. A director in the company your father and I built together.'

This wasn't entirely true and Lampton knew it. That they had been friends, through business, for years was true enough. But Baron's Haberdashers had been two thriving stores, Lampton's just a largish shop selling dress materials. Fred Baron had ploughed in the most money, had had the controlling interest until they'd floated shares within the family and Henry's brother Robert Lampton had bought enough to secure him a place on the board. Obviously Lampton had bought some for Madge as his daughter, and of course David had a like amount. He had also inherited his father's shares on his death, which virtually gave him the deciding interest in the expanding company. All as it should have been – if he and Madge had been happy together. But there was one more important element: Henry Lampton. Had one ace up his sleeve, had he?

'Since you have inherited your father's share,' he went on, 'there is nothing I can do, but my greatest pleasure would be to see you resign, lock, stock and barrel, sell out and get out. Although I am powerless to ask you to do so, of course.'

David wanted to laugh, tried not to feel

triumphant, knew he must not because Henry might be dangerous. The old man had expected to die before his card could be played. The danger was that, if forced, he might play it before his demise, by deed of gift to Madge.

David did not laugh. It took only the stroke of a pen to leave Madge holding a threatening amount of control in the business and Robert Lampton, her uncle, would not take much persuading to side with her. Madge could be very persuasive. But so far Robert Lampton, ten years younger than his brother, had always had a kindly attitude to Fred Baron's son . . . Hopefully it would continue.

David hugged that hope to him, said evenly: 'I'm sorry you feel that way. But I've no intention of resigning or selling out. Do you think I'd do that and let the name my father built die out in some takeover?'

Lampton gave a chuckle. 'I wouldn't dream of letting my old friend's name die. I honour his memory too, you see. Always will. Pity I can't feel the same for his son. And I tell you this, David, I don't suppose I have many years ahead of me. But things won't be plain sailing for you when I'm gone. As long as you and Madge remain married, my shares in the company go to both of you. But a divorce will make her my sole heir. With my shares and those she has now, she only has to acquire a few remaining in my family to sell out over your head if she has a mind to. There'd be nothing you could do about it. You could be out on your ear, your father's name vanished for all your fine intentions. So if I were you, David, I'd think twice about separations and divorces. But then you know that already, don't you? That's why you've not left her before, isn't it?'

David, seeing the old man's smile, his eyes gleaming craftily, remained silent. He had known he was beaten before he'd begun.

CHAPTER 28

Letty shrugged off her fox fur, and let it fall on to the armchair. Throwing up the sash of the window, she leaned out to look down. Oxford Street had been a scene of jubilation all day. All of London had. All of Britain. Flags and decorations were strung out in the May sunshine; bunting and pictures of Their Majesties hung in windows; stores displayed red, white and blue and gold and silver – masses of silver – appropriate for the Silver Jubilee of King George and Queen Mary.

It was dark now. No, not dark. Every large store glowed with decorative lights, Selfridge's virtually ablaze with floodlighting – the first time anyone had seen such a thing here – that lit up the sky, not including the brilliant flashes from fireworks in all the parks.

'It's almost like daytime,' Letty whispered as David took off his white silk scarf and trilby, dropping them on top of the fox fur.

It was nearly midnight but groups of revellers still roamed the street below, loath to say goodbye to what had been a glorious day.

Earlier she and David had made their way down

Charing Cross Road to the Strand, pushed this way and that by crowds trying to catch a glimpse of the king and queen as they passed, together with Prince Edward, heir to the throne, looking somewhat detached from it all, the Duke and Duchess of York and their two pretty girls, Elizabeth and Margaret Rose, and all the rest of the royal family; coaches gleaming, cavalry glittering and jingling, bands playing, everyone cheering. It had been marvellous.

This evening dancing at the Waldorf, then in Trafalgar Square, half crushed to death, she and David had drunk champagne. Now back at the flat, Letty felt just a little tipsy and rather exhausted.

David stood behind her, his hand on her shoulders. She felt their warmth through the narrow straps of her Schiaparelli satin evening dress as he slowly turned her to face him, lifting her chin to kiss him.

'Haven't you had enough for one day?' he asked, relinquishing the kiss for a moment to pull the window further down. She breathed in the sweetness of his breath, touched a little with celebratory champagne.

'Not enough of you, David,' she whispered, wanting nothing more but him.

He kissed her again while below them people passed by. From a radiogram a voice recounted the joyful events of the day but Letty hardly heard, twining her arms around David's neck, holding his lips firmly upon her own.

'Early night?' he whispered within the kiss.

Again she nodded, and with his arm about her guided her away from the bright window, switching off the radiogram, the happy sounds of the outside world receding as together they went into the bedroom.

She should have been was happy. But there was the underlying knowledge of the hospital's findings. It had taken David more than six months to tell her. Something about a narrowing of the arteries that would cause him problems as the years went on. Now he took tablets to allay the pain; had to beware of too much stress. That was a laugh! Letty told herself. He had nothing but stress, the way Madge treated him. Sometimes Letty felt she was doing it on purpose. David had told her about how he had almost walked out on Madge at Christmas, prevented only by the intrigue he knew was going on between his wife and his father-in-law over the business.

Letty had been furious, said he was weak, said the business meant more to him than she did. Deaf to explanations, she'd finally paused in a welter of fear and remorse only when David's hand had moved towards his chest, the pain he'd suffered this past year returning sharply.

From that day in April she had said no more about it. Dared not. Better to have him as he was than not have him at all. In the small hours she would lie awake visualising life without him.

Numbed by fear, she vowed to do everything possible to make life easy for him, vowed to avoid anything that might endanger his well-being. If it helped to lessen the stress he could even return to his wife, with Letty's blessing. Once she had tried to tell him that. He'd laughed and said that would be the day!

Even after all these years they still had only the weekends together. There was some consolation in the knowledge that this was the lot of many a professional couple. She was still occupied by her business, though with time it had lost some of its sparkle, its romance. David's working life was taken up with all that the smooth running of a large departmental store entailed. Letty knew now that this would be all she would ever have of him; she fashioned her life around that knowledge and tried to be happy with what she had.

It was summer 1936. A year had gone by and David's health had not deteriorated as Letty had fearfully imagined it would. She thanked God for it. She viewed everything philosophically, even the lack of change in their lives together, making the most of those brief weekends, amazed how the time flew by – so fast, at times it worried her.

Elsewhere there had been change. In January King George had died; the nation was plunged into mourning. Like most people Letty had felt terribly sad. It was hardly a year since his Jubilee broadcast. It had touched everyone, that speech:

'How can I express what is in my heart? I can only say to you, my very, very dear people . . .' He had been so loved.

Edward VIII was popular, handsome, had that little boy lost look that appealed to women young and old, and Letty was no exception; she had to endure David's taunts when she too enthused over their new king.

'For pity's sake! You're forty-six, Letty. He's only forty-one.'

'Should that matter?' she laughed.

She *was* forty-six. Still slim, her neck was smooth, but certain lights could reveal those fine lines about her green eyes, strands of silver amid the auburn of her short wavy hair that needed no permanent wave to make it so.

There was grey in David's hair too, fast replacing its dark glossiness. Fortunately it suited him, made him appear the distinguished man of business that he was. If only he didn't look so drawn these days.

He wouldn't have looked so had it not been for that niggling pain he suffered. He had begun to smoke too. But he didn't look so bad for a man of fifty-six, still very upright. His eyes, still dark and clear, held a soft faraway expression at times, and his smile was gentle. Oh, how she loved him, wanted to take away the pressure of all that bore down upon him!

Henry Lampton was growing weaker by the month, and David's fear of Madge's influencing the old man before he finally died wasn't doing him any good. Letty had accepted now that a divorce could cost him all he'd worked for. She knew he was hoping to pass his share of the business on to Chris, his heir, when the time came. That, even more than his wish to carry on his own father's name, had become paramount in David's mind.

This warm July morning they lay in the double bed, her head resting on his arm, while the summer sun filtered into the room.

'What if she stops you seeing me altogether?' Letty shivered in spite of the warmth, feeling David's muscles move spontaneously beneath her head.

'I don't want to think about that,' he said in a tight voice. 'She still enjoys her own life.'

But Letty could see the day coming when Madge would begin to tire of the good life and settle down to middle age, as everyone did in time. Letty herself could feel that phenomenon coming on.

In time, Madge would begin to feel lonely. No children to comfort her in her later years, she would demand David back. What then? Would he defy her, tell her to do her damnedest, risk losing a business which was growing from strength to strength? Somehow, Letty couldn't see him allowing it. He had already made a will (it had terrified Letty, even with her business mind, making his death seem so much more imminent), leaving all his shares to Chris. What lengths would he go to in order to safeguard the business for his son?

What if anything did happen to him? Where would Chris stand in all this? What clash of interests would arise between him and his father's true wife?

'I don't want to think about it either,' she said, shuddering at the immensity of it all.

David's arm tightened about her. 'So long as I keep out of her way, don't antagonise her, I think everything's all right. She taunts me about you, but I keep quiet and she soon tires of it. We don't argue any more. So long as her father doesn't alter his will, once he goes I can get our lives sorted out. I must avoid letting Madge use her shares to ruin the company. She will, you know. Out of sheer vindictiveness.'

Lapsing into silence, he lay wrapped in his own thoughts then suddenly leaned over and kissed Letty, the kiss growing strong and lingering.

'Let's forget what might be,' he whispered. 'Just think of what is. You and me.'

'Mmm!' Letty moaned longingly. Her mind closing to everything else, she melted luxuriously against hands that held a sort of desperation in their touch.

Chris was home. Twenty-one in a few weeks' time, he had left Cambridge for good. Letty proudly noted how handsome her son was; noted too that three years of study hadn't given him the slightest idea what he wanted to do in life.

'Plenty of time to worry about that,' he said. He'd been home for three weeks and had already brought home two girls, one after the other. Neither lasting more than a week, he had now brought home a third.

'She won't last either,' Letty said to David with an impatient lift of her chin. 'It's his not wanting to settle down that worries me.'

'He will in time,' David said with proud parental tolerance.

David would have liked to have been closer to his son, Letty could sense it. There had never been that bond between them she'd imagined there would be. From the very start Chris had treated him more as an uncle than a father; in fact, she suspected, he still looked on Billy as more of a father figure. He still talked of Billy, a reminiscent smile lighting his clear, handsome features.

It pained her to see David trying so hard to be close to him, and Chris casually fending him off. Still slightly immature despite his college education, he had absolutely no idea how deep his father's need of him went.

For all his broad shoulders, his height, his twenty-one years, he was a boy still. He had a likeable arrogance about him that made him popular, that made Letty proud of him, but which did nothing towards making him a man.

David booked a table at the Waldorf Hotel for his birthday. He had suggested a proper birthday party for whoever Chris cared to invite, but he had shrugged, said that his friends wouldn't come to a family birthday party. Getting together in someone's room with a few chums from university, yes. But family parties? He didn't think so.

Letty, knowing his university chums, was glad. She persuaded David to limit it to just a small dinner for themselves and Chris, then afterwards he could do whatever he wanted. Fortunately Chris seemed quite happy about the arrangement, though insisted on inviting a friend – a strange female he called Bunny who wore horn rimmed spectacles, had slightly protruding teeth and talked incessantly about politics.

She monopolised most of the conversation with unswerving venom against the Jarrow marchers who had walked three hundred miles to London to state their case – so poor, yet they could afford the boot leather, she observed. She herself was obviously well off. She also denounced the German Chancellor, Adolf Hitler, for marching into the Rhineland, and wondered where that would lead; and she pontificated against the Rome/Berlin/Tokyo Axis pact which she said the British saw as a threat to future peace, though Letty herself hadn't thought it a threat as such, if she thought about it at all. Lastly she spoke of War that had broken out in Spain in July.

'Of course, the majority of us are for the Royalists, aren't we, Chris?' she said, 'us' meaning people like her, Letty deduced. 'Lots of us are thinking of going to Spain to support them. We have to fight for the rights of others, not just ourselves, even if it does mean with our lives! You're thinking of going, aren't you, Chris?'

She laid a hand, heavy with huge rings and chunky bracelets, over his, blue eyes gazing very intensely into his dark ones, while Chris gave his parents a sidelong glance, and half nodded.

Letty drew in a sharp breath, fear spreading through her like spilled oil. 'Christopher! You're not!'

'I was only thinking of it.' He toyed idly with his crêpes suzette, stuffing a large piece into his mouth to prevent the need to say more, prevented too by the loquacious Bunny going off at another tangent.

'I say, this business of Edward and Mrs Simpson is rather off, don't you think? He'll never be allowed to marry a divorcee. Imagine . . . Queen Wallis!' She gave a peal of laughter that made heads turn.

Letty smiled, wishing this birthday dinner would hurry to its end.

'What's this about going to fight in Spain?' she taxed Chris later. 'Don't you think you should first sort out your life here?'

'It's only an idea,' he said, not meeting her eyes so that she knew it was more than that. 'It's just that I can't see myself settling down to some boring old job. There's nothing in England.'

'What about all this law you've been studying? If that doesn't interest you any more, your father could find you a good position with him if you wanted it. It's an expanding business. Employs hundreds of staff. As managing director, your father would find you something worth while.'

The handsome young face grimaced. 'I want to see a bit of the world. Have a bit of excitement.'

'Then go abroad on holiday!' she railed at him, beset by fear. 'There are so many places you can go. It needn't cost you a penny. Your father and I will pay for it. Why not take a cruise to America or somewhere? But not Spain, darling. You can't want to go there.'

'They'll need men. It's serious, you know, Mum. I don't want to holiday. I want to help in preventing upstarts from imposing their will on a country – like Mussolini's doing in Abyssinia. We have to help prevent tyrants and dictators from invading other countries.'

'No one's *invaded* Spain,' she argued desperately. 'It's their own quarrel. It had nothing to do with anyone else. And, anyway, what can you do on your own?'

'There are thousands who think the same as me, Mum. If everyone went, like they did in the last war, it would help stop it. Bunny says it's the thin end of the wedge.'

Letty's mouth was bone dry. 'Don't you realise, you could be killed?' She saw him smile nonchalantly.

'Don't be silly, Mum! It won't be that kind of war – just peasants fighting the government. And we'll be with the government troops with heavy artillery. I'll be all right. Don't worry.'

It was like hearing a little boy about to meet an opposing rugby team. But she remembered the war of twenty years ago. Albert Worth, Vinny's first husband and Chris's foster father, a slightly rotund, pompous but kindly man, had been killed; Billy, a strong young man, was gassed, wrecked for the rest of his life before dying prematurely; David, Chris's own father, was taken prisoner by the Turks and to this day had never spoken about it.

What in God's name did Chris know about what he saw as the excitement of war? Of bullets that tore away jawbones, shell splinters that blinded, bombs that shredded men to pieces, gas that choked them to death? And now they had even more horrific weapons: planes that flew at four hundred miles an hour to drop bigger, more devastating bombs.

To Chris going to war held a similar pull as it had for men like Billy – a promise of adventure, excitement and noble heroism.

The truth was, he wasn't settled here at home. How could he be? David arriving at weekends, sharing her bedroom, then returning to his home in Barnet on the Sunday. To Chris it must seem sordid, embarrassing. She knew how he must feel, but to wish himself into a war . . . it was unthinkable.

Her blood going cold, she recalled her sister Vinny's words at her dad's funeral: 'I hope you never have to lose him, like I had to do.'

It sounded frighteningly prophetic now – almost like a curse.

★　★　★

The last days of 1936 were full of portents. The country's new king announced his decision to abdicate rather than take the crown without Wallis Simpson; people felt for him as he gave his reasons. Some, like Letty, knew only too well the pain he must have experienced to come to this. But to everyone it was a blow. Preparations for his coronation were quickly transferred to his brother, to be crowned George VI on 12 May 1937.

In December Crystal Palace burned to the ground. Having become an institution, many considered it an ominous sign and weren't so much surprised as alarmed by the abdication a few weeks later.

In December too David was told that his father-in-law was slipping away fast. He and Madge hurried to the bedside, sat until the early hours, but Lampton passed away without regaining consciousness.

They attended the funeral some days later, then with the solicitor and interested parties heard Lampton's will. Letty waited that weekend, but when David didn't show up, was left in a ferment of anxiety as to why. She dared not telephone, Madge possibly being there, she had no wish to put the cat among the pigeons – cat being the operative word in Letty's thoughts where Madge was concerned.

A week of heart-rending uncertainty, indecision, insomnia, niggling anger which she managed to submerge when David turned up the following weekend. Anger that dissipated as he came in from the wintry weather, offering her a kiss that was just as cold. His face was bleak as he took off his trilby, scarf and overcoat, hung them in the hall.

'How did it go – the funeral?' she asked as they went on into the living room. She couldn't bring herself to ask the reason for his not seeing her, but busied herself mixing him a warming scotch and soda while he sat down in the armchair by the brightly glowing gasfire.

'Like most funerals,' he said woodenly. 'Though there wasn't much crying done. Most were more eager to hear what he'd left them. He'd outgrown their love years ago, I think. His brother Robert seemed the most upset.'

'And Madge?'

'Madge!'

His scathing tone made her look at him as she handed him the drink.

'What's wrong, David?' she asked.

It was a while before he answered, sipping his scotch, staring into the fire while she went and sat opposite.

'He said once that as long as I was married to her, he would divide his shares in the company equally between us. He left me one hundred. To Madge, he left nine hundred.'

Letty's heart went out to him. 'Oh, David, that's really hateful. He must have been as vindictive as she is.'

'He was all right,' David excused quickly. 'It was her – she got to him. She must have done.'

'Does that mean she has control?'

'No.' He smiled bitterly. 'Not quite. Oddly enough, I have. But only by a fraction. The shares my father left me just about give me the edge over her. Trouble is, the rest are held by Lampton's brother Robert, and my cousin Freddy.'

The shareholders in Baron & Lampton's had never strictly interested Letty before now. With her own business to deal with and all that it entailed – hers still a one woman band and shares of little concern – she'd heard the names mentioned, but had taken little account of them.

Now they assumed momentous significance in her mind. David supplied the reason within seconds.

'All she has to do now is to nobble her uncle.'

'But you said he doesn't like her, that you and he get on well.'

'True. But it doesn't mean that she might not try to twist him round her finger.'

'I don't think she could,' Letty said with conviction.

'You don't know her,' David said despondently, but Letty still felt confident.

'There's still your cousin Freddy. He's on your side, isn't he?'

David nodded without speaking, remained gazing into the fire, and Letty could see he wasn't convinced, realised then just what damage Madge could do, knew just how keen she would be to do it.

Not knowing quite what to say, how to comfort

him, she came and sat on the arm of his chair, wordlessly putting her arm about him. It mattered little to her if David had no business, had not a penny in the world, but it mattered to him – it mattered that he hoped to leave his shares to Chris, for his future, a future he could now see being plucked away from his son by the wife he detested.

CHAPTER 29

It was quite wrong to expect Chris to settle down, even if Madge hadn't hit the roof when David suggested finding somewhere for him in the company. 'The last thing I would sanction would be having your bastard around,' she said in front of everyone prior to their monthly board meeting. Mr Hawke of Hawke & Walsall, Company Secretary, had frowned his disapproval of her remark.

'Most uncalled for,' he said when they had gone into the meeting. 'A most unseemly remark. She may hold a tidy investment in this concern, but she does not sit on the board and has no say here. She certainly should not be coming here for the sole purpose of stirring up dissension no matter how you and she, Mr Baron, conduct your private lives.'

'I can't stop her coming here,' David said stiffly, as he took his seat at the head of the long polished oak table, a secretary with her notebook and pencil at his side. 'And Mrs Baron and myself consider our private lives to be private, you understand?'

Mr Hawke had frowned even deeper, the lines

on his face forming canyons. 'Quite. But if I may venture to say so, you might think it best, under the circumstances, not to allow your boy . . . er, your son . . . to come into the company – at least for the time being. Better all round, don't you think?'

David nodded wordlessly, wondering how to explain to Chris.

In fact Chris had no interest in being found a job in his father's firm.

'It's nice of Dad, but I want to see what I can do off my own bat.'

'Are you thinking of going in for law?' Letty probed with purpose.

'I'm sorry, Mum,' he said apologetically. 'Can't see myself in it somehow. Stuffy lot, solicitors. Wouldn't mind a stab at politics though. Bit young for it yet perhaps, but I'd like to make a start.'

Somehow, Letty couldn't see much future in counting local votes, canvassing, listening to speakers, or whatever budding politicians of twenty-two got up to. But he was at least thinking of something.

Ideas of going to fight in Spain had faded with the going of Bunny. He had a different girl now, had been with her for six months which Letty thought encouraging. A pretty girl – tall and skinny, with a pleasant face and extremely fair fluffy hair which Letty suspected was ten per cent natural, ninety per cent peroxide. Her name was Eileen Cochrane, a sister of one of Chris's erstwhile college chums.

At least, if anything came of it, Letty thought hopefully, she'd not have the name Beans. Chris had kept the name of Bancroft until last year when he'd agreed to take his father's name. David in his wisdom had sewn the seed several years ago but hadn't pursed it until Chris was absolutely sure in his own mind that was what he wanted.

He had also explained about his investments in Baron & Lampton's, his intention to leave them to Chris, and about his heart trouble. Chris had emerged from the talk with his father more subdued than Letty had seen him in years, and had finally agreed to his name becoming Baron. Letty thought Eileen Baron would sound very nice and looked forward to something coming of this budding relationship, overwhelmingly relieved that Chris appeared to be smitten enough to make him forget about Spain, death and glory. It was an immense relief to Letty who took to Eileen like a duck to water for that reason alone.

Chris and Eileen got engaged the following April, a month which in their case turned lovers' thoughts rather heavily to romance. A month in which Letty had thought of David, thought of her life, her beginnings, where it had led her; sometimes wondered what it had all been for. Over the last two years she had lost interest in her business. With a manager now, a competent buyer and a gifted dealer who practically ran everything, including exhibitions, she could sit back.

Over the years she had gained fame, prestige,

wealth, the things Dad had always dreamed of, had never achieved. She had time now to notice the passing of her days without David, bringing a sense of foreboding. She awaited her weekends with him with a longing more suited to someone half her age. She was forty-eight and had begun to study each tiny new crease on her long, still graceful neck, every fine vein on her once fresh cheeks; she had also begun to colour her hair, discreetly, endeavouring to push back an onrush of grey and retain the once vital auburn.

David's hair was entirely grey now – a distinguished pure grey that enhanced his looks for all that his fifty-eight years were taking a toll. His life with Madge wasn't easy, was even less easy with all that hurrying here from Barnet and back again each weekend. Trying to pretend to Madge that he wasn't seeing his mistress – for that was what Letty was – was telling on him. Even though Madge knew full well what he was doing it pleased her to keep him on a leash, it was destroying him. He was suffering ever increasing pain in his chest that worried Letty terribly.

He said nothing to Madge about it, preferring her not to know, but Letty knew how bad it was at times when she saw him grimace, watched him furtively take one of his tiny tablets and perk up a few minutes later. But the intervals between were becoming shorter and shorter. He had regular check-ups at the hospital, always coming back with a smile saying everything was fine. He was smoking more than ever, and that, Letty concluded with loathing, was Madge's fault.

'She won't leave a thing alone,' he told her. 'Every time there's a board meeting she presents herself at the office, hovering outside until it's over. She says she should be a director. Freddy Wheeler, my idiotic cousin, thinks so too, but Mr Hawke and Robert Lampton are against it. They're of the older school, think women have their place in the home and not running businesses.'

'Huh!' Letty exploded, making him grin and cuddle her to him, telling her she was different.

But David was a worried man with Madge turning up at the board meeting in May to make a nuisance of herself, as usual, Freddy going on about her rights to have a say in the firm as its second largest shareholder after the MD himself, and David compelled to shut him up rather sharply, which reaped a baleful glance from his cousin.

Madge was still hovering when they came out of the boardroom, her face creased with pique. She made towards Mr Hawke who, hurriedly evading her, mumbled something to David about another engagement and took his leave without waiting for the glass of brandy David's secretary was pouring for directors and managers.

David would have shouldered his way towards Madge through the small knot of colleagues, but Freddy was already there, handing her a drink as though she had every right to be present.

It was hard to say anything to her before Freddy Wheeler. The moment he moved away, David intended to manoeuvre Madge gently out of the offices, going with her to make sure of it. She had no place here.

Seeing her talking closely to his cousin, it struck David that they were a well-matched pair. At fifty Freddy wasn't so much young in looks as behaved as if he was, delighting in retaining that ridiculously boyish name of his. It was hard for Freddy to be serious for long. He had always sported a debonair attitude in some ways matching the sense of frivolity which Madge too assumed despite being forty-eight. It was the same age as Letty. But Letty could give her a ten-yard lead for poise and elegance even now, and she hadn't been born into it as Madge had – in her it had been born, even though she'd started life in the slums of East London.

They were amusing each other now, sharing some joke, Madge's bubbling laughter dominating the room. She had a hand on Freddy's arm, letting it lie there, her eyes fixed upon his cousin's, his upon hers. The sight made David frown but he thrust away the thought as quickly as it had come to him, turning aside to talk to one of his managers.

Britain was in the grip of nervous anxiety. Germany had been rearming for years while Britain had failed to do so, implicitly believing that another war like the last one couldn't possibly be repeated.

Baldwin's Government had believed it, and while the new coalition Government under Chamberlain had still teetered along upon the path of indecision, Germany had walked into Austria and was readying itself for its next move, pressurising Czechoslovakia none too gently into handing over large areas of its country.

Letty, like everyone, went in fear of war. Many of her clients were Jewish and had opened their homes to relatives, refugees from Germany and German-dominated areas, all with horrifying tales to tell of Hitler's regime with its satanic hatred of their race. As summer wore on, it looked as though these horrors might easily happen here.

'They're digging trenches in Hyde Park,' she told David when he came one weekend in September.

One beautiful Friday she'd gone there on her own and seen the smooth grassy tracts disfigured by the long dirt gashes and piles of soil, in anticipation of bombs over London itself. In its way it struck her as even more ominous than the strange silvery whale-like objects called barrage balloons that during the week had been floating some hundred feet above the city on the ends of steel cables anchored to the ground. She'd watched them moving with almost comical majesty one way and then the other in the warm air currents above London, feeling far from laughter. Then had come the first issue of gas-masks, terrifying the life out of her, seeing again the men in the trenches engulfed in creeping yellow fog, coughing up their lungs, temporarily or permanently blinded. Now it might all happen here in her own city. It was unthinkable.

There was frantic talk of evacuating the children, rumour of enforced conscription – every male between eighteen and forty-one. It was fiercely contested by the Labour and Liberal Parties, but all the same very possible, and Letty thought of Chris and nightly died a small death for him.

It was all so different to the onset of 1914 when suddenly the country had found itself at war, everyone excited, going crazy with war fever. 'It'll be over by Christmas!' Those words still rang in her head.

Not so this time. That there was going to be a war, Letty was in no doubt, but this one was creeping up on them all – visible but unstoppable – all the more ominous for their having to watch its approach helpless to prevent it.

'I'm so frightened.' Letty echoed the fear of every woman in the land. She dared not voice that fear before Chris, somehow believing that keeping it from him might prevent his running headlong into enlisting as he had almost done during the civil war in Spain.

'We're all edgy,' David said. 'But somehow I don't think it will come to war. We won't make the mistakes we made twenty-four years ago. We'd be fools to be drawn into a quarrel that's none of our concern.'

'God, I hope you're right!' Letty said fervently

as they stood in the park gazing up at a barrage balloon.

David was right. At the beginning of October the Prime Minister, Neville Chamberlain, went to Munich to meet Germany's dictator. He returned triumphant. War had been averted. He had promises, signed by Hitler himself. Relief swept the nation like a refreshing wind.

'Thank God for that!' Letty sighed when David came that weekend. In a whimsical mood he bought her a bag of sweets – sugared umbrellas – replicas of that comforting utilitarian object the Prime Minster carried wherever he went and which had become his personal trademark. Opening the bag, her laughter swept away every last vestige of fear as she drew out tiny pink umbrellas.

Everything in life was sublime. Chris had got himself on the staff of the *News Chronicle*. With his university education he had been given a position as one of its political journalists – nothing special as yet but he was doing well, he and Eileen planning to get married next August. They had peace. She had David – or at least half of him, Madge clinging remorselessly to the other half, which prompted David to vow with a sort of desperate determination to spend this Christmas with Letty.

'What about Madge?' she asked. Unbelievable that they should be together at Christmas for the first time ever. Madge would find some way to stop him, she could almost bet on it, and loathed her afresh.

'She's not coming!' he said with slow drollery, sweeping away Letty's disquiet.

Heartened, she pushed him playfully down on to the sofa, a new one – all her furniture was new, beautifully made especially for her. The flat was full of lovely things, expensive things, tasteful things. It was her delight, her haven, her love-nest when David was there. She leaned over him, kissed him, suddenly serious.

'Dear God, I wish you were free, David. I wish we were married.'

He returned her kiss tenderly, gently, the urgency gone with the years. Even so, Letty yearned to have him to herself wholly, to share him with no one, least of all a wife.

David, on his way to his own bedroom at the far end of the passage from Madge's, stopped abruptly and turned to stare down at her standing at the foot of the curved staircase, disbelief slowly permeating his brain.

'What did you say?'

Madge's smile as she stared up at him was mocking.

'I said, if you want your divorce, you can have it.'

The mocking smile broadened. She stood, clad in slinky black, one hand resting elegantly on her hip, the other holding a cigarette from which a tendril of smoke wafted lazily upward.

'Bit of a shock, darling? You've waited long

499

enough, haven't you? Though I suppose coming this late in life it's a bit of a damp squib, the ardour gone off somewhat. I expect you lost all your get up and go long ago. Never mind, darling, better late than never. You're still capable of doing a geriatric scramble over her, aren't you? Or do you get too out of breath now?'

David ignored the crudeness, and said stiffly: 'The divorce – when?'

'Oh, any time, darling! As soon as you like. Aren't you excited?'

She remained looking up, his silence causing her lips to compress. 'Don't you want to know what's brought about my change of heart?' she questioned sharply.

He longed to say 'Not particularly', but anything like that might make her change her mind. Unless she was merely taunting him, had no intention of letting go of him?

'I shall tell you,' she went on. 'You see, ever since last year, your cousin Freddy and I have had something going. I bet you never even suspected. In fact, Freddy has proposed. Trouble is you're rather in the way, darling. So, if you want your divorce, by all means. Although I'd rather it be me divorcing you, and naturally your Letitia will be cited as co-respondent. Those are my only terms. Oh, yes, and of course an adequate settlement from you.'

David's thoughts flew immediately to the shares he held in Baron & Lampton's. They belonged to

Christopher. It was in his will and no one, not even Madge, could contest it. Once he and Letitia were married, Chris could fight off anyone who tried.

'Whatever you like,' he said harshly. 'Except, of course, my shares in Baron & Lampton's.'

Did he see her face drop a little? Even with her and Freddy's share combined, they wouldn't have a majority vote. And there was always the possibility that Freddy wouldn't want to see the business go. But David was certain that above all else Madge would have liked to have seen him grovel, to see his fear of takeover. The business meant nothing to her. To him it meant everything – his father's name, his son's future, Letitia's peace of mind. And she knew it.

He steeled himself against Madge's withdrawing her magnanimous offer of divorce, but after a long tense pause, saw her shrug and relax, her face breaking again into that mocking smile.

'That suits me,' she said airily.

Why did he get the feeling there was something up her sleeve?

'Do you love him? Freddy?' he queried. She was only using his cousin, surely?

The softening look in her eyes, even from this distance, conveyed the complete opposite, a misty glow of love he had forgotten her to be capable of. The next moment her eyes had become veiled. She lifted one eyebrow very slightly.

'Now why should you care, darling? You have what you've always wanted. Be satisfied.'

It was all too easy. She knew something he didn't. Had she got to Robert Lampton? Robert hadn't been too well lately, might very well be making an arrangement. He had no one else to leave his shares to – his wife died years ago and, David had been told, was never able to have children. That Robert didn't like Madge meant nothing – blood was thicker than water. It seemed he'd have to keep an eye on Robert. With all these thoughts running through his head, David nodded tersely and turned towards his bedroom.

'We're in agreement then?' her voice followed him. 'I shall start divorce proceedings tomorrow?' Again he nodded, went into his room and closed the door. Tomorrow he would tell Letitia the news. She would hardly believe it – this turn-around. He hardly believed it himself. One thing was certain: from tomorrow he would spend every day with Letitia, and that included spending the whole of Christmas with her.

CHAPTER 30

There was a gleam in Madge's eyes these days whenever he came face to face with her – malevolent, taunting. Perhaps I know something you don't, it intimated. You think you're getting away with it, it challenged. Go and see my uncle. Suck up to him – if you can. You'll get nothing out of him.

Robert Lampton, sitting up in bed in his rambling Victorian Middlesex mansion, looked waxy – an old age waxiness, eyes watery behind dusty spectacles, mouth sunken, teeth in a glass beside him. Like his home with its redundant gas mantles, thinning carpets, dusty drapes, its great domed mirrors, huge dark pictures and high cobwebbed ceilings, he was of another age. But he was as welcoming and pleasant towards David as ever he'd been.

At seventy-three he had finally resigned his directorship – Babbington, the store's Chief Buyer, and Taylor its General Manager, had been elected on to the Board at last year's AGM. But Robert still held the shares that could give a majority vote to either David or Madge. With the perversity of old age, he evaded any query as to what he intended to do with them, and said to David in cracked cheery tones: 'I'll see the both of you all right when me time comes, me boy, don't worry. Always been fair.'

The toothless smile of reassurance, David suspected, was the same as he'd given to Madge – insurance against any faltering in the loyalty to him which he seemed so much in need of, forcing each of them to visit him regularly once a week.

Meeting Madge by accident last week with that taunting gleam in her eyes, David hoped their visits wouldn't clash this morning. He yearned to be away, on edge with nerves. You perverse old bugger, he thought, smiled, shook the narrow blue-veined hand, the old-man odour of the house following him as he left to go to see how the store was doing.

Like a man who fears he might be asked to bid farewell to a loving friend at any moment, David visited the emporium as regularly as he visited Robert Lampton. Wandering slowly, nostalgically, through its departments, he returned the friendly nods of the staff he passed, each time the knowledge that this could be the last time, knowing just how he'd feel when it finally came.

Every department was always bustling with customers. He strolled through the shop with an ache in his heart for what could so easily cease to be his as each floor manager came to greet him.

'Good morning, sir!'

'Good morning, Mr Seymour. How are things?'

'Very well, sir. Thriving.'

'Fine.'

'Good morning, sir! Nice to see you here.'

'Nice to be here, Mr Wells. Looks busy.'

'Oh, it is, sir, it is!'

The cylindrical metal money boxes rattled as spring pulleys were tugged by sales assistants, whirring along overhead tramways to the cashier's office behind its glass windows to be emptied, filled with whatever change was needed, the tops screwed back on to be whizzed back. A somewhat old-fashioned store but people loved it, didn't want modern ways. They flocked in through the revolving doors, breathing in the welcome smell of this emporium as they entered – a smell of carpets, fabric and furniture. David took a deep breath, filling his own lungs with its nostalgia, and felt he could cry.

It seemed to be taking ages, solicitors' letters passing to and fro. A simple case they'd said – no one contesting it. Solicitors, however, Letty concluded, never seemed to feel justified in earning their fees unless they were seen to earn it, and that meant reams of correspondence, wodges of Instructions to Counsel, Further Instructions and Affidavits, all held together by a myriad of rusting pins and cracked sealing wax, prevented from sliding out of scruffy beige files by a mile of faded pink tape. That was the way Letty saw it.

Always patient, David soothed her.

'A couple more weeks, my sweet. Three at the most.'

'It feels like three years!' she moaned. It had been horrible to be termed 'the Woman Named'. Made her feel dirty, unsavoury; made a sordid affair of her and David's love for each other.

'It's already August,' she went on angrily. 'What the hell are they doing? If you ask me, she's deliberately holding things up.'

David's arm tightened encouragingly. 'Be patient, darling.'

They sat on a bench under the trees of Kensington Gardens, glad of the shade. Couples and families strolled by, women and girls in bright summer dresses and wide hats, the men shirtsleeves and lightweight trilbies, braces on show, coats slung across their shoulders.

David leaned away to fish in his pocket for his cigarette case – the gold one she'd bought him two years ago for his birthday in March with his initials engraved on it.

Listlessly she watched him take out a cigarette. He smoked strong Players Navy Cut. As he lit up, she looked away towards a small cluster of pigeons, pink feet kicking up tiny puffs of dust as they plodded about in search of crumbs. At least the females were – indifferent to the males, pea brains still on sex, iridescent breasts puffed up while they warbled futilely.

Acrid smoke was floating by her face. Without switching her gaze, she knew it trickled lazily from his nostrils, its toxic enjoyment held in his lungs for as long as possible.

'You smoke too much,' she remarked, heard a small grunt of ironic acknowledgement escape him.

He knew he did. How could he not? She knew the tensions, felt them herself – waiting, waiting. She worried about the persistence of that pain he kept getting. All due to tension. Perhaps when this was over . . . Letty closed her eyes. Dear God, please let his divorce come soon.

The sun had moved round from the heavy summer foliage above them. Its warmth touched her short hair. She lifted her face to it, drank it in. Behind her the well-stocked flower beds wafted a scent of lavender and roses and the tangy perfume of the box hedge.

There was going to be a war. Everyone knew that now. No dodging it like last year. Hitler had made up his mind to march into Poland, and Britain had promised Poland its support. If Hitler did carry out his intentions, and there were no indications that he wouldn't, then Britain would go to war.

Terrified, Letty saw the inescapability of conscription, had hoped that perhaps Chris's job on the newspaper might make him exempt. But for all he was twenty-four, was engaged to be married, he still had that sense of adventure that had nearly got him into the Spanish venture.

'If the balloon goes up, I'd much sooner volunteer than be called up,' he'd told her last week – had then dropped his bombshell. 'I've already written off applying to train as a pilot in the RAF.'

She'd been terrified all right. Had burst out, 'Chris! No!'

'Don't worry, Mum,' he'd told her, his clean-cut handsome features only concerned that she was fearful for him.

'But what about Eileen?' she had gasped.

'She understands,' he'd said. 'I'd be called up anyway if there is a war. Everyone will. And I'd love to fly. I'm waiting to hear from them. I've had a university education so I'm bound to be accepted.'

He had decided to postpone his wedding for the time being – much against the wishes of Eileen and her family – this when hundreds of couples were rushing headlong into marriage as though it were their last ever chance before the balloon did go up.

As August moved towards its close, everywhere there was this haste, this rush to do things that for years had been left undone. The whole country was in flux as September arrived and Hitler marched on into Poland, cocking a snook at the British Government. Troops commandeered nearly all the trains. If it wasn't troops, it was children – hordes of them evacuated out of the city, from the vulnerable East End with its industry and its docks, into the country away from the bombing that everyone knew would come.

Anderson shelters, named after Sir John Anderson who had designed them, were being delivered to be installed in suburban gardens. Lucy told Letty that they had paid a man to put theirs in, and were building a rockery over it to try to make it look a bit more presentable.

In town brick public shelters were being constructed on any odd piece of ground. All done at a frantic pace, giving the feeling of life as they knew it coming to an end. Letty, quite expecting to see those down-at-heel sandwich men on every street corner, boards displaying the words: BEWARE – THE END OF THE WORLD IS NIGH! was surprised to see so few. Two days later, it felt her world was indeed coming to an end.

On Sunday morning, with Chris standing by the window, she and David on the sofa, they listened to the radiogram. She felt David's hands come over hers and grip convulsively. She smiled at him, trying to make it encouraging even as he tried to encourage her while from the radiogram droned the sad, flat, disillusioned voice of Chamberlain telling them the country was at war with Germany.

His voice dying away, the National Anthem swelled from the fretted loudspeaker of the radiogram in an almost desperate crashing crescendo of national pride. As one Letty and David stood up, her hand in his, Letty's chin held high, her eyes on Chris in a silent prayer for his safety.

Wordlessly her tall handsome son gazed back at her, his dark eyes concealing what he was thinking. And she couldn't ask. She merely murmured, 'All right, Chris?' saw him nod slowly and went to distract herself by putting on the kettle for a much needed cup of tea.

It had hardly started to steam when in the distance came a strange eerie wailing, rising and falling at slow regular intervals.

'Air raid!' The words were wrenched from her. Turning off the kettle, virtually yanking its plug from the socket, she hurried into the sitting room to stare helplessly at David.

Instantly he took charge, ushering her and Chris ahead of him downstairs to the closed gallery and through the door to the cellar below, already shored up against the bombs that could be falling seconds from now.

Half an hour later they were back upstairs, laughing with relief as the sweet single note of the All Clear shivered the air over the City. Within seconds the telephone was ringing, Lucy's voice near to panic as it always was in any crisis. Lucy, twice a grandmother, was still as highly strung as ever she'd been as a youngster.

'Oh, Letty! It's dreadful. My daughter's husbands – if they're called up. Them with young children too. And an air raid only a few moments ago.'

'It must have been a false alarm,' Letty told her, in control of herself. 'Nothing happened. It was so quiet. You heard nothing?'

'It doesn't mean a thing!' Lucy screeched. 'We're at war – anything could happen. We could be killed when we're not looking!'

It took a while to soothe her, Jack audible in the

background on the same quest, his quiet voice on the phone he'd wrested off Lucy deep with reassurance, talking to David long after Letty had gone back upstairs.

Chris left two weeks later, stopping off on the way to say goodbye to Eileen and go on from there to Cramwell in Lincolnshire. David and Letty waved him off, watching him carrying his suitcase, his back ramrod straight, his face full of anticipation.

Wiping away the tears that had been held back until he was out of sight, Letty went back inside to gather up the morning mail and open the gallery. Life had to go on. They couldn't stop because a son was off to war.

Not that there'd be much trade this morning – people much too occupied thinking of themselves, hiding away their own treasures, to bother about buying more. In the office while David went on upstairs she sorted listlessly through the bills, invoices, brochures, and a few letters. She stopped at the envelope with Garen, Polder & Stanway, Solicitors stamped across the top. Excitement gripped her. At last! She let the rest of the mail fall back on to the desk.

'David! I think it's come! This must be it!'

Without waiting for his reply, she raced up the stairs, burst into the sitting room where she knew he'd be, perhaps pouring himself a drink before leaving to pop into his office later or to the store.

He was sitting in the armchair. No, sprawling. His face, screwed up in pain, was a pasty grey, and perspiring. Groaning softly, eyes closed, he was rubbing one hand along his chest and shoulder, head limp against the chairback.

The envelope fell from Letty's hand as she rushed forward.

'Oh, God, David! What is it? What's the matter?'

'It's terrible, the pain . . .'

'Where?'

'Everywhere.'

She hesitated no longer but threw herself at the phone and was dialling the exchange before she had even steadied herself. Frantic at the delay she waited to be put through to the hospital. And all the time she could hear David groaning. The sound went right through her.

It seemed wrong, the sun shining so brilliantly outside the green-curtained waiting room. It was hard to sit in one place for any length of time. Her mind a turmoil, Letty sat first on one chair, then another, went to the window to stare out, to the door in the hope of someone, anyone, coming to tell her what was happening.

She'd telephoned Lucy who had squealed as though it were her own husband stricken. She said she'd get Jack to phone back, blubbered a lot of sympathetic nonsense into the phone and rang off – most likely to indulge in a good cry. Jack had phoned back within ten minute from his print works just off Lea Bridge Road in Walthamstow, a large and thriving firm now.

'I'll be over straight away,' he'd said. 'You need someone with you.' That was all. She'd returned to the waiting room feeling easier.

She knew she could depend on him. As tall and skinny as ever he'd been when she'd first known him, though now with a noticeable stoop, she would never have believed in those days he could become a rock for her sister to anchor her high-strung emotions to. And now Letty too needed him at this moment, such a floundering ship she had become. But he hadn't arrived yet and she quaked with fear as she waited.

She had tried to telephone Chris at Eileen's but had missed him by quarter of an hour. By that time the ambulance had come and they'd got David into the hospital. And what with talking to the sister, and finally being installed here in this dingy green-painted waiting room, she had missed her son who was now somewhere between here and Lincolnshire. She had got in touch with the station he was destined for and left a message for him. Now she could only wait, hope they'd send him back on compassionate grounds.

Jack arrived just after eleven, strode in to catch her as she leapt up to throw herself at him in the relief of having someone to share her vigil. It was a few moments before she became aware of Lucy standing behind him, full bosom heaving, face as distraught as Letty guessed her own must be.

Letty freed herself from Jack as Lucy came forward to clasp her in an emotional hug. Letty was not certain who was comforting who, her sister in a flood of tears.

'What an awful thing to happen! Oh, God, Letty, how you must be feeling!'

'How bad is he?' Jack asked, although she'd already told him over the phone. 'Have you heard anything?'

'No,' she said tightly. 'He's still in a special ward. No one's been near me, except to give me a cup of tea.'

She gazed at the cup sitting on the window sill where she'd left it half drunk, too distressed to finish it, the contents cold, the milk congealing. 'And they couldn't tell me anything.'

They waited a further half an hour that seemed like half a year, Lucy persistently sighing, Letty sitting rigidly in one place now, and Jack pacing the floor without a pause. It was good to have them with her, despite Lucy's sighing and Jack's pacing.

Jack stopped suddenly. 'I'm going to find out what's going on,' he announced.

As if on cue the door opened. A white-coated man with greying hair stood there, announced himself to be Mr Baron's doctor. As the two women leapt from their seats, he glanced from one to the other.

'Which of you is Mrs Baron?'

Letty stepped forward. No point going into explanations.

'Is he all right?'

The doctor smiled gently at her – to Letty not a good sign. Doctors either smiled briskly or gently, depending on whether their news was good or bad, and this smile conveyed nothing but ill omen.

'I'd like a word with you, if I may. If you would like to come with me, Mrs Baron?'

Letty steeled herself, wanting to say she'd rather have someone with her, but Lucy would be an encumbrance. She didn't want floods of tears when the news was broken to her. She didn't want Jack's firm arm about her either, when she stood ashen-faced, blank-eyed, as the news was broken to her, gently or otherwise. She wanted David's arm. But David would never hold her again, she knew that now.

Wordlessly she followed behind the white coat, was shown into a small room a few yards down the corridor. In it was a desk, quite bare but for a single forgotten pencil; by the wall three green metal filing cabinets, a waste paper basket and two chairs. The room was painted green and cream like the one she'd left, the curtains the same washed out green all over printed pattern which she gathered must be endemic to the whole hospital, knew she would never forget this room. Whatever in the future she would think of today, this scene would leap to mind as starkly as it now presented itself.

'Sit down please, Mrs Baron.'

Letty sat, an automaton now. She wouldn't cry. She knew that. She had never cried at death. Perhaps it would have been better if she had – more bearable.

The doctor seated himself on the table, one leg on the floor to support him, the other dangling; folded one hand over the other on his tilted lap. His stethoscope hung just a few inches from Letty's eyes. The grave face looked down at her from a height.

'I'm afraid your husband has had a rather hefty heart attack,' he began carefully. 'We have done everything we could, and I'm glad to say that he is now out of danger . . . For the time being,' he added hurriedly as an expression of unadulterated relief passed across Letty's face and she half rose from her chair.

'I say for the time being, Mrs Baron,' he went on as she sank back. 'An attack such as your husband has had could recur at any time. One can never say how long that interval might be. It could be hours, days, weeks, months. Even years. No one can predict . . .'

What he was saying seemed to be coming from a distance through a thick haze. Letty felt worse than if she had received the news she'd conditioned herself so firmly to expect. His voice echoed hollowly as though he was talking into a bucket. Meaningless sounds whirling in a noisy vortex that seemed to be forming inside her skull. And she was falling, plunging downward . . .

She came awake lying on a hard bed, tried to lift her head to look around.

'It's all right,' came a soft friendly Irish brogue. 'You just fainted. You're in a side ward,' it went on, obliterating the need for Letty to ask more. 'You just give yourself a minute to come round fully now, then you can sit up.'

Looking towards the voice, Letty saw the round young face above the blue-striped uniform and white apron, cheeks rosy and shiny, as though they'd been washed with soap that she'd forgotten to rinse off properly. Black hair showed glossy beneath the stiff nurse's cap and her eyes were as blue as a summer sky.

She smiled a sweet and ready smile as after a moment Letty sat up slowly. 'That's it, just take it carefully now. You'll be as right as rain in a second or two.'

Letty half expected to find herself in a hospital gown, but she was fully dressed, her handbag on a chair beside her, her hat laid neatly on top.

Her thoughts, however, were with David. 'Do you know how Mr Baron is?' she asked. It seemed odd asking that question; a moment ago she had never expected to ask ever again. And then the impact of what she had expected to face hit her. She gazed imploringly into the girl's face, expecting her to shake her head, the doctor's words just a dream. The nurse gazed back, her blue eyes twinkling, and Letty knew it wasn't a dream. In that second all her pent up feelings surfaced and she was suddenly engulfed by a fit of weeping such as she could not remember happening in years, not even when Billy had died. It took over completely as, lying against the young nurse's soft shoulder, the girl holding her to her, murmuring, 'There, there . . . A good cry'll do you good,' she let it wash over her.

Lucy and Jack left about four o'clock. Letty stayed on, holding David's hand as he dozed. She had vowed, not to leave him until forced by hospital rules to do so, and then was determined to argue against them with all her might.

She had a terrible superstition that were she to leave, something dreadful would happen to David; that so long as she stayed here at his bedside, all would be well. A superstition she knew was quite ridiculous but which she couldn't shake off.

There had been a message for her that Chris was being sent back for a short period to be with his father before returning to Lincolnshire. She would wait until he arrived.

She had left David for a minute or two earlier on to telephone Madge Baron from the public phone box outside. Her heart had been in her mouth at forsaking him for even this short time. Why she had even bothered she did not know, though Madge did at least confirm that the envelope David had received had indeed been the decree absolute of the divorce. Madge's reply to Letty's urgent message about David's heart attack was that she had no intention of tearing off to any hospital to see an ex-husband.

'No business of mine, darling,' she sighed offhandedly. 'He's your problem now.' And she had hung up, leaving Letty utterly appalled at such cold-heartedness.

Guilty at having left him, she ran all the way back to David to find him still sleeping. She calmed herself and vowed to sit for as long as it took for him to wake up and see her, praying as the hours ticked by that he would wake up, that he would live and not have another attack.

Letty gazed at David as he smiled at her from his pillow. He was recovering well, she thought. What Doctor Harper had said, couldn't have been right. And yet, deep in her heart, she knew it was; that she must make the most of what she had. Only she hoped it would be for years, not months or weeks. She prayed for that, taking in David's face, storing its picture in her mind so it would never fade.

He had the letter from the solicitors and she watched him open it, take out the document and the covering letter, scan them briefly.

And then he smiled at her, his dark eyes deep with his love for her. But only for a moment. Within seconds they clouded.

'Doctor Harper's spoken to you?' he asked.

She nodded, not knowing how to answer. He answered for her.

'He told you what could happen?'

Again she nodded as he went on sombrely now, not looking at her.

'I love you, Letitia. Always remember that I love you. Don't ever stop thinking that. But knowing what we know, I couldn't in all fairness ask you to marry me now. It'd break my heart knowing I'll leave you a widow . . .'

In Letty's body every nerve, every fibre, jumped at once, like a pain. Her voice trembling, she spoke urgently.

'I want you to listen, David. This country's at war and thousands of couples are rushing off to get married. None of them knows if they will ever see each other again and they've probably only known each other a year or two. I've known you nearly all my life. We've been lovers for more than half that time. I'm lucky to have had what I've had, and if I marry you and am widowed next week, I shall still count myself the most fortunate of women in having been loved by you. I've had more love than anyone could ever have wished for. So I shall marry you, David, and no more talk of . . .'

She couldn't say it, could only lean towards him and feel his arms close around her, feel their pressure against her conveying that he was in full agreement with her.